THE
ORPHEUS DESCENT

TOM HARPER

THE
ORPHEUS DESCENT

HODDER &
STOUGHTON

First published in Great Britain in 2013 by Hodder & Stoughton
An Hachette UK company

I

A CIP catalogue record for this title is available from the British Library

Hardback ISBN 978 1 444 73135 4
Trade Paperback ISBN 978 1 444 73136 1

Printed and bound by Clays Ltd, St Ives plc

Hodder & Stoughton policy is to use papers that are natural, renewable and recyclable
products and made from wood grown in sustainable forests. The logging and
manufacturing processes are expected to conform to the environmental
regulations of the country of origin.

Hodder & Stoughton Ltd
338 Euston Road
London NW1 3BH

www.hodder.co.uk

For Matthew
Beauty and Truth

No one in his right mind would try to express his deepest thoughts in words – let alone put them down in writing.

Plato, *Letter* 7

Imagine our situation something like this.

There's a cave. There are men inside it, collared and chained so that they can't move, can't even turn their heads. There's a fire behind them – which they can't see – and puppets dancing in front of the fire. All the prisoners see is shadows thrown on the cave wall.

They've been in that position their whole lives. They think the shadows are reality. How could they know any different?

What happens if one of them escapes?

I don't have to imagine the cave: I'm already in it. There's no fire and no sun. The only shadows here are projections from my own mind.

The hard floor bruises my bones; a knot in the rock digs into my skull. But the pain fades eventually. The stone swallows me, the warmth of my body melting me into it.

I went down . . .

Poets rhapsodise about the silence of the grave. Now that I'm here, I have to conclude they're beautifully misinformed. It isn't silent. Water drips like a heartbeat. The hiss of stone rushes through my ears, the melody of the earth turning on its axis.

The darkness gives me strange sight. I can't see my hand in front of my face, but I can peer over the rim of the world and see all space combined. I can dip in my hand and scoop up bubbles of time, twisting them this way and that to see how they catch the light.

I went down . . .

In a glistening bowl, I see the gilded city, its temples proud on the high rock of the acropolis. In the harbour beyond the walls, there's a wooden ship with bright red eyes, and an iron ship whose eyes are rusted shut. The iron ship has no sails. It's the ship of the dead.

I can hear the silence and see through darkness. I'm awake and dreaming. I'm dead, and more alive than I've ever been.

In the dry air, I catch the impossible smell of ripe figs. The goddess must be near.

I went down to the Piraeus. It's so clear, it could have been yesterday.

One

Under no circumstances should anyone under forty ever be allowed to travel abroad.

Plato, *Laws*

Athens – 389 BC

I went down to the Piraeus yesterday with Glaucon, my brother. I told him not to waste his time, but he insisted.

Flutes piped me away at dawn. The best parties were just letting out: musicians played a last song, while tired guests dressed and dragged themselves into the streets. Rain licked the air; a dark cloud brooded motionless over the greatest city on earth.

At the eastern gate, I paused for one last look. Civic Athens had already turned her back on me: the agora, the law courts, the Assembly houses and gaols were all hidden behind the shoulders of the acropolis. Only the Parthenon remained, hovering above the city: a marble phantom among the clouds.

For a second, delicious melancholy drowned out my worries. I whispered a silent prayer and tried to swallow the moment whole, to carry it with me on my journey.

'Take a good look,' Glaucon said. 'You'll miss it when you're gone.'

I turned away. In front of me, a two-foot god with a

3

three-foot erection leered out at me from the gate. Glaucon spat on his hand and touched the herm's well-worn cock for luck.

'At least he's pleased to see you go.'

I frowned, cross that he'd spoiled the moment with a cheap joke. Glaucon's face fell, wounded that I'd taken offence. A space opened between us.

Beyond the gate, the road to Piraeus is a long straight corridor between the walls, a no-man's-land of graffiti, allotments and tombs. Walking there reminds me of a prison yard, especially on the days when the executioners are at work outside the north wall, and the screams of condemned men follow you all the way down to the sea. That early, the executioners were still in bed; the road was almost empty. Our few fellow-travellers merely showed as shadows in the distance.

It was a lonely walk, but if there were bag-cutters and cloak-snatchers skulking among the tombs, they left us alone. The Aristids have always been big men. Even at our ages, just touching either side of forty, you could still see shades of the war hero in Glaucon, the wrestler in me. Pollux and Castor, Socrates used to call us: the divine brothers, boxer and horseman. His star pupils.

A muscle tightened across my chest, as it always does when I think of him. Ten years on, his absurd death still takes my breath away. Athens has been empty since – I should have left years ago. All it wanted was courage.

Glaucon looked at the sky. 'Could be a storm coming. Not a good day for going to sea.'

I walked faster. I've dreamed the same dream three nights running: drowning, sucked down into a void from which even my screams can't escape.

I don't want to go on this voyage.

★　★　★

Athenians have never been easy with the world. We're exceptional people, only comfortable with each other. Even our fitful attempts at empire feel solipsistic, an attempt to engage the world by making it more like us. The rest of the time, we keep it at arm's length.

And the end of that arm is the Piraeus, the Athenian hand that holds back the world, or extends – tentatively – to greet it. Every nation is here: dark-skinned Carthaginians jabbering in their quickfire tongue; crafty Sicilians who smell of cheese; Black Sea colonists like bears, and Egyptians who can give you the look of eternity even while haggling three coppers off a bale of cloth. Hens peck at the corn that the grain wagons have spilled lumbering up to Athens, while two-obol whores try to distract men from their work. A few tried to proposition me and Glaucon. Even at my age, I found myself blushing, not knowing where to look.

'Perhaps it would settle your nerves,' Glaucon suggested. 'You look seasick already.'

I couldn't deny it. Through all the imported scents in the air, I could taste the bitter note of the sea. It turned my stomach. I wished, again, that I could abandon this trip.

My hand moved to my waist, touching the bag where I kept Agathon's letter. I had to go.

We carried on, past the Emporium and the shrine of the Thracian goddess Bendis. Burnt-out sticks littered the street from the torchlit procession the night before; street sweepers swiped brushes at the crushed garlands and broken pots left behind from her festival.

And then there was the harbour.

I suppose everyone looks at the sea and finds a mirror of his own possibilities. A merchant sees profit; an admiral, glory; a hero, adventure. To me, it was a black mouth, unfathomable and vast. Ships clustered around the basin like teeth; yellow foam and effluent flecked the pilings like spit. Worst of all was the water. Its trackless waves opened in front of me and sucked me into my nightmare. The ground swelled beneath me. Sweat beaded on my face.

Glaucon caught my arm. 'Are you ill?'

I waved him off and forced my attention away from the water. Behind the stoa, I noticed the widow's-peak roof of Aphrodite's temple.

'I thought perhaps I should say a prayer to the goddess before I go.'

He didn't believe me. 'Wasn't going to Delphi enough? And what about the ram we sacrificed to Poseidon yesterday?'

I hadn't forgotten it. The beast nodding while I sprinkled water over his head; the sickly gleam of the priest's knife; the blood gushing into the basin and the entrails quivering like a heap of eels.

'The priest said the omens were good,' Glaucon reminded me. *His mouth twitched as he said it.* 'If you don't like the auguries, perhaps you should stay.'

I risked another glance at the harbour. The vision had passed: all I saw was boats.

'Let's go.'

We found my ship moored up at the Sicilian docks on the east side of the basin, the busiest part of the harbour. She watched me approach, two red eyes painted on her prow just above the waterline, while slaves fed jars of olive oil into her belly. An unattended pile of baggage sat on the wharf by the gangplank.

Glaucon sized up the bags, which a wagon had brought down yesterday. 'Are those all yours?'

'It's mostly books.'

'You won't see much of Italy if you've got your head rolled up in a scroll.'

I didn't try to explain. Glaucon loves learning, but he'd never miss a meal for it.

'You never saw Socrates with a book,' Glaucon persisted.

'I'm not Socrates.'

'He wouldn't have left the city.' There was a point to this, and Glaucon meant to get there. 'He never left, except on military service. Athens was everything to him.'

'I'm not him,' I repeated.

'Are you sure you're doing the right thing?'

'It depends how you define right action.'

Running footsteps from behind cut me short. A tug on my coat almost pulled me off my feet. A breathless slave, his tunic bearded with sweat despite the cloudy day, stared up at us.

'Philebus wants you to wait,' he said baldly.

'Where is he?'

The slave pointed back to the crowds around the stoa. I snuck a glance at the gangplank. Even my terror of the sea might compromise to avoid a man like Philebus. But I could already see him, a round figure poling himself along on his stick. A bedraggled garland sat crooked on his white curls, and a spray of wine dregs flecked his cheek, as if someone had slapped him. He must have just come from dinner.

He hailed us as he came close.

'Ariston's boys. I knew it was you.' He made a show of looking from the baggage to the boat, and back to us. 'Are you two going somewhere? It looks as if you're off on a voyage.'

'I'm staying.' Glaucon gave me an unforgiving nod. 'He's going.'

'Where?'

'Italy.'

Philebus smacked his lips. 'Of course. The food, the boys – you'll come back twice the man you are now.' He jabbed me in the stomach. 'Careful what you put in your mouth, eh?'

I shuddered, but Philebus didn't notice. His restless eye had moved on over my shoulder, so that I had to turn awkwardly to see. A tall man with a distinguished mane of hair, a handsome face and a robe worn casually over one shoulder was climbing the gangplank. A gaggle of porters trailed behind him, swaying perilously as they tried to carry all his baggage.

Philebus' hooded eyes widened. 'That's Euphemus,' he announced. 'The philosopher.' He snorted. 'He's got even more luggage than you do. At this rate, your ship won't make it out of the harbour without capsizing.'

My stomach turned. 'Euphemus isn't a philosopher,' I said. 'He's a sophist.'

'A thinker.' Philebus tapped the side of his head. 'Proper, useful stuff. Not like your old friend Socrates, wasps farting and suchlike. Euphemus could have taught him a few things. By the time you reach Italy, you'll be so full up with learning you'll hardly have room for the food.'

He was standing near the edge of the dock: it would have been quite easy to knock him in the water. A grab of his stick, a twist, and he'd have been licking barnacles off the ship's hull. I put a hand on Glaucon's arm in case he'd had the same idea. Unlike me, he might actually have done it.

'At least you'll have plenty of conversation on your voyage,' Glaucon told me. He kept a straight face, though I didn't appreciate the joke. If there was one thing to dread more than a voyage in solitude, it was a voyage in company with a man like Euphemus.

Are you sure you're doing the right thing? Avoiding the question was easy; answering it, even with all the wisdom Socrates taught me, impossible. That's why I had to go.

I will always risk a possible good over a certain evil, he said. A month later he drank the hemlock.

A punch in the stomach brought me back to the shore.

'Dreaming, eh? One foot in the fleshpots already, I bet.'

'I'm going to meet a friend.'

A vile wink. 'Of course you are.' He almost doubled over at his own wit. 'I wish I was coming with you.'

He rapped the slave with his staff like a goatherd, then upended the stick and poled himself off into the crowd. Glaucon glared after him.

'I don't suppose there's another berth on your ship?'

It was a graceful concession. I met his eyes in thanks, and saw the doubts still raw behind them. He looked away.

'Be careful. Italy's a dangerous place. Beyond the coasts, there's nothing but wilderness and barbarians. I won't be there to look out for you.'

We embraced. The moment I touched him I felt a pang: not the satisfying melancholy of leaving the city, but something bitter and irrevocable. I held him as long as I could.

As I pulled away, he pressed something into my hand – a glossy green pebble polished smooth by the sea.

'It's a shipwreck stone. If the boat goes down, cling on and it'll whisk you back to land. So they say.'

I held it in my fingers like the pick of a lyre. Of course I knew it was superstition – but I was sensitive that morning. I could almost imagine I felt the magic of the stone vibrating inside it like a plucked string.

'Where did you get it?'

'A wanderer sold it to me – a priest of Orpheus.' He laughed, embarrassed. 'Well, you never know.'

'I hope I won't need it.'

'Of course. Go well. And come back a better man.'

The moment I set foot aboard, the nausea returned with a vengeance. The deck seemed to roll like a bottle, though the boat was tied up and motionless. That didn't bode well. I gripped the side and stared down at the wharf, looking for Glaucon and reassurance. He'd gone.

Something struck me on the back of the leg, almost knocking me over the side. An angry porter swore at me to get out of the way; an amphora nearly crushed my toe. Smarting, I edged my way to the stern, around the side of the deckhouse. I was trembling. I sat down on the deck and waited for the panic to subside.

Are you sure you're doing the right thing?

I reached my hand inside my bag and extracted the letter. The crew were too busy getting ready for sea to pay me any attention. The sophist Euphemus had disappeared inside.

I unfolded the flattened scroll, though I'd read it so often I had it word perfect.

> *I have learned many things which I cannot put in this letter: some would truly amaze you. But Italy is a strange place, full of wonders and dangers. There is no one here I trust with these secrets.*

For the thousandth time, I wondered: *What secrets?*

Cargo was stowed and lines tightened. The sun traced its course around the world. An afternoon breeze came down off the mountains, snapping the halyards like whips, though the clouds didn't lift. In the offing, the sea and sky were welded together without a join.

A longboat pulled us out of the harbour, hidden from the deck so that the ship seemed to move of its own volition, without oars or sails. The white tower of Themistocles' tomb watched from the headland as we passed.

I surrendered myself to the sea.

Two

Berlin – Present Day

It started slowly. A shuffle on the cymbal, like water trapped in your ear; a brushing sound that emerged imperceptibly from the noise in the club. It crept through the crowd, taking over conversations, leaving behind a wash of silence. The audience turned towards the darkened stage.

The drum kicked in. Slow, forty beats a minute, the pulse of a sleeping heart. The crowded bodies pressed towards the stage, closer to the music. The whole room had become a single organ, breathing in and out with the throb of the drum.

Jonah sucked the plectrum between his teeth and let the beat take a hold of him. His left-hand fingers slid up the neck of the guitar and settled on the chord. The music was a vector, channelling the crowd's energy into him so that he could feed it through the strings and deliver it back to them.

The bass joined in, matching the drum and then slowly pulling it forward. A freight train gathering pace, stretching the weight on its couplings. Jonah took the plectrum out of his mouth and held it above the strings. He closed his eyes. He didn't have to count off the time: he knew what was coming.

The beat was accelerating, the pulse drawn out of sleep into life. The keyboard sprinkled in notes that glittered like powdered glass. Spotlights chased over the crowd. Caught out in the moonbeam, he saw a willowy girl with a thin face, her long hair tied back with a circlet of cloth. Her head was tipped back, her mouth open, her body moving in perfect time with the music. In perfect time with him.

He thought of Lily. One more day . . .

He hit the first chord and the stage exploded in light.

Sibari, Italy – 24 hours later

The security lights exploded over the yard as Lily let herself in the gate. She crossed the lot quickly, painfully exposed to the surrounding darkness. She had every right to be there, though it didn't feel that way. She pulled her hat lower over her face.

She climbed the stairs and unlocked the lab. She'd thought about bringing a torch, but that would have looked suspicious. She flicked on the fluorescents and hoped the window shutters were thick enough to cover it.

I'm the site director, she reminded herself. *I'm in charge here.* She unlocked the Finds room and dialled in the combination to the safe. The gold tablet lay on its cushion, bright where the conservator had cleaned off twenty-four centuries of mud. The tiny gold letters winked out at her.

A creak behind her: she almost dropped the tablet. She stuffed it back in its drawer and peered back into the lab. No one was there. Next to a half-cleaned skull, the door swung loose on its hinges.

She was getting paranoid.

She closed the door firmly, checking it had latched, then retrieved the tablet. The writing was almost too small to read with the naked eye. She slid it under a microscope, pen and paper ready. It bulged and shrank as she fiddled with the dial, until suddenly the lettering leapt into focus.

Her Greek was rough – she left that to others – but she knew the first line by heart.

The words of Memory, carved in gold . . .
It always made her think of Jonah.

Berlin

Jonah leaned back on the wicker couch and took a long drink from the bottle. He barely tasted the beer, but the cold felt good. Even at 2 a.m., the night was warm, and his T-shirt still stuck heavy with the sweat from the club.

The world spun slowly – nothing to do with the beer, nor even the pot smoke drifting over from the next table. He was coming down, shrinking back. The music had stopped, the audience gone. The energy they'd poured into him had all drained out and he was himself again. Nothing more.

That was the hardest thing about coming off stage. Some musicians tried to beat it with drugs, but he knew that didn't solve anything. Just multiplied the falls. All you could do was ease the way down with a few beers and a few friends, hold on to the night as long as she'd let you.

There were stars in the water and lights in the sky. They'd come to a bar on the bank of a river, a laid-back haunt spilling over old industrial terraces under the road bridge. Fairy lights snaked through the trees, and Spartan techno drifted off the dance floor that they'd crammed into a brick bunker no bigger than a meat locker. A clutch of empty-eyed ravers stood outside like lost souls, their bodies jerking spasmodically to the music that still possessed them. It was a long time since they'd touched reality.

Shadow pushed through the crowd with six bottles of beer in one arm and a girl on the other. He always said drummers needed good hands.

'One more for the road?'

Alex, who played bass, took two. 'Isn't this the end of the road?'

'Not for me.' Jonah leaned over and took another bottle. Shadow dropped himself onto a wicker cube-stool and balanced the rest of the beers on the table. The girl behind him squeezed onto the couch between Jonah and Alex.

'This is Astrid,' Shadow said. 'She was at the show.'

Jonah remembered her – the girl in the moonbeam. She wore a slim black T-shirt with short sleeves and a sharp V opening down to her breasts. Her hair fell in long ringlets almost down to her waist, bound back with a circlet so she looked like some ancient prophetess.

'You're in the band too, right?' She had to put her mouth right up against him to be heard above the music. 'You're Jonah.'

The couch was tight, no doubt about that. When she put her drink down, there was nowhere for her hand to rest except on his thigh.

'You played a great show tonight,' she said. The tip of her tongue grazed his ear. 'Your songs . . . ' She put her hand on her midriff. 'I feel them so deep.'

'Thanks.' It sounded gruff. He never knew how to handle praise.

'Are you playing any more here in Berlin? I would like to see you again.'

'This was our last night. The tour's over.'

'Then we should celebrate. You want to party some more? I know some clubs in Kreuzberg I can get us inside. It's near my apartment.'

And it would have been so easy. The night made everything possible, and morning was just a rumour. The lights and the water and the music all whispered that he could have her, forget the dawn and everything that came with it. So easy to forget.

The temptation must have shown on his face. Alex, who'd

drunk more than the others, was nodding his head, perhaps in time with the music. Shadow, wise to the danger, was trying to catch Jonah's eye.

But some things were worth remembering. Jonah stood, leaving the unfinished beer on the table.

'I need to get to bed. I've got a long drive tomorrow.'

Astrid started to rise with him. 'It's no problem. We—'

'I'm going to see my wife.'

Sibari

Jumping at shadows meant you often missed the real thing. Focussed on the golden letters, Lily didn't hear the car pull up outside. The shutters hid the sudden flare of the security lights.

She adjusted the tablet under the microscope to read the last two lines. They called it a tablet, but that implied solidity. In fact, every time she touched it she expected it to curl up like a flower petal. The gold was beaten to a thin foil; the elusive letters shifted with every change of the light. The conservator had done an amazing job reclaiming it from the mud where it had rested so long.

Until Adam sacked her.

The door banged downstairs – she must not have shut it properly. She copied out the last few letters, squinting hard at the unfamiliar shapes. The person who originally wrote the text had made plenty of mistakes, and she didn't want to add more. She tried to imagine the first scribe, pressing the words into the foil with the haste of a lover. Or a thief.

She shivered, breaking her concentration. In the gap, she heard a sound from the stairs. It wasn't her imagination. There were footsteps, nearly at the top.

There was no time to get back to the safe. She whipped

15

the tablet off the microscope, snapped it into an old sweets tin and stuck it in her shorts pocket, then grabbed the Field Journal from the table just as the door opened.

'Working late?'

It was Richard, dressed in a white linen suit that made him look a million years old. She peered over his shoulder, but he seemed to have come alone.

She waved the journal at him. 'Just wanted to make sure it's up to date. You?'

'I was driving back, saw the lights from the road and thought I'd better check.' His eyes sidled towards the store-room, the door she'd left open. Her pulse raced.

'How was Ari?'

'Fine.'

'Did you make him understand he can't just take what he wants?' That was rich, with the tablet burning a hole against her thigh.

'You should have come. You can't go picking fights with our sponsor and then sulk off.'

'Should I have stuck around to fight some more?' She crossed to the store-room and locked the door, feeling the weight of Richard's gaze on her back. She bit her lip, and turned back with what she hoped was a complicit smile.

'If I promise to be good, will you give me a ride back?'

Berlin

The van was a white Ford Econoline, dented and filthy, with SOUTH PECKHAM CHURCH OF THE REDEEMER painted down the side. Jonah had never been to the church, but he reckoned he probably owed them a few prayers of thanks. In seven years covering almost every road in Europe, it had never been stolen or broken into.

'You're good to drive?'

Shadow had come to see him off, dressed in his boxers and still clutching a beer. The others were AWOL, though it didn't matter. No one liked goodbyes at the end of a tour.

'I'm fine.' He threw his bag on the passenger seat, together with a thermos of coffee he'd filled from the breakfast bar. He'd need more. He'd had four hours of sleep, and had eighteen hours of driving ahead.

'Did anyone go home with the girl from the club?'

'She wasn't interested in us.' Shadow mock-pouted. 'They never are – just want our boy-band reject. Shame you're taken.'

'Not really.'

'You must be the only guy in the only band in the world who finishes a tour and goes back to his wife. Rock and roll.'

Jonah climbed into the cab, brushing aside the food wrappers and drinks cans carpeting the floor. He closed the door and opened the window. At ten a.m. it was already twenty-five degrees, and he was heading south in a van whose air-conditioning was strictly wind-down technology.

'How long are you going to be down there?' Shadow asked.

'Two, three weeks. Lily's got another few days on the dig, then we'll head up. Take our time.'

'Sounds nice. Give my regards to Yoko.'

'You know the Beatles only split up because they couldn't live with Zeppelin.'

They smiled, but there was a harder truth behind the jokes. Neither of them knew if there'd be another tour. The band had been together ten years, a minor miracle, but each time it got more difficult. Each new song was more of a struggle, each tour rougher than the last. The great shows, the ones where they walked off stage buzzing like gods, were fewer and further between, but the terrible hotels were there every night.

Now wasn't the time. They bumped fists through the open window. Jonah said a prayer to the God of South Peckham, and started the engine.

'So long.'

Shadow waved him away with the beer bottle. 'Go to hell.'

Jonah had spent so long on the road, he thought he could swallow the distance without feeling a thing. But this was different. The end of the road wasn't another sticky club and hasty soundcheck: it was Lily. Every time he thought of her, impatience raced away with him; the odometer couldn't possibly keep up.

From the flat Prussian plain, the land gradually rose across hundreds of miles until he could see the snow-capped peaks of the Alps on the horizon. He crossed into Austria, deep in the shadow of the mountains, then into Italy. He wolfed down a sandwich and a Coke at a *Rasthof* just below the Brenner pass, took a lungful of mountain air and hurried back to the van. He had to get to the sole of the Italian boot, and he wasn't yet halfway there.

His phone buzzed. He glanced down from the road to read the text message.

Drive safely, but don't hang around. Need you here. {o} L

He wondered what she meant. Driving one-handed, he thumbed a reply:

On my way. Everything OK?

A minute later:

All fine. Can't wait to have you back to myself. {o} L

He ate again near Florence, slept a few hours in a truck stop near Rome, and breakfasted outside Naples as the breaking sun touched the summit of Vesuvius. Then it was through the mountains once more before the heady descent to Sibari. He could see the plain spread out before him, hemmed in by the mountains, and the blue sea shimmering through the distant haze. Just before nine o'clock, he rolled into the resort of Laghi di Sibari and cut the engine for the last time.

Once, Sybaris had been a byword for hedonism. Twenty-five hundred years later, the only trace was a white-elephant marina complex, with hotels and condominiums built on long fingers into an artificial lagoon. The ancient city had been washed away; the modern one was just falling victim to the traditional Italian fate of neglect. Plaster peeled off the whitewashed buildings; several were missing shutters. Rubbish overflowed the bins and littered the streets. The boats still looked nice enough, but they were just passing through.

Lily's dig had block-booked rooms at a three-star hotel near the end of one of the quays: not somewhere you'd want to have a holiday, but better than a tent. From the receptionist, who spoke no English but smiled a lot, Jonah gathered the archaeologists had already left for the day.

He felt a stab of disappointment – the hope of catching Lily at breakfast had kept him going ever since Naples. And it got worse when the receptionist showed him up to the room. All Lily's stuff was there: clothes laid over a chair, books lined up on the dresser next to a small perfume bottle, the laptop open on the desk. The bikini draped over the balcony rail was still dripping from her morning swim. Everything except her.

Not quite thinking, he sat down on the bed and kicked off his shoes. He wanted her so badly, but he'd slept six hours in forty-eight and his eyes felt like lead. He lay down, burrowing his face into the pillow to breathe in her scent. *So badly.*

Half an hour. Then he'd go and find her.

Three

If you were at sea, would you be up on deck wrestling with the helm? Or would you let the captain take care of all that, and relax?

Plato, *Alcibiades*

The philosopher Heraclitus said, famously, that you can't step into the same river twice. The world moves too much; everything's in flow. The only constant is that nothing stands fast. The stream you dip your toe in is not the stream where you take the plunge. You're not the same you, either.

Aboard ship is the wrong place to read Heraclitus, who makes me queasy at the best of times. Here, his river has flooded into the sea, and the sea's become the whole world. Everything moves. The crew bustle about trying to tame the ship; sails flap and ropes flex; the deck rises and falls; words swim, and endless waves bend the horizon. Not a place to look for truth.

We were a day out from the Piraeus and making good speed. The purple mountains of the Peloponnese crawled by, the sun shone through the thin sail and made shadows of the ropes behind it. The lines and brails made a regular grid on the sail's face, overwritten by the arcs and diagonals of stays, halyards, braces and shrouds. A mathematical beauty.

Checking that no one was watching, I pulled out Agathon's letter and flattened it against the scroll in my hand.

A PYTHAGOREAN TEACHER HAS A BOOK OF WISDOM HE IS WILLING TO SELL, BUT HE WANTS ONE HUNDRED DRACHMAS FOR IT. CAN YOU SEND THE MONEY – OR, BETTER YET, BRING IT YOURSELF?

I PRAY YOU WILL COME. I HAVE LEARNED MANY THINGS WHICH I CANNOT PUT IN THIS LETTER: SOME WOULD TRULY AMAZE YOU. BUT ITALY IS A STRANGE PLACE, FULL OF WONDERS AND DANGERS. THERE IS NO ONE HERE I TRUST WITH THESE SECRETS.

I HAVE BEEN STAYING WITH DIMOS IN THURII, BUT WILL WAIT FOR YOU IN TARAS. I HAVE MADE CERTAIN FRIENDS I WOULD LIKE YOU TO MEET.

Agathon. Of all Socrates' pupils, his star burned brightest. After the execution, when we scattered, he and I lived together in Megara studying for a time. I had five years on him and still couldn't keep up. I was a donkey, trudging the winding path; he was a sure-footed goat who bounded up the mountain in great leaps, never falling because he never looked down. For ten years, it was Agathon who led us from city to city and island to island in search of some teacher he'd heard of, and Agathon who got bored first when we found him. Agathon who wanted more, and Agathon who first caught the whispers that perhaps the answers we sought were in Italy.

A shadow fell over me, with a breath of narcissus perfume. I looked up and winced as the boat came around and the sun blazed over the edge of the sail. I'd avoided the sophist until then: he had a berth in the deckhouse with the officers and the syndicate merchants, while I slept on deck with the other passengers. Whenever I saw him moving forward, I went aft to the latrine; if he came aft, I went down to the galley to beg some bread off the ship's cook. Even on a hundred-foot wooden prison, there are ways of avoiding people.

But nowhere to run once you're cornered. I tucked the letter into my Heraclitus, not fast enough to escape notice.

'What are you reading?'

'Heraclitus.'

'What does he say?'

'He says the sea is a paradox: both good and bad.'

'Good for fish, bad for people.' Euphemus peered over the side. 'I do hope we don't end up with the fish. I have my doubts about the captain, you know.'

I didn't want to know. I didn't want to talk to him. Euphemus folded himself carefully and sat cross-legged on the deck beside me. The narcissus smell blossomed.

'If you need anything else to read, I'd be happy to lend you something. I've written a little book myself – you probably know it – *On Virtue*.'

'Didn't you ever hear the expression, "Write what you know"?'

He laughed and smiled, though the two didn't quite connect. 'Very quick. You know, I saw you at the Isthmian games when you won the wrestling title. You were quick then, too.'

I accepted the compliment with a nod.

'And they tell me you knew Socrates.'

They tell me. *They* always do: men like Philebus who snipe and gossip and mistake it for knowledge.

'A long time ago.'

'What was he like?'

I shifted my weight on the deck. 'The wisest man who ever lived.'

'Everyone says that.'

'Now that he's safely dead.'

'I mean, what was he really *like*?'

I didn't answer. I can no more describe Socrates than I can the surface of the sun. Even if I squint, it hurts too much to look.

'What takes you to Italy?' I asked.

Changing the subject got me another smile. He had one for every occasion. 'I'm bored with Athens. I've had a better offer.'

He waited for me to take the bait. When I stayed silent, he carried on anyway.

'I'm going to Sicily. The tyrant of Syracuse fancies himself as a patron of the arts. He'll pay top price for anyone who'll come to his court. Particularly someone with my skills.'

'Which are . . . ?'

'I'm a teacher of virtue – like your Socrates. As I'm sure you know perfectly well.' He eyed me suspiciously, a dog wary of having his tail tweaked.

'Are you any good?'

No hesitation. 'The best. Virtue is my trade, and I teach it better and faster than any man in the business. If you attend my lectures, the very first day you'll go home a better man than when you came; and better on the second day than on the first; and better every day after that than the one before.'

I pretended to be impressed, though it was obviously a well-rehearsed patter. 'Can virtue really be taught? I always thought it was inherent in a man's character?'

'Of course it's inherent. But it's no good trapped inside. It needs a teacher like me to draw it out, buff it up a bit.'

'And do you think,' I concluded, 'that prostituting yourself to a tyrant is the best thing for a self-styled teacher of virtue to do?'

It was clumsy, but I've seen his type preening in the agora or the gymnasiums so often that I have no patience. I wanted to make him go away. But Euphemus had another smile ready: indulgent, and just a little disappointed.

'I'd say that a sophist who only taught good men to be better would be wasting his talents. Much better to try and make a bad man good. Your uncle, for example, could have used a dose of my teaching.'

My uncle. Fifteen years ago, he led the coup which overthrew a democratic government and sold out Athens to our arch-enemies, the Spartans. His junta barely lasted a year – but long enough for the blood of all the people he murdered and tortured to leave an indelible stain. For a family which traces itself back to Solon the Lawgiver, it wasn't our proudest moment.

I rolled up my scroll, got to my feet and stalked off. Which is to say I lurched across the heaving deck, managed not to fall over, and dropped in a heap next to a coiled rope about ten feet away.

It's always a mistake to argue with a sophist.

A red sky bled the horizon that evening, and the wind freshened. I took Glaucon's shipwreck stone out of its pouch and turned it in my fingers as I stared out across the wine-dark sea. In the distance, a hazy shape broke the line of the waves.

'Is that a sail?' Euphemus' voice, pitched high with anxiety. 'I heard there are pirates near here. Should we perhaps keep a little more distance?'

The Master stepped up to the rail beside me.

'Not pirates,' he declared.

'That's a relief.'

'It's the mouth of Hell.'

He cackled, and took a swig from the bottle in his hand. When a loose rope snapped in the breeze, Euphemus actually jumped.

The Master laughed again. 'Cape Tainaron,' he explained. 'Where Orpheus went down.'

I peered into the twilight. Now that I knew, it was obviously just a lump of land, a hillside blurred in the blue haze. Yet it still held me in thrall. *This is the place,* the Voice of

Desire whispered in me. The cave where Orpheus went down to Hades to play his lyre and charm the gods into releasing his wife.

Legendary nonsense, the Voice of Reason replied. But it couldn't stop me looking, trying to find the dark mouth of a cave in the hillside. All I saw was spots in front of my eyes.

I stole a glance at Euphemus. Even he looked less certain than usual.

'Does that mean we're close to where we're going?' he asked hopefully.

'It's where we're all going in the end.'

'That's not exactly . . . '

The Master shook his bottle towards the headland, now fading into the darkness behind us, then dropped it in the water. The waves swallowed it.

'How close we are – only the gods know that.'

Our ship was called *Calliste*, after the sea nymph. Whoever named her must have been an incurable optimist, or blind, for there was nothing nymph-like in her swollen, functional body. She didn't dance through the waves: she waddled. It needed a gale to move her faster than a crawl, and at the least hint of a wave she rolled so hard I feared she'd tip us all into the sea. Every night, I lay listening to the ship creak, and imagined the planks pulling apart, letting the ocean flood in. Every night I dreamed my drowning dream.

The sea still terrified me. But what the poets fail to capture when they write about danger and torment, is how something terrifying can also be utterly monotonous. The Trojan War lasted ten years: there's a reason Homer only wrote about a few weeks of it.

During the days, I read. I read Herodotus and Thucydides, Pittacus and Simonides. I forced my way through Heraclitus without throwing him overboard. And when all those were exhausted, I read Euphemus. He'd left it on my blanket roll that first evening after we spoke.

I tried not to let him catch me reading it. But, like a dog, he had an unerring nose for his own mess. He gave me half an hour; then there was the narcissus scent breathing over my shoulder.

'I see you've picked up my little pamphlet.'

He waited awkwardly, wanting the compliment and wanting it to come spontaneously. I left him hanging.

'And . . . ?' he prompted at last.

'It's called *On Virtue.*'

'Yes?'

'But in it, you say there's no such thing as virtue.' I scrolled through the text. '*The only law that nature gives is life and death. Life comes from what helps us; death from what hinders us. Nature commands us, therefore, to help ourselves and pursue pleasure if we want to live.* You sound like Heraclitus.'

'Thank you.'

'Not in a good way. If the only law is selfishness, then how can a man be good?'

Triumph spilled over his face. 'He can't. That's my point. All we can do is react to our circumstances according to nature. And the only truth that nature gives us is: *survive.*'

I could feel my blood heating up, my voice getting louder. Socrates, who would have stood at the gates of Hades looking amiably puzzled, always teased me that I didn't have the temper for debate. Not that he did any better when they put him on trial.

'If there's no such thing as virtue, how can you claim you teach men to be good?'

'It depends what you mean by good.'

'No, it doesn't.' I was rising to his bait; I couldn't help myself. 'If we can't agree on what goodness is – if it's just every man's self-interest – then what is there to teach?'

'You're assuming that there's some fixed measure of *goodness* that we can rate every man against. A scale of one to seven. I say that *man* is the measure, and goodness is just a quality. A man isn't simply good *of himself* – he's good *at something.*'

'But by that reasoning, a thief could be good – if he was good at stealing things.'

'He'd be a good thief,' Euphemus agreed.

'But not a good man.'

'He could be.' A sophist's trick is never to lose patience, never stop smiling. 'You remember we agreed that nature's law is that a man should pursue his desires.'

'I didn't agree anything.'

'So to be a good man is to be good at getting what you want. A good thief is good at getting what he wants. Therefore – a good man.'

'And virtue has nothing to do with that?'

'Of course it does – it's essential.'

I eyed him suspiciously. 'How?'

'You have to play by society's rules to get ahead. A man with a bad reputation will never get as far as a man known for his morals. If everyone knew the man stole, they'd lock him up and he'd no longer be any good as a thief.'

His diabolical amorality left me dizzier than the ship ever had. In his terms, bad was good and worse was better.

'So that's all you teach your clients? How to *appear* good, never mind the reality?'

'Appearances are reality – and none of my customers has ever complained.' He chuckled. 'I teach men to be good at getting what they want. At using words to sway juries and legislators. At framing arguments to win. At charming boys, and prospective in-laws. In case that doesn't work, I even teach martial arts.'

My arms twitched to give him a martial arts lesson of my

own. Somehow, he seemed to have robbed me of every other weapon.

'Is there anything you can't do?'

He missed the sarcasm and puffed out his chest. He cocked his head, stroking his chin as he fathomed the vastness of his own competence. Then, with a sheepish grin, he nodded to the heaving sea.

'I can't swim.'

It would be easy to dismiss Euphemus as a complete fraud. But give him more credit than that. I think he honestly believes what he's saying, his world of change and strife and greed that's only restrained by fear. It's philosophically rigorous in its total amorality – more so, in truth, than anything I can offer.

Having to concede the philosophical high ground to Euphemus makes me want to throw myself overboard.

It's not just that I can't stand him. His system offends me. It sounds so persuasive, almost reasonable, but all it explains is itself. It can't account for the things we know to be true and good. The glow of helping a stranger in distress, and the beauty of the sun setting over Cape Sounion. The strength of a soldier dragging his comrade back from the carnage of a failed assault. The lift of your heart when you hear a friend at the door.

I don't *want* to live in a world defined by Euphemus' brutal constraints. It's a world without love or beauty. A world with no hope for improvement.

Wanting something to be true isn't an intellectually coherent position.

We were eight days at sea, and I'd be happy to report that by the end of the voyage, Euphemus and I had resolved our philosophical differences through discussion and reached a conclusive friendship. If I'd been Socrates, I'm sure that's exactly what would have happened. But every day, I found something new to loathe. In fact, I thought, looking out over the stern one evening, I would happily have endured twice as long on that ship to be rid of Euphemus.

I admit I was complacent. The most dangerous part of the trip, the stretch over open water from Corfu to Italy, had passed in a day and a night with a calm sea and a fair wind. When dawn broke and we saw the Italian shore off our bow, I poured a cup of wine over the ship's altar and thanked the gods for our safe passage. Surely now the worst was over?

It was an idle fancy – I never said a word. But the gods have ways of listening in to our souls. The waves chattered under the hull, whispering my thoughts down into the coldest depths where the gods heard them. And laughed.

We doubled the cape and coasted towards Taras, the first port of call, where Agathon was waiting. Not that the gods seemed in any hurry to deliver me. Ever since we entered the bay, all life had gone out of the air. The heat rose over us like a blanket; the wind barely moved us. The whole ship sweated the smells of wood and tar, while olive oil boiled out of the hold and made every surface slick to touch.

I sat in the shade of the sail and watched the shoreline creep by. I came of age when Athens' imperial pretensions had sunk once and for all on the rock of her own hubris, so I never had to fight abroad. Nearing forty, the furthest I'd ever travelled to now was Olympia, for the games. I stared at the coast, the deserted beaches and thick forests choking the shore. I thought of Agathon's letter.

Italy is a strange place, full of wonders and dangers.

The air stirred. A breeze crept up and chilled the sweat on the back of my neck. The day suddenly seemed darker. The sail filled and snapped taut. A flinty tang charged the air, spelling rain.

Night came quickly that evening. Euphemus came out on deck and stared up at the sky.

'No stars.' He turned to the Master. 'Do you think that's a bad sign?'

The Master looked sober. *That*, I thought, was a bad sign. 'Nothing to worry about.'

'Should we anchor nearer the coast for the night?' Euphemus persisted. 'Wouldn't that be safer?'

The Master put down his chin and spat into the sea. 'The wind's wrong. If we go any closer, it'll drive us onto the shore.'

The waves were rising. The ship, never still, now heaved and fell like a galloping horse. I slipped the shipwreck stone out of its pouch and rubbed it between my fingers. It was smooth as glass: I wondered how many other anxious hands had polished it on other voyages. Logically, if I was holding it now, it must have worked for them.

I'm not sure you can apply logic to the concept of a life-saving pebble.

The Master slapped Euphemus on the back. 'We can't be more than a few leagues from Taras. If we make harbour, there's no safer anchorage.'

I stared over the side, willing the land to appear out of the darkness. I knew it must be there. But no fires showed, and no moon broke the clouds. The only light in the world was the tiny oil lamp spluttering on the roof of the deckhouse, where two sailors had now joined the steersman in trying to wrestle the steering oar straight.

If they can't see the land, and they can't see the stars, how do they know where to go?

Heavy rain began to fall. Waves broke over the deck and snatched at my legs, knocking me to my knees. I was trapped in chaos, one more fragment in a world of strife. Every time I moved, the ship did its best to shake me off, bucking like a titan trying to loose his chains. The wind screamed through the rigging. At the stern, I could hear the master bellowing at the helmsman as they fought the steering oar. Lightning forked the sky. Moments later, thunder replied, drowning all noise so that the wind, the storm, the sea and the ship seemed to move in dumbshow silence.

And then it stopped.

A vast groan shuddered through the ship. All of us were flung to the deck like leaves from a tree. The lamp spilled and went out. I heard a shriek overhead, and a rattle like drums. In the perfect darkness, something big and brutal swung through the air and struck the ship with a crash, pinning me to the deck. I thrashed around, but couldn't move. Were my legs crushed?

I wanted to lie still – but nothing could be still in that fury. A wave raced over the deck and slapped me in the face. My eyes stung, I gagged on salt water. I tried to spit it out, but another wave chased in and forced it down my throat.

It was my drowning nightmare made real. I put out my hand, searching the chaos for a single thing I could hold onto. All I touched was turbulence. Water and air boiled through my fingers: I raged at the injustice, that waves and wind could hit me hard as rocks, yet melt away when I tried to grasp them.

Something snaked out of the darkness and wrapped itself around my wrist. I tried to shake it off, but firm fingers dug into my skin.

'She's going down,' a sailor's voice shouted.

He dragged me up the sloping deck. Something slithered off me, and I realised it hadn't been the mast that had crushed me but the sail, smothering me with its sodden canvas. I got up onto my knees and crawled forward. The further I climbed, the further the deck seemed to tip me back.

I felt the edge of the ship, now upright like a blade, and

reached for the rail. It wasn't there, but I managed to get a grip on the hull just as another wave broke over the side.

Out in the water, a frantic voice was screaming for help. I don't know how I heard it over the storm – perhaps some trick of the wind, or an echo off the waves – but for an instant it was so clear he could have been beside me. Euphemus.

A flash of a conversation. My sarcastic question: *Is there anything you can't do?* And his disarming answer.

I can't swim.

I'd been here before. I leapt off the ship, and plunged into my dream.

Four

Jonah – Sibari

He'd been dreaming of the sea, though it vanished the moment he woke. He lay on the bed, deciphering his surroundings. The hotel sheet had twisted around him; the water glass on the bedside table had fallen over and spilled on the floor. Did he do that? He didn't think he'd been asleep more than five minutes.

Hard light beat through the gap in the curtains. The room baked. The door was open.

'Lily?'

A man stood in the doorway, dark and tough with a spanner in his hand. He wore a tight-fitting white polo shirt, Lacoste crocodile on the breast, and designer jeans.

Jonah sat up. His eyes were like pebbles, and his head felt as if someone had squeezed a ten-ton weight into it.

'Can I help?'

'Bathroom.' The man made two turns of the spanner in the air, and pointed to the bathroom door. 'For shower. She want me to fix.'

'OK.' His brain was nowhere near awake yet. 'Can you come back?'

The man gave Jonah a nonchalant stare. For no reason he could understand, Jonah felt unsettled by it, vulnerable. He swung himself off the bed and stood up.

'I come back.'

'Wait,' Jonah said. 'Who asked you? Was it Lily – the woman who's staying here? Is she here now?'

The man shrugged. He tossed the spanner and caught it easily, a bicep bulging under the short sleeve.

'I come back.'

The door slammed loud behind him, echoing through the hotel until it faded into the sprinklers ticking around outside. What time was it?

Lily's alarm clock had fallen over with the glass. He turned it over and winced. Twenty past two. How had he slept so long?

The man said he'd come to fix the shower, but Jonah tried it anyway. The water came out straight away, hot and strong. Jonah spun it down as cold as it would go and tried to force some adrenaline. All he got was a headache, but at least it had a certain clarity.

He could have waited for Lily – she'd be back soon, he was pretty sure – but the hotel was dead and he was impatient. He'd been boxed up for the last six weeks in clubs, hotels, vans; living away the summer by night. He missed daylight and fresh air. He missed *her*. So he decided to walk.

Down in the lobby, the handyman was sitting in a plastic chair, watching the TV that played twenty-four hours a day over the reception desk. His eyes followed Jonah out of the door, a smirk fixed on his face.

'The shower's fine,' Jonah called to the receptionist as he passed. She gave him an uncomprehending smile.

For a few seconds, outside actually seemed cooler than in. Then he hit his stride, and the sweat began flooding out of him. At three o'clock on an August afternoon, most of Italy had sensibly retreated to its beds: the resort complex felt like a ghost town. Out in the fields, a few labourers shimmered in the distance. Otherwise, it was just the crunch

34

of his footsteps on the sandy verge as he walked the road between twin rows of poplars.

He heard a car coming and stepped into the long grass by the roadside. Even from a distance, the car filled the road, growing to monstrous proportions as it sped towards him. A boxy black Mercedes, as big as a tank. He had a brief flash of tinted windows, shadows behind and a slap of air that almost knocked him into the ditch. Then it had passed. A cloud of dust chased it down the road, sticking to his skin as it settled.

Nice to know someone's still got money.

A concrete slab bridged the ditch. On the other side, a pair of monumental iron gates stood in the field in splendid, pointless isolation. Whether they were the down payment on a house that never got built, or the last relic of a vanished estate, he didn't know. The shadow of the gateposts blocked the sun for a moment as he crossed the arbitrary threshold: afterwards, he'd remember that fleeting chill, a ghostly breath, and wonder what exactly he'd crossed. A little way off, he could see cars parked in the field, circled around the trench. He quickened his pace.

The first time he met Lily he'd been ten feet down a hole. That he'd been there at all was so random, so unlikely, that afterwards he had to believe it was fate. He'd been dating another girl, Amy, an archaeology student from Preston whose course required her to volunteer on a dig over the summer. She'd picked somewhere in Greece. No experience was necessary, and Jonah figured he could get some sunshine and time with Amy on the cheap, so he'd signed up too. Three days before they were supposed to go out, Amy had had second thoughts. About the dig, about the course, and about Jonah. All she left him with was three hundred pounds paid in a non-refundable deposit, another broken heart, and a return ticket to Athens (also non-refundable). He didn't have so much money he could afford to waste it – he hadn't really had enough to pay it in the first place. So he went.

He quickly regretted it. The dig was in an out-of-the-way corner of Greece, led by an elderly professor more worried about his pension than the project. There were only four other volunteers, all undergraduates from Oxford, all good friends. In the afternoons, when it got too hot to dig, the rest of them decamped to the beach and worked their tans or read Evelyn Waugh. Jonah, never good at sitting still, had hiked into the mountains, or swum far down the beach. At supper together, he drank too much and baited the students, who took it in a strained, embarrassed silence that only made him try harder. If he could have changed his flight, he'd have quit.

And then Lily arrived. He didn't see her come. He heard the stir, the others putting down their tools and going over to welcome her, but he stayed scraping away at the wall he was excavating. The first he saw of her was when a pair of creased hiking boots stepped into the trench opposite.

'So you're the rock star?'

The others called him that. A way of classifying him, an Oxford-minted insult that sounded like a compliment. But her voice wasn't private-school pony-club like he'd expected: it had a flinty edge that reminded him of grey mountains, burnt heather and home in the north.

He looked up. Honey-blonde hair pulled back in a ponytail, short shorts and a straw cowboy hat tipped back. Her eyes were pale blue and smiling.

'Richard said you're a moody bastard.' She knelt down opposite him and began probing the stones with the point of her trowel. 'I'm Lily.'

That was all she said, but somehow it was enough. So he stayed, to see what happened.

★　★　★

One thing Jonah learned that first week with Lily: any time an archaeologist sticks a spade in the ground, it's called a trench. If he'd ever heard the term before, he'd imagined something like you saw in First World War films, a narrow cut shored up with planks. But an archaeologist's trench could be anything from a few inches to dozens of yards long, and as wide as they could make it. Holes, in other words.

He could see the edge of the latest trench now, the steps dug into the earth leading down. The hum of generators displaced the summer silence, but he'd forgotten his headache. Any moment now, she'd be there.

He looked down. It was a busy dig, almost twenty people working in twos and threes, brushing and scraping and skimming off the centuries five centimetres at a time. Most were on their hands and knees; a few stood around a table under a green awning stretched on guy ropes.

None of them was wearing a straw cowboy hat.

Jonah went down the steps. It was hotter in the trench, no shade except at the very edge and under the awning. A few of the volunteers looked up with blank half-smiles. They were mostly students, none of them familiar. He still couldn't see Lily.

'The rock star returns. Did you play Wembley?'

A man in a pink shirt and a white panama hat had come out from under the awning. He walked briskly towards Jonah, hand right-angled in greeting. He'd spent six weeks in the Italian summer and his face was still pale as death, with a sweaty sheen that made him look like a waxwork. The only colour in his face came from his lips, flushed permanent and vivid red.

'Welcome to the lost city of Sybaris,' he said. 'Good trip?'

'Hi Richard.' Jonah shook his hand and looked past him. 'Is Lily here?'

'She had to go to the lab – bad day; she'll be back any minute. Can I get you something to drink?'

Jonah realised he was thirsty as hell. A student handed him a bottle of water from a cooler, and Jonah rubbed it against his forehead before draining it. It went through him like a rod of ice.

Above ground, the earth was baked solid; down in the pit it was damp underfoot. He remembered Lily telling him how the ancient city had been washed away in a man-made flood. He wondered if this was that same water, locked underground for twenty-five hundred years.

'Has it been raining?'

'Fat chance. We're under the water table.' Richard pointed to the yellow plastic pipes that fed out of the trench, linked by a series of humming electric pumps. 'Those run twenty-four hours a day. If they fail, we'll all go the way of the original inhabitants.'

'Looks like it's happening already.' A pool of black water had filled a corner of the trench, lapping over the ruins of an excavated wall.

'One of the pumps failed this morning. Water was up to our knees before we got it mended.' Richard lifted his hat to wipe his brow, revealing a sweaty mess of hair underneath. 'Really, it's been one thing after another today.'

A tall girl in an Edmonton Oilers baseball cap came up and cut in, ignoring Jonah. 'Can you look at something for me, Richard?'

'Of course. If you give me a minute . . . '

Jonah looked up at the top of the trench, but there was still no sign of Lily. 'I'll go to the lab.'

'Have you got a car?'

'Is it far?'

'In this bloody heat? I'll drive you over as soon as I've got this sorted out. Won't be a minute.'

Jonah almost walked anyway. It couldn't be that far, and he was desperate to see Lily. And something felt wrong. Even in the burning sunshine, a black aura seemed to hang over the trench. No one looked as if they were working very hard, and none of the supervisors were trying to encourage them. The volunteers clustered together in small groups, looking over their shoulders, as if afraid of being overheard. As if they were talking about him.

He was too tired and too hot: it was easy to get paranoid. They probably *were* talking about him. After six weeks' digging, anyone new was bound to be more interesting than another shovelful of dust.

Impatience won out: it would be faster to drive. He sat down on a flat column base in the shade of the trench wall and took out his phone.

I'm here! Richard's giving me lift to the lab in a minute. Hold on to your hat.

He sent the message and waited. Two minutes passed, then five. Across the trench, Richard was now deep in conversation on his mobile, frowning hard. Jonah looked back at his own phone, waiting for Lily to reply.

The minutes stretched on.

Five

Sailor, beware! At sea, or by land,
The castaway's grave is ever at hand.

Plato, *Epigram 15*

Two orbs like black stars eyeballed me from their stalks. They swivelled slowly side to side, taking me in. Judging me.

'What do you want?' I asked the monster.

A pink arm reached out for me. There was no hand: instead, it ended in a vast, serrated claw. I stayed very still. If I moved, it would probably snap me in two.

The claw touched my nose and I twitched. The eyes blinked. The crab yanked back its claw and scuttled away across the sand. It wasn't as big as I'd thought.

I was so thirsty I was sure I must have died. My whole body ached. I felt like sand that's been left in the sun too long, that a gust of wind might blow me to atoms.

I looked around and saw colours: green trees, blue sky, white sand. Foamy waves lapped at the edges of my vision. The crab had vanished.

I pulled myself to my feet. A coil of seaweed slithered off my head. The sky was clear, the trees still, the waves chattering gently. The only evidence of the storm was the jetsam strewn across the shore. Among the weed and shells and driftwood I saw a length of rope, a curved plank that looked like part of the hull. And, at my feet, Euphemus, sprawled on the sand, snoring like a drunkard.

I remembered everything like a dream. The voice in the sea. My arm around his chest, fighting the water until I was sure I'd die. Sand under my feet. I couldn't believe how heavy he was.

I turned a full circle, taking in the compass of our new world. The beach curved out into a long bay, hemmed by pines and cypresses. A little way off, *Calliste*'s hulk lay cock-eyed on a sandbar lapped by the waves. Her mast had gone; a jagged gash ran through her hull. A brown oil slick stained the water around her. In terms of survivors, there was only Euphemus. And me.

I opened my fist, still clenched in a ball. The green ship-wreck stone gleamed smooth and wet in my palm. I squinted at it, wondering. Had I really clung on to it through all the storm and drowning?

I knelt and shook Euphemus awake. He sat up.

'Where are we?'

'Italy.' It hurt to say it.

He rubbed his eyes. Dry salt streaked his face. 'I thought I was dead.'

'We need water.'

The forest pressed close against the beach, but a little way along I thought I saw a break in the trees. I hauled Euphemus up, leaning on him for balance. After so long at sea, the sand lurched under me. My stomach was bruised, as if I'd just fought a wrestling bout. Twice, I nearly fell as we made our way towards the treeline.

'What's that?'

I looked down at my feet and stopped. Storm waves had washed the beach smooth, but here – just beyond the tide-mark – someone had disturbed it. Or, rather, rearranged it. Rows of white pebbles marked out a square, and in the centre someone had drawn a series of geometric figures. Three squares, two identical and one slightly larger, arranged so that their edges met in a triangle.

Euphemus shied away with a dark murmur that sounded like 'witchcraft'. I almost managed a smile.

'Not magic,' I croaked. 'Maths. We must be near civilisation.'

A path took us off the beach into the trees. The pine-needle carpet stifled our footsteps; the forest swallowed the noise of the sea so that all we heard was the breeze hissing in the branches. An enchanted quiet hung in the air. I wondered who had cut the path we were following. The same men who drew the figures on the beach?

A gust of wind made the forest sigh – and brought something else. Strange music, meandering notes that had no melody, but seemed to move according to some hidden pattern. Not a flute or a lyre, but the low ripple of bells.

We hurried on. Soon the path opened onto a clearing, where a round stone wall held back the forest. Inside the enclosure, a gravel path wound in spirals to a small circular temple. In front of it was an altar and, in front of that – in the very centre of the circle – a spring welling up into a stone basin.

We went through the gate, ignored the spiral path and cut straight across to the basin. My hands were inches from the water when Euphemus stopped me.

'Do you think it's safe?'

I paused. I wanted to ignore him, to plunge headfirst into that pool and drink until I'd forgotten there was ever such a thing as thirst. But he was right. We were in a strange country with strange gods. What if there was some prohibition?

The water flashed darkly, daring me to drink it. The weird music played again, much closer. I looked around.

Whichever god guarded that place, he wanted strange

offerings. Wooden frames lashed together with ropes lay scattered around the precinct like the pieces of some enormous machine. Shallow sandpits had been dug into the soil, with more figures like the one on the beach laid out inside them. Seven metal pipes of different lengths dangled on strings from a tree branch, knocking into each with the wind to create the ever-shifting music I'd heard. A horned Bacchus watched proceedings from a plinth. And still the water tempted me.

'What could be wrong with having a drink?'

Without warning, something flew out of the forest and struck me hard on the head. Weak, off-balance, I toppled over and fell splash into the pool.

Euphemus grabbed me and hauled me out. I shook myself off. An apple lay on the ground beside me, with a big brown bruise to match the bruise swelling on my forehead. And on the edge of the clearing, behind the boundary wall, a man was watching us.

I jumped at the sight of him. He was a beanpole of a man, with a round head that he seemed to have borrowed from someone much larger. Grey hair burst out in all directions, matted with leaves; leaves clung to his white tunic, too, as if he'd slept the night in the forest. He didn't look strong enough to have thrown the apple so hard.

'Is it safe to drink?' Euphemus called.

The man shook his head.

'We need water,' I croaked

He considered this. Very deliberately, he walked around the wall to the gate and bowed. He followed the path, spiralling round us three times before he finally reached the centre.

'I am Eurytus,' he announced, as though it should mean something.

He looked like an outlaw, or an escaped slave. But he

obviously wasn't entirely destitute. A round gold disc, carved with tiny writing, dangled at his throat on a leather cord.

I caught his eye and realised I didn't look any better. 'Our ship sank,' I whispered. 'We need water.'

'Come with me.'

He made us follow the path all the way back to the gate, muttering to himself all the while. The wind-chime music died away as we left the precinct and carried on into the forest. Not far off, we came to a shallow stream running between poplars.

'You may drink.'

We knelt down on the bank and slurped up the water like dogs. I almost drowned myself all over again. Eurytus leaned against a tree, watching.

'Are you from Athens?'

I nodded, surprised. How could he tell? Did so many bedraggled Athenians come traipsing through these woods that we were a common sight?

'Our ship was going to Taras,' Euphemus said. 'Is it far?'

'Nine miles.'

'Can you take us there?'

He looked us up and down. 'You should rest, first.'

From Eurytus' appearance, I'd expected his house would be a lean-to made of moss and branches, the sort of place the centaurs might have taken the young Achilles to nurse him on berries. In fact, he lived in a good-sized farmhouse beyond the forest, overlooking a cultivated plain. That was as much as I saw before I collapsed into his surprisingly comfortable bed.

I only meant to sleep for a couple of hours, but when I woke, a soft sunset was glowing orange through the window. Fresh clothes had been left on a stool. Euphemus lay on the bed beside me, snoring like a marble saw.

I dressed and went out. The main living room was empty,

but I could hear a soft, irregular tapping, like loom weights, coming from outside.

Eurytus sat on his knees in the courtyard. For a moment, I didn't recognise him. He'd changed into a clean, white woollen tunic and combed his hair almost respectably straight. But it hadn't made him normal. He scrabbled on the ground, kneeling over a sandpit and making patterns out of white pebbles, murmuring under his breath. Every so often, he'd lean over to the counting frame beside him and shuttle a counter from one side to the other with a sharp *clack*. Then he'd go back to the pebbles.

There were plenty more important questions pending, but I couldn't help asking: 'What are you doing?'

'Experiments.' He didn't look up.

'Some kind of art?'

'Philosophy.'

They looked like children's pictures to me, stick men and stick animals standing outside stick houses, surrounded by other, more abstract figures. A lot of triangles.

I remembered the figure on the beach. 'Is this geometry?'

'Geometry is the study of shapes. I'm concerned with number.'

'I don't see any numbers.'

'You have to count them.'

He swept up the pebbles and started laying them out again, heavy and deliberate. 'The world is made of numbers. One is a point. Two make a line. Three points defines a surface, and the fourth' – the pebble went down – 'creates volume. Solid objects.'

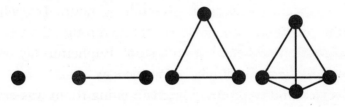

He drew lines in the sand with his finger to connect the stones. 'You see? One, two, three, four. Do you think that's a coincidence?'

'Um . . . '

'All things that exist have a number.' He dealt out more pebbles, making another stick man. 'If we can work out the number of each thing, we can understand how the world works.'

'Who decided that?' said Euphemus, from behind. He'd come down unnoticed and was peering over Eurytus' shoulder at the picture in the sand.

'The Philosopher. The first and greatest.'

'Which philosopher?'

Eurytus wouldn't answer. But staring at the triangles he'd drawn, I suddenly realised the answer. And I remembered Agathon's letter. *A Pythagorean teacher has a book of wisdom he is willing to sell . . .*

'Was it Pythagoras? Are *you* a Pythagorean?'

He made a strange twisting gesture with his hand, and touched the gold locket at his neck. 'Only the enlightened should say his name.'

'I've come to Italy to find a friend of mine. He said he was studying with a Pythagorean' – Eurytus flinched as I said the name again – 'teacher. Did you meet him? He's called Agathon.'

The question had an extraordinary effect. Eurytus looked as if he'd swallowed one of his own stones. He swept the pebbles up and rattled them into a small sack. 'Truth is sacred,' he muttered. 'Not to be spoken.'

'So many prohibitions,' Euphemus observed. 'Do you ever manage to say anything?'

I waved him to shut up. 'Did Agathon come here? Stay with you?' Agathon is one of the gentlest souls I know, but he has a razor-sharp mind – and he isn't afraid to draw blood.

46

I could imagine how the conversation might have gone if Eurytus had started showing him his stones.

The old man shook his head.

'But you knew him?'

'Archytas dealt with it. He can tell you.'

'Dealt with what?'

'Archytas can tell you,' he repeated.

'Who's Archytas?'

He shut the bag with a drawstring and stood up.

'I'll take you to him.'

Six

Jonah – Sibari

The shadows spread across the trench, creeping over the drowned city. Volunteers gathered tools and stretched plastic sheeting over the remains. Lily still hadn't come back.

He should have walked – he'd have been there by now. Now, he worried he'd miss her if she drove back while he was walking over. He dialled her number: it rang and rang until he almost tuned out the sound, but she didn't answer.

He couldn't wait any more. He jumped up and found Richard on the far side of the trench with two volunteers, examining a pot-handle embedded in the ground.

'I'm going,' Jonah said. 'If Lily comes, tell her to call me.'

Richard's head jerked up. 'Sorry.' He flapped a hand. 'It's all mad today. I'll just be another minute.'

'Forget it.'

'OK, OK.' Richard tossed his notebook to one of the volunteers and took a bunch of keys out of his pocket. 'We'll go now.'

Jonah followed him out of the trench and strapped himself into one of the pickups. The headache was back. The warmth of anticipation had cooled to a lump in his stomach, disappointed and uncertain. He took out his mobile. Still nothing.

Richard piloted the car along the dirt track and onto the coastal highway. Jonah stared out the window as they drove half a mile down the road, then turned in at a stonemason's.

Beyond it, along a track, a two-storey farmhouse stood on the edge of a field circled by citrus trees and shiny barbed wire. The drive had taken three minutes.

He could have walked it in ten, fifteen tops. Instead, he'd wasted almost three-quarters of an hour waiting for Richard. He stamped against the footwell in frustration as Richard opened the gate.

The house had a porch, where half a dozen volunteers sat cross-legged with buckets of muddy water, scrubbing pink pot fragments with toothbrushes. Clean pieces lay out on mesh racks in the sun: they reminded Jonah of the pictures you saw after air crashes, warehouses where investigators tried to reverse-engineer a catastrophe out of its debris.

'Is Lily here?'

A muscled boy in a green vest looked up. 'Haven't seen her.'

'We just got here a half-hour ago,' added the girl beside him, in an American accent. 'She could be upstairs.'

Jonah took the steps two at a time. The lab was a plain room with a few wooden tables pushed together in the middle that reminded him of a school science lab. There was a dirty sink, a microscope, a computer, and plastic bags filled with pottery. A half-assembled black vase stood on the table, next to a grinning skull.

Lily wasn't there.

'She must have gone back to the hotel.' Richard had come up behind him. 'She said she'd been feeling the heat.'

Jonah stared around the room, as if Lily might emerge from under the table, or step out of one of the pictures on the wall. The sweat on his face felt ice cold.

Richard was in a different world. 'I'll run you back to the hotel,' he offered. 'She's probably in the pool.'

Lily was a waterbaby. That first dig in Greece, she'd paced him stroke for stroke as they swam out to the little islet just

49

off shore, hauling themselves up on the rocks, careful to avoid the sea urchins that could stab your feet like needles. He told her she was a dolphin in a past life; the first present he ever bought her was a dolphin pendant.

A door opened, an office beyond. A girl popped her head out. She was young, like the rest of them, with long brown hair and minimal clothing. She noticed Jonah, and her eyes seemed to stay on him a moment longer than necessary.

'Can I help?'

'I'm looking for Lily.'

Unselfconsciously, the girl put a hand to her shoulder and straightened her bra strap. 'You're Jonah, right? She said you were coming today.'

'Is she here?'

'Um, I'm not really sure.' She looked back to Richard. 'There's something you need to look at in here.'

'Won't be a minute.'

Without apology, Richard went in and closed the door behind him. Jonah almost knocked it down to take his car keys so he could get back to the hotel. After hanging around at the dig, now this, he thought something would explode inside him.

Richard always was a prick, he thought. He flopped onto one of the battered chairs and closed his eyes. Ever since he woke up he'd been feeling he'd come into a different world, that someone had rearranged the furniture on him while he slept.

You're not thinking straight, he told himself. The heat, the tiredness, the end-of-tour emptiness. Of course Lily was back at the hotel. If he hadn't stopped for that last coffee at the Autogrill, he'd have caught her at breakfast.

He opened his eyes. On the table, the incomplete skull stared back at him. It had one eye socket, and a hard ball of earth filling the space where the brain used to be.

I know how you feel.

He looked around, trying to find Lily in the lab's clutter. Minor artefacts covered the table in ziplocked bags, each one with a slip of paper noting where it had been found. Some of the writing looked like Lily's. A photocopied cartoon had been pinned to the wall, an old Far Side he recognised from her office in London. A pitchfork-toting Satan prodding a hapless nerd towards two doors marked 'Damned if you do' and 'Damned if you don't'. *'You've got to choose,'* said the caption. A black-and-white exercise book lay on the cupboard underneath it.

Richard was still in the office. Jonah went over and picked up the exercise book. The cover said *Field Journal,* printed in Lily's plain handwriting. He flicked through page after page of Lily's meticulous observations, her neat line drawings of the artefacts they'd found. Coins, pots, a comb with a handle like a centaur.

One drawing filled almost the entire page, a thin cylinder, dented and bent like a cigarette that had been dropped on the ground. Two loops fastened it to a chain, which Lily had also drawn. Underneath she'd labelled it *R27: tablet/pendant/case,* and drawn a scale, showing it was about four centimetres long.

He was about to turn over when he noticed a gap, a rough edge where the facing page had been torn out. It surprised him. Archaeologists obsessed about preserving everything they did: they had to. It was a one-shot discipline – the moment the spade hit the ground, they were destroying the very thing they wanted to study. If it wasn't documented, it didn't exist.

'Trying to put yourself to sleep?' Richard stood in the office doorway. 'That's confidential, you know.'

'Just seeing what Lily's been up to.' Jonah closed the book and pushed it away. 'There's a page missing.'

Richard's face froze. 'Really?'

'Just so you don't think I stole it.'

'Too paranoid.' Richard jangled the car keys at him. 'Let's go and find Lily.'

Back at the hotel, the marina was coming to life as the shadows lengthened. Children kicked a football in the road using dumpsters for goals; nut-brown men in Speedos hosed off their yachts. Jonah went straight up to the room. He wanted the day to end, the day that had begun in Berlin and ended on the shore of the Mediterranean. He wanted to see Lily, to touch her and fall asleep and wake up with her beside him. It wasn't complicated.

The room was unlocked. The tension inside him began to dissolve. 'Lily?' he called. He pushed open the door.

The room was empty, so empty it took him a moment to really process it. No Lily – no anything. The clothes on the chair, the alarm clock, the shoes and the laptop – all gone. New towels lay folded on the freshly made bed. As if she'd never existed.

He checked the number on the door to make sure it was the right room. He slid open the cupboards. Empty. Ditto the bedside drawers, ditto the bathroom. When he pulled open the shutters, the red towel and bikini had gone from the balcony rail.

He swivelled around slowly. Or perhaps the room turned, and he simply took it in. His legs had turned to wax. In the pool, a girl shrieked. He sat down on the bed.

Water gleamed on the tile floor next to the bedside table. The water from the glass he'd knocked over while he slept. This was definitely the room.

The phone vibrated against his thigh as if he'd been stabbed in the leg. He snatched it out of his pocket and read the message that had arrived.

Family emergency – had to dash home. So sorry I missed you. Will explain later.

He read through it again, trying to understand. But that wasn't possible – it made no sense. Why hadn't she called? He dialled her number, his sweaty fingers fumbling the phone.

Once again, it rang into infinity. The flat monotone of the continental phone system, not the homely *ring-ring* of home. At least she was still in the country. Perhaps she was driving, or couldn't answer.

He hung up and punched out an urgent message.

Are you OK? Where are you? What's going on?

The ten minutes that passed were some of the longest of his life. Then:

Mum had another fall. I need to be with her. Low on battery. Will call when I get to London.

He fell back on the bed and watched the ceiling fan spin. *When I get to London?* He'd driven almost twenty-four hours to reach her, and now she was flying to London? Without seeing him.

'So why the hell am I in Italy?' he said to the room.

He sat up and went out onto the balcony. Below, children were splashing and fighting in the pool, while their parents lay on their sunloungers with their phones and cigarettes. And among the tanned bodies, a pair of hideously white legs in beige shorts, sticking out from the shade of a sun umbrella.

Jonah ran downstairs and out to the pool. Richard was sitting up, a novel tented open on his lap and a phone in his hand. He slipped the phone in his pocket and looked at Jonah from behind a pair of oversize sunglasses.

'I was just coming to find you. I got a message from Lily.'

'So did I,' said Jonah. 'She's gone.'

'Rather short notice.'

Short notice? She knew he was coming today. She must have known he'd arrived: she couldn't have missed the van parked outside. So why didn't she find him before she left? All she had to do was call.

'Did she say what it was? Richard asked.

'Her mum had another fall.' Two years earlier, Lily's mother had fallen on the stairs and broken her hip. The leg had recovered, but not her confidence: she lived in terror that it would happen again.

But Lily's sister lived virtually next door. Couldn't she have looked after her mother? Why the race to be home?

He should call her family and find out what was going on. But first . . .

'Where's the nearest airport?'

'We usually use Bari. Naples and Brindisi are a similar distance.'

The hotel's wi-fi reached the pool terrace. Jonah used his phone to connect and started searching for flights. Precious minutes passed: the internet crawled along as if somewhere down the line, someone was laboriously hand-writing every word.

'What time is it now?' he asked Richard, not looking up.

'Nearly five thirty.'

The last flight was at ten to nine. 'How far to the airports?'

'They're all about three hours away.'

Jonah swore. Richard took the phone from him and read the flight times off the screen.

'You'll never make it – not on a Friday night. Looks like you're stuck with us. Unless you're thinking of driving back?'

Jonah put his hand in his pocket and felt the van keys. For a moment, he really considered it. If it would have got him to Lily sooner, he'd have been behind the wheel that instant, even though the thought of twenty-four hours more driving made him sick.

But it wouldn't gain him any time. There was an early flight next morning: he could be in London for lunch, about the time the van would be crossing the Alps if he drove.

'I'm sure it'll all work out,' Richard said. 'Just one of those things. We meet for supper on the terrace at eight – you're welcome to join us.'

He stood up, then remembered he was still holding Jonah's phone. He stretched out his hand to give it back.

With a slap of wet feet, a small girl in a frilly swimsuit came racing around the pool, chased by her big brother. Richard jerked out of the way, slipped on the wet stones and threw out his arms to balance.

'*Shit.*'

Jonah's phone flew out of Richard's hand. Jonah lunged towards it, but it was too far and he was too late. It dropped into the water with a splash. Tiny bubbles popped out of the case as it sank towards the pool floor.

Jonah grabbed Richard's arm. 'What the—?'

'I'm so sorry.'

Behind sunglasses and newspapers, every pair of eyes around the pool was watching them. A boy duck-dived to the bottom and surfaced with the phone. He handed it up to Jonah, then kicked away in a plume of spray. Jonah stared at the dead slab of metal and glass in his palm.

'Don't try turning it on,' Richard warned. 'You need to let it dry out.'

Jonah's look would have turned Richard to stone, if he'd had the power.

At five to eight there was a knock on his door. Jonah groaned and didn't answer. He didn't want to go to dinner. He didn't want to see anyone. He hadn't moved since he came back from the pool, his thoughts racing the same circles until they blurred into static. Not thinking or feeling, not asleep and not awake, just *being*. The only sensation was a vague nausea, like the hum of a light that was about to pop.

His arms were cramped from so much driving. He stretched out to the end of the bed, curling his fingers around the end of the mattress.

And felt something. A book, fallen between the mattress and the wall. She must have missed it when she packed. He could imagine her reading it in bed, up too late, slipping it under the pillow and then pushing it down the back of the bed in her sleep. He tugged it out.

The book fell open at the first page. His eye read it automatically.

I went down to the Piraeus, yesterday, with Glaucon . . .

He flipped back to the cover. Plato's *Republic*. Not exactly beach reading, he guessed: she must have had it for work.

As the cover flapped open, an inscription on the inside caught his eye.

To Lily—

Love is Truth, Adam

A dull ache, like heartburn, passed through him. It must be an old book: she hadn't seen Adam in years. He wondered why she'd brought it to Italy.

Another pang – and he realised it wasn't anything more complicated than hunger coming back with a vengeance. He hadn't eaten since breakfast, a rest-stop somewhere up near Naples. At least he could do something about that.

He put down the book, got up and splashed water on his face. His T-shirt was filthy, and he had no clothes in the room, so he went down to the van and dug out something fresh. He looked into the lobby to see if he could use their phone to call Lily, but the receptionist was away.

He found the dig crew at the back of the hotel, on a terrace overlooking the marina. They sat out at a long table, laughing and flirting in the glow of the fairy lights strung along the rails. Richard sat at the head. There was no seat for Jonah.

'Weren't sure if you were coming. I'll get them to lay another place.'

Jonah loitered awkwardly while the volunteers shuffled along and a new chair was fetched. His presence seemed to cramp the conversation.

'I spoke to the office,' Richard said. 'They were very sympathetic. They've booked you onto the first flight out of Bari tomorrow morning.'

'Has Lily called?' He felt desperate without his phone, locked out of his life. He needed to hear from her.

'She'll be on the plane now, I suppose.' Richard looked into the sky, as if they might see Lily's flight winking among the stars.

Jonah tore open a piece of bread and stuffed it in his mouth. Yacht lights shone off the water; on the far side of the marina he could see an enormous motor-cruiser lit up like a stage.

Antipasti plates had arrived. Richard reached over and speared a sun-blushed tomato, clumsily. Jonah had to grab his wine glass to stop it knocking over.

Another kick of anger hit him as he remembered the phone. The one time he needed to speak to Lily more than ever, and he was impotent. He couldn't call her family, their friends . . . all their numbers were in the phone. Hers was the only one he knew by heart – and she wasn't answering.

'Lily didn't say anything about her mother before she left?'

'Not a thing.' Oil oozed out of the tomato as Richard bit into it, dribbling onto his pink shirt. He'd always been a careless eater. 'She just said she was going to the lab.'

Across the marina, a car pulled up on the dock beside the

cruiser. Vast and black, it looked like the Mercedes that had nearly run Jonah off the road. There couldn't be two cars that size in the area.

He kept watching as four men got out of the car. Even at a distance, there was something predatory in the way they moved: spread out, heads turning slowly as if they anticipated danger. Two climbed the gangplank and disappeared inside the boat. Two others returned to the car and pulled a large package out of the back. It needed both of them to lift it.

Along the table, Jonah heard one of the volunteers make a crack about Mafia. Others laughed, some nervously. This was southern Italy, after all.

But one of the men looked familiar. So much had happened to him that day that it took a moment for the answer to come. He was dressed differently, too: a black shirt and jeans, not the white T-shirt with the alligator on the chest.

It was the plumber who'd come to fix the shower – the shower that worked perfectly well. So what was he doing here?

Nothing made sense. He pushed back his chair and stood. Blood rushed out of his head, he swayed and grabbed the table. The students looked at him as if he was drunk. Fragments of foreign conversations kicked around him like dust.

'It's so bling.'

'Sandi didn't think so.'

'Ari's such a creep.'

As he turned, he caught the woman at the next table staring at him – not a casual glance, but full bore. She was strikingly beautiful: black hair cut straight across the fringe, delicate features made golden in the fairy lights. A lotus-flower tattoo blossomed on her bare shoulder. He had the nagging feeling he knew her from somewhere, though it might just have been implicit in her too-familiar gaze. Maybe a gig?

She looked back at her food and he decided he'd imagined it. Every night, for the last six weeks, he'd seen hundreds of faces flashed up at him as the lights framed them for an instant. Subliminal overload. Somewhere, his brain probably stored them all. It would explain why he felt déjà vu so often.

But unless he'd imagined the whole incident with the plumber, the man on the dock was no false memory. He ran out of the hotel, down the street. The resort was staggered around the marinas, the condos and hotels built on long fingers divided by moorings. The dock opposite was only fifty yards across the water, but to reach it without swimming was most of a mile. He ran it in ten minutes and felt like throwing up before he was halfway there.

Two blocks away, a macho rumble told him he was too late. He tried to run faster, but the harder he tried, the slower he seemed to go. The engines throttled up; he heard the gassy sound of propellers churning water. He reached the dock just in time to see the lights on the fly-bridge floating away into the night. The wake glowed luminous white; across the transom, he read the name NESTIS.

A blazing white light picked him up. The Mercedes had been waiting in the shadows; now it came to life. The driver, invisible behind the lights, gunned the engine, then dropped the clutch so suddenly the whole three-ton car leaped forward. The light swamped him: for a moment, Jonah thought it would run him right into the water.

The car stopped at the last minute, executed a sharp three-point turn and raced away. Jonah's eyes swam. Behind him, he heard running footsteps.

'What on earth are you doing?' Richard's face was red as a balloon. His shirt-tails flapped untucked, and one of his shoelaces had come undone. He doubled over, clutching a stitch. 'Jesus.'

'I thought . . . ' *What?* The energy drained out of him.

Had he really seen the plumber on the dock – in the dark, over the water? Or was his overtired mind just throwing up images at him? More déjà vu.

A bird swooped over the marina. Across the harbour, he saw the others watching from the hotel terrace. A billion miles away. He realised how ridiculous he must look to them. The water was still, only a few gentle waves lapping the pilings to show the boat had ever been there.

Richard tucked in his shirt and wiped the sweat off his glasses.

'It'll all be fine tomorrow.'

Seven

A stranger who makes his way into the major cities, and persuades the best young men there to associate with him, must take extreme care. Jealousy is quickly aroused, and he can attract a lot of hostility and conspiracies against himself.

Plato, *Protagoras*

I was drowning again. I thrashed for the surface, but the water was thick and my arms barely moved. I screamed. The sea rushed in, filling me up until I no longer felt it because I had *become* it.

I was breathing water. It flowed through me, calming my panic. Now when I looked up I could see the sun, a white orb shimmering through the waves. Even underwater, it burned my eyes. I had to reach it. I started to float upwards, but however fast I rose, the sun never came any closer.

Now I was on land. Black clouds plated the sky, scudding over the plain, and a forked mountain loomed in the distance. The goddess approached me across a flower-strewn meadow, barefoot. The wind blew her dress taut against her marble skin; the ivy in her hair rustled. Her face was solemn, beautiful but hard as stone. When I woke up, drenched in sweat, I knew she'd just told me something vital.

I wracked my brains, but I couldn't remember what.

★   ★   ★

Eurytus was eager to get rid of us. After a quick breakfast, we set off for Taras. My first impression of Italy, beyond the beach and the forest, surprised me. I'd expected a primal wilderness: instead, neat lines of olive and citrus trees divided the holdings, with thick wheat growing green in between. The road was good, the houses well-kept – we could have been near Thebes. Except that a high plateau walled off the horizon, laying a sharp line across the limit of civilisation. And, when we reached Taras – across a causeway through a salt marsh – the walls were thick, the mortar still white. You couldn't forget that this colony still clung to the fringes of a wild, unknown country.

The city stood on a neck of land between the sea and an inland lagoon, natural defences that also made a superb harbour (if only our ship had reached it). Eurytus led us through busy streets, with handsome temples and houses squeezed close together. He, too, was less wild than I'd first assumed: plenty of respectable-looking men greeted him in the streets and paused to talk business, more and more often as we entered the agora.

He steered us across the plaza to a fountain of Poseidon standing in a chariot drawn by four dolphins. Opposite him, almost as high, a man in a blue cloak stood on the steps of the Assembly house, deep in debate with a score of men around him. Some were dressed like soldiers, some like merchants and some like lawyers – but all of them looked important.

Eurytus pushed through the crowd to the man at the top and managed to get his attention. He whispered in his ear, pointing out me and Euphemus. A moment later, the man excused himself and came down. The others pretended to continue their conversation, though I saw every pair of eyes latch onto us.

'These are the castaways,' was the apologetic introduction Eurytus gave us. 'This is Archytas.'

He was tall and civilised, with strong arms and the clipped stride you get from marching in formation with a hoplite shield banging against your knees. I found out later he was the same age as me, though he looked older. His hair was streaked a handsome grey, and the shrewd eyes that examined me seemed to have seen and understood more than I ever would.

'So,' he said. 'Tell me your country, your nation and your city, and all the places you have wandered.'

Quoting Homer doesn't impress me, though I'm sure it's exactly the sort of thing Euphemus loves. Before he could reply in kind, I said, 'We came from Athens. Our ship was wrecked.'

'And what brought you to Italy?'

A simple enough question. But behind him, I could see twenty heads leaning forward to hear my answer.

'I came to look for a friend.'

'Agathon,' Eurytus said. He and Archytas shared a look.

'You know him?'

'A mutual acquaintance introduced us,' said Archytas. 'He stayed with me.'

I didn't understand the past tense. '*Stayed?*'

'He had to leave suddenly.'

'He's supposed to meet me here.'

'Why did he go?' asked Euphemus, alert to scandal.

'Where did he go?' I wanted to know.

'I imagine he went back to Thurii. He had a friend there.'

I have been staying with Dimos in Thurii. 'My stepbrother, Dimos.' My mind spun, thrown off by the unexpected news. 'Is it far from here?'

Archytas' shrewd eyes examined me. They seemed to be saying something, but I couldn't work out what.

'You can walk to Thurii in three days. By boat, it's quicker.'

'We're not going in another boat,' said Euphemus, emphatically.

I didn't know where I was going. Just walking to town had exhausted me again. I didn't have anything except the clothes on my back (and those were borrowed from Eurytus); I couldn't afford lunch, let alone a passage to Thurii. And there were things about Agathon that Archytas seemed unwilling to say, that I was desperate to know.

Archytas must have read it all in my eyes. He took mercy on me.

'It's too late to set off now. You can stay in my house tonight.'

Archytas' house, near the agora, dwarfed anything you'd see in Athens, big enough that Euphemus and I were given separate rooms. Archytas excused himself with business in town; Euphemus invited himself along, no doubt hoping to tout for business. I lay on the bed and stretched out, trying to unknot my battered muscles.

I flexed my fingers around the end of the mattress. To my surprise, instead of soft cloth, my hand felt something brittle and hard that crinkled under my touch. I pulled it out.

It was a scroll, battered and dented. I unrolled the first column's worth to see what it was.

The Way of Truth, by Parmenides.

Of course I've studied Parmenides, but never with much success. He writes his philosophy in such dense, elusive language it's impossible to know what to think. Half of me – the Voice of Desire – is utterly seduced by the dark fantasies and vivid images. The other half – the Voice of Reason – insists that if he had anything worth saying, he'd just get it out.

I lay on the bed and turned through the scroll. I wondered who had left it there.

The path you came down is far from the well-trodden roads of mortals. But it was not cruel Fate who brought you here, but

*Truth and Justice, in order for you to learn everything there is
to know.*

*There are two paths of enquiry – the way that is, and the way
that is not. And one is impossible, for you cannot travel the way
that is not, and nothing that goes down that road comes back.*

Perhaps it was reading him on Italian soil, where his ideas
germinated. Perhaps the shocks of the last two days had
cracked my rational defences. Whatever it was, I found the
Voice of Reason unusually submissive as I read it.

Do not let habit drag you into the well-worn rut,
Guiding yourself with blind eyes, deaf ears and a dumb tongue,
But use reason; by thought, look clearly on things which though
they are not there
Are there.

I was still looking at the manuscript, trying to see things that
might or might not be there, when I heard commotion downstairs, and Archytas' strong voice issuing orders to his slaves.
I went down.

Archytas was in the *andron*, the men's quarters. Like the
man himself, the decoration was spare and masculine: black-
and-white tiles tessellating triangles on the floor; a few fine
pieces of dinnerware hanging from the whitewashed walls,
and bronze armour displayed in an alcove.

I walked through the door and was almost bowled over as
a small boy barrelled into my knees, bounced off, and wrig-
gled through my legs. I stepped back, just in time to avoid
another child hurling himself after the first. In the corner, by
a chest, a naked baby sat on the floor, tugging at a wheeled
wooden duck that quacked as it rolled.

'Have I come into the nursery?' I wondered aloud.

'Children keep us young,' Archytas said. 'Sometimes they
see things more clearly than grown-ups.'

He tickled the baby's cheek as a slave woman bundled it away. I handed him the scroll. 'I found this in my bedroom. I think it belongs in your library.'

Archytas checked the title. 'I wondered where it had gone.'

'It fell behind the bed.' I paused. 'Did Agathon have that room before me?'

'Yes.'

Again, Agathon's name was like sand on a fire. All the light went out of him and the warmth cooled. This time, I decided to poke around to see what I could stir up.

'Tell me about Agathon. Is he well?'

'The last time I saw him.'

'You said he left in a hurry.'

'Yes.'

'Why did he go?'

'He didn't tell me.'

The bitterness in his answer practically invited the next question. 'Had you argued?'

He picked up the duck and examined the underside, tightening one of the wheels. 'Is Agathon a close friend of yours?'

'The best friend I have.'

I could see him wondering how to interpret that. If I'm honest, I'm not sure myself. On one level, it's entirely true that Agathon is my dearest friend, the one I love best. When I talk to him, it can feel as if my soul is on my lips. But it's also true that he can be wilful, evasive, cruel, and often gives the impression he wouldn't notice if you came or went. Like asking you to cross the sea to meet him, and then leaving before you get there.

'I know Agathon's sometimes difficult,' I offered, trying to make an opening. 'He gets impatient.'

Archytas nodded slowly.

'Was he bored of waiting?'

66

'He thought I could teach him something I wouldn't tell him.'

I didn't understand. Agathon had come to Taras to meet me off the boat, not to study.

So why isn't he here?

I looked at the armour on the wall. It was nicely made, but not impractical. Light pooled in the hollows where dents had been hammered out, and the cuts scored into the leather greaves were too deep to have come from drills and sparring.

'Was Agathon interested in warfare?' Unlikely: he's the most peaceful man I know. 'Politics?'

'Philosophy.'

He laughed at my obvious surprise. 'Not all philosophers are shoeless loiterers haranguing strangers.'

I remembered the way the men in the agora had deferred to him – even the older ones. 'I didn't realise you were a philosopher. I thought you were somebody . . . '

'Important?'

'Respectable.'

'I'm the captain of the city's defences, if you count that as important.' He smiled. 'In Italy, philosophy isn't incompatible with other occupations. You can even be respectable.'

That was a whole different conversation I would love to have had. But not now.

'What did Agathon want from you?'

'He'd become fascinated by Pythagoras.'

I stared at my host. In every pore of his being, he couldn't have looked more different from Eurytus. 'Are you a Pythagorean?'

'I'm a mathematician.'

'Like Eurytus?'

'We both believe that the key to the world is numbers. But he thinks that the numbers themselves are what matters. He looks at the particulars and thinks he can make rules from them, some sort of meaning. I'm doing the opposite.'

He put his thumbs and index fingers together, making a crude triangle. 'You might see this as a triangle, but it isn't really. My fingers aren't straight, the angles aren't exact. If you tried to generalise about triangles from this, you'd get gibberish. But there's another way. When I think about a triangle, I'm not thinking about this one or that one. They're just images of a prototype which isn't defined physically, but logically. Not *a* triangle, but *the* triangle *itself*. Pythagoras' genius was discovering that the world has an underlying order, a system which – and this is the really miraculous bit – we can understand through reason.'

'I can see it works for triangles,' I said doubtfully.

Archytas reached into a chest and took out a handsome eight-string lyre, with a tortoiseshell sounding box and double-scrolled arms. He cupped it to his breast and plucked two strings in succession.

'This is a note, and so is this.' He plucked again, this time both strings simultaneously. 'Together, you get harmony – a third thing that unites its component parts.'

The chord rang with a kind of sad beauty. 'But what does that have to do with mathematics?'

'Music *is* mathematics.' Archytas played the chord again. 'Look at the strings. If you measure them, you'll find that the first harmonious pair is made by making the second string four-thirds as long as the first. The next harmonious pair is on the ratio three to two, and the octave comes by doubling the length.

He wrote the ratios on a wax tablet. *1:2 – 2:3 – 3:4*.

'I thought you weren't interested in numbers.'

He plucked a few more notes, improvising a short tune. It reminded me of the deathless music the wind chimes had made in the forest.

'The universe is motion, and everything that moves makes a sound. If we could hear it all, and understand the formulas that govern it, there'd be a lot more harmony in the world.'

'Is that what Agathon wanted to learn about?'

The music died away. Archytas laid the lyre back in its box.

'Agathon thought there was more, and I was hiding it from him.'

'Were you?'

A grave look. 'The beauty of mathematics is that you can't hide anything. There are no rituals or mysteries. Each step comes logically from the last. Anyone can see it if he takes the time to think it through.'

'But you parted on bad terms.'

'Not when he left. When I found out what he'd done—'

Just then, the door banged open and Euphemus walked in.

'Good news,' he announced. 'I've hired mules to take me as far as Rhegion.'

Obviously, he expected me to make something of it. I just stared.

'Thurii's on the way.' Another pause. 'If you want to find your friend there, you're welcome to come with me.'

Everything I owned was fishbait – including my purse. 'I can't afford . . . How are you paying for it?'

He showed me a palmful of gold coins, heavy archers minted in Persia.

'Did you rob someone?'

'I keep them sewn into my belt for when things go wrong. Which they usually do, in my experience.'

'No wonder you were so heavy to drag out of the sea.'

'And now I'm showing my gratitude. Do you want to come?'

I hesitated. There was so much more I wanted to ask

Archytas – and having to endure Euphemus' company on the road was a dismal prospect. But . . .

There are two ways, says Parmenides, *and one is impossible.* 'I'll come.'

Archytas was out to dinner that night. Euphemus angled for an invitation, but Archytas artfully outmanoeuvred him. I spent the evening in my room with a lamp, trying to make sense of Parmenides. I couldn't concentrate. I kept listening for Archytas' return, but all I heard was an empty house: a slave singing, water splashing out of the well, a broom knocking the wall as it swept out some corner.

The place I began is where I shall return.

Somewhere in the house, the wooden duck quacked. I rubbed my eyes. I'd been staring at the same column for the last twenty minutes, thinking about Agathon. I rolled up the scroll and laid it on my chest.

The goddess visited me again that night, holding my hand as we flew over the golden sea. She told me something, but the rushing wind snatched the words away and I didn't hear. She wanted me to repeat it; when I couldn't, she got angry. She let go of my wrist, and I was falling, falling, falling towards the water, until I hit the mattress and jerked up in the dark, silent house.

Then it was morning, and everything was forgotten in the rush to be ready. I had nothing to pack, but Euphemus seemed to have bought enough new clothes and provisions to outfit an army. Archytas said he would walk the first stretch with us.

We took a ferry across the mouth of the lagoon. On the far side, we picked up a shady road leading south, through the ripe fields along the coastal plain. I wanted to ask Archytas about Agathon again – I could feel the time slipping away with every step – but somehow it never seemed like the right moment.

We hadn't gone far when I saw a cluster of low mounds, too small and isolated to be hills, bulging up on our right under a stand of poplars.

Archytas stopped. 'Let me show you something.'

Tethering the mules, he led us off the road down a path through the grass. Asphodels and daisies licked at our feet; I could smell thyme and wild onions.

Coming closer, we entered a sort of valley between the mounds. They rose above head height, each with a stone doorframe set into the side, sealed with a clay slab. Blackened lamps, long burned out, sat in niches cut into the lintels. Weeds grew from cracks in the stones, and grass had begun filling in the spaces between the doorposts.

I supposed they must be tombs. I wondered why they were so far back from the road, on this isolated patch.

One was different. A dark tongue of earth trailed from its door where something had been dug or dragged out of it. Fragments of a smashed clay slab lay on the ground; the opening had been blocked by a few planks hastily jammed across.

Archytas paused in front of it, making sure I saw.

'What happened?'

'Someone broke in two weeks ago. They opened the coffin and stole some grave goods.'

'That's terrible.'

It sounds like a platitude – but I meant it. Disrespecting the dead is about the worst thing you can do to provoke the gods: no Greek in his right mind would want to do it. If you've seen *Antigone*, you'll know what I'm talking about.

'Did they catch the person who did it?'

Archytas picked up one of the clay shards, turning it in his hand.

71

'Not yet.'

He was trying to tell me something, but I couldn't understand what. Perhaps I was naïve; perhaps I had too generous a view of my friend.

Euphemus, with no illusions to confuse him, got it at once. He coughed, with the contrived sorrow of a doctor giving a diagnosis which will be immensely profitable to him.

'I think what our friend is trying to tell us is: Agathon did it.'

Eight

Jonah – London

He'd seen films where astronauts passed their journeys in hypersleep, dreaming away the light years in glass cocoons until they reached their distant star. There were no cocoons on Ryanair, but it felt the same. He was numb, oblivious, moving through space in suspended animation. Even when he arrived, he didn't feel he'd woken up.

He'd rung Lily's mobile from the hotel phone before he went to bed, but her mobile was still switched off. No answer from their home number, either. The thought that she might have tried to call him on his dead phone ate away at him: without it, he felt as though he'd lost a limb. The moment he reached the terminal at Stansted, he found a phone shop and paid over the odds for a new handset, praying his old SIM card would work.

The new phone switched on. A circle spun in infinite loops on screen as it looked for a network, twisting his hopes into knots.

It's only a phone, he reminded himself. But it was more than that. It was his lifeline.

Network found.

He checked the Contacts and saw all his old numbers had come with the SIM. The feeling of relief was embarrassing – but he didn't care. He found Lily's mother's number and dialled.

Julie, Lily's sister, answered after three rings. It made sense she'd be there. She sounded surprised to hear him.

'Is everything OK?' she asked.

That's what I want to know. 'How's your mum doing?'

'Not too bad.'

'Is Lily there?'

A pause. 'Isn't she with you?'

'She flew back last night to be with your mum.'

'What are you talking about?'

'Your mum. The fall. Lily came back.' He kept waiting for her to agree, some sort of affirmation, but none of his words were getting a response. 'Didn't she?' he concluded lamely.

'Mum's here right now doing her crossword,' Julie said definitively. 'I just came over for a cup of tea. What's all this about a fall?'

'Lily said . . . ' He needed to get out of this conversation. 'I think I must have had a crossed wire somewhere.'

'Is something wrong with Lily?'

That's what I want to know. The whole conversation was backwards. 'I don't know.' He told her what had happened.

'I've no idea where she got that from. Mum's fine.'

'That's good.' But that wasn't the question hammering in his mind. 'So where's Lily?'

An uneasy silence as Julie weighed up the options. 'Maybe she's gone home.'

He knew she wasn't there the moment he saw the house.

The curtains were half drawn to suggest the occupants might be in or out, the same way they'd been for the last six weeks. The lights were off, though on a rainy afternoon the basement flat would be dark as mud. And he could feel her absence, the same way you could pick up a CD case and tell if it was empty by the weight.

He opened the door, sweeping back the pile of post that clogged the doormat. More post was stacked in neat piles on the table. Someone had been here, but not today and not Lily.

He listened. All he could hear was the rumble of traffic heading towards Wandsworth Bridge, the drip of the kitchen tap. Had that been going on for six weeks?

'Lily?' he called.

The flat had three rooms and Lily wasn't in any of them. Nor was her luggage, nor any sign she'd passed through. When Jonah had checked all three, he went upstairs and rang the bell of the ground-floor flat.

Alice answered the door, eventually, in bare feet and a painting smock. Her long grey hair was knotted into a bun that let go more than it held; she had a smudge of blue paint on her cheek. She looked puzzled.

'I thought you weren't back for another three weeks.'

'Change of plan. Lily and I flew back separately. Have you seen her?'

Alice pushed her glasses up onto her forehead and peered at him. 'Is everything all right?'

All right? Nothing was right. But how did you tell that to the upstairs neighbour who'd been watering your plants?

'She'll probably be here soon,' he said. He felt her eyes on his back all the way down the steps.

'Thanks for doing the plants,' he remembered at the bottom.

The flat was dark, cramped, and damp. It cost more than they could afford, and its only public transport links were the buses that rumbled past twenty-four hours a day, shaking the foundations and keeping them awake. Similar parts of London had been colonised with organic delis and shops that sold thousand-pound bathroom fittings. Here, gentrification was an estate agent's myth.

But at the back of the flat, double doors opened into a small paved yard that ended in three concrete steps down to the river. Not the Thames, but one of its tributaries: a forgotten stream that had once watered green hills, then washed the city's industrial sprawl, and finally inconvenienced its middle-class suburbs. The moment Lily glimpsed it from the bedroom, she'd known this was the place.

Jonah had thought about the cost, vaguely wondered about flood risks, and agreed. There was something in Lily that he recognised but didn't understand, a kinship with water that responded to it, needed to be close. The night they moved in, she stripped off in the garden and waded in from the steps, careless of Jonah's warnings and the neighbours' windows. She splashed in the black water, swimming circles on her back and laughing with cold. When she came out, she huddled against Jonah under a blanket – even now, he shivered remembering the chill of her body against his – and sat on the steps, looking for the stars that the city hid with its false glow.

'Will you marry me?' he asked her.

The stars were gone now. It was mid-afternoon on a cool late-August day. Jonah sat on the steps, sipping a beer. Trees covered the far bank, with a park beyond: if you focussed, you could imagine the city away. He watched the water and thought about Lily. The river flowed, but his thoughts just went in circles.

Part of him still tried to argue that really it was fine. There'd been a crossed wire, a mixed message, and somehow they'd each ended up in the wrong place. If he stayed put, sooner or later the door would open or the phone would ring, and everything would be right again. That was how normal life worked.

But he knew it wasn't true. The theory had too many holes to even pretend it made sense.

She'd been in Sibari yesterday morning. Richard said so; Jonah had seen the swimsuit dripping on the balcony, barely taken off before he got there. And, by mid-afternoon, she'd packed up her room and vanished.

He knew why he wanted to believe it was just an honest mistake: because the alternatives were too bizarre and terrifying to contemplate.

But that was where he had to go.

He picked up his new phone and called Richard in Sibari. It rang a long time – any other time, he'd have given up – before Richard answered.

'Is everything all right?' he said. 'Did Lily get back safely?'

Jonah let the pause run so long Richard must have thought he'd hung up. He was staring over the edge of a precipice and couldn't see bottom.

'She's not here. She never came back.'

He blanked out the predictable exclamations and questions, answering with his eyes closed. *I'm sure. Not at all. Nothing.* All he could feel was falling.

'You haven't seen her either?'

'Not a thing.'

'Can you find out what time she checked out of the hotel? Did the receptionist see her?'

'I'll ask. I'm at the site at the moment.'

'Ask the others, too. See if she told them anything.'

'I will.' He sounded impatient, eager to be off the phone. Jonah didn't let him go.

'Do you know if she was worried about anything?'

'Only dig stuff.'

He remembered the yacht and the big car on the dock, the certainty he'd felt that it had something to do with Lily. At the time, he thought he'd just embarrassed himself.

'There was a car there that day – a big black Mercedes.

And the yacht. Can you find out if anyone saw them around, anything suspicious?'

'I'll look into it,' Richard promised. 'I've got to go now.'

Jonah finished the beer and went to the kitchen for another. He needed the sedation: without it, his thoughts would have been too much to live with. A thousand hideous images, dredged from every film and news report he'd ever watched, played around him. He had to find a way through.

As he opened the fridge, a Post-it note on the door caught his eye. It had been there since before they left for the summer and had started to curl around the edges. Another artefact of Lily.

Buy: Milk, Spaghetti, Ham, Beer. {o} L

The {o} was her ideogram – a stylised lily-flower, if you looked at it right. Whatever she wrote to him – notes, e-mails, texts – she always signed off with it.

But not those last two texts she'd sent him in Sibari. He'd noticed it, though at the time it had been the least of his worries. He'd assumed she was too upset about her mum to bother.

Except her mum was fine, and there was no family emergency. That was a lie.

Lily would never lie to him.

He went back to the river but didn't open the beer. He needed to think. Someone could have stolen her phone and sent the messages as a sick prank. In the circumstances, that was almost the best he could hope for. But it didn't account for the one fact that mattered.

She's missing.

He said it aloud, letting the river take the words and spin them away on the current. Then he started to think what he could do about it.

Greece

The moment he saw Lily, he felt he must have known her forever. He just needed to find out who she was.

Lily made it six of them on the dig: her, Richard and Julian, Charis, Adam and Jonah. Jonah hadn't realised how much the others had been waiting for her until she arrived. Those first three days, they looked like a closed circle, sufficient with each other, not much interested in him. It was only when she got there that he saw the change. As if they'd all been holding something back. Lily was the one who made sense of the group, the hub at the centre. Much later, he wondered if they even liked each other much without her.

Because picking broken pots out of the ground didn't tax his concentration, he had plenty of time to think about the others. Even the way they dressed was totally different, to each other or anyone else he knew back home. Richard wore long-sleeved shirts and a ridiculous Panama hat to keep the sun off; Charis exposed every inch of her golden body that she could get away with. Julian, twenty going on forty, dressed like a banker on casual Friday. Adam wore nothing but black, even shovelling soil in the Greek midday heat. Jonah would have said good riddance to all of them – if Lily hadn't shown up.

It was hard to prise them apart at first. Always in and out of each other's rooms, rubbing sunscreen on each other's backs, clambering over each other in the sea. The first day, he thought Lily and Adam were an item; the next, perhaps Lily and Julian. Richard, he assumed, was gay. Through all of it, Jonah sat apart with his headphones on, watching and wondering.

Sunday was a day off: they'd hired a car to go and visit Delphi. They'd spoken about it all week and never included

Jonah, but after breakfast that morning, Lily found him in the lobby.

'Are you coming?'

'Is there space?'

'They can squeeze up.' She grinned. 'You might have to get out on the hills and push.'

Lily drove. Jonah, being the oldest and tallest, got the passenger seat. The other four crammed into the back; Charis sat on Julian's lap. They wound down the windows and turned up the radio, a Greek station that seemed to have fallen through a 1970s timewarp. 'Don't Bring Me Down', sang the Electric Light Orchestra. Richard fretted about pollen. Adam hunched over the guidebook.

'The oracle at Delphi issued its prophecies for over eight hundred years. Incredible, when you think about it.'

'Mystic Meg,' said Julian. 'She was high as a kite.'

'The temple's built on a geological fault.' Richard fiddled with his hat. 'Ethylene fumes seeped out and the oracle breathed them in.'

'Richard's got an explanation for everything,' Lily told Jonah. 'No romance.'

'Archaeology's the search for fact . . . ' Richard began.

'If it's truth you're looking for, Doctor Tyree's philosophy class is right down the hall,' they all chorused.

In ancient times, the Delphic oracle had been big business – a cross between Mecca and the United Nations, according to the guidebook, a huge complex spilling down the slopes of Mount Parnassus. They started off together, but gradually the sheer size of the site separated them. Julian and Charis drifted ahead, Richard and Adam wanted to pore over every scrap of marble. By the time they reached the temple of Apollo, Jonah and Lily were alone. It was just past noon, and the sun was brutal. Most of the tourists had gone back to their buses, or down to the café to get a Slush

Puppie. It felt as though they had the whole site to themselves.

Lily sat on a fallen piece of masonry and considered the temple. Half a dozen ribbed columns stood at one end; otherwise, all that had survived was the base. Even that was big enough: as long as a cathedral, built of stones as big as cars. A hole at the far end showed where the oracle had once sat in her cave and given the answers that defined her civilisation.

'If you only had one question, what would you ask her?'

Jonah looked into Lily's eyes, shaded under the brim of her hat.

'You'd have to be careful, though,' Lily warned. 'Sometimes her answers were trickier than the questions.'

'I'd ask if she had a date.'

Lily laughed. 'I think she was supposed to be celibate. Otherwise, the whole vision thing didn't work.'

She stood and pirouetted away, heading further up the mountain. Jonah stood in the dust, wondering if he'd blown his chance, offended her, if she'd even noticed?

Three steps later, she looked back.

'She doesn't, by the way.'

London

He sat by the river with his laptop. His finger trembled as he tapped out the words on the screen.

MISSING PERSONS

Why *persons*? It was a phrase that somehow arrived fully formed in his consciousness, a cultural shorthand. Was it so common that society needed a shorthand?

Common enough that the government had a whole section of their website devoted to it. It told him to report the case to the Foreign Office. He went in and dialled the number they gave, hovering over the last digit so long the phone gave up. Like being a teenager, calling the girl who'd broken your heart. He tried again.

He told the switchboard what he wanted and they put him through to a young voice called Martin. Martin offered scripted sympathy and took Lily's name, description, last known location.

'Do you know her passport number?'

'She had it with her.'

'A mobile phone number? An e-mail?'

He gave both. 'But she's not been answering her phone. I think someone's using it to send fake text messages.'

Did that sound crazy? Martin acted as if he hadn't said it. 'You need to make a full statement to the police. They'll pass it to Interpol, who'll contact the Italians. The local police in Sibari will lead any investigation.'

It was all too slow. Did they think they'd find her by filling in forms and passing them from desk to desk. 'Can't I go back and report it directly?' Not that he had a lot of faith in the Italian police.

'You can go out, of course. But you ought to think about what you might achieve. Do you speak Italian? We wouldn't be able to help you out there, or provide any resources. It's entirely in the Italians' hands.'

'Are you saying there's nothing I can do?'

'We can arrange a statement to the media. We can also arrange for flyers or posters to be distributed in the area.'

Flyers and posters. Was that the best they could do? Bedraggled sheets of A4 taped to a lamppost, as if he was looking for a lost kitten.

'Whatever you decide,' Martin continued. 'Contact your local police first. That'll get the ball rolling.'

'Right.'

But Martin still had more of the script to get through. The

fine print. 'Of course, one has to remember that sometimes people go missing because they choose to. That they may not want you to know where they are. If that's the case, we can't tell you their whereabouts even if we do find them.'

'*Choose to go missing?*' Jonah echoed.

'Though we would certainly tell you if we discovered they were alive and well.' He turned the page of his script and his voice brightened. 'Tens of thousands of people are reported missing every year, you know. For most, there's a harmless explanation and the cases are quickly resolved.'

Nine

Anyone with an ounce of common sense will do his utmost to steer clear of any crime involving foreigners.

Plato, *Laws*

I stared into the broken-mouthed tomb. The poplars shivered in the wind; the long grass whispered its secrets. I half convinced myself I could hear some dreadful creature slithering down the tunnel, drawn to the light.

'You think Agathon did this?' I mumbled.

'It happened the night he left.'

A piece of the clay slab that had closed the tomb lay by my feet. I picked it up. A hooded woman sat on a throne: I guessed it was Persephone, though the broken tablet had torn off her face.

'That doesn't prove—'

'A mourner had come here to light a grave lamp. She saw him.'

I didn't know what to say. 'Who's buried here?' We were a long way from the public necropolis I'd seen on the approach to Taras, or the grand monuments that lined the road. A private place.

'Someone who died a long time ago.'

'Then what did Agathon think he'd find?' The tomb yawned black, an open question. 'Were these Pythagoreans?'

'They belong to a religion which is older than Pythagoras.'

Archytas picked a pair of asphodels and laid them across the tomb's entrance. An apology. 'Pythagoras wasn't enough. Agathon wanted to go further, to find what came before. The source of Pythagoras' ideas.'

'What was that?'

A firm stare. 'I couldn't tell him.'

We walked back in silence, except for the buzz of flies and the croak of crows from a split cypress tree. It didn't surprise me that when we got to the road, Archytas turned towards Taras. He'd shown me what I needed to see.

'Did Agathon find what he wanted in that tomb?' I said quickly. Euphemus was fussing with the saddlebags. For a last, brief moment, I had Archytas to myself.

'No.'

'So where will he look next?'

'Are you going to follow him?'

'That's what I came for.' And everything I'd heard since I got there suggested he was in some awful kind of trouble.

Archytas rubbed a smudge of dust from the neck of his tunic.

'Let me ask you a hypothetical question,' he said. 'Imagine the gods gave you mechanical wings, and you flew into the air, past the sun and the planets and the stars, all the way to the very edge of the universe. And as you stood there, you raised your arm and tried to push it beyond the limit. What would happen?'

'I don't know.' I thought about it. 'If I was at the very edge of the universe, I suppose my arm wouldn't be able to go any further.'

'But what could block it? A wall, some sort of barrier beyond?'

I saw the problem. 'Then that would be part of the universe, too – so I wouldn't be at the absolute limit.'

'But if your arm went through, then there would have to be space beyond for it to go into. So, again, you wouldn't really be at the limit either.'

It sounded suspiciously like sophistry to me. I gave him a hard look. 'Is there an answer to the riddle?'

'It's a paradox. There is no answer.' He met my gaze, forcing my doubts back on me. 'As for the meaning . . . '

Whatever he was going to say, he thought better of it.

'Something for you to think about on the road.'

'And Agathon?' I prompted, reminding him of my original question.

'Try your stepbrother's house in Thurii.'

I could see he was eager to go. But just before he went, a final, unexplained question jumped into my mind.

'Did Agathon ever mention a book he wanted to buy? Something expensive, probably rare?'

A curt shake of his head. 'He never mentioned a book.'

It seemed like the longest, flattest road in the world. The land merged with the sea, and then the sea with the sky, to make a perfect geometric plane, uncluttered by any solid object. At least I had space to think. Mile after mile through the heat and tedium, I continued the silent conversation I've been having for ten years.

Socrates: Are you regretting coming to Italy yet?
Me: I'm worried about Agathon.
Socrates: The business with the tomb?
Me: It makes no sense. Agathon wouldn't steal. And he'd never desecrate a grave.
Socrates: Because he's a good man?
Me: Yes.
Socrates: And a good man . . .
Me: . . . would never do something he knew was bad.

You drilled that into me.

Socrates: But he might do a bad thing that he mistakenly believed was good, wouldn't you say?

Me: Agathon knows right from wrong. He's obsessed with doing the right thing.

Socrates: But does it seem to you that when a man does something, he wants the thing he's doing for its own sake, or for the sake of what he's trying to achieve? For example, when you sailed to Italy, did you want the hazards of the voyage and the hardships of travel, or did you want to find Agathon?

Me: I assume that's a rhetorical question.

Socrates: And isn't that always the case? When a man does something, he wants the end and not the means?

Me: Certainly.

Socrates: And what is the object of every action?

Me: From previous conversations we've had, I'd say it has to be something good.

Socrates: So is it possible that Agathon could have committed the act of stealing from the tomb because he believed it was better to do so than not?

Me: I suppose so.

Socrates: Because he aimed at some good.

Me: Yes.

Socrates: And what is the supreme good?

Me: Wisdom.

I trudged on, leading my mule by the bridle to give it a rest. I was sweating, and only partly from the midday heat. Dark images blotted my mind; the faceless goddess lingered at the back of my thoughts. I tried to distract myself by looking at the landscape, but there was nothing in that monotony to get hold of.

Socrates: On the subject of wisdom, what did you think of your first encounter with the Pythagoreans?

Me: I thought Archytas made more sense than Eurytus. And I still only understood about half of what he said.

Socrates: Agathon obviously thought they had something worth knowing.

Me: I suppose you're going to tell me he's right.

Socrates: Didn't Heraclitus say there are no certainties in the world because everything is in flux?

Me: You can't step in the same river twice.

Socrates: But Pythagoras proves there are certainties. A triangle's corners always add up to 180 degrees.

Me: A doubled string always sounds the octave.

Socrates: So Heraclitus is refuted. You *can* step in the same river twice – if the river is defined mathematically.

Me: That's just it. I can see mathematics is all very well applied to triangles. But is there a mathematics of virtue? Laws that will tell you the right thing to do, as certainly as they'll tell you what note will sound harmonious?

Socrates: Why not? Do you think most people can hear music and tell if it's in tune or not?

Me: Yes.

Socrates: Everyone?

Me: Not everyone. Some people are tone deaf.

Socrates: And, by and large, can people tell whether an action is good or not?

Me: Some, I suppose.

Socrates: Perhaps people who can't tell right from wrong have something equivalent to being tone deaf. A sort of moral deafness.

Me: Euphemus certainly suffers from it.

Socrates: He's making the same mistake as Heraclitus. He makes deductions based on what he sees in the world – and because he sees so much chaos, he deduces there are no rules.

Me: So you're saying there *are* moral laws too? Laws which govern the things that people know are right and wrong, even if they don't understand why?

Socrates: Listen to Parmenides: *Use reason to look clearly on things which though they are not there, are there.*

Me: I don't suppose you're going to tell me what these rules are?

Socrates: There's a long way to go yet.

Socrates loved walking. He loved to walk and talk, and walk and think, up and down and around every street in Athens. *Walking is good for thinking*, he said, though it never worked for me. My thoughts don't flow until my body is settled, with a pen in my hand and a fresh tablet on the desk.

But perhaps I understand the attraction now. So often with Socrates, I left feeling that I'd travelled a great distance without ever reaching a destination.

At least walking guarantees you'll get somewhere.

Further south, the scenery began to change. Mountain peaks broke the monotony of the ridge on the horizon. The road grew empty, the settlements fewer and further apart. At night, I heard wolves howling in the distance – or perhaps it was the wild tribes of the interior. Sadly, it didn't intimidate Euphemus. He told me early and proudly that one of his best courtroom tricks was to speak without seeming to breathe, so that the opposing advocate couldn't get a word in. It was a skill he demonstrated *ad nauseam*.

'Why do you despise the world so much?'

We were climbing over a spur of a mountain, part of the ridge that guarded the plain of Thurii. I'd blanked him out: it was only when he went quiet that I realised he actually wanted me to say something. He repeated the question.

'I don't despise the world.'

'Then why are you so hostile to the sophists?'

'I hate to tell you this, but despising sophists isn't the same as despising the world.'

'But it's our worldliness that offends you. While philosophers sit on their mountaintops drawing triangles, we're down in the law courts and the Assembly wrestling with the problems of real life.'

'*Real* life?' I echoed. 'There's nothing real about it. You don't try to explain the world: you argue it whichever way you're paid. You'll happily claim that black is white, bad is good and the weaker argument is actually stronger.'

'If enough people can be made to believe that, then perhaps the weaker argument isn't as weak as you suppose.'

'It's not a question of being weak or strong. It's about true and false.'

He smiled indulgently. 'Do you think that anyone would believe something he knew was untrue?'

'Of course not.'

'Then if something's demonstrably untrue, how could I possibly persuade anyone otherwise?'

I backtracked. 'Socrates said at his trial, "Anyone who really cares about justice, and wants to stay alive for any length of time, needs to keep out of public life."'

'"*Socrates said*. . . "You go around quoting him like Homer. Why don't you just say what *you* think?'

I rounded on him. 'What *I* think? Do you really want to know?'

'Very much.'

'I grew up being told that it was the best men who should rule the state because *we* were the best educated. That *we* were the only ones wise and clever enough to really understand justice. Then *we* took charge – as you know – and butchered our opponents like sheep. Anyone who disagreed, anyone who argued – and once those were out of the way, anyone *we* didn't like the look of. No trials, just daggers in the night. They even tried to force Socrates to carry out an execution, just so they could discredit him.'

They also came to me. Not *for* me, *to* me. They played on my vanity. They made me think that the killings and torture were necessary evils to protect Athens, that soon the cancer would be cut away and then we could heal the city. They flattered me that I could use my learning, if only I would help them, to set up the sort of perfect society we'd always talked about.

And the worst of it, my eternal shame, is that I was tempted. When they offered me the blade, I very nearly took it. I saw the surgeon's scalpel, not the murderer's knife. I was blinded. Only Socrates had the wisdom to help me see through the illusion.

'And then the democracy was restored. The new men said we should let the past lie; they passed an amnesty law. It all seemed very just. But they still needed a scapegoat, a sacrifice to appease the people. They executed Socrates, which even the junta didn't dare to, because democrats hate having their hypocrisy exposed even more than tyrants. And do you know who did the dirty work? Who brought the charges against Socrates? A poet, a businessman and a sophist.

'That's why I despise your *real* world. Because men fight over it like a tug of war, trying to pull it to their advantage without any regard for what's really *true*.'

A second later, I realised I'd conceded Euphemus' original point. But if he noticed, the look on my face made him think better of mentioning it.

At the side of the road, a boundary stone said we were ten miles from Thurii.

For any philosopher thinking of taking up a public career, Pythagoras' life offers a cautionary tale.

One hundred and fifty-odd years ago, he sailed out of the east in a blaze of mystery and settled in the Greek colony at Croton, towards the southwestern end of Italy. Pupils flocked to him. In short order, most of the city's eminent citizens had signed up to his school, including a local strongman called Milo. Pythagoras taught ascetism, contemplation and mathematics. When his zealous pupils noticed that their local rivals, the Sybarites, lived a decidedly un-Pythagorean life of hedonistic luxury, they destroyed Sybaris.

But not everyone took to Pythagoras. Government by the wise is necessarily elitist: the unwise and foolish feel excluded, and tend to resent it. And there's never any shortage of fools. One night, Pythagoras' enemies in Croton rose up, burned down his home and massacred his followers. Pythagoras barely escaped. He lived out the rest of his days in exile, not far from Taras. You can still see his house from the road, though it's now built into a temple complex.

We passed it on the second day, and I insisted on dragging Euphemus over to have a look.

'Where did Pythagoras get his wisdom from?' I asked aloud, remembering Agathon's question to Archytas. 'You hear a lot about his students and followers, but nothing about his teachers.'

Euphemus studied the plain little house. Next to the stout-pillared temple, it didn't look like much more than a lamp store.

'I met a man from Croton, once, on Crete. He told a tale that Pythagoras went down to the underworld, like Orpheus, but instead of bringing back a woman, he brought back wisdom.'

I remembered the tomb that Agathon had cracked open, the gaping hole in the hillside. 'What could you possibly learn that would be worth that journey?'

Euphemus shrugged. 'It's just superstition.'

★ ★ ★

On a dark day when the clouds raced low, we reached Thurii. I saw it from far off, a city on the plain, hemmed in by mountains and the grey sea. As we crossed the bridge over the Cratus, past the white temple to Artemis that marked the city limits, Euphemus pointed to the river below. Thick weeds billowed in the stream, clutching the fragments of fallen columns that littered the riverbed like the bones of a lost army.

'The drowned city of Sybaris. Say what you like about the Pythagoreans, but you don't want to get on the wrong side of them.'

Thunder rolled down off the mountains and rumbled across the plain. The clouds closed ranks like a shield wall. Raindrops punched rings in the river surface.

Euphemus looked at the sky. 'It's going to be bad.'

By the time we reached the city walls, we were both wet as fish. I had to shout to the gateman to make myself heard. 'Dimos' house?'

The storm had swept the streets bare. We hurried down the broad avenue, past empty shops and grand temples. Dim figures crowded under the porticoes like the shades of Hades; above, carved monsters crouched on the gutters and spat streams of water at us.

'The city's going to be drowned again if we're not careful,' Euphemus bellowed in my ear.

'At least we're not at sea.'

Lightning flashed, thunder hard on its heels. With a bray of terror, one of our mules jerked his bridle out of my hand and galloped down the street out of sight. There was no point trying to catch him. Euphemus and I dragged the other mule another hundred yards, to the house the gateman had described.

A slave opened the door, hanging back to avoid the rain spattering the threshold.

'Is this Dimos' house?'

The slave nodded.

'Is Agathon here?'

'For all the gods' sakes.' Euphemus elbowed me out of the way, pushed past the slave and shook himself off like a dog. 'Does it matter? Let's get out of this rain.'

We stood in the hall while the slave fetched water and washed the mud off our feet. Another slave went to find his master. A third had the thankless task of unloading our mule in the rain. Soon Euphemus' baggage was dripping another puddle onto the floor.

'Welcome,' said a not-terribly-welcoming voice. A body eclipsed the lamp at the end of the corridor: a stout man with sloped shoulders and oily grey hair. He dug his thumbs into his belt, rocked back a little and considered us, like a bale of goods landed unexpectedly outside a warehouse.

'Do we have business?'

'Don't you recognise your own brother?'

Sort of. There's no blood shared between us. His father married my mother, a second marriage for both of them. Dimos was fifteen years my senior and out of the house before I could remember. His father named him in a fit of enthusiasm for the Democracy, which gave the wags of Athens plenty of material when the rest of the family threw in their lot with the dictators. Dimos, who has nothing in common with the common man, found it so unbearable he emigrated.

'And this is Euphemus, the famous sophist and rhetorician.'

If Euphemus had any use at all, I'd hoped he could at least impress my stepbrother. But Dimos barely registered him. 'My house isn't an inn for you and your idle friends,' he muttered as he led us down the corridor. 'I'm still recovering from the last one you sent here.'

The cold was forgotten. 'Agathon?'

'Some would say you're taking advantage.'

'Is he here?'

'Not any more.'

'When did he leave?'

'A month ago.'

I stopped on the threshold of the *andron*. 'But that's impossible. He was in Taras two weeks ago.'

'Then that's where he must have gone.' He dropped heavily onto a bench and leaned back. 'Wine! I was glad to get him out of the house.'

'His host in Taras said he'd come back here.'

'He could have gone to the moon for all I care. He's not welcome here.'

His face had gone a vivid red; his shoulders twitched with anger. It seemed an excessive reaction. I put it down to the shock of finding me on his doorstep.

I tried to be nice. 'It's good to see you, brother. You look well.'

That wasn't entirely true. In Athens, when he was young and I was younger, Dimos lived a gilded life: handsome, rich, desirable. Thirty years later, some of the gold has definitely worn off. Scratched and dented, you can see the lead underneath.

'No one warned me you were coming,' he grumbled. A slave brought cups of warmed wine. 'What are you doing in Italy?'

I didn't dare mention Agathon again. 'I wanted to study.'

'You'll find no philosophy here.' Dimos is one of those Athenians who emigrated chiefly so he could tell the colonists how much better things are at home. 'And your friend?'

'He's going to work for the tyrant of Syracuse.'

Euphemus made an awkward bow from his couch, like a starfish curling up. 'Allow me to thank you for your generous hospitality . . . '

I was sick of the sound of Euphemus' voice. I drank the wine and listened to the storm, and thought of a hole in the ground that was the last place anyone had seen Agathon.

95

Ten

Jonah – London

At Wandsworth police station, a heavy-set constable took him to an interview room and gave him a cup of coffee. She said her name was Ruth. The fluorescent lights flickered and burned as she took his details.

'Profession?'

'Musician. I play in a band.'

She looked up. 'Should I have heard of you?'

He guessed not. Their first album had kindled a small blaze of hype: a profile in the *NME*, a fawning write-up in *Uncut* and a sniffier notice from *The Face*. A couple of singles had lingered around the lower echelons of the charts: they might have broken the Top 20 if they'd sold their song for a mobile phone ad, but Jonah had refused. At the time, he thought it meant they had integrity. But the label had lost interest, and suddenly they weren't a hot new band but just another group trying to be heard above the noise. The songs got better, the fans were as loyal as ever – but, year by year, it became clear they were never going to make the leap.

'We once toured with LCD Soundsystem,' he offered.

'I'll take that as a "No",' she said, smiling as if it were a joke. 'Moving on . . . '

Ruth asked the same questions as the Foreign Office, and got the same answers.

'So as far as you're aware, the last time anyone saw her was yesterday morning.'

'Or afternoon. She got her things from the hotel. The receptionist might have seen her . . . ' He tailed off, thinking of all the things he could have done differently, the questions he'd have asked in Italy if he'd known Lily wouldn't be here.

'Can you think of any reason she might have for wanting to disappear like this?'

'*Wanting?*' Jonah echoed. 'You think this is something she *wanted?*'

Ruth acted as if he hadn't spoken. 'There's no evidence of any crime. That's a good thing,' she reminded him. 'In most cases like this there's a straightforward explanation.'

Cases like this.

'What about the text messages?'

'What about them?'

'She can't have sent them herself. Someone else must have.'

Ruth was too professional to let him see what she thought of that. 'We'll look into it. Were there any issues in your relationship? Any problems?'

'Everything was fine.'

'When was the last time you saw her?'

'Six weeks ago. I took her to the airport.'

'It's a long time to be apart.'

Jonah tried to read her expression, but it was perfectly neutral.

'It happens every summer. She has to dig, I need to tour.'

'Can't be easy.'

'No.'

'Did you keep in touch?'

'Every day.'

Another note. 'Did she talk about anything that was worrying her. Conflicts with her colleagues, her private life?' Jonah shook his head. 'Any arguments?'

He was still shaking his head when he realised the last question was about him. 'No,' he said emphatically.

Her eyebrows arched up as she made another note. 'It's not uncommon for couples to argue.'

Jonah didn't answer.

'You drove all the way from Berlin, overnight. Any particular reason for the hurry?'

'I wanted to see her.'

'You must have been very tired.'

'I slept on the way.' What was she trying to say? That he might have missed Lily because he'd nodded off? He felt the anger rising inside him and tried to keep it in check.

She waited, watching him to see if he'd say more. When he didn't, she leaned forward and wrote something down. It seemed to take a long time.

'That's enough to be going on with.' She stood. 'We'll inform Interpol, who'll pass it on to the Italian police. They'll conduct the investigation. In the meantime, we'll arrange a press conference to try and raise some awareness.'

She showed him the door.

'Someone out there knows where your wife is. We just have to reach them.'

Greece – ten years ago

Another Sunday, another drive packed into the hire car, part of Adam's apparent plan to visit every ancient column in Greece. This time Jonah let Richard take the front seat, while he squeezed in the back. Charis sat sideways on his lap, her bare legs folded against his, her chest inches from his face.

On the radio, Richard had managed to find the only station in Greece that played classical music, much to the others' disgust. Charis, in particular, teased him relentlessly.

'I mean, it all sounds exactly the same. I bet you don't even know what this song's called. You're just being pretentious.'

'You don't have to know what something's called to like it.'

'Plato would say you have to know something's proper name to understand its essence,' Adam said from the other side of the car. Charis reached across and flicked him on the nose.

'Stuff Plato.'

'It's called the "Queen of the Night",' Jonah said. 'From *The Magic Flute*. By Mozart.'

Richard twisted around in his seat. 'Ten points to Jonah. I didn't think this was your thing.'

'Quite the opera buff, aren't you?' said Charis. She pinched his cheek.

'My mother's a singer,' he said. It made him think of lying in bed, listening to the songs come through the floor as she practised in the sitting room. But Julian had started telling a long story about a girl at school they'd called the queen of the night, and no one cared.

The temple was a let-down, just a few blocks overgrown with grass and weeds, surrounded by a low chain-link fence. There was no guard. They climbed over the fence and poked around for a few minutes, but even Adam couldn't make much of it.

Charis put her hands on her hips and surveyed the ruins. 'Adam, darling, you've found the one thing that actually makes digging look interesting.'

'Good view, though.' Julian had wandered to the far edge of the site, where steep cliffs fell to the waves.

'The book says there's a sea cave underneath,' said Adam. 'There's a local legend it used to be an entrance to Hades.'

'Oh, fab.'

They'd brought a coolbox. Julian took out a can of beer, opened it, and poured a good measure over the ruins.

'You can't do that.' Richard looked over his shoulder, in case a caretaker should appear. 'It's a site.'

'Libation to the gods.' Julian splashed another slug over the ruins, then took a deep swig for himself. 'Anyone else?'

Jonah took one. In the heat, dust and salt in the air, it tasted like nectar. He offered the can to Lily.

'Want some?'

'Thanks.'

Adam was still staring over the edge of the cliff. 'Does anyone want to see about this cave?'

'I will.' Jonah jumped up and went over. The cliffs were steep but not sheer, with plenty of fissures in the rock to hold onto.

'You'll break your necks,' said Richard. 'Or drown.'

'Getting up'll be harder than getting down,' Julian added. 'You'll end up marooned.'

'Like Philoctetes,' said Charis.

'I'll go first.' Jonah set his beer carefully on a column base. He sat down on the cliff edge, then pivoted around and lowered himself down. The rocks were hot under his fingers, but not as steep as they'd looked from above, and his arms were strong from the digging.

The cliff ended in a rocky shelf, a couple of feet wide, before a short drop into the sea. He couldn't see a cave, but a few yards along a sea channel cut through the rock and disappeared into the cliff. Not far off, he could hear a roar like a motorway.

Pebbles and grit rattled down the cliff. He looked up to see a pair of bare legs and battered boots almost on top of him. Lily slithered down the last few feet and landed off-balance. Jonah grabbed her arm.

'Steady. You don't want to prove Richard right.'

'I want to see it.'

She pushed past to the end of the ledge and lay on her stomach. Leaning out over the sea channel, she craned her head to look in.

'It definitely goes somewhere.'

Jonah lay down next to her. The channel disappeared into the cliff, a low dark mouth, invisible inside.

'That's too small to be a cave.'

Another clatter of stones. Adam had come down. He wiped his hands on his jeans.

'Is it there?'

Lily got out of the way so Adam could see. Jonah rolled aside to give him more room. Behind him on the ledge, Lily had stood up.

'I want to see where it goes.'

She raised her arms and pulled off her T-shirt; kicked off her boots, unzipped her shorts and stepped out of them. She stood there in her underwear, blushing a little, defying him to look. She had little pink bows on her bra straps.

She padded to the edge of the rock. A wave surfed through the channel. Adam looked up, then hurriedly down again.

'What about currents?' said Jonah.

'You can wait here, if you like,' said Lily.

Jonah glanced at Adam, both trying not to stare at Lily. Without a word, they both stripped to their boxers.

The moment they jumped in, all awkwardness disappeared. The narrow channel squeezed the waves dangerously fast: Jonah took one in the face and was slapped straight into Lily. He bobbed up and felt the roof graze his head; he opened his mouth in surprise, and took in a lungful of water. Lily's arm snaked around his neck and pulled him forward. Another wave broke over him, blinding him, but he kicked on.

He felt the darkness cool his shoulders as he passed under the rock. He put out an arm, expecting to meet a dead end, but all he felt was water. The snare-drum crash of the waves was gone, replaced with a low murmur all around him like distant laughter. Lily had let go. He opened his eyes.

The channel had opened into a long, high cave. By some trick of nature, sunlight from outside flowed through and reflected onto the walls, throwing rippling lines of light across the stone. The whole cave glowed golden blue.

They trod water and drank in the wonder of the place. No one spoke. As his eyes adjusted to the dimness, Jonah saw the walls arching into space above them like a cathedral.

Lily kicked across to the far side. Little splashes echoed around the cave. She reached up and put her hand in a small hollow.

'This was carved by someone. You can still see the chisel marks.' She felt around the niche. 'Perhaps there was a statue here.'

'It's a sacred place.' Adam's voice was distant, distracted. He was staring into the depths of the cave, where the walls tapered to darkness.

Jonah tried to imagine ancient hands patiently chipping away the wet rock, hour after hour in the sea-lit gloom. Time was fluid here. When something brushed his hand, for a wild moment he imagined it was a sea nymph, or the ancient carver returning with an offering for the goddess.

Fingers twined with his. He looked across and saw Lily floating at arm's length, her hair slicked back, her face shining. In the instant his eyes met hers, something passed between them that left Jonah suddenly struggling for breath.

'This is unbelievable,' Adam called from further up the cave. 'Open your mouths. Drink it.'

Still holding his hand, Lily let herself sink until the water reached her nose, then opened her mouth and let it flow in.

She bobbed up, gasping. 'Try it.'

Jonah parted his lips, letting the water trickle over his

tongue. It was cold and clear, just a faint hint of salt around the edges.

'It's fresh.' Jonah glanced at the niche in the wall again, feeling the strangeness of the place beginning to bend reality. 'But—'

'It must be the mouth of an underground river,' said Adam. He had his back to them, staring into the darkness. 'I wonder how far back it goes.'

'Don't,' said Lily.

'I won't go far.'

He dived forward and disappeared. The splashes of his strokes slowly receded into echoes. Lily and Jonah were left alone.

Afterwards, he couldn't say whether she came to him, or he to her, or both to each other. All he remembered was the heavy magic of the cave pushing them together, the sparkling ripples and the drone of the waves and her body suddenly wrapped around his. Their lips touched. Her body was cold as the water, as good as naked, but all Jonah felt inside was a golden warmth turning him to light.

They'd stopped kicking to keep afloat. They sank, oblivious, until the water covered them, until they felt the sandy floor of the cave underfoot. Jonah pushed off. They broke the surface, gasping and laughing, staring at each other with wonder.

From the depths of the cave, they heard a fluttering sound which firmed into the rhythm of swimming. They pulled apart, though she kept her foot crooked around the back of his leg.

Adam came into the light, breathing hard. 'It goes back for miles.'

He looked between them, suspicion chasing across his face. 'Are you OK?'

Jonah couldn't speak. All he wanted was to taste Lily again.

'Should we come back with torches?' Lily swept her hair back. 'Explore?'

'It's better in the dark. Floating there, listening to it. You should come.'

Jonah took Lily's hand. 'We should get back.'

London

The next day was Sunday. Jonah spent it in the flat, staring at the phone and willing it to ring while he tapped out hopeless messages on his laptop. There were so many ways to contact people, and he tried them all. He e-mailed, he posted, he messaged – and those generated more e-mails, replies, questions, sympathy. But the only thing that mattered was answers – and there were none of those.

He logged into their bank account, looking for any transactions that might hint where Lily had gone. It hadn't been touched since he took out money in Berlin to pay for petrol. He rang Sibari – three times to the hotel, twice to the lab. The lab was shut, their day off; the hotel answered, but the receptionist spoke no English. He left messages for Richard.

Speaking to the hotel reminded him again of the boat he'd seen. With the computer open in front of him, it occurred to him that there were probably people on the internet who obsessed about that sort of thing. A search for NESTIS YACHT quickly proved him right.

In a short while, he'd established that the yacht belonged to a Greek called Ari Maroussis, heir to a fortune courtesy of a company called Ophion Shipping. For a few minutes, it felt as though he was being flooded with information. Wikipedia articles, magazine profiles, the occasional news story about the company, speculation on succession. Ari's father was rumoured to be in poor health, holed up in his villa on the Aegean island of Spetses. But even in the vastness of the World Wide Web, the flow soon dried up; he found himself rereading the same few facts. None of the boat spotters had reported any sightings of NESTIS in the last couple of months. And nothing suggested why Ari would have even known Lily existed.

What did it mean? Probably nothing. He shut the laptop and lay on the sofa. He didn't read, didn't eat, didn't watch TV, didn't even listen to the radio in case he missed the phone. He floated, waiting for a call or a key in the door that would make the world start again. He got her photo down from the bookshelf and stared at it until it blurred. Lily in the sun, her hat tipped back, red earth smudged on her cheek. *Where are you?* he asked the photo. But though it might be worth a thousand words, it only said the same thing over and over.

It was like all the come-downs after all the gigs he'd ever played – the greyness in the world, the emptiness inside – but a thousand times worse. So he managed it the way he always had, and poured another drink.

Monday morning he was back at the police station. The conference room was smaller than he'd expected – and still three-quarters empty. When you saw these things on the news, they always looked packed: flashguns, TV lights and questions firing nonstop at the desperate family. Here, there was one unattended video camera, and half a dozen journalists standing at the back cracking jokes. A trestle table with a microphone stood facing them, below the Metropolitan Police logo.

Ruth led him out through a side door. 'We'll wait a few minutes to see if anyone else shows up.'

'I thought there'd be more,' Jonah said.

'You know how it is.'

She looked as though she was about to say something else, but bit it back. Jonah could guess. Lily's case wasn't juicy enough or bloody enough to attract the feeding frenzy. The ones who'd come today were just outriders, sniffing around on the off-chance.

Ruth ushered him into a waiting room. A potted plant, a water cooler, a few blue chairs – and Lily's mother and sister sitting in a corner. Her mother wore a grey skirt and a pink cardigan, as if she'd taken a wrong turn on the way to church; her face looked small and grey. Julie was wearing a blue jersey dress that came down to her knees, revealing tanned legs and slim, firm arms. Her dark hair was pulled back in a functional ponytail. She looked so unlike Lily that lots of people, Jonah included, wondered if they'd had different fathers. He'd never asked. The father, whoever he was, had never been around to answer.

He leaned in and gave her mother an awkward hug. She was so thin he worried he might snap her. She hadn't been the same since the fall two years ago: the light inside her had gone out. And now this.

'You poor thing,' she murmured.

'It's good of you to come.'

'We came down this morning,' Julie said. 'You haven't heard anything?'

He shook his head. 'You?'

'Nothing. I'd have thought she'd have called to check in on Mum. Even if you . . . '

She caught herself. Jonah felt his chest tighten.

'We were fine.'

Her mother looked up. 'She'll come back. Or at least let us know.'

'That reminds me,' said Julie. 'There's something—'

She broke off. Ruth had popped her head in. 'Let's get this over with.'

She led them back into the conference room. Jonah didn't count any more reporters than before. A couple of the photographers held up their cameras for pictures; the rest just looked bored. Jonah felt the anger rising inside him and tried to force it back. It only increased the pressure.

They took their seats and Ruth leaned in to the microphone. 'Thanks for coming. As you know, Lily Barnes went missing in Italy on Friday. Her husband is going to read a short statement, and then we'll take questions.'

She turned the microphone towards Jonah. He took the creased paper out of his pocket and unfolded it, squinting at the words. It was the hardest thing he'd ever written, and he dreaded having to read it out. Most nights, for the past six weeks, he'd performed in front of hundreds – sometimes thousands – of people. These were half a dozen bored journalists in a shabby police station. But there was no song that would make these words sound right. He was telling the world that Lily was gone. Making it public was like opening a door, letting out all the terrible possibilities he'd bottled up inside himself and giving them life.

'My wife Lily . . . '

'Could you speak up, please?' called one of the journalists.

The room was too hot; his mouth was dry. He cleared his throat and took a drink from the glass of water in front of him. 'Sorry.' He just wanted this to be over. 'My wife Lily . . . '

He paused. A uniformed officer had come through the side door and was whispering something in Ruth's ear. Ruth nodded, and put a hand over Jonah's microphone.

'Hold on a sec.'

They went out into the corridor. Jonah watched them through the window in the door but couldn't hear a thing. In front of him, the journalists had started to look interested. One took out his notepad and started scribbling, glancing up every few seconds at Jonah. Was he writing about him?

Jonah felt another rush of anger. This was supposed to be about Lily.

The door opened. Ruth came in but didn't sit down.

'I'm afraid this conference is cancelled,' she announced.

The journalists started to grumble, but Ruth stared them down with the sort of look they probably taught in the first week of police school. Jonah just gazed at her, echoing the question that several of the reporters had shot back.

'Why?'

Ruth half turned towards Jonah and Lily's family. 'They've found her.' And then, seeing the journalists' noses twitch, added, 'She's fine.'

Ruth took them back into the waiting room, leaving the journalists to pack up. A couple shot Jonah looks as he went out, as if they blamed him for spoiling their fun. He didn't care. He balled up the statement and threw it in the bin, dizzy with the relief flooding his system.

But there was so much he needed to know. 'Where is she? Is she OK?'

'She's well,' Ruth said.

'How did they find her?' Julie asked.

'The Italian police spoke to her on her mobile. I don't have details yet – they just rang through. They'll send a full report later. But she's fine.'

'*They spoke to her on her mobile?*' He must have rung it a hundred times in the last three days and it had never been switched on. The relief suddenly wasn't flowing quite as hard as it had.

'When's she coming back?' said Lily's mother.

'I don't know.' Ruth smiled – but behind her brisk manner, there was something evasive. Something she was keeping from him.

'Where is she?' Jonah said again.

Ruth squared her shoulders, bracing herself. She looked Jonah dead in the eye.

'She asked them to keep that confidential.'

Jonah went cold. This couldn't be right.

'She told the police she's sorry about worrying you all with the story about her mother, and causing all this fuss. She didn't know what to say. She needed some time to herself.'

'Can I speak to her?'

'I don't know what happened between her and yourself, but that's between you two. This isn't a matter for the police any more.'

She was moving, shepherding them down the corridor towards the front door. Jonah wanted to stand his ground, to stay there until he got answers, but he had to follow her to be heard.

'How did they know it was Lily? It could have been anyone using her phone. Did they actually go and see her? Did they trace her phone?'

'It'll all be in the report,' said Ruth. Too late, he realised she'd managed to get him through the big double doors into the reception area.

Something like pity creased her face. 'I'm sorry you had to find out this way.'

Find out? Everyone was acting as if something had been settled, but in Jonah's world there were only more questions. Why couldn't they see it? Why weren't they as desperate to know as he was?

Julie took his arm and pulled him out onto the street. Her mother was already down there, leaning on the metal rail that separated her from the traffic crawling down towards the gyratory.

'Did you have a fight?' Julie asked.

'I didn't even see her.' He tried to play back every conversation, every message and e-mail they'd exchanged in the last six weeks. 'We didn't argue about anything. We just wanted to be back together.'

He could see she didn't believe him. 'Everyone argues – just ask my Rob. She'll come round.'

'There was nothing,' he insisted.

'Go home and get some rest. And don't call unless you've got good news. You've worried Mum enough.'

She left him standing on the steps as she headed for the taxi rank outside the shopping centre. A moment later, she looked back and fumbled in her bag. 'I almost forgot. This arrived this morning.'

She came back and gave him a white cardboard envelope covered in courier's stickers. Jonah's heart jolted as he saw the address on the front: Lily's writing, sent to Julie.

The date on the sticker was Friday. She must have sent it just before she disappeared. Hand trembling, he slid out two pieces of paper. The top sheet had a brief note: *Can you look after this until I get back?* Underneath, the second sheet was covered in writing: strange, angular letters that looked like a child's. It took Jonah a moment to realise it wasn't English, another moment to realise it wasn't even the normal alphabet. Greek, maybe?

'I suppose it's something to do with her work,' said Julie. 'You keep it. She might want it when she comes back.'

If she comes back. He tried not to think it, but the cruel voice inside him slipped through his defences.

He checked his phone but there were no messages. He tried Lily's mobile again, but it was switched off. Of course. At the bottom of the hill, traffic crawled in circles around the Wandsworth gyratory. Jonah watched them go round and wondered if that would be the rest of his life.

Unless . . . He looked at the paper Julie had given him again – dead words in a dead language – and wondered if they could bring Lily back.

Eleven

My first impressions of Italy disgusted me. I despised the sort
of life which they called the life of happiness, stuffed full with
the banquets of the Italian Greeks and Syracusans, who ate to
bursting twice a day, and never went to bed alone.

Plato, *Letter VII*

'Actually, I can answer your question perfectly well.' Dimos
dunked his bread in wine, then sucked until there was nothing
left but the crust. 'Is Dionysius a good thing for Syracuse?
Absolutely. The city needs a strong hand, or Sicily will be
overrun by Carthaginians.'

His own strong hand reached for a peach, squeezing so
hard the skin split. Nectar oozed between his fingers.

'But Dionysius has forgotten who he's supposed to be
fighting. He's like a man who picks his wife, only to discover
that he prefers her sister, and then the sister's cousin, and
then the cousin's son . . . ' He made a gesture with his dripping fingers. 'He's insatiable.'

'Show me a tyrant who isn't,' I muttered through my
breakfast.

'Has Dionysius invaded the mainland?' Euphemus asked.

'Two years ago we formed a coalition, Thurii and the other
cities, to resist him. It was a disaster. We fought two battles,
and both times he routed us. Total embarrassment. And
Dionysius behaved impeccably. He let our men retreat in

good order, ransomed the prisoners and offered peace with dignity. That's the mark of greatness.'

He sounded almost proud, as if by going down to defeat they'd somehow earned a share of the glory. I've never fought on a battlefield, but I saw the corpses stacked in the agora when my uncle and his friends took charge. Dead eyes, denied any future. The mark of greatness.

Dimos was still talking. 'There are plenty of sensible men who think we could do with a dose of strong leadership here in Thurii.'

Euphemus fastidiously peeled his own peach. 'A home-grown tyrant? Or would you invite in Dionysius himself?'

'There's no denying we'd benefit from a leader who could do the right thing. Not just talking around everything in the Assembly all day, getting nowhere.'

I was in a disagreeable mood. My stepbrother has that effect on me – plus I had a runny nose from the storm the day before, and I'd slept badly.

'Do you think a tyrant always does the right thing?'

It was the first thing I'd said that he'd noticed. The question surprised him. 'Some do, some don't. I'm saying, at least they have the freedom to do the right thing.'

'Tyrants aren't free.'

'They do whatever they please.'

'They're slaves to their appetites.'

'But they have the power to satisfy them.' Euphemus spoke lightly, trying to take the heat out of the conversation.

'Any immoderate desire is tyrannical,' I persisted. 'You're a slave to it. Lust, for example.'

'Maybe.'

'Or gluttony.'

'Yes.'

'And every drunkard turns into a tyrant.'

Dimos smiled. For most people, a smile shows their face at its best. With Dimos, it was an ugly thing.

'If that's true, we'll all be tyrants tonight.'

I didn't understand.

'I'm throwing a dinner party.'

I spent the day wandering around Thurii, asking about Agathon. Thurii's a modern town, like the Piraeus, with straight streets and paint still fresh on the temples. You could almost believe there's no history at all – until you remember the drowned Sybarites slowly mouldering under its foundations.

Nobody had seen Agathon since he left a month ago. At least they didn't seem to think he'd committed any crime. I came home after lunch, napped, and then dressed for dinner. The first guests arrived just before sunset.

In Athens, the chief business of a dinner party is drinking. The meal is simply a foundation to give the evening some ballast. In Italy, they take the eating much more seriously. We had songbirds and gamebirds, five kinds of fish and three of eel, peppers stuffed with raisins and sweet almond cakes baked in the shape of the goddess. Well before the others finished, my stomach had bloated like a corpse. Euphemus, two couches away and in his element, couldn't resist teasing me.

'Not hungry?'

'It's too much.'

'I don't know why you bothered coming to Italy, if you're just going to leave all your food on the table.'

The men around us laughed. The man sharing my couch, a merchant, reached around and jabbed me in the ribs.

'You Athenians need feeding up.'

He was fat as an ass, and put away every plate that came near him. I faked a smile and replied to Euphemus.

'Do you have to embarrass yourself, showing our hosts how greedy you are?'

'I'm not greedy: you're just a prig.'

'You eat like a Pythagorean,' the merchant told me. Hilarity ensued.

'Don't,' said Euphemus. 'He's already obsessed with triangles.'

Dimos found a wedge of bread and offered it to me. 'Perhaps this would be more to your taste.'

'Just don't serve him lentils.'

'If he farts too much it'll break his concentration.'

'He'll come back as a flea.'

I hated them, but Euphemus most of all. I lay on my couch, trapped by the man in front of me, and soaked up the insults. Looking back, I don't suppose they wanted to be cruel. They expected me to join in. They kept tossing stones because they thought I'd find a stick and hit them back. That was what passed for entertainment in their lives.

Eventually, they got bored and moved on to the drinking. Slaves came and cleared the tables, then washed our hands and feet and crowned us with wreathes of myrtle and rose. We offered libations, sang a hymn to the goddess, and performed the usual ceremonies. I mumbled along as best I could, unfamiliar prayers to unfamiliar gods. In Athens, we honour Athena and Zeus: cold wisdom, hard power. In Italy, they prefer Demeter and her daughter: ripe, soft and susceptible. Their mysteries yield to the touch like the petals of a flower, deeper and deeper until you lose yourself in the darkness.

The others elected Dimos as *symposiarch*, though they grumbled when he suggested mixing the drink at three parts of water to one of wine.

'Haven't you got the stamina?'

'Are you in such a bad way after yesterday's session?'

'He's counting his pennies, the old miser.'

Dimos waved them down with bad humour, and ordered the slaves to mix the wine at two to one. The cup they poured it in was a two-handled krater, broad-rimmed and deep.

'Bigger than Nestor's cup,' the merchant cackled. I wondered if Homer was his way of trying to make nice to me. I had a different tag in mind.

Unwelcome revellers, whose lawless joy
Pains the sage ear, and hurts the sober eye.

Dimos slapped the side of his couch for silence. 'As Homer says, "Music and dancing crown the banquet." Shall we have some entertainment?'

'I've heard Diotima may grace us with her presence tonight,' said the merchant in my ear.

Cheers, catcalls and the thud of heels drumming on the couches. Everyone stared at the door.

The sun had set by now, but the heat in the room kept growing. Every man there was stripped to the waist. The lamps shone on their smooth-oiled chests, on fat and muscle; on the polished tables, on the olives and chickpeas that glistened in their dishes. The perfume the slaves had splashed on us made the air almost too sweet to breathe. I could feel something about to snap.

A slave opened the door. Four dancers came in: three young women and a boy of about fifteen. The boy wore a loincloth; the girls slightly less. A flute player followed them in and took a stool in the corner.

The guests watched appreciatively as the dancers went through their routine, a little pageant meant to mimic the judgement of Paris. The three girls tugged the boy this way and that, trying to persuade him, while the flute music accelerated to a frenzy. By the time it was finished, all four of them had lost their clothes. Hera and Athena retreated to the sidelines, while Paris and Aphrodite engaged in an orgy of eye-popping gymnastics.

The merchant who was sharing my couch nudged me. His buttocks pressed against my groin.

'I bet you don't get a show like this in Athens.'

'In Athens, we usually entertain ourselves with conversation.'

Euphemus disagreed. 'Maybe at the parties you go to. I once saw—'

But Dimos had heard me as well. 'I'm sure we wouldn't want my little brother to go back to Athens thinking Thurii was any less civilised than Athens.' He snapped his fingers. The dancers gathered their clothes and left the room.

'What should we discuss?'

A thin man three couches to my left – an aspiring playwright, I think – said, 'All this music and beauty makes me think of love.'

'So we see.' This from the doctor, an older man with bushy eyebrows and thick white fleece covering his chest like a ram. He pointed to the bulge under the playwright's tunic. 'It obviously stimulates you.'

Before the playwright could reply, there was a knocking at the door of the house, as if some revellers had decided to crash the party. Dimos told the slaves to go and see who it was.

'If it's friends of ours, invite them in. If not, say they've missed the drinking and we've gone to bed.'

The laughter and ribbing subsided as we all listened to see who it was.

A breath of cool air washed in. A woman entered, barefoot, wrapped in a long cloak and carrying a double-barrel flute, an *aulos*. A sigh went through the men in the room.

Diotima.

I won't try to describe her. I could pile up words like bricks, but they'd be a wall, not a window. I could try chiselling her out of adjectives, but the best they'd give you is a statue –

and that would be worse than saying nothing, for Diotima was more alive than anyone I've ever known. Like a reflection in water or on polished stone, the image you saw was never the same. Unless, if you watched so long that you no longer noticed the movement, you might eventually catch sight of the deep stillness at her core.

She shrugged off the cloak and gave it to a slave. Underneath, her dress was thin and clear as moonlight, trimmed with silver thread. It hid nothing.

I felt the mood change – like being among wolves when a lamb wanders into the cave.

'You're late,' said Dimos.

'I was with someone else.'

She didn't belong in that fleshy, sweaty room. In fact, it was hard to think where she *could* belong, except possibly in a temple precinct, where she might have kept company with the goddess. Any other woman would have shrunk under the scrutiny of those men. Diotima was cool and adamant.

She took the flute out of its wrapping. 'Shall I play?'

The men agreed.

The moment she put the reed to her lips, the room changed. The world changed. I could feel the wine coupling with the blood in my veins; I believed Pythagoras, when he said music is the language of the universe. But at the same time, I knew he hadn't got it right. This wasn't music in the key of reason, a mathematical construct laid out like a grid of streets. This was the music that maenads play on the mountains in spring; music that makes you crave warm flesh and oblivion; music that Orpheus might have used to play his way out of the underworld.

The last note died away. Diotima sat on the edge of Dimos' couch, eyes closed, practically naked yet utterly untouchable.

A gust of air hissed through the room as we remembered to breathe again.

'Is there anything better than getting drunk to the sound of the flute?' the playwright rhapsodised.

Diotima eyed him like a sphinx. 'Be careful. It's a dangerous pastime.'

'How?' I asked. It wasn't a considered question. I just wanted her to notice me.

She turned her eyes on me and I trembled. The music's enchantment still echoed in her gaze.

'Flutes have magic. Drop your guard, and they can bewitch you almost without your noticing. Remember the Sybarite horses?'

'No.'

She looked surprised. 'I heard you were a Pythagorean.'

Where did she hear that? 'I'm not.'

'When the Crotonians came to attack Sybaris, they knew the biggest danger was the Sybarite cavalry, so they put their flute-players in the front row. They played, and the Sybarite horses were so enchanted by the music they abandoned their riders and trotted across the battlefield to join the Crotonians. Without their horses, the Sybarites were doomed. That's a true story,' she added with quiet authority, as if she'd witnessed it herself.

'A warning not to get carried away.' Dimos clapped his hands as if to break a spell. A look passed between him and Diotima. 'Before you arrived, my dear, we were about to move onto the speeches in honour of our Athenian guests.'

She slipped onto his couch and leaned against him. He stroked her hair.

'What's the topic?'

'Love.'

The cup had come around to me. I drank deeply. Thasian wine – almost the best. Wasted on me.

Diotima hugged her arms under her chest. 'I'm waiting.'

'We'll let the Athenians start us off, show us how it's done.'

He nodded to Euphemus. 'You must have something clever to say about love.'

'Euphemus has something clever to say about everything,' I pointed out.

Euphemus propped himself up on his elbow and took a sip from the cup.

'To understand love, you have to understand human nature. And to grasp that, we have to go right back to the dawn of time.'

Was it my imagination, or did he keep staring at Diotima's breasts?

'In the beginning, primeval man was round. His back and sides made a sphere, and he had four hands and four feet, one head with two faces, looking opposite ways but identical; and four ears, eyes and all the rest.'

'What about his private parts?' asked the doctor – inevitably.

'He had both, male and female. And he could walk upright like we do, backwards or forwards, and when he wanted to run fast he could roll over and over at a great pace, spinning on all those hands and feet like a gymnast. And they were so strong, these early men, that they planned to scale heaven and overthrow the gods.'

'Does this have anything to do with love?'

'Listen and see.' Euphemus straightened the wreath on his head. 'Zeus devised a plan: he cut them in two, just as you might split an egg with a hair. After the division, each part longed for his other half, hugging each other in hopes they could grow back into one. And that's the ancient desire we all have, to reunite our original natures. We're always looking for our other half: without them, we're like a flat fish, or a figure on a frieze which is only half carved. And this intense pursuit of wholeness, even though we only dimly understand it, is what we call love; and when we find our other half we want to melt into them, to live every minute together until even death can't divide us.'

I would have liked his speech, if I'd trusted him. I kept waiting for the punchline. But he finished with a slight bow, and a quick glance at Diotima. She gave no sign of having heard a word.

There were other speeches, though all I remember from them is looking at Diotima as often as I dared. Both times the cup came around, I drank more than I should.

When it came to the merchant's turn, he was seized with a fit of hiccups from overeating and couldn't speak.

'Hold your breath.'

'Try sneezing.'

'Gargle.'

'He can't get a word out. Let Pythagoras take his turn.'

By Pythagoras, of course, they meant me. I've never had a gift for speaking. Part of me would happily have stayed in the corner, hiding behind the merchant, who was holding his nose while hanging off the couch trying to drink a cup of water upside down. But I was tired of listening to the sound of their voices – the sort of men who'd held the stage ever since they got rid of Socrates. And I had something to say.

'I don't know much about love,' I said. 'Certainly nothing I can put into words. You can make jokes about it, or discuss its effects and the crazy things it makes men and women do. You can describe the physical act.'

Lewd cheers, and shouts of '*Do, do.*'

'But what it really *is*, I couldn't tell you, any more than I can tell you what fire or light or truth really are.'

'Don't get philosophical,' said Dimos. 'We're talking about love.'

Diotima took an almond from the bowl and popped it in Dimos' mouth. 'Isn't love a sort of wisdom?'

Dimos squeezed her breast. 'In my house, it's a technical subject.'

More laughter. Diotima let his hand rest there a moment, then pirouetted out and slid to the floor, leaning against the foot of the couch. Dimos' arm twitched.

The cup had come around again. I took it by both handles and drank deeply. The wine was heavy as lead. I didn't notice the water.

On my right, the merchant started trying to say his piece, but Dimos cut him off, pointing at me.

'Let him finish.'

'Let Pythagoras have his say,' the others chorused. 'Otherwise he'll make a stink.'

I could have ridden it out until they got bored. But as I tried to ignore them, I noticed Diotima watching me from the floor, a faint smile parting her lips. Not sympathetic, certainly not inviting, but . . . curious.

I sat up, and raised a hand until they had no choice but to pay me attention.

'I'm going to talk about the only man I ever loved.' Inevitable, obvious jokes. 'His name was Socrates.'

Suddenly, I was a celebrity.

'Did you know him?'

'*The* Socrates?'

'Were you his lover?'

'Is it true he corrupted little boys?'

I sat up on the couch, dangling my legs over the edge. I could feel them watching me, Diotima most of all, but that was nothing more than background noise, like waves crashing on a beach. I stared into the flame flickering from the lamp-spout, fixing on the clearest part, until I was back in the agora, twenty years younger. He stood among the placards and handbills posted on the Heroes' Memorial, looking like a man who'd lost his way. Old, even then, but with an intense playfulness, like a child.

'It's not easy to describe Socrates. Most men, you describe them by comparing them, either to someone you know, or to characters from literature or history. Socrates was unlike anyone who is or ever has been.'

I paused, working out an idea I'd had once before.

'If I describe him, it'll sound like a caricature. But it's the truth.'

'Just get on with it.'

'In Athens, the shops sell little busts of Silenus the satyr, with pipes and flutes in his mouth. Do you have those here? On the outside they're grotesque, all hair and squashed features, but there are hinges. Open them up, and inside there's an image of the god.'

Some of them seemed to know what I was talking about.

'Socrates was like that satyr. The face the world saw was the carved head of Silenus. His nostrils flared, his eyes bulged, his hair grew wild. He had a snub nose, and fat lips like a donkey. He always went barefoot, so his feet were cracked and calloused. The best thing you could say about his clothes is that sometimes his wife washed them.

'And the things he taught were the same. Outwardly, common to the point of being ridiculous. He didn't show off his learning. He didn't illustrate his points with ancient heroes and poetic quotations. They didn't interest him. He dressed his arguments in the skin of the everyday: pack-asses and smiths and cobblers and tanners.'

I heard a few chuckles around the room.

'Ignorant people laughed at him. They didn't understand – you had to open the door and look inside. And if you did, if you got close enough to open it, you'd see golden images of such fascinating beauty you couldn't stop looking.'

'He was a subversive rabble-rouser,' said Dimos.

'He was subversive,' I agreed. 'In the best, most dangerous way. He made me realise that I shouldn't live the way I had done, feeding the expectations I thought other people had of me. Everything that society teaches you to respect, wealth and honour and power, he despised. He brought me to the point where I could hardly endure the life I was leading.'

'You're supposed to be talking about love,' Dimos scolded me. 'This sounds like hard going.'

'No,' said Diotima. 'That's exactly what love is.'

'The more I heard him, the more I wanted him to speak. And when I finally got close enough to open him up, to see what he really meant, I would have done anything for him.'

'*Anything?*' In case I'd misunderstood the question, the playwright illustrated it by waggling his bottom in the air.

'Were you there when he . . . ?' The Syracusan made an imaginary cup with his hand and mimed drinking, then tipped back his head and pretended to choke.

Diotima frowned. I just stared, and imagined throttling him for real.

'I was ill that day,' I lied, with great effort.

'I think it's my turn,' said the merchant. 'Sneezing did the trick.'

No one cared. At that moment, careless as a cat, Diotima uncurled herself from the foot of Dimos' couch and stood.

'Shall I tell you about love?'

'Will you give a demonstration?' the doctor asked.

She fixed him with a mocking smile that would have stopped a Gorgon. 'You couldn't keep up.'

The lamplight caught the golden skin of her face, her bare arms and the skin at her throat. A gold chain sparkled around her neck, dangling a gold pendant between her breasts. I was reminded of those moments in Homer when the goddess shrugs off her disguise and lets the hapless hero see who she really is. Her grey eyes looked at me, and I felt I'd turned to water.

'You loved Socrates?

'I did.'

'And how did that feel?'

'I felt . . . ' My soul seemed to inflate at the very thought, the way muscles flex at the memory of a fight. 'I felt like Euphemus' primitive man – that I'd found the other half of me.'

'Why was that?'

'I don't know.'

There were only the two of us in the room. The others were as flat as the painted men dining on the walls behind them.

'Let me tell you about love,' she said. 'Love isn't kind or fair or good, like the playwright says. He isn't a god – he isn't even immortal. One moment he can be brimming with life; the next moment dead in a cave; then alive again.

'Love is a poor man huddled in a doorway, rough and squalid, with bare feet and bare earth clinging to his clothes. He's a sophist, a conspirator and a sorcerer. An ingenious hero. He's the child of Want and Plenty, the grandchild of Cunning. He's needy, ruthless and tricky. And do you know what he craves most of all?'

'No.'

'Immortality.'

Widespread groans. 'She's as bad as him,' someone said.

'I can think of a few other things love wants.' The doctor unwound his tunic and spread it apart, in case we lacked imagination. Diotima allowed a small smirk at the corner of her mouth.

'It's true, love infects us with a lust for sex. Every creature – man, bird or beast – suffers untold agonies longing to procreate.' A cool glance at the doctor's exposed member. 'Some quite shrivel up with desire. Why?'

'Come into the courtyard and I'll show you,' said the doctor, unpleasantly.

'Love wants beauty.'

'You said it was immortality.'

She shook her head. Even that simple gesture held me. The play of light on the sweat at her throat. The flash of her earrings. The way the ivy leaves fluttered, and the sickle-strand of dark hair hanging down by her cheek.

'Love wants beauty. He wants it for himself, and he wants it forever. Sex isn't love's objective: it's the method he uses. It's the closest most of us can come to feeling so alive we escape our mortality.'

Dimos leaned forward, overhanging his couch like the prow of a ship. The lamplight scored deep red cracks in his face.

'And who do you love, Diotima?'

She thought for a moment, then looked straight at me. Every atom in my body seemed to turn to fire.

'Someone who isn't here.'

A crash shattered the hush in the room. Dimos was standing. A marble table lolled on the floor, rocking back and forth among the scattered dates and nuts.

'Perhaps it's time you left,' he said. 'Unless you have any more to say about love?'

She had her back to me; I couldn't see the look she gave him. All I know is that it seemed to freeze time.

'Even you might be able to get yourself initiated into love's lesser mysteries,' she told him. 'But if you're thinking you might go all the way . . . ' She crooked her little finger at him. 'You'll never get in the door.'

By the time he could think of a retort, she'd gone. Dimos sat heavily, then clapped his hands.

'Let's have some more entertainment.

The dancing girls came back. While we were talking, they'd oiled up their bodies, lubrication for what was to come. The mood in the room improved. The flute-boy started playing again, though after hearing Diotima play, he might as well have been farting through a straw.

I ignored the dancing girls, and the slaves sweeping up the mess Dimos had spilled. For me, the room was empty. Through the open door, I could see Diotima in the courtyard putting on her cloak. I stared at the slim ankle below the hem of her dress, the sway of her hips as she wrapped the cloak around her.

A cloak's a simple garment – the first thing a girl makes once she's learned to weave. No two are exactly the same, but they all look alike. That's why you dress it up with a pin or a ribbon or a piece of embroidery, so you can identify it at the end of an evening when your eyes are tired and there are ten to choose from.

This one had a monogram, an A in a circle stitched on the back, just below the nape of the neck. Wholly unremarkable. Except that I'd seen it before, many times, most recently on the dockside at the Piraeus, wrapping the shoulders of the friend I was seeing off. I still remember the moment he turned to board his ship, the flash of the monogram across his shoulders.

Of course I do. It was the last time I saw Agathon.

Twelve

Jonah – London

Charis lived in an imposing townhouse in a whitewashed enclave of north London. Two bay trees flanked the front door; on the raked gravel at the bottom of the steps, a winged god, one arm missing, watched the street. A red ball lolled against his foot.

Jonah climbed the stairs and rang the bell. A young woman answered, slim and pretty in figure-hugging jeans and a tight pink T-shirt. Probably the nanny. She smiled at him, in the way women often did.

'Is Charis in?'

From inside, a muffled voice called, 'It's OK, Yolanda, I'll get it.' He heard a flurry on the stairs, a bang and a well-spoken *shit*. The nanny stepped back. The door opened wider.

'Can't you get the children to clear up their toys, Yolanda?' A pause as she registered Jonah. 'Darling?'

When he first met her, Charis was the girl they all wanted. Everyone has an age where they look their best: Charis's came on young and strong. Too strong, perhaps, for her own good. She'd had a girlish innocence in a body that had raced ahead; her skin glowed with youth, her long, dark hair framed puppy-fat cheeks. She laughed loudly, and threw her arms around people she'd just met. When you looked into her blue eyes, there was no hint of self-consciousness, only wide-open delight inviting you in. Even Jonah had felt the pull – before Lily turned up.

And now . . . thirty really shouldn't seem so old. The puppy-fat had come off, leaving a hard and angular face; her hair, fashionably bobbed, had lost its lustre. Her eyes looked tired. Only the hug she gave him hadn't changed.

'I didn't know you were coming – you should have said.'

'I called yesterday.' One phone call in dozens, ringing round every friend he could think of to look for Lily. 'I left a message.'

'Sorry. We had Bill's parents down for the weekend – they've just left – and then this morning's been murder with the kids.' She gave him the sort of smile pretty girls use instead of apologies. 'I would have called back, I promise. Was it urgent?'

He couldn't explain on the doorstep. 'Can we talk somewhere?'

'Mysterious.' A hint of her old energy. 'Come through. Can you keep the kids away, Yolanda – and put the kettle on. You take sugar, don't you? Excuse the mess.'

She brought him into a conservatory filled with wicker furniture and plastic toys. Summer had mounted one last charge and the city was sweating, not a cloud in the sky. Office workers would be packing the parks at lunchtime, rolling up sleeves and sliding straps off shoulders to even out their fading tans. But even with the heat in the conservatory, Charis didn't open the doors.

The nanny brought tea. Charis glanced at her watch. 'It's after twelve,' she said, happily surprised. 'Perhaps we can manage something stronger.'

'Tea's fine.'

'Bo-ring.' She sprang down from her chair, went out, and came back with a bottle of white wine and two glasses. She filled them to the rim.

'Cheers.'

The wine was so cold it tasted almost like water. Charis slipped off her shoes and curled her legs under her in the chair. 'So what's going on?'

'Lily's missing.' He blurted it out, took another gulp of wine, and told the story. By the time he'd finished, his glass was empty. Charis refilled it.

'I'm so sorry. If she calls me . . . '

'It's not that.' He could tell what she was thinking from her tone, and didn't want to hear it. 'Just before she disappeared, Lily posted a letter – she must have sent it from the hotel that morning. I thought if anyone could understand it, you could.'

He took the FedEx envelope from his bag and slid the piece of paper out of it. Charis's hand brushed his as she took it.

'It's ancient Greek.'

'So you can read it?'

He didn't really have to ask. Charis had got a First in Classics at Oxford. The doctorate followed, then a research post which quickly became a full fellowship at her college. At the same time, she burned through a string of hapless boyfriends, had a torrid affair with her supervisor, then abruptly married an old Etonian twenty years older who worked in hedge funds and took it as a point of principle that his wife shouldn't work.

'It's a bit messy.' She stroked a lock of hair back from her face. 'She must have copied it from somewhere. Maybe something she dug up. Do you know what this is?'

She pointed to the top left corner of the page, where Lily had written and circled 'R27'.

'I don't know – maybe some reference number.' He scratched his stubble. 'That's the bit I *can* read.'

Charis mumbled under her breath, then made a small grunt of surprise.

'*The words of Memory.* That's what it says. *The words of Memory, carved in gold, for the hour of your death.*'

Even in the stifling conservatory, a chill went through Jonah.

'What does that mean?'

'Just a minute.'

Charis slid off her chair and went into the living room. Jonah took the paper back and stared at it. Compared with Lily's regular writing, the page was a mess. The lines were crooked, the letters badly spaced. Like a child just learning to write.

For the hour of your death.

On the bookshelf, he noticed Lily staring at him out of a photograph in an old, cheap frame. He picked it up and studied it. She was with Richard, Charis and Adam, arms around each other – somewhere cold and wet, judging by the coats and damp hair. Probably Oxford. Had he been there? It must have been ages ago. Their faces were fresh as the rain – and it was a long time since she'd had her arm around Adam.

He drained his glass and poured more, splashing it over the rim.

'Those were good times.' Charis had come back with a book in her hand and perched on the arm of his chair. Jonah looked at the picture again.

'Have you spoken to Adam recently?'

She shook her head. 'He doesn't do Christmas cards. I think he went off to Greece to play at being Socrates.'

Jonah put the photograph back on the shelf, though his eyes kept darting to Lily. Charis opened her book and spread out the glossy pages in the middle. Against a black background, Jonah saw what he took to be a golden sheet of paper, creased into eighths where it had been folded, its edges torn and ragged. There was writing on it, though not in ink. It looked as though it had been pressed into with a blunt nib, or through another sheet.

'Is that parchment?'

Charis laughed and ruffled his hair. 'Too cheap, darling. It's gold.'

'It must be worth a fortune.'

'This is blown up. The real thing's about the size of a credit card.'

Jonah looked closer. The writing resembled what Lily had written, block letters meandering across the page. Even enlarged, the writing was no bigger than you might use for a shopping list. He could hardly imagine how small it must be in real life, how hard it must have been for someone to engrave those letters. Or why they'd bothered.

'What is it?'

'It's a golden grave tablet. There was some sort of cult in the ancient world: people would be buried with these things to take to the afterlife. This one in the book dates from about 400 BC.'

'There's more than one?'

'They've been found all over the Med. There's one down the road in the British Museum, I think.'

Jonah sipped his wine. The heat had made it sour.

'Could Lily have found one?'

'Where she was is more or less ground zero for these tablets. I think some actually came up in other excavations at Sybaris. Yes.' She scanned a few pages of the book, reminding herself. 'Three were found at Thurii, which was the city they built on top of Sybaris after it was flooded.'

'So you don't have to translate it. You know what it says already.'

'More or less. The tablets vary a bit on the details.'

'Details of what?'

She blinked. 'Didn't I say? They're directions to the under-world.'

Greece

Jonah wasn't there when it happened. He got the story afterwards. He'd been at the lab with Menelaos, the professor, fetching some tools; the others had been playing Frisbee in the olive grove next to the trench. Menelaos often warned them about the snakes, but he was a worried old man and paranoid like all Greeks, so they didn't pay any attention.

At first, they said, she barely felt a thing. A bit of pain where the fangs had punctured her calf, just over the top of her boot. A trickle of blood running into her sock. They even carried on the game for a few vital moments while she sat under a tree, rubbing the wound and chatting quite normally. The snake had vanished into the ground; Lily said it was no longer than her arm.

Five minutes later, the poison hit. Her face and neck puffed red as a balloon; her veins popped, her eyes bulged, her tongue swelled until it forced its way out of her mouth. She writhed on the ground as the pain shot through her back.

It was Adam who saved her. While Charis cried and Richard talked about calling an ambulance, Adam lifted her in his arms and got Julian to help him carry her out of the meadow. He laid her on the back seat of the hire car, and drove her fifteen kilometres to the hospital at Aegion. When Julian suggested that he might kill all three of them, the way he was driving, he almost kicked him out of the car.

Jonah got back fifteen minutes later. Menelaos had the only other car but he wouldn't take him: he said there was nothing they could do. Jonah walked two miles to the main road and flagged down a lorry going in the right direction. It dropped him on the outskirts of town; after that, it took almost an hour to find the hospital. Julian met him in the crowded waiting room.

'She's unconscious. The doctors say she's fifty-fifty.'

'Fifty-fifty *what?*'

Julian pulled out a handkerchief and wiped his forehead. 'Fifty-fifty that she'll make it.'

He chattered on with words that Jonah barely heard: *antivenom . . . organ failure . . . sedation . . .*

'I have to see her.'

'Adam's with her.' Julian laid a hand on his arm. 'Let the doctors do their thing.'

Jonah shook him off. 'I have to see her,' he repeated. He looked around for someone to help, though he didn't speak Greek. Instead, he saw Adam coming through a pair of double doors. His face was white as death, his shoulders hunched.

'How—?'

'No change. They won't know for ages. They said to wait out here.'

That night, Adam and Jonah sat together in the waiting room, barely talking. When a nurse told them they could visit again, they both trooped through and took seats on opposite sides of Lily's bed. She looked like a prisoner. A breathing tube snaked down her open mouth into her throat, while fat bundles of tubes and cables stuck to her like cobwebs.

Eventually, Adam looked up, 'There's no point us both being here. The doctor said it could be hours, even days. Better to take turns.'

'No.' There was so much poison in her body, and she was so weak. She needed him there. 'You can go, if you want.'

He was too tired to pretend. The emotion in his voice was raw and explicit. No way to mistake it. Adam stared at him.

'Are you and Lily . . . ?'

Jonah nodded. Since that day in the sea cave, he and Lily had been behaving like fifteen year olds on a family holiday. Sneaking away at every opportunity, swimming round to the next beach, legs touching under the table at supper. Every moment snatched, illicit. Somehow, it would have felt like a betrayal of the group to confess.

And I don't want to upset Adam, she'd said. *He'll take it badly.*

'I thought so.' Adam took a sip from his water bottle. His face was pinched in furious concentration, as though this was some sort of mathematical problem he could solve with his intellect. 'She likes you.'

Jonah didn't know what to say. They stood on opposite sides of the bed, Lily between them. All he could hear was the hiss of the air pipe, the soft pulse of the machines.

Adam stroked Lily's arm, strapped to the bed so she didn't pull out the tubes by moving it.

'Call me if anything changes.'

A universe of space seemed to hang between them. Jonah said, 'You saved her life. The doctors said another five minutes and it would have been too late.'

A tear ran down Adam's nose and he wiped it away angrily. 'You'd have done the same if you'd been there.'

Lily spent forty-two hours unconscious. The whole time, Jonah was either at her bedside during visiting hours, or dozing in the waiting room. The second night, one of the nurses took pity on him and let him stay in the room after curfew. He sat in the chair, drifting into rapid-fire dreams that always ended with hours still to go until dawn.

He must have fallen asleep because at last the sun woke him, pale gold coming through the window. The light fell on Lily's face through the cocoon of cables, painting life onto the pale skin.

She stirred, blinked, and opened her eyes. Jonah gaped, then lunged across the room for the call button. Lily wanted to say something, but the tube in her throat prevented her. He kissed her forehead and held her gaze, saying it all with his eyes.

It was only when he knew she'd make it that he finally understood it might have been different. Until then, he'd refused to let himself admit the possibility, because to admit it was to let it in, and he'd been holding back death for three days. He just had enough time to call Adam before he collapsed from exhaustion.

Once the poison had worn off, the doctors said, the symptoms should pass quickly. They discharged Lily the same afternoon. That night, he went to the room she shared with Charis. Charis answered his knock.

'She's sleeping. I was just going down to see if Adam wants a drink. He's been pretty cut up about all this.'

'I'll keep her company.'

The air-conditioner above the window was going full blast, so cold that Lily had pulled a blanket over herself. Jonah sat on Charis's bed, feet on the floor, hands clasped like a prayer.

'I love you,' he said aloud.

Lily opened her eyes. He didn't know if she'd heard.

'Can you open the window?' she said. 'It's freezing in here.'

'The doctors said to keep you cool.'

'I need fresh air. Please.'

Jonah pulled open the window. After so long in the sterile hospital, the taste of life in the air overwhelmed him. He turned off the air-conditioner. For long moments, they luxuriated in the silence.

'How's Adam?'

'Glad you're better.' He didn't want to think about Adam now, but he could see she expected more. 'He wants to know what you felt, before you got to hospital. If you saw shining lights, met God, anything like that.'

She pulled him down onto the bed. He lay beside her, outside the blanket, feeling her body rise and fall against him as she breathed.

'It was dark and frightening – no stars or shining lights. I didn't see God, I'm afraid, or any big revelation. All I could think was, there's so much more I want to do in life. With you.'

She pushed back the blanket. Underneath, she was wearing a T-shirt, one of his, though he hadn't lent it to her. She must have taken it when he wasn't looking. She raised her arms and he tugged it off, so that she lay perfectly naked beside him.

'Is it safe?' he whispered.

'I'm not going to poison you.'

'That's not what I meant.'

'Life's too short.' She hugged her arms to herself. 'Unless you don't want . . . '

Gently, carefully, Jonah manoeuvred himself over her and kissed the nape of her neck.

'I do.'

London

The glass room seemed to turn inside out. The wall behind him throbbed with the sound of a ball being thrown against it.

'I've told Yolanda not to let them – not inside the house,' Charis fretted. She looked back at the paper, mouthing words to herself.

'Why did she send this?' Jonah asked aloud.

'Something to work on over the winter? The Italians would never have let her take the original out of the country.'

'She could have stuck the copy in her bag and brought it with us. Why send it?'

He caught Charis giving him a funny look. Her chest shone with sweat; the strap of her top had fallen off her shoulder.

'What?'

'Listen to yourself, darling. Do you really think an ancient Greek tablet is going to tell you where Lily is?'

'She put it in the post the day she vanished. There has to be a connection.'

You've got nothing else, said a voice inside him.

'So what do you want me to do?'

'Can you translate it? See if there's anything unusual about it?'

'It'll take time – it's a tricky text. Can I keep it for a bit?'

'It's all I've got.'

'I'll take a copy.' She jumped up, pulled him to his feet and led him upstairs. In another room, a child screamed as though its world had ended. A second child joined in, punctuated by the nanny's exasperated shouts. Charis didn't seem to notice.

The study was cool after the oven-heat of the conservatory. A white computer stood on a white desk; white bookshelves lined the room. There was a white bed with white sheets, presumably in case the guests overflowed the other five bedrooms. A black bare-breasted goddess stood on a side table, head tipped back and arms offering two snakes to the heavens.

The printer-copier hummed as Charis ran the paper through it. Jonah stood by the window, staring down at the lawn. The crying had stopped. All he could hear was the drone of the city on an August day.

Her naked feet made no sound on the white carpet, but suddenly her voice was very close behind him.

'Can you stay for supper?'

'I should get back.'

'We can have the place to ourselves. I'll have Yolanda take the kids to the cinema. Bill's in Frankfurt,' she added.

He turned. Charis stood almost touching him, back arched, head tipped back. Her musky perfume filled the room.

Jonah put his hand on her bare shoulder. The wine turned his thoughts to haze: he felt drunk.

He pushed her away. She took two steps back and sat down on the bed. She started to unbutton her top.

'What are you doing?'

She paused, surprised. 'Darling . . . '

She reached out for his belt. A wave of fury crackled through him: he slapped her hand away. To be doing this when Lily needed him – to be doing it at all – was wrong wrong wrong. Like . . .

Like dancing on Lily's grave, his brain supplied.

Charis stood and straightened her top. Her face had gone hard and grey.

'You don't have to play Sir Galahad. What do you think Lily's doing right now?'

'She's missing.'

'She isn't missing, darling. She's left you.'

The wine had softened him up, but the words still hit him like a punch in the gut.

'She's missing,' he repeated, hiding behind the phrase like a wall. Charis's laugh knocked it down again.

'Be a grown-up. You said the police spoke to her this morning. Listen to what they're saying, what she's saying. Do you have any idea what she was getting up to in Italy?'

He shook his head. He wanted to make her understand, but all the things he could say – *She would have called; she wouldn't leave me* – didn't scratch the surface of what he felt. He just *knew*.

Charis hugged her arms across her chest. 'Believe what you want. I just felt sorry for you.'

Jonah took the paper from the printer and left the copy in the tray.

'If you want to help, tell me what that says.'

He walked out the door. He heard her coming after him

on the stairs but didn't look back. In the kitchen, the ball had started bouncing again. He fumbled with the front door latch.

'Jonah?'

He looked, despite himself. Charis stood halfway down the stairs, her face in shadow. She looked as if she'd started to cry, though it was probably just sweat.

'I hope you find her.'

He walked and walked, meandering through the sticky city. It was easier than thinking.

He drifted south, like a raindrop trickling down to the river without ever understanding the gravity that pulls it. He'd have to go back to the flat, but he couldn't bear even thinking about the emptiness there.

Eventually, he found himself on the Tottenham Court Road. A black sign with gold lettering pointed left to the British Museum.

There's one down the road in the British Museum, I think.

He followed the sign, climbed the steps between the soaring Ionic columns, and got directions to a distant gallery far removed from the noise of the Great Court.

The gold lay sandwiched between cloudy Perspex, locked in a display case in a corner of the room. It was even smaller than Charis had said, not much bigger than a large postage stamp. He had to stoop and shade the glare with his hands to see the tiny writing. Next to it, a cylindrical gold case hung on a gold chain. A card carried a typed translation of the text.

Gold tablet with an Orphic inscription and the pendant case that contained it, the label informed him.

He looked at it for a long time. No one disturbed him or asked him to move: this part of the museum was too far from the gift shops and cafés for most people to bother with. Even if they'd asked, he wouldn't have heard them. His gaze was fixed – not on the tablet, but on the case beside it.

He'd seen it before – or one just like it. Three days ago, sketched in Lily's drawing in the Field Journal at Sibari.

He took out his phone.

Thirteen

Perhaps it would be easiest if I recounted a conversation I once had with Diotima, and the questions she asked me.

Plato, *Symposium*

Akolouthei.

A single word printed in the mud outside the doorstep, wet where the slaves had tipped out their washing water. *Follow me.*

In the *andron* behind me, Euphemus, Dimos and the doctor were still snoring on their couches where they'd passed out, naked. One of the dancers – Aphrodite, I think – lay curled up against Euphemus' chest. For a moment, when I saw her, I thought she might be Diotima. I would have killed him.

I'd made it to bed the night before, but it hadn't helped. My head hurt; my stomach felt as if I'd swallowed a stone. I wanted to vomit. Judging by the smell, I wouldn't have been the first. I tottered to the door, threw it open – and saw the word in the mud.

Akolouthei. Follow me.

I rubbed my eyes. One step further it appeared again. And again. A trail of words leading up the street, each a pace apart. Fainter, where the earth was dry and footsteps had scuffed the dust, but still legible.

I've seen marks like this before. Whores in the Kerameikos

use them: little boots with words carved on the sole, advertising their bodies wherever they go, like cats putting down scent.

The ground was newly wet, and the footprint newer still. Whoever left the marks, she must have left the house recently – and by the men's entrance. Had she stayed the night, after all?

Follow me.

I was in a susceptible state. I followed.

The prints avoided the main boulevards, sticking to the sidestreets and back alleys where fewer feet could overwrite them. The further I went, the more certain I was that they were a message – a message for *me*. What it might be, or why, I couldn't think. That's why I followed.

The trail ended at the door of a large house near the edge of town, where the streets began to unwind from their strict symmetry. Across marshy fields, the forked peak of Mount Apollion punctured the sky. Two columns supported a porch, one with a herm facing out of it and a bell hanging from his outstretched phallus. I rang it.

A slave answered, a stooped woman with grey hair tied up in a bun.

'Whose house is this?' I asked.

She held open the door with a mute smile, letting me in to a shady courtyard. A fruiting apricot tree grew in the centre, surrounded by a tiled floor which showed birds nesting among vines and ivy. On a table under the tree, a real bird sat silent in a wicker cage.

The air was sweet with the smell of apricots – and figs too. I looked for another tree, but didn't see one. And it was too early in the season for figs, anyway.

'Don't trust your senses?'

Diotima slipped out from behind a pillar. I started, though only because the sound surprised me. The fact of her being there seemed entirely logical, as if I'd known it already.

Don't trust your senses. Was it a question?

'I followed your footsteps.'

'I thought you might.' She took another step closer. 'You look like a man looking for something to follow.'

I didn't know what to say. I could have told her *no*, that I wasn't looking for someone to follow but someone I'd lost, a friend whose cloak she'd worn last night. I could have asked how she came by it.

I wasn't ready for the answers, so I studied her instead. She had a face that somehow escaped age, the character so strong that nothing could touch it. Her skin was smooth; her features firm; her eyes deep as time. She wore a simple linen dress, with a necklace of beads and dried figs at her throat. I thought that might be what I'd smelled, though the ripe scent didn't belong with those shrivelled husks.

I have a weakness for figs. Socrates always used to tease me about it. He said it was the only time I was willing to get my hands sticky.

Her grey eyes caught me looking and I blushed. I'd seen her virtually naked the night before, but this felt more guiltily intimate. I took cover behind banality.

'You have a beautiful house.'

'Thank you.'

Even in Italy, it must have cost a small fortune. 'Do you have estates in the country?'

'No.'

'Some kind of workshop?'

'What are you trying to imply?'

I winced. The word I'd used, *ergasterion*, can mean any sort of workshop. It can also mean a more specific, intimate sort of commercial establishment.

'I didn't mean to imply . . . '

She wasn't offended. 'Men want to be friends with me.'

'Naturally.'

'Some of them choose to show their feelings with gifts.'

I looked around the room: the paintings on the wall; the expensive ceramics displayed in an alcove; a pair of gilded sandals put together under a chair.

'You must have generous friends.'

'When I let them get close.'

There was a name for her line of work, though even Socrates wouldn't have used it to her face. *Hetaira*. Not bought like a prostitute, but far more expensive to maintain than a wife. Available, but not for sale. Respected, occasionally, but a long way from respectable.

'Is Dimos a friend?' I tried to sound casual. Inside, the Voice of Desire was screaming to know whether she'd spent the night with him.

'He's very attentive.'

'You came to his dinner party.'

'I heard he had a famous Athenian philosopher visiting. I wanted to see for myself.'

'I hope Euphemus didn't disappoint.'

She gave a small, private smile that didn't seem meant for me. Behind its wicker bars, the caged bird preened itself. I wondered why she kept it.

'Shall we take a walk?'

She'd changed her shoes: these ones didn't say anything. Nor was she wearing Agathon's cloak. She led me back through the city, pointing out the temples, the public statues, the theatre. She chattered away about Hippodamus, the architect who designed the city; and Protagoras, the sophist who wrote its law code. I followed and listened. It felt strange, to be walking with a woman as companionably as if we were two men going to the gymnasium. But then, everything about Diotima was strange.

And, in truth, I didn't have much idea what you say to

women. Perhaps if I'd been born Spartan, it wouldn't have been a problem. I'd have grown up side by side with them, fighting and wrestling them just like boys. In Athens, we bury women in our homes like treasure.

'Are you from Thurii?' I asked, when a pause seemed to demand I should say something.

'Nobody's from Thurii,' she said tartly. 'It's a city of immigrants.'

'Where do you come from, then?'

I knew she wasn't Greek. She didn't look or sound any different, but I could feel it, like listening to a foreigner playing a familiar song. The notes were pitch-perfect, the rhythm exact, but in the cadences – the spaces between – you heard something else.

She'd gone ahead and didn't hear my question. We'd come into the agora, a wide square lined with matched porticoes and newly minted statues. Symmetry reigned: every building had its mirror, every column its twin. In their centre, the navel of the newborn city, a handsome tomb stood on a plinth.

'The mausoleum of Herodotus,' Diotima announced, like a tour guide on the Acropolis. And then, as if it mattered a great deal to her, 'Do you like it?'

I considered the tomb. It was a pretty thing: pillars supporting a canopy, with scenes from the Persian wars carved on a frieze. I could see Leonidas and his three hundred Spartans; Xerxes carried on a litter; a Persian sailor screaming for help as his trireme sank under him at Salamis. The figures were lifelike, the colours vivid. The entire structure was dressed in marble and must have cost a fortune.

'It's not Herodotus' monument,' I said. 'His monument is the *History*.'

'His monument is history,' she said.

I puzzled over what she'd said. Did she mean that the

grand stone tomb was a historical artefact? Or that one day it would be nothing but dust? That his real legacy was the field of history, which he broke open for other men to plough? Or was she simply repeating what I'd said?

Words speak as if they had meaning, but when you question them they always say the same thing, Socrates said. Diotima's words always seemed to be saying three things at once.

'Herodotus achieved a sort of immortality,' I said, remembering what she'd said the night before. *Love craves immortality.* 'He wrote his history, he says, "so that time will not bleach out the colours of men's deeds." But, in fact, it's him that survives, more than Darius or Themistocles or the three hundred Spartans.'

I stared at the figures on the frieze – carved images not of reality, but of the image of reality that Herodotus had made with his words. Did they have any truth against the men whose hands blistered on the trireme oars, who kissed their wives when they left, and screamed as they drowned in the clear sea at Salamis?

'Herodotus tells a story about Gyges the Lydian,' Diotima said. 'Do you know it?'

I nodded. She made a gesture with her eyes, inviting me to tell it.

'Gyges was a bodyguard to the Lydian king.' I'd lost my Herodotus in the wreck of the *Calliste*, but I remembered the story well enough. It's almost the first thing you read in chapter one – as far as some people get. 'The king wanted to show Gyges how beautiful his queen was, so he hid him in the bedroom where he could see her undress. But the queen saw Gyges watching, and realised what her husband had done.

'The queen was mortified and offered Gyges a choice. To kill the king for his temerity, or be put to death himself. Gyges chose the first option. He murdered the king, married the queen and became ruler of Lydia. And all because he saw her naked.'

'A woman's body is a dangerous thing.'

I bit my lip, trying to put away the image of Diotima in her translucent dress the night before.

'But I've heard a different version of the story,' she said. 'In this one, Gyges is a shepherd, not a bodyguard. One day, while he's pasturing his sheep, an earthquake opens a cave in the mountain. He goes down. Inside, he finds a mechanical horse made entirely of bronze, and the skeleton of a giant man, with a gold ring on one of its fingers.'

Her voice conjured the images in my mind. A deep defile where the earth had been torn apart; the sky nothing more than a jagged scar. The bronze horse lying on its side as if fallen in battle, gleaming dully. The giant bones, half sunk in the cave floor, and the shepherd's rough hands snapping the knuckle in their haste to remove the ring.

'He takes the ring and goes back up. Except, when he meets his fellow shepherds, they can't see him. The ring has made him invisible, he realises, which puts an idea in his head. He goes to the palace. As soon as he's inside, he uses the ring to get past the guards, seduce the queen and murder the king.'

'Just like that?'

'Just like that.'

I considered it. 'I prefer Herodotus' story.'

'Why?'

'In Herodotus, the king gets his comeuppance for betraying the queen. Gyges is executing a sort of justice, obeying his fate. In your version, Gyges simply kills the king because he can. He has no motive. So he must have been bad to start with.'

'Really?' Her dress swayed on her hips. 'Do you think if there were a second ring, and a good man found it, he wouldn't eventually do everything that Gyges does? He could take anything, sleep with anyone, even kill people – and never be caught. There'd be no limits on his power.'

'Then he'd be a god.'

'But if he had the power and didn't use it, people would say he was an idiot. In their hearts, all men think that behaving badly will get them further than doing the right thing. Good men are just too frightened of getting caught.'

'That's what Euphemus would say,' I said glumly.

We walked another block in silence. Thurii's civic grandeur was behind us: we were heading back to the edge of town. The forked mountain rose over me, until I could feel its weight pressing down on my shoulders.

'Last night, you said that there was more to know about love than you'd revealed,' I said. 'Did you mean it? Or were you just teasing Dimos?'

'I meant it.'

'Can you tell me? Or is there some initiation rite I have to undergo?'

She paused, turned, and studied my face until I thought it would burn.

'You've already been born into those mysteries. You just haven't opened your eyes yet.'

I flushed scarlet: offended, tantalised, frustrated beyond reason. I was beginning to understand the dress she'd worn the night before. She could wear something that covered nothing because her mind remained perfectly opaque, like a city with no walls but an impregnable acropolis. *You can have everything*, she seemed to say, *but it counts for nothing.*

'Socrates said that wisdom lives inside people; he was just the midwife bringing it into the world.'

'Socrates understood the mysteries.'

She said it so certainly, it reminded me of the way she talked about the Sybarite horses. As if she'd been there.

'Did you ever meet Socrates?'

Another one of her elusive, inward-looking smiles. 'How old do you think I am?'

There was no good answer to that question, and I was wise enough to know it. I suppose they must never have met, or Socrates would surely have mentioned her. Formally, they were opposites – a sphinx and a satyr, Aphrodite and Hephaestus. But the same divine intelligence burned in both of them. If they'd ever married, their children would have been immortal.

'Did Socrates say how people came by the wisdom he delivered?' she asked. 'If he's the midwife, who's the father?'

I shrugged. 'The gods, I suppose.'

We were back near her house again. The closer we came, the more my mood darkened. I couldn't bear it to end. And I hadn't asked about Agathon's cloak yet. Honestly, I'd almost forgotten it.

She paused outside her own front door. 'Do you mind if I show you one more thing? It won't take long.'

Relief put a giddy smile all over my face. I followed her happily, out through the gates and onto a causeway that carried the road between green marshes full of lilies and weeds. Strange hummocks bulged uncomfortably out of the ground. Where the water ran clear, stone blocks lurked below the surface.

'This was Sybaris,' Diotima said.

This one I knew. When the Pythagorean army from Croton decided that the Sybarites' decadence offended them, they didn't just try to defeat or enslave the city. They wiped it off the earth. They came here one night and diverted the river Crathis, turning it against the town and drowning it. The sleeping Sybarites had no chance. The site was a wilderness for seventy years, until Athens decided to resettle it. Even then, the colonists didn't dare use the old name, and the new city occupied a shrunken plot compared to its predecessor. The long, lonely marshes gave silent proof of that.

149

Out in the reeds, a heron stood perfectly still, head bowed, waiting. I wondered how something so bleak could also be so beautiful.

'Have you ever been to Egypt?'

I was getting used to Diotima's sudden changes of subject. 'No.'

'They remember events there that were old when Homer wrote.'

Someone had erected a fence on the edge of the marsh to keep animals from straying into it. She climbed over, scrambled down the bank and stepped onto a stone capital sunk into the earth. Water bubbled out of the grass around it.

'The Egyptians tell the story of a sacred island that existed nine thousand years ago, beyond the Pillars of Hercules, larger than Libya and Asia put together. It belonged to Poseidon, who called it Atlantis.'

I followed her down and stood on the edge of the marsh. Cold mud oozed around my sandals.

'The city they built was a marvel for the ages. The walls were dressed with bronze, and the temples sheathed in gold and silver. The canals and harbours were full of ships and merchants from all over the world.'

Again, her voice spun fabulous pictures before my eyes, as if she was charming the old stones out of the swamp and reassembling them into something even more magnificent than they'd been before.

'For generations, the Atlanteans had sufficient wisdom to despise everything but virtue. They refused to succumb to luxury. But, over the centuries, they lost their divine spark. Human nature took over, and although to an external observer they seemed richer, happier and more powerful than ever, in fact they were leading themselves to disaster.

'They provoked a terrible war with Athens, the worst the world had ever seen. And when they were defeated, Poseidon took his island back. After a day and a night of terror, there were great earthquakes and floods, and the island of Atlantis sank into the sea. Even today, the Egyptians say, ships can't navigate that stretch of ocean because of the mud shallows near the surface.'

A breeze blew off the marsh. She snapped off a piece of mortar and skimmed it over the stagnant water. It bounced twice, then sank.

I wanted to say something – something profound or insightful, something to impress her. But I was tongue-tied. My mind had become a desert where no words grew.

'Why did the others call you Pythagoras last night?' she asked.

'They were teasing me about my appetite.' I paused, then told her a measure of truth. 'I came to Italy looking for a friend who'd been studying with a Pythagorean teacher.'

'Have you met any Pythagoreans?'

'Only one who made any sense – and he wouldn't call himself a Pythagorean.'

'Archytas?'

Again, I felt there was nothing I could say that she didn't know already. It made me despair. 'Have you met him?'

'He's a friend.' Careless of the jealousy burning my face, she continued, 'Did you learn anything from Archytas?'

'He said the world is an instrument.'

She stared into my eyes. I felt she was unscrolling my soul and reading it like a manuscript.

'You liked his theory.'

'When Socrates died, I felt that the world had broken.' I'd rarely spoken so honestly to anyone, let alone a woman. 'Archytas' theory shows how the divided world can be united, like the harmony produced from two strings.'

'But it's only a metaphor.'

'It isn't. That's what Pythagoras discovered. Music's

151

governed by mathematical ratios, made of the same numbers which underpin the whole universe. Mathematics explains everything. You probably know that,' I realised.

'But the mathematics isn't perfect. Did he tell you that? If you tune a lyre to the mathematical ratios, the interval between each pair of strings sounds perfect. But they don't add up. The more strings you add, the further they get from the base note. A good musician knows that you have to adjust each note a fraction so that the whole scale is in tune with itself.'

I was no musician. 'I don't understand.'

'Perfect mathematical intervals create an imperfect scale. It's as if you wanted to fill a jug that holds exactly eight cups. You pour in the water, one cup at a time, but with the eighth cup the jug overflows. The only way to stop it from over-flowing is to make each cup slightly less than full.'

'That doesn't make sense.'

'That's the point. The world isn't sensible. Either our senses aren't made to appreciate perfection – or else the perfect world that mathematics describes isn't our world.'

I remembered Archytas' paradox, the edge of the universe that can never be reached.

'You sound like a sophist. Up is down, left is right, good is bad.'

She parted her lips and held me with her eyes. 'Haven't you ever done a bad thing that made you feel good?'

A warm feeling spread through me. I could feel myself getting hard. Worse, I could see she'd noticed.

'It's strange to talk about these things with a woman,' I stammered.

She gave me her sphinx smile. 'Can't women talk philosophy?' Are there major differences between men's and women's natures, other than that one sows the seed and the other bears the fruit?'

'Men tend to be stronger.'

It was a feeble answer and her expression let me know it. 'Is that difference relevant to philosophy?'

'No.'

'Aren't a lot of women better than a lot of men at a lot of things?'

It had never occurred to me. You don't see women doing many things in Athens.

'Do you think natural capacity is parcelled out differently between the sexes? That a woman is necessarily lazier, feebler, stupider and less able than a man?'

I might not know women, but I know enough men. 'I doubt it.'

That wasn't good enough for her. She looked away impatiently, back towards her house. I was losing her.

'Why are you wearing Agathon's cloak?' I blurted out.

She turned back, with a stare that went through me like sunlight through a curtain.

'I wondered when you were going to ask me about that.'

'How—?'

'Agathon never stopped talking about you. He thinks you're the wisest friend he has.'

'Why are you wearing his cloak?' I repeated.

'He forgot it at my house, the night before he left Thurii.'

'He was at your house?'

'The night before he left,' she answered evenly. *You can think what you like,* her eyes said. *I'm not going to tell you.*

'I thought he was staying with Dimos.'

'They'd quarrelled. When Agathon came back, he came to my house.'

'What do you mean, *When Agathon came back*?'

'Two weeks ago. He'd gone to Taras to meet you, but something bad happened.'

153

I remembered the broken tomb. For a man so obsessed with virtue, a lot of bad things seemed to have been happening to Agathon. 'Why didn't he wait for me here, then?'

'A letter had come, from Locris. The moment he read it, he said he had to go.'

'Did he say what it said?'

'No.' A smile crossed her lips. 'But I found out.'

She reached into her shoe and pulled out a small fold of papyrus. I took it and read it.

I have another customer. If you want the book, find me before the end of the month. I am on the porch of the Great Temple.

The handwriting was a scattered mess, barely literate – as if it had been written by someone thrashing around in a nightmare. It wasn't signed. 'Do you know who sent it?'

'There's a man in Locris, a Pythagorean called Timaeus. Agathon had been trying to buy a book from him, but he wanted too much money.'

A hundred drachmas – now scattered over the seabed in the Bay of Taras. I started to say something, but trailed off. A nasty thought had struck me. I saw the tomb again. *They opened the coffin and stole some grave goods.* Was there money in there? Gold?

Diotima put me out of my misery. 'He didn't have the money.'

'How do you know?'

'Because he asked me for it. I said no.'

'So what was he planning to do when he got to Locris?'

'He wouldn't tell me. He didn't even say if he was coming back.'

A cold tremor went up my leg. While I'd stood there, the wet ground had been slowly swallowing my feet. I pulled them out, almost losing a sandal, and retreated up the bank.

Diotima was watching me.

'There was something else.' She reached up and unclasped

a gold chain from around her neck. The necklace of figs had hidden it, though I remembered seeing it the night before. Along with so much else.

'He said if you got here before he came back, I should give you this.'

The chain ended in a cylindrical gold locket. She fished it out from where it had hung between her breasts and tossed it to me. It smelled of figs.

I undid the locket. A slim piece of gold fell into my palm – a golden leaf rolled delicately into a scroll.

'Open it.'

I unravelled the gold until it made a sheet about the size of my thumb. Tiny incised letters covered almost every grain of it, squeezed into the space with almost desperate urgency.

The words of Memory, carved in gold . . .

Fourteen

Jonah – London

He stared at the tablet in its Perspex coffin and pressed the phone to his ear. Richard answered unusually quickly.

'You've heard the news about Lily? The police? Apparently they found her.'

Jonah didn't bother to answer. 'Tell me about . . . ' He read it off the museum label. ' . . . The Orphic gold tablet.'

From the corner of his eye, he saw a guard staring at him from the doorway. Just then, it didn't make any difference. Richard had gone as quiet as the museum.

'I don't know what you're talking about,' he said at last.

'I saw the picture in the Field Journal.' He was about to mention Lily's copy of the text, but suddenly decided not to. There was too much he didn't understand yet.

'We signed non-disclosure agreements,' Richard pleaded. 'Lily shouldn't have said anything.'

'She didn't.' The guard gave him a warning stare. Jonah ignored him. 'I think it's got something to do with her disappearing.'

'But they've found her. Haven't they?'

'Have you heard from her?'

Richard hesitated. 'No.'

'Neither have I. So I need to know about the tablet.'

The line hissed. Jonah glanced over at the guard, but he'd

been distracted by a Japanese woman who'd taken a flash photograph of one of the exhibits.

'You need to ask the funding body.'

'Don't give me that. You're her friend, aren't you?'

'Of course,' Richard protested. 'And I want to help. But I'm not the one who says she's missing.'

'If you can't tell me, I'll go to the press. They're sniffing around this story already.' He could hardly get the lie out as he remembered the press conference that morning. But Richard swallowed it.

'I'll call the foundation. They'll explain.'

'Who?'

'The Eikasia Foundation – the people funding the dig. There's an office in London.'

The Japanese woman had gone; the guard was advancing towards him, gesturing towards the phone. But he knew the answer wasn't in London. 'What was going on in Sibari before I got there?'

'*Excuse me*,' said the guard, far more loudly than anything Jonah had said.

'OK, OK.' Back to Richard. 'Arrange a time and tell me when. Soon.'

He put the phone away, and rode out the guard's stare until the man retreated back to his stool. He didn't give a damn.

He gazed at the tablet, trapped in its case. He felt its anguish: alive and dead, visible to the world but unable to touch it.

I am the words of Memory, the tablet told him, *carved in gold, ready for the hour of your death.*

'Is Lily dead?' he asked.

No. He'd have known if she was, would have felt it. Instead, he felt nothing. She was far away, perhaps trapped behind her own invisible wall like the tablet. But alive.

How can I find her?

Two words seemed to swell out at him from the translation on the card in the case. *Stay away.*

A beat filled Jonah's ears, rhythmic and relentless. With a shock, he realised it was the tick of his watch. He glanced around, but no one else in the gallery seemed to have heard it.

Am I going mad?

He glanced at the watch. His hearing reset itself; all he heard now was the hiss of air-conditioning and voices in the distance.

Jonah sat at the table in his flat with the pile of torn-open post, his laptop and a beer. Lily watched him from a photograph on the screen. She was sitting inside a giant *pithos* vase that would have been almost taller than her if it hadn't been buried up to its neck. She smiled up at the camera, glowing with delight and breaking Jonah's heart.

It was her Facebook page. He ran through the posts for anything significant. Worried notes from friends he'd called on Sunday, hoping she was OK, cut off with a quick line from Julie that the Italian police had traced her. No one else knew anything. No answers.

He typed out a quick message.

I still haven't heard from Lily. If anyone was on the dig and saw something unusual, or knows where she might be, please get in touch.

The words appeared in her timeline and went grey. While he waited for a reply, he opened another tab and logged in to their bank account. Still no transactions since he left Berlin.

Charis's question came back to him. *Do you have any idea what she was getting up to in Italy?* He started scrolling back through the bank statement, looking at what had happened before Lily went missing.

If life had been normal that previous week, it would have stood out straight away. But Lily had been in Italy and he'd been all over the place: every cashpoint he'd touched had spoken a different language. French, Dutch, Italian, Greek, German . . .

Greek?

He read the line on the statement.

22 AUG 2012
ATM SYNTAGMA SQUARE, ATHENS GR EUR 100.00

Touring was a dislocating experience. Clubs, hotels, fast-food joints – the same brands in different languages, and everyone speaking English regardless. It was easy to forget where you where, even easier to forget where you'd been. But he knew he hadn't gone within five hundred miles of Athens on that tour.

The card might have been stolen – but there was still money in the account, and Jonah didn't think a thief would have taken it all the way to Athens just for a hundred Euros.

But Lily had been in Sibari that week. He'd spoken to her every night.

Or maybe not. Perhaps there'd been one night: the promoter had taken them to a club, the bass so loud he never heard his phone. When he finally got out, Lily had sent him a text message saying she'd gone to bed. Was that Monday? Tuesday? Rotterdam or Ghent?

Still, she would have mentioned if she'd been in Athens. Wouldn't she?

He clicked back to her Facebook page and stared at the photograph, wishing it could answer. Wondering what a gold tablet and a trip to Athens had to do with why she'd vanished out of his life. Suddenly, the smile on her face became something desperate. *Get me out of here*, she said, buried in the earth.

His phone beeped with a text message. Richard – he hadn't had the guts to call. Jonah thought about calling him straight back, but knew he wouldn't answer.

What have you got to hide? he wondered.

He read the message.

They'll see you at two tomorrow.

★　★　★

It had once been the biggest port on earth, moving goods from every corner of the world. Now, the only thing they traded in Docklands was paper. Jonah slouched through the crowds of suits and felt like a tramp in his skinny jeans and Beta Band T-shirt.

He walked into the lobby and wondered whether he had the right building. The sign behind the reception desk didn't say anything about the Eikasia Foundation. In large brass letters it said: OPHION SHIPPING SA.

A second later he realised he knew the name. He'd read it on the internet two days ago, but not in connection with the foundation or Richard. It was the family firm of Ari Maroussis, the shipping heir who owned the yacht *Nestis*. The yacht that he'd watched sail into the night the day Lily vanished – vanished from the dig sponsored by the Eikasia Foundation. Whose offices Richard had sent him to. Except that actually the offices belonged to Ophion Shipping.

The receptionist didn't smile as he approached.

'I'm looking for the Eikasia Foundation,' he told her.

'Do you have an appointment?' Her face said she found it unlikely.

'Jonah Barnes. They're expecting me.'

She gave him a pass and sent him to another reception area on the fourteenth floor. No one was there to meet him. He sat down on a coffin-sized leather sofa, comfortable and cold, and took a brochure from a glass table. He flipped through, scanning the photos for any sign of Lily among the scientists and smiling field workers. A lot of the projects didn't seem to have anything to do with archaeologists: there were physicists, philosophers, marine biologists. Obviously the foundation had plenty of money to splash around.

A glass door opened and a grey-suited man stepped through. He was tall and tanned, with wiry black hair and a chiselled, alpha-male face.

'Mr Barnes.' He didn't smile. 'I'm Andreas Maniatis, the executive director. Thank you for coming to see us.'

His English had the sheen of something foreign that had been expensively perfected. He led Jonah through double glass doors, into a private office. Full-length windows showed the building's reflection mirrored in the opposite block.

'I'm sorry about your wife. This must be a difficult time for you.'

Difficult? The word implied some sort of relative degree, a continuum that stretched from easy to hard. Jonah was several steps beyond impossible.

'Doctor Andrews will join us in a moment. He will have more precise answers to your questions.'

A secretary brought two pots of coffee and cream.

'I thought I had the wrong place,' Jonah said, while she poured the coffee. 'What's the connection with Ophion Shipping?'

'Ophion's owners also fund our foundation.'

'Ari Maroussis.'

'Among others.'

'He was there, wasn't he? On site, the day Lily went missing.'

Andreas tapped a silver pen on the table. 'The Maroussis family are interested in where their money goes. Naturally.'

'Can you hear me?' a tinny voice interrupted. Jonah turned to the door. But it was closed – and the voice had come from behind his back, though he hadn't heard anyone enter. He spun round on his chair.

A screen on the wall had burst into life, a widescreen Richard sitting at a desk. It looked like the lab in Sibari. He'd put the camera too high and too close, so that it squashed him down into his chair and magnified his nose.

'Thank you for joining us, Doctor Andrews,' said Andreas. 'You know Jonah Barnes.'

Jonah hadn't made the connection. To him, Richard had always been Richard, never Doctor Andrews. He shifted his chair closer to the middle of the room, not sure where he should be. He couldn't see the camera on his end.

'As Richard knows, I want to hear about the Orphic gold tablet you found at Sibari,' he said to Andreas.

Andreas studied him a moment, as if Jonah were a pair of cufflinks he was thinking about buying.

'I am not an archaeologist. Here, we just write the cheques.' He tapped the pen on the table again, emphasising the point. 'And we have made nothing public yet from the Sibari dig.'

His tone was so patronising, Jonah wondered if it was deliberate. Designed to wind him up.

'They found a tablet,' he said. 'You know what they are, the Orphic tablets? Ancient little scraps of gold with writing on them. There's one in the British Museum. Lily found another on the Sibari dig.'

'All our staff sign confidentiality agreements.'

'This is about my wife,' Jonah reminded him.

'Doctor Andrews says the police have found her already.'

'They haven't. And I think the tablet is part of the reason.'

A three-way silence. Andreas's pen had stopped moving. Jonah turned to the screen, trying to stare Richard down. It was hard without knowing where the camera was, but he must have found it. Richard squirmed.

'We're not supposed to talk about it.'

'What's so secret?'

Richard's eyes darted over Jonah's shoulder to Andreas's desk. The class swot, always seeking the teacher's permission.

'It's a major find. We need to authenticate it, study it . . . There are procedures.'

'But you did find it?'

An unhappy nod.

'Was there anything special about it?'

'Special?' Richard scratched an itch on his nose. 'What do you mean?'

I wish I knew. I wish I knew why Lily copied it out and posted it to her sister the morning she disappeared. But he didn't want to tell them about her letter.

'Can I see the tablet?'

Richard and Andreas exchanged another look. Richard's mouth opened, but the lips didn't move.

'What?'

'Tell him,' Andreas said.

Richard leaned towards the camera. His face filled the screen.

'There was a break-in at the lab last week. Someone opened the safe and stole the tablet.'

It took him a moment to process what he'd just heard. 'Did you tell the police?'

'Of course.'

'When they asked about Lily, I mean? First the tablet went missing, then she did. There must be a connection.' Was he the only one who could see it? They were still holding something

163

back. 'Christ, Richard, don't give me your fucking procedures. She's your friend.'

Richard's head had bowed so low his face was almost hidden.

'Jonah?'

Andreas's voice, cool and commanding. Jonah spun slowly on his chair.

'What my colleague is trying to say is that only three people on the dig knew the safe combination where the tablet was stored. Doctor Andrews himself, the conservator . . . and your wife.'

Greece

Together in the trench – the first time, before the snakebite, before the sea cave. Squeezed together in what had once been a store-room. Now it was just four low stone walls making a rough square. Lily was on her knees, scraping away the ground; Jonah swept up the earth with a wicker brush and carried it away in a bucket. It was hot, tedious work. He'd drunk too much at dinner the night before and slept badly, kept awake by Julian's snoring.

'Is this really what you want to do with your life?' he asked. It came out more surly than he'd meant.

'If someone gives me a job.'

'You couldn't pay me to do this.'

'You paid to be here,' she pointed out.

'Don't remind me.'

The bucket was full. He took it to the spoil heap and dumped it out. He came back and sat on the ancient wall, watching Lily closely. Her face was a mask of concentration, pigtails tucked back behind her ears. There was something intimate about seeing her so fixed on what she was doing.

'I never know what you're thinking,' she said suddenly. 'You watch everything from behind your fringe, like some kind of animal hiding in the long grass, and never say a word.'

Jonah glanced to the far side of the trench, where Julian and Charis were cleaning out a *pithos* vase and having a loud discussion about Julian's love life. 'Just because someone talks the whole time, it doesn't mean you know what they're thinking.'

'At supper last night, you didn't say a single thing for fifty-seven minutes. I timed you – I wanted to see if you could go a full hour.'

Jonah shrugged. Lily sighed.

'How are you ever going to be a rock star if you're so quiet?'

'They give me an amp on stage.'

'And do you just stand there scowling at the audience like you scowl at me?'

He didn't try to explain. He didn't really understand it himself. Off stage, he was happy to stand at the back of the room, watching. Not shy or nervous: he just didn't have much to say. Not in words. The things that mattered he put into his music: feelings and colours, shades of emotion and longing.

'I'm not scowling at you.' He bared his teeth in a forced, ferocious grin. 'I'm concentrating.' He reached in front of her and swept the dirt away, letting his shoulder touch her arm. 'Come and see a gig when we're back in the UK.' In the lights, plugged into something awesome and beautiful, that was where he came alive. 'I'm different on stage.'

She wrinkled her nose. 'Maybe I don't want you different.'

'You don't even know what I'm thinking.'

She offered him the hand-pick. 'Shall we swap?'

He took the pick gingerly and squatted over the hole

Lily had made. The sun had baked the ground so hard that the only way in was to hack it apart, then scrape away the lumps. Each time the blade bit the earth, he had his heart in his mouth, in case some priceless vase took the hit. Lily did it like surgery; Jonah felt like he was chopping wood.

'You want to know what I'm thinking,' he said after a while. 'I'm wondering how a person like you wants to do the world's most boring job.'

She flicked him with the brush. 'You're as bad as Julian. It's only boring if you're boring.'

'Sell me.'

'Didn't you ever want a time machine? You'll never walk in ancient Athens, but if you dig in the right place you can stand on the same stones that Plato or Euripides might have trodden on. You can pick up a cup or a coin, and the last person who touched it before you lived two thousand years ago. Hand to hand. Not like in a museum, where everything's in airless boxes and you can't touch it. This is real.'

She lifted her hat and wiped her forehead. 'Adam says it's like quantum superposition. You know the theory that every possible world exists simultaneously? Archaeology's a way of reaching through the dimensions and touching something from a different reality.'

Jonah wasn't much interested in what Adam said, even if he'd understood it. He glanced at Lily, trying to read her face. *Adam says.* He'd have loved to know what she thought about Adam.

'*Wait!*'

Lily shot out her arm to block the pick mid-air. 'Look there.'

He'd missed it – predictably. A blush of pink in the grey earth, flush with the floor. A millimetre deeper and he'd have smashed it.

'Your turn.' He handed her the pick and got out of the way. Lily knelt, tapping the soil like a builder testing a wall.

'Can I have the triangle tool?'

He gave it to her, a nine-inch wooden handle with a triangular iron scraper on the end. She pulled it across the hard earth, taking off fractions of dust each time.

'It's a big piece,' she announced. 'Better go and get the professor.'

The others came over to watch. They stood in a circle around Lily as she scratched and brushed and chiselled around the piece of pottery. She never once looked up. She was like a sculptor or a potter, drawing a form out of the clay that was invisible to everyone but her. Jonah wished the others would go away.

It took almost an hour. By the time Lily had finished, the piece that had been buried now lay free in a flat crater, though she hadn't touched it once. You could pick it up as if it had been dropped five minutes ago. They measured the position and photographed it; the professor entered the details in the Field Journal.

It was a figurine, a clay woman with wide hips and full breasts, arms raised in power. Her face had been wiped almost smooth: all that remained was a thin crescent groove that might once have been a knowing smile.

Lily cradled her in her hand while the professor wrote the tag for the bag. Her face shone with sweat and pride, as if she'd just given birth.

'You see?'

London

Jonah felt as if the chair had dropped out from under him.

'Lily wouldn't . . .'

He remembered the bank statement, the trip to Athens she hadn't told him about. The family emergency that never happened.

Do you have any idea what she was getting up to in Italy?

Andreas jabbed the pen at him. 'Perhaps now you could tell us exactly what Lily said about the tablet.'

He stuck to the lie. 'Just that she was worried about it.' Did that sound too empty to be true? 'That's not the point.'

'I think it's precisely the point.'

He wanted to breathe, but no air came. He wanted to be able to explain, to convince them there was no way on earth Lily would have stolen an artefact. But the words weren't there.

'We're as keen to find her as you are,' Richard put in.

'So why didn't the police try to arrest her when they traced her?' At that moment, even having Lily in a cell seemed like it would be a step forward. At least he'd know where she was.

'The Italian police.' Andreas made a face as if he'd tasted a glass of wine and found it corked. 'Your missing person request went to a different office from the one that was investigating the theft. By the time they had made the connection, Lily had escaped again.'

He still didn't believe it. 'You said there was a third person who had the combination. The conservator.'

'She wasn't there. She left the dig . . . early.'

Again, Jonah noticed the gap in his words. A missing piece, something unsaid. 'Why did she go?'

'She had a prior obligation,' said Andreas smoothly. 'It's quite normal. When you hire the best people, they're in great demand.'

'We've confirmed she wasn't in the country,' Richard added.

A nasty thought. 'What if someone forced Lily to open the safe?'

'It's possible.' *Unlikely*, Andreas's eyes said.

'Was anyone worried about safety? Anything suspicious?'

'Not in the least. It's Italy. We have projects across the Middle East, north Africa, Balkans . . . ' He waved at the window. 'Italy, it's like digging in your own back garden.'

Jonah remembered something one of the volunteers had said at dinner, a passing crack about the Mafia. 'What about organised crime?'

'The Mafia?' Andreas shrugged. 'For sure, they're down there. But archaeology, it's not really what they do.'

'A priceless gold tablet might have got them interested.'

'All the staff signed confidentiality agreements. No one outside the dig knew the tablet was there. Except you, apparently.'

Andreas let the statement hang until there was no mistaking the suggestion.

'If you're trying to say . . . '

'I am stating facts. I should warn you, also, the Italian police are aware of these facts. They may want to ask you some questions.'

'They think I helped Lily steal the tablet?'

'You are the only other person who knew about it. In contravention of the non-disclosure agreement.'

He wanted to explain that he hadn't known a thing, not until the letter arrived and he saw the case in the museum. But he'd told his lie, and now he was caught in it. Perhaps, if he spoke to the police, he'd be able to set it straight.

'Lily and the tablet have a connection,' Andreas said decisively. 'One will surely lead us to the other.'

Nothing added up, but his head was spinning so fast all his thoughts were a blur. There was more he needed to know, but he'd forgotten what it was. He had to get out.

He stood. Andreas pressed a button on his desk and the door clicked open. Jonah hadn't realised it was locked.

'We understand your concern completely,' Andreas assured him. 'We want Lily back as much as you do. If this is a misunderstanding, or if she is innocent, only she can answer the questions.'

He walked him to the lift.

'But what you must ask yourself is: does she want you to find her?'

Fifteen

If you don't know where you started, and you don't know your
destination or any of the waypoints, how can you ever get anywhere?
Plato, *Republic*

Diotima glanced at the sky. High clouds wove a screen over the sun; the mountain peaks seemed larger than ever.

'I ought to go. I have to meet a friend.'

'Wait.' Mud oozed around my feet; I felt I was sinking. I held up the golden leaf. 'What is this?'

'Ask Agathon, when you find him.' She skipped off the stone capital and climbed up to the road. 'But don't waste time.'

'Won't you help me?'

She stopped at the top of the embankment and looked down, a solemn goddess silhouetted against the sky. The look she gave me broke my heart.

'Thank you for listening to my stories. I enjoyed it.'

'When can I see you again?'

I didn't quite catch what she said. It sounded like, 'In your dreams.'

★   ★   ★

The words of Memory, carved in gold
For the hour of your death,
When darkness covers you and leads you down the dreadful
path.

The Mansion of Night, the right-hand spring,
Black water and a shining white cypress
Where descending souls cool their fall.
Stay away.

Next, cold water from the pool of Mnemosyne
Flowing beneath the Guardians,
Watching, all-knowing.
'What are you looking for
In the dark shadows of Hades?'
'I am a son of Earth and starlit Sky,
Drained dry with thirst, dying.
Let me drink quickly from the cold water
That flows from the pool of Mnemosyne.'

More questions.
They will consult the Queen of Hell.
You will drink cold water from the pool of Mnemosyne,
Fly out of the circle of suffering,
And travel further down the sacred road
In glory, with the other initiated souls.
Folded in the breasts of the Queen of Hell
A kid in milk, pure, no longer mortal.
A god.

I put down the tablet. My eyes hurt from puzzling out the flea-sized letters on the gold leaf, twisting it this way and that to catch the light. Even now, I couldn't be sure I had it right.

Who could blame the scribe? Reading the words was hard; how much worse must it have been trying to write the minuscule letters in gold? Whoever did it, he must have thought his life depended on it.

When darkness covers you and leads you down the dreadful path . . .

The verses were hexameters, the heroic rhythm of Homer. More or less. The metre was choppy. Some of the words were misspelled; others seemed to be missing or abbreviated. But that wasn't what bothered me.

I held the gold leaf, so thin I could feel my thumb through it. I sniffed it. Gold shouldn't smell of anything except the person who's worn it, but behind Diotima's fig scent I caught something cold and earthy, as if it had lain underground for a long time. The poem described a journey to the underworld. Just the sort of thing you might bury in a tomb, to help the deceased find their way.

They opened the coffin and stole some grave goods.

That bothered me more: how Agathon, that paragon of virtue, had come by it, and why he'd left it for me. If he was so desperate for money, why didn't he sell it?

But what troubled me most, as the gold glinted in the light and the grooves pressed against the whorls on my thumb, was its authenticity. This poem wasn't a story. These were instructions, meant in deadly earnest, from someone who had been there – and come back.

A noise at the door. Euphemus had come into the room, sniffing the air like a fox. A casual smile couldn't hide the curiosity in his eyes. Too late, I put my hand flat on the table to hide the gold leaf.

'Have you been out?' he asked.

'Seeing the sights. Did you know Herodotus is buried here?' I tried to slide the gold sheet towards me without attracting attention. 'Where's Dimos?'

'He's out.'

'Who with?'

'Probably some boy he met at the gym. He stank of perfume.' Euphemus sat heavily on my bed and stretched himself out. 'All that talk of love last night. What did you think of the girl?'

'Diotima?' The name flashed out of my mouth too quick to stop. Euphemus' eyes narrowed.

'I don't suppose you know where to find her?'

'You can't buy a woman like that,' I warned him.

'I don't have to. A well-placed gift and the right words will open her legs like Pandora's box.'

Diotima's too clever for you, the Voice of Will insisted.

You know what she is, the Voice of thwarted Desire replied.

'Did you have the same idea?'

'What?' I hadn't heard him properly.

He leaned forward. 'You did, didn't you. I thought I smelled her perfume when I came in. Was she here?' He patted the bed and sniffed his fingers. 'Did you have her here?'

'Don't be ridiculous.'

'It's nothing to be embarrassed about – I'm not jealous. Well, perhaps a bit. But I'll get my turn.'

'She wasn't here.'

'And you're still mooning like a teenager. Are you in love?' That seemed to amuse him even more. 'For sure, she's better looking than Socrates.'

'Get out.'

He stepped towards the door, then remembered something.

'I went down to the harbour this morning. There's a ship leaving for Syracuse tomorrow.'

'You said you weren't trusting the sea ever again, after *Calliste*.'

'Sicily's an island – I've got to get there somehow. What are you going to do?'

What am I going to do? Should I stay there, enduring Dimos' hospitality, hoping Agathon would turn up?

The gold throbbed under my hand and whispered words into my blood. *Fly out of the circle of suffering, and travel further down the sacred road.* Suddenly, I knew what I wanted to do.

'I'm going to see Locris.'

It turned out that Locris was on the way to Syracuse, and that Euphemus' ship would be calling there. It meant two more days at sea and two more days with Euphemus, which didn't appeal. But travelling by road would have taken over a week, and I needed to make up time on Agathon.

Dimos was thrilled when I suggested I might be leaving – less so when I explained it would cost him a hundred and twenty drachmas. Five to get me to Locris, fifteen back to Athens, and a hundred for the book.

'Even your friend had enough manners not to ask me for money.'

'I'm family,' I said, stretching the definition. 'And I'll pay you back when I get home.'

'What if you don't make it?' I could see he was worried about his loan. 'That end of the peninsula's a war-zone. Dionysius has an army down there besieging Rhegion, and there's nothing Syracusans like more than sending Athenians down to rot in their quarries.'

I faked nonchalance. If I'd shown the least crack, he'd never have given me the money.

'I'm not going any further than Locris. That's peaceful, isn't it?'

'For the moment.'

I had one more question for him – something I cared about far more than his money.

'The flute-girl who played at your party. Diotima . . . '

He flinched at the sound of her name.

'Diotima . . . ' I said it again, just to see the effect. 'Have you known her long?'

'Why are you interested in her?'

'I heard she was a friend of Agathon's.'

If I'd claimed to have seduced his wife, he could hardly have reacted more violently. 'I was worried that might get out.'

'Worried?'

'She came while Agathon was here. He took a shine to her . . . well, why not? Every man in Thurii's got a hard-on for Diotima. But there was a scene, Agathon made a pest of himself. Treated her like a two-obol whore. When I told him to calm down, he attacked me. In my own house.'

I considered this. Agathon has a slight build, reed-thin arms, and only ever sets foot in a gymnasium if there's a lecture on. Dimos is a big man who wears his weight well. A fight between them would be as short and painful as Dimos chose to make it.

'I know he's your friend – still . . . '

'What did Diotima say?'

'She blamed us both. Silly cunt.' A reflective tone. 'They say she's half barbarian. Her mother was a Sicel.'

'A what?'

'Sicilian. Wild people, from the old days before we got there. We've mostly got rid of them, now.'

How had I spent most of a morning with Diotima swapping stories about lost cities and magic rings, and never heard about this? Why didn't she tell me about the fight? And if Agathon had behaved so outrageously, why did he stay with her when he came back?

What else hadn't she told me?

So many things I should have asked her. But time in her company passed like a dream, and going into conversation was like wading into the ocean. The ground shifted, and even rocks got swallowed.

One thing I did know. There was only one person in the

world whose honour Dimos would defend, and it wasn't a flute-girl. Not even one as desirable as Diotima. If there'd been a fight – and that much I did believe – there was only one likely reason.

'Did she prefer Agathon to you? Was that what made you angry?'

Dimos stood with a terrifying smile. 'I'll get the money now. I don't want to delay you.'

The morning we left, I went back to Diotima's house. The door was locked; the windows shuttered. I knocked until my knuckles bled, but nobody answered.

I wandered around Thurii for what seemed like hours, eyes down, reading the dust for her footprints. I lingered at Herodotus' tomb, Aphrodite's temple, the theatre. I spent an hour staring at the ruins of Sybaris. Out in the marsh, gulls perched on a pair of old columns that thrust out of the water, a gateway to nowhere. Sunlight flashed on the water between them. I imagined Diotima approaching the gates, gliding across the surface like a swan, then vanishing in a twist of light.

It was as likely an answer as any.

'Do you know the story of the ring of Gyges?'

We were back on a ship, coasting down to Locris. I think. In memory, the ship and the sea and the sky and Euphemus and I are all archetypes, a collage assembled from stock parts. What I really remember is the feeling. All I wanted, that short voyage, was to talk about Diotima.

Euphemus didn't know Gyges' story the way she'd told it. I paraphrased it, not mentioning Diotima. When I'd finished, he nodded approvingly.

'I think that rather proves my point.'

'Because the law of nature tells us to pursue pleasure and take everything we can get?' I pressed.

'Indeed.'

'And the only reason we pretend to be virtuous is so that other people don't realise we're trying to get something from them?'

'Ye-es.' More cautiously, sensing a trap.

'But if you picked up the ring of Gyges, would you really turn into a thieving, murdering libertine? Is all that's preventing you from stealing my money and throwing me in the water right now the fact that I can see you?'

Euphemus' constant smile stretched tight. The motion of the sea seemed to be upsetting him.

'It's a hypothetical situation.'

'You can't say it.' Now I was smiling. I could feel the sun warm on my back. 'You say the world is a cauldron, all boiling against all. You say we use convention to mask the grasping, selfish truth. But I think you're hiding the opposite. Strip away convention and social expectation, like the ring of Gyges, and you might find you actually have some good in you.'

He picked at the end of a rope, pulling apart its strands. 'Who can be sure what we'd do in extreme circumstances?'

'Are you saying that in extreme circumstances, if you had absolutely no choice, you might actually do the right thing?'

'Very good. No, I'm thinking of Orpheus.'

I didn't see the connection.

'When Hades snatched his wife, he wanted to go down to the underworld to rescue her. He said he'd do anything for her. But he tricked his way in. That's why the gods didn't let him bring her back – because he wouldn't make the ultimate sacrifice. He thought his love was perfect, but when it came down to it, it wasn't. He didn't dare die for love, so the gods didn't feel compelled to let her live.'

The crack in the earth. A lone man picking his way over the rocks that are loose as ashes. He has a lyre slung over his back and a crown of black ivy wrapped in his hair. It could be Gyges.

But there's no ring or bronze horse at the bottom of the ravine – only a dark hole leading deeper into the earth. If you put your ear to it, you can hear waves crashing.

We must have changed course while Euphemus was speaking. The sail shaded the sun. 'That's an extreme situation,' I murmured.

'Extreme situations reveal the truth.' The rope-end had become three separate strands, twisting into the air like the triple-headed serpent of Apollo. 'Your elusive friend, Agathon. Is he a good man?'

'One of the best.'

'Just? Virtuous?'

'Absolutely.'

'And yet he broke open the tomb and stole something.'

His eyes tracked me like a hawk following a mouse. How much had he seen in my bedroom? Did he know what the tablet was? Did he guess? I balled my hand into a fist so that I wouldn't touch the locket hanging around my neck.

I wanted to change the subject – but so much talk of Orpheus and tombs reminded me of something I'd been meaning to ask.

'That story you told me, that Pythagoras found his knowledge in the underworld. Did it say if he wrote anything down about it?'

He shook his head. 'Pythagoras never wrote anything down. He's notorious for it. That's why you get people like Archytas and Eurytus, all arguing about what he actually said. Why?'

Pythagoras wasn't enough. Agathon wanted to go further, to find what came before. The source of Pythagoras' ideas.

Agathon hadn't gone down to the underworld like some latter-day Orpheus, I told myself firmly. He'd gone to Locris, to buy a book.

Euphemus tossed the rope aside. 'Perhaps he did find it.'

'Find what?'

'The ring of Gyges.' He saw I'd lost him. 'Agathon. That would explain why you've travelled the length of Italy and never seen him.'

A crack from above. Even in that split second, I knew it was different from the usual run of the ship's sounds. Perhaps I started to look up.

Shouted warnings came too late. It was already in motion.

Something tore through the air and landed hard on my head.

Sixteen

It was only Tuesday and the torture had already become routine. The trembling as he unlocked the door, like waiting to go on stage. Imagining her there – her smile, her arms around him – the vision so painfully real it *had* to be true. There was no reason in the world why she *couldn't* be there, so why *shouldn't* she be?

Calling her name through the open door. Looking into each room, just in case she'd fallen asleep, waiting. The slump of despair. Checking voicemails, text messages, e-mails, missed calls. Each piece of nothing seemed to take a bite out of his soul. He wondered how long before it was all gone?

The warm day had made him sweat, and the sweat had cooled to something sticky and unpleasant. He was furious with himself. He'd gone to the Eikasia Foundation with so many unanswered questions – the tablet, Ari, her trip to Athens – and instead he'd been blindsided by their story that Lily was a thief.

Was it true?

Lily's letter, the tablet transcription, lay on the sofa beside him. He held it to his face, sniffing for any trace of scent, but Lily never wore perfume on the digs. *Your hands always smell like earth anyway*, she said.

Why did she send it?

She was a self-confessed trowel monkey. She didn't date

pottery, or piece things together, or read ancient Greek. She left conservators and academics to explain the things she found: she just pulled them out of the ground. So why did she spend the last hours before she disappeared copying the text?

If she was going to steal it, why would she bother to copy it out and send it to her sister beforehand?

Why *did* she bother?

He called Charis. Her voice went artificially bright when she heard him.

'Haven't got long – Bill's got a do. Just getting ready now. Any news of Lily?'

No mention of how they'd parted. By mutual agreement, it had never happened.

'Nothing yet.' *Yet.* In the cold hard corner of his mind that provided a running commentary, he wondered when *yet* became *ever.*

'Did you translate the tablet?' he said.

'I did what I could. There's not a lot there, darling. More or less the same as the others that have already been published.'

'Can you send it to me?'

'If you like. I'll e-mail it. I'd better go now and get dressed. Look after yourself.'

He put the phone down. On the bookcase, he saw the book he'd brought back from Sibari, the battered old Penguin Classic of Plato's *Republic.* He took it down and flipped through, wondering if it had anything to do with Orphic tablets. But there wasn't an index, and he was too tired to process the snatches he read.

He saw the inscription on the inside cover again.

To Lily—

Love is Truth, Adam

He snapped the book shut and went to the fridge. He was out of beer, but he found vodka in the cupboard. He splashed it over a couple of ice cubes and drank quickly, glad of the cold in his mouth. It calmed the shaking inside him. He poured another glass.

A chime from the open laptop said an e-mail had arrived. The familiar stab of hope subsided as he saw it was from Charis, sending through her translation. He started reading but stopped halfway.

The text was no different – and it unnerved him. Reading it seemed to lock up his brain, to drop him in a dream chasing down an endless tunnel.

The words of Memory, carved in gold
For the hour of your death.

Why was that the last thing Lily wrote?

While he had the computer on, he tabbed back to Lily's Facebook page. The message he'd left the day before was still at the top – but now there was a comment underneath it. Someone called Sandi McConn had replied.

I was on the dig. I was the conservator.

The message had come through five minutes ago – she was still online. He hit the chat button.

Jonah: Can I talk to you? About the dig?
Sandi: NDA
Jonah: ?
Sandi: Non-disclosure agreement. I signed one

They were in a public thread. Did that have something to do with it?

Jonah: Where are you in the real world?
Sandi: Right now London. Flying home tomorrow
Jonah: Can we meet?

This time, he had to wait for her answer. Time for doubts to flood in. Had she wandered off? Was she really in London? Was she even who she said she was – or just words on a screen?

Sandi: Can you come to Paddington?
Jonah: When?
Sandi: Now

Sandi McConn was a slim, pretty woman, about the same age as Jonah, with a short brown bob and three silver rings in each ear. She stood and waved at him across the coffee shop.

'I recognised you from your photos. Lily liked to show you off.'

Jonah flushed. His throat tightened; tears threatened, though he knew they wouldn't come. Watertight, Lily used to call him.

'I'll get a coffee.'

By the time he'd navigated the queue, he'd calmed down. He sat opposite her and stirred swirls in his cup.

Only three people on the dig knew the safe combination. Doctor Andrews himself, the conservator . . .

'I saw what you put on Facebook about Lily,' Sandi said. She hesitated. 'I hope she turns up.'

'Thanks. And thanks for seeing me. It's lucky you were in London.'

'For you, I guess.'

'I know how busy you are.'

She gave him an odd look. 'Yeah?'

184

'Richard said you were off to another job.'

'Did he?'

He was missing something. 'Is that not true?'

Sandi leaned back. 'I told you, I signed a non-disclosure agreement when I started, and another one when I left. They don't like people talking about the dig. And they *really* don't like people talking about how they got fired.'

'You? But they said you were one of the best people they had.'

'Gee, that's nice.' A savage smile. 'Maybe they'll give me a reference.'

He held up his hands in a 'way over my head' gesture.

'I was supposed to finish the dig yesterday, lay over a day in London and head back to Canada tomorrow. I've been sitting on my ass in London for the last week because I couldn't change my flight.'

'What happened?'

'That would be the "non-disclosure" part of my non-disclosure agreement.'

'Was it to do with the gold tablet?' he guessed.

Sandi leaned back on the seat. Her slim fingers wrapped around her coffee mug. 'Unless I read it wrong, that's covered by the NDA too.'

'I spoke to Richard Andrews this afternoon. He told me all about it.'

'Really?'

'The tablet's been stolen. He said the only three people who had the safe code were himself, Lily and you.'

'Is he trying to frame me for stealing now?'

Jonah hesitated, then decided he had nothing to lose. 'He thinks Lily did it.'

'Maybe he's right.'

'No way.' His voice rose; he could feel himself losing control. 'She'd never.'

'Are you sure?'

'Of course I'm sure.'

But something in her voice made him pause. A coded warning, a sly poke in the ribs. *You don't know as much as you think you do.*

'Tell me something,' Sandi said. 'You went to Sibari, right? Were you there when the tablet got stolen?'

Jonah nodded.

'Was it a big deal? Police crawling everywhere, searching everyone's rooms, that kind of thing?'

'I didn't see any police.' In fact, now that he thought about it, Richard hadn't mentioned it once that day. The whole dig team had sat down to dinner as normal that night, and no one had said a thing.

Only three people on the dig knew the safe combination. Doctor Andrews himself, the conservator, and Lily.

Sandi hadn't been there. He was certain Lily couldn't have done it. That left . . .

'Did Richard take it?'

A long pause. Sandi stared at her coffee. Jonah wanted to lift her off her seat and shake the truth out of her.

'Am I right? Is that why he fired you?' He took out Andreas's card and started dialling the number.

'Who are you calling?'

'Richard's still in Sibari. I need to alert the Eikasia people so they can get him.' He fumbled over the numbers, his fingers jabbing the screen. *Richard stole the tablet and made Lily disappear to cover it up. He took her phone and used it to send the bogus messages. That was how he knew about her mother, to make it plausible. He knocked my phone into the pool, so I couldn't call England and find out it was a lie.*

Sandi put out her hand and laid it over the phone's screen. 'The problem with what you're saying is, he didn't fire Lily.'

'He made her disappear.'

She glanced over her shoulder. 'You want to be careful saying things like that. Especially about people who have lots of money and scary lawyers. And it's not like these guys are the Illuminati. If they wanted Lily off their case, they'd give her a plane ticket and a payoff and an NDA.'

'She must have surprised him. He didn't have a choice.'

'You're very confident about Lily.'

'Yes.'

'You trust her.'

He stared into her eyes. Anger throbbed through him – but didn't make him completely deaf.

'What are you saying?'

Sandi turned the coffee spoon between her fingers, watching her reflection bow and distort in the bowl. 'I trusted her too. I thought she was one of the good guys. Until she came back from Athens.'

Reality check. He remembered the bank statement, the trip to Athens Lily never mentioned.

'What happened in Athens?'

'Richard wanted me out. Lily went out to speak with the Eikasia Foundation guys who were funding the dig. She said she'd get them to change their mind. Instead, she brought one of them back to fire me.'

Part of him was relieved to hear there was a simple reason for Lily's trip to Athens. Part of him said if it was that simple, why hadn't she told him about it?

'She must have done her best.'

Sandi dropped the spoon in her cup and fixed him with a look.

'Don't you get it? They were all in this together. All college friends, all in each other's pockets. Once Adam got me out of the way, they could do what they wanted.'

He must have heard wrong. The coffee shop was filling

up; a group of students at the next table were all trying to out-shout each other. '*Who?*'

'Adam, the program director. Weird, uptight guy. He was the one who fired me.'

'Adam *who?*'

'Adam Shaw.' She saw the look on his face and raised an eyebrow.

'I guess you've met him too.'

Seventeen

*Here is Timaeus, from Locris in Italy, a city which has fine
laws, and who is himself in the first rank of his fellow-citizens;
he has held the most important and honourable offices in his
own state, and, I believe, has scaled the heights of all philosophy.*

Plato, Timaeus (20)

Another city, another port. Locris occupied a sandy coastal
strip beneath the high mountains which marched towards
the sea. The sun was hotter here, the air thicker. The moment
you stopped moving, swarms of flies descended. In that heat,
I suppose they struggled to tell the living from the dead.

The city was a blur. The block that fell from the yard only
glanced me: they said that was lucky, though I didn't feel
lucky. I felt like one of those Homeric heroes who'd got on
the wrong side of Achilles, my brains dashed out of my skull.
The bandage on my head kept coming loose and flopping
down over my face like a veil, though at least that protected
my eyes from the dazzling sun. Bolts of pain shot through
my skull every time I moved.

I almost fell in the sea as I stumbled down the gangplank
off the ship. Euphemus caught me. As we entered Locris
through the massive walls, I began to understand why the
flies flocked here. There were temples everywhere, altars
sticky with blood. All Italians live in the shadow of the dark
goddess: in Locris, she's closer than ever. We passed two

temples to Aphrodite, heavily decorated and thronged with women. Golden figures gleamed within, while white doves pecked corn off the precinct floor. The statues in the front flaunted all Aphrodite's charms. I tried not to look, but couldn't help myself – like some bursting adolescent staring at the *porne* down by the city gates. They made me think of . . .

Agathon, I reminded myself, trying to get a grip on my delirious thoughts. I'd come for Agathon.

There's a man in Locris, a Pythagorean called Timaeus. Agathon had been trying to buy a book from him, but he wanted too much money.

Diotima told me that, sitting in the ruins of Sybaris, silhouetted against the water. I remembered the curve of her breasts under her transparent gown at dinner, breasts like ivory, the nipples small and upturned and—

Agathon.

I knew the routine by now, as well as Sisyphus knew his boulder. Taras, Thurii, now Locris: go to the agora, ask for Agathon, draw a blank. Once I'd established no one knew him, I decided to look for Timaeus.

If you still want the book, find me before the end of the month. I will be on the porch of the Great Temple.

Our ship had cargo to unload – it wouldn't sail until the next morning – so Euphemus offered to come with me. I clenched my teeth and willed him to go away, but he wanted to see the temple.

'It's the most famous temple in Italy. I'd hate to miss it.'

I climbed the hill, wrapped in a cloud of pain and heat and despair. Flies nibbled the blood that had seeped through my bandage. By the time we'd come to the top of the town, I stank with sweat and the bandage was the only thing holding my skull together.

The building was magnificent. It stood on a terrace on the edge of a ravine, a little way beyond the city walls. In spring, I could imagine torrents of meltwater foaming down off the mountains; now, the river was just a trickle among bone-white stones. Thick columns like tree-trunks supported a vast pediment. Caryatids, Persephone's hand-maidens, watched me with cold eyes as they held up the roof.

The Guardians.Watching, all-knowing. My burned-out eyes made them sway on their pedestals. I imagined them stepping down, shrugging off their burden and letting the temple fall in on me. Their stony faces said they could do it without a flicker of guilt.

Hushed voices murmured around me like flowing water as we stepped into the shade of the portico: whispered hymns, desperate prayers. Worshippers, mostly women, passed by, carrying their offerings into the sanctuary. Some came out crying, others beaming with joy. The air was sticky with blood and wine and pomegranate juice.

I did a lap of the colonnade, trying not to trip over the stray women and dogs. I didn't see anyone who fitted my picture of what a Pythagorean bookseller should look like, so I accosted a priest on his way into the temple and asked him if he knew Timaeus.

He didn't. But the name got a reaction: over the priest's shoulder, I saw a slumped head suddenly jerk up. A filthy, hooded beggar, lying against the temple wall.

I knelt down beside him. The fly that had been crawling up his arm buzzed away indignantly.

'Do you know who Timaeus is?'

I wished I stayed standing. He stank rotten. His fingernails were black, and he had strange growths coming off his feet. Even in the shade, he kept his hood so low it hid his eyes completely. The only detail I had of his face was the straggling orange beard that escaped the hood, too long and too thin. Behind the beard, his lips never stopped squirming, as if he had something horrible in his mouth he couldn't get down and couldn't get out.

'Timaeus.' He giggled as he said the name. 'I knew Timaeus.'

'Where is he?' I looked at the crowds around us. 'Can you point him out?'

He extended a filthy finger, swinging it around like a drunk. I tried to see where he was pointing, until suddenly he reversed his hand and planted the finger on his own chest.

'You're Timaeus.'

He didn't deny it.

'I'm looking for a friend. Agathon. He wanted to buy a book from you.'

'Do you want the book?'

'I want Agathon. Is he here?'

The hooded face swivelled theatrically, first right, then all the way round in an arc.

'Not *here*,' I said impatiently. 'I meant, in Locris.'

His head dropped as if his neck had snapped. He stared at his feet.

'Is that a no?'

No answer.

'But you know who I'm talking about. Was he here recently?'

'There is no *was* or *will be*. Only *is*.'

'Where did he go?'

More silence. Then, as if someone had turned a key to unlock him, he suddenly spat out, 'Down over the mountain. No escape, no escape that way. Nine years we kept that siege, against Ilium's windy walls. And for what?'

'Rhegion?' guessed Euphemus. He'd kept his distance, standing well back from the beggar like something he didn't want to step in.

'Yes.' Timaeus seized on it eagerly. 'Yes, yes – Rhegion. He went to Rhegion.'

'Why would he go there?' Dimos had told me about Rhegion – the city on the tip of Italy that the tyrant Dionysius had spent two years trying to batter into submission. 'Is it even possible to get in?'

'In, yes. Out?' A splenetic laugh that devolved into a wet fit of coughing. 'Against that dreadful path, I hold you back. Stay away. Stay away. Nothing comes back that way.'

'Then why did Agathon go there?'

Timaeus held up his hands and stared at his palms, jerking his head from side to side in a crazy parody of reading.

'For the book?' I interpreted.

'What was the book?' Euphemus asked.

He cupped his hands in a wide bowl. '*The Krater.* We called it *The Krater.*'

'What's in it?'

Abruptly, he slapped his hands hard against his face. 'Secrets.'

'Pythagorean secrets?'

'He wouldn't pay the price.'

Now we were getting to the heart of the matter. I held out my purse, right in front of his face so he couldn't miss it.

'I can pay.'

He craned forward. From under his hood, I felt his gaze hook onto me.

'How much do you think it is worth?' he asked slyly.

'Agathon said it was a hundred drachmas.'

'More!' he barked.

I considered my finances. 'I could go to a hundred and ten?'

'No book's worth that,' Euphemus objected.

'Only a fool thinks he knows the price of wisdom,' Timaeus told him.

'If you're trying to say—'

Timaeus' hand moved for the purse. I snatched it back, then realised he was pushing it away anyway.

'Knowledge is cheap,' he sneered. 'Cheap as dying. But not the book, not at any price.'

'You won't sell it?'

'Can't.'

'Why not?' And then, making a leap: 'You don't have it. You sold it.'

A hissing chuckle, like a kettle boiling, told me I'd got it right. 'To Agathon?'

More hissing – but no answer.

'Who bought it?'

He giggled. 'A Lydian trickster, a sorcerer, with golden hair and perfumed locks, and the flush of wine on his face.' A flash of anger and a sudden roaring voice. '*I'll cut off his head if I find him!*'

I tried to ignore the theatrics. 'Did he have a name? Is he here in Locris?'

'Told you. You guide yourself with blind eyes, deaf ears.'

He was quoting Parmenides at me, I realised. If I'd been thinking more clearly, I might have asked how a raving beggar knew such esoteric philosophy. But my head hurt, and I was fed up with his half-truths and babbled nonsense. I wanted to look him in the eye. I reached forward and yanked back his hood.

His scream tore open the temple, loud enough – it seemed – to crack the stone goddesses. I leapt back. Timaeus writhed on the floor, howling like a dog and clutching his eyes. Or, at least, the part of his face where his eyes should have been. In the split second when I pulled back the hood, I'd seen there was nothing there except horrible knots of scar tissue.

Someone or something had burned his eyes away.

★   ★   ★

'You're not seriously going to Rhegion?'

Euphemus stared at me across the table in the wineshop. I wished he'd keep his voice down. Timaeus' screams were still ringing in my ears.

'Haven't you listened to anything they've told us since we landed in Italy?' he persisted. 'Rhegion's at war. Dionysius the tyrant has his army camped around it and he's choking it to death. You won't get within ten miles of the gates.'

I didn't want to talk to Euphemus.

'I know you think you're better than this world. But reality won't go away just because you ignore it. You know what they'll do if they capture you sneaking into the city? They'll sell you as a slave, or send you to the stone quarries of Syracuse. Have you read Thucydides' book? He's very eloquent on the subject.'

'I have to go.'

'For Agathon? You've visited every colony in Italy looking for him. Did you ever think that if he wanted to see you, he could have made the slightest effort to help you find him?'

'He might be in trouble.'

'He'll be in trouble if he's gone to Rhegion. And so will you.'

My whole head seemed to have shrunk in, boiled dry by the heat. I had nothing to say. And nor, finally, did Euphemus. Except:

'I'm going to Syracuse. If you end up in the quarries there, don't think I'll be able to help you.'

I took out Dimos' purse, still heavy with the unspent coins. 'How much do you want?'

'What?'

'For what you've spent on our trip since Taras. How much?'

If I'd cared about his good opinion, the disgust on his face would have cut deep.

'I know you think all I care about is money. So let me prove you wrong.' He stood to go.

'Wait.' I fumbled in the bottom of the purse. Among the flat-pressed coins, the pebble had a solid reality that made it easy to find. 'Take this.'

I held out the shipwreck stone in my palm. Euphemus hesitated.

'It worked before,' I pointed out.

He still couldn't tell if I was mocking him. 'Won't you need it to get back to Athens?'

'I can swim.'

He swept it off the table.

'I hope you find Agathon. And I hope he's worth it.'

Euphemus had one thing right: getting to Rhegion by sea was impossible. The Syracusan fleet had it blockaded. I asked around the harbour, but even a hundred drachmas couldn't tempt anyone.

'Go over the mountain,' one leather-tanned captain told me from the deck of his boat. 'It's the only way.'

'Is there a road?'

He shook his head and spat on the deck. 'But I know someone who can take you.'

Locris had become a bad dream. The next thing I knew, I was standing in an alley behind the merchant's stoa, negotiating with three scarred men who looked like murderers and stank of goats. With a bloodied head and wine on my breath, I fitted right in.

'Three days over the mountain to Rhegion,' the leader told me. He was called Polus. 'What are you bringing?'

'Just what I'm carrying.'

He looked surprised – which I understood when we assembled outside the city. We were four men, a boy and twenty donkeys, backs breaking under the weight of the sacks loaded onto them.

'Lots of hungry people in Rhegion,' Polus said, by way of

explanation. 'They've been locked nearly two years. A hungry man pays a lot to eat.'

Why would Agathon go there? Why would he even think he could? Had he paid smugglers to take him over the mountain too? What possessed him? Did he think he could raise money for a book that Timaeus had already sold?

If I'd stopped to consider any of those questions, I probably wouldn't have gone. But my head hurt too much to think about it. Instead, I stared up at the mountain and the sun hanging off its shoulder. Perhaps things would be clearer from the top.

Any Athenian – any Greek – lives with mountains from the day he's born. But familiarity doesn't make us comfortable. We huddle in the narrow plains; we'd rather take to the sea than climb. Mountains are hard, cruel places. Thin air makes hearts cold. Artemis the huntress lives there; so does Dionysius, the god of wine and frenzy. It was on a mountain that King Pentheus' own mother ripped him to pieces, and where Oedipus' father left him to die.

The sea's dangerous, but we risk it because there's always movement, always the promise of change. Mountains confront us with the eternal and offer no way out.

Those, roughly, were the thoughts I had as I trudged up the mountains with the donkeys. My guides were terse as Spartans and left me to myself; once I'd persuaded myself they weren't going to murder me, I forgot about them. The clop of hooves, the panting of breathless men and beasts, the hiss of insects chirping in the grass were the only conversation I had.

We trudged up a stony gorge and made camp on the riverbed. The wind roared through the gorge in the night, as if a great wave was massing just around the corner: I had horrible dreams. Next day, we continued up the river, twisting through thickly wooded slopes, always climbing. When I looked up, I despaired at how high we had to climb – and even those summits were only steps on the way to the true peak, hidden behind them.

My head throbbed. By mid-morning, the sun had forced the shadows out of the valley. The stones baked; the air boiled. Now we walked in the stream, to wet our feet and keep them cool. I was parched with thirst, but whenever I knelt to quench it, the icy water sent needles through my skull.

> *Black water and a shining white cypress*
> *Where descending souls cool their fall.*
> *Stay away.*

In the afternoon, we left the river and struck out up a flank of the mountain, where fire had burned the trees away. The slope was brutal, steep and utterly featureless. We walked, hour after hour without water, kicking up plumes of ash until our legs turned black.

Halfway up, I started to shiver uncontrollably as if I had a fever. Despite the sun, the world seemed dark to my eyes. As the dust blew by, I imagined I saw Socrates walking beside me. Even on that mountainside he moved with graceful, effortless strides.

'I wish you were really here,' I told him.

I couldn't see his face, but I think he smiled. 'I'd have stuck with the city. Trees and pretty views are all very well, but they don't teach you much.'

'Do you think I'll find Agathon if I get to Rhegion?'

'Do you trust Timaeus?'

'Not really,' I admitted.

'You knew that when you set out.'

'I suppose so.'

'Starting the journey is what matters.'

'I know that. I've heard the *Odyssey*.'

'You just have to keep going. However steep the climb.'

'It's hard when you can't see the top of the mountain.'

'It is,' he agreed. 'That's why I always stayed at the bottom.'

'Should I turn back?'

He didn't answer. I tried to read his face, but the dust hid it.

'It's a long, weary road before you reach the truth,' he said at last.

'Is there a shorter way?'

'I suppose not. Though you might manage better if you stick to the task at hand.'

Somehow, I knew he was talking about Diotima.

'She knew where Agathon had gone,' I pointed out.

'Is that *all* you wanted from her?'

'I know I should have better self-control.'

'Not at all. Every philosopher should fall in love, or he wouldn't know his subject.'

'Loving wisdom isn't quite the same thing.'

'But we need the other kind too. The sticky, sweaty, human kind. It opens our eyes.'

'To what?'

'Beauty. And that's the first step into a much wider world.'

'What world?'

He shook his head. 'You know what I told them. How did you put it in the dialogue?'

'*If I have any wisdom, it's that I don't claim to know what I don't.*' It felt absurd to be quoting me quoting him. The incongruity amused him.

'I showed people they didn't know anything – and they didn't thank me for it. You want to show them *what* they don't know, and that's much harder.'

'They probably won't thank me, either.'

'You'll find what you're looking for,' Socrates said. And even though he wasn't there, it lifted my spirits.

All the while we'd been talking, I'd been climbing. It was late in the day, but at last we were getting somewhere. The first I noticed was the air growing cooler. Even without looking back, I could tell we'd reached a high place by the silence around me. The light had softened. For a few minutes, the dreary mountainside became a magical place.

We crested a ridge and the world opened out to the horizon. The sun had begun to set: the sky was a crimson canvas stretched from the earth to the heavens, with a low line of purple cloud pencilled across. And in its centre, a crown.

At first I thought it was just another cloud. But the lines were too clear, the shape too exact. I looked closer, and realised it was the top of a mountain. In the evening light, it seemed to float in mid-air.

'Etna,' said my guide.

There are lots of stories about Etna. Some I knew then; others, I learned later. That it's the home of Hephaestus, the gods' craftsman. That an ancient Titan, the hundred-headed Typhos, lies in Tartarus pinned down by the mountain, causing its eruptions as he writhes under its weight. That Empedocles the philosopher hurled himself into its crater in hopes of becoming a god, leaving behind only a single bronze sandal. That it's the gateway to Hell.

Lines from Pindar I learned at school came back to me:

Pure springs of unapproachable fire
Burst out from its inmost depths:
By day, the lava-streams pour forth
A lurid rush of smoke;
But in the darkness, a red rolling flame sweeps whole rocks
Down to the wide deep sea.

There were no fountains of fire now, just a thin wisp of smoke rising off the summit. In a way, I was disappointed.

'We'd better get down,' said the guide. 'You freeze up here at night.'

Etna faded into the twilight as we began our descent. In the cool evening, my head had stopped throbbing. The awe of seeing Etna seemed to have cleaned something out of me.

We reached a grove of oaks and chestnuts, and called a halt. The others unloaded the donkeys and turned them out to pasture on the mountain grass; someone made a fire. I took a bucket and went to find water. The sun had vanished, but the night didn't frighten me. Not far off, I could hear the chatter of a stream. I followed the sound to the source and crouched to fill the bucket, scooping up handfuls to wash the ash off my face.

Stars were coming out. I sat back on the rocks and stared up at them. The world looks different at night. By moonlight or starlight, we see it dimly or not at all – even though we're looking at the same things we'd see clearly in daylight. The world hasn't changed. Our eyes are the same. It's just the lack of light.

What if there was a different sort of sun? A sun that didn't illuminate the world with light, but with reason? Are there things that we'd see differently, things we grasp dimly or not at all at the moment? What *would* we see?

My breath quickened. I was groping towards something in the darkness – I couldn't see it, but I could feel it was important. Something I'd been searching for all my life.

Heraclitus says we can't know the world because it's in constant motion. The sophists say we can't know it because we only know what our senses tell us – and they're so inadequate they tell us different things at different times of day.

Ten feet away from where I'm sitting, there's an oak tree split by lightning. I can't see it at the moment, but I know it's there: I remember it from when I was coming down the hill. Even if my eyes don't see it, my mind does. It *knows*.

If there's a sun that could rise on the mind, how much more would we perceive instead of the twilight shadows of this world we live in?

And if the things we apprehend in this world are just shadows, what are they shadows *of*?

I heard shouts from back at the campsite. The others must have been getting impatient. Reluctantly, I scrambled to my feet, lifted the bucket and carefully retraced my steps back towards the fire that flickered between the trees.

I stepped into the glade. The fire had taken well: it leaped into the night, throwing long shadows across the earth. Figures of men and animals, some talking, others silent. If I'd have bothered to count, I might have noticed there were more than when I'd left.

There must have been a struggle. One of my companions lay on the ground, bleeding; the others had been herded against the trees. A dozen soldiers in bronze armour and red tunics guarded them. I'd been so busy dreaming of other worlds I hadn't paid attention to what was happening right behind me.

I told you so, Euphemus said.

I didn't try to run. I wouldn't have got ten paces.

They bound me, gagged me, and marched me off into the darkness.

Eighteen

Jonah – London

Don't you get it? They were all in this together. All college friends, all in each other's pockets.

He stood in the street outside Paddington, in the maze of money shops, newsagents and dry cleaners. He needed a drink. He found a pub and sank a pint of beer without tasting it. He needed something stronger. He went back to the bar and got two vodka tonics.

Lily went to Athens to see Adam. That was why she didn't tell him. They came back together, and Adam fired Sandi because she objected to their plan to steal the tablet. Then Lily stole the tablet and disappeared.

He told himself he didn't believe it.

Really? For four days he'd insisted that Lily was the victim. He'd clung to the certainty, clear and hard as glass, ignoring the cracks that were beginning to spread. But there were only so many hits it could take before it shattered.

He had to speak to Adam, but the last number he had for Adam was in Oxford. He tried Charis, but her phone was off – he remembered she'd said she was going out.

The Eikasia Foundation website didn't give much away, but it did provide a phone number in Athens. Jonah rang it, and got an answering machine babbling in Greek. He checked the time. It was seven o'clock, nine in Athens. He guessed it was telling him the office was shut.

He couldn't call Richard. There was only one other person he could think of. He only had an office number, but that didn't matter because he was usually there. At this time of night, the secretaries had gone home and he answered the phone himself.

'Julian?'

'Jonah.' A rich voice, booming through the little speaker. 'How the hell are you?'

'I've been better.'

'Any joy with Lily?'

'No.'

'I'm sure she'll turn up.'

From anyone else, it would have sounded like a platitude. When Julian said it, you believed he really meant it. His world was a comfortable, well-upholstered place, where people behaved properly and bad things only happened on the pages of the *Telegraph*.

'I need to speak to Adam. Do you have a number for him?'

A *you'd-be-lucky* sort of laugh. 'Somewhere.' A pause. 'Not in my phone. Might have it in an e-mail. God knows the last time I used it. Not really one for chitchat, is our Adam.'

'If you can find it, I could really use it. I think he might know something about Lily.'

'Not a problem.' Silence, punctuated by clicks as Julian did something with his computer. 'Listen, I'm actually heading out your way this evening. Shall I pop by? You sound as if you need a shoulder to cry on – or a pint to cry into, at any rate.'

Of all the people he knew, Julian was one of the last he could imagine opening his heart to. But the alcohol was dissolving all the certainties he'd clung to, leaving a desolate void inside. He'd never been so lonely.

He named a pub in Wandsworth and agreed to meet in an hour.

Oxford

Some people said Oxford was a city of dreams. For Jonah, it was a slow, fantastical nightmare.

His mother cried when he told her he was going. His friends back home told him it would be full of southern wankers. The band almost split up. He went anyway – because he wanted to be with Lily, and because he was stubborn. After two months, trying to squeeze in moments with Lily between her lectures and his shifts behind the bar at The Bear, he was almost ready to admit they'd been right. In Greece it had seemed so natural. In Oxford, nothing was easy. The students acted as if they knew a secret you didn't; they hurried wherever they went with hidden purpose, and spoke a strange language riddled with medievalisms like 'Michaelmas' and 'subfusc' and 'quads'. Older, harder, uninterested in the schools where they'd been or the jobs where they'd go, he didn't belong in their universe, however much Lily tried to make him fit.

By December, he knew that if he went home for Christmas, he wouldn't come back.

Lily had other friends at Oxford, but it was the ones who'd been in Greece he saw most often. Unexpectedly, it was Adam he got closest to. He couldn't say he liked him, and never got anything like warmth or friendliness in return. But there was something inside each of them, an intensity of purpose, that they responded to in each other.

'We're both following our muses,' was how Adam put it, one time when Charis asked. And Jonah thought he was right.

One day in December, Adam came to Jonah's room with a large shopping bag. Jonah sat on the one chair and drank a beer; Adam perched on the bed with a glass of water.

'What's in the bag?'

Adam ignored the question. 'Do you know what a symposium is?'

'Some kind of party?'

'In ancient Greece, it was a drinking party. Plato and Xenophon both wrote famous descriptions of them. Cultured men would get together in their homes and discuss the great questions of philosophy.'

'Sounds like a hoot.'

'I'm going to have one. On Thursday.' He pushed down the sides of the bag. Inside stood a strange instrument: a rounded wooden bowl that tapered up to two arms, with seven strings stretched across the opening.

'Do you know what this is?'

'A sort of mandolin?' Jonah guessed.

'It's an ancient Greek lyre.'

'Did you dig it up under the college lawn?'

'It's a replica. I borrowed it from the Classics faculty.'

He passed it across. Jonah felt the weight of it, the sturdy construction, and guessed it had been built as a science project rather than an instrument. But when he plucked the first string, the note sounded clear and in tune. Less resonant than a guitar, less depth than a harp, it had a flat, cold quality.

'Can you play it?'

Jonah rummaged in his guitar case for a plectrum. He picked a few of the strings, then strummed them together, damping the notes with his fingers. Even cradled against his chest, the music sounded strangely removed.

'Do you know any tunes?'

Adam took a sheaf of papers from his satchel. 'I photocopied some things for you. A few articles on classical musicology. According to Plato, the Dorian mode is the most Greek.'

Jonah flicked through the papers. A lot of words like *hypolidian* and *diazeuxis*, but nothing that looked like chords or notes.

'This isn't going to work. You can't analyse music like . . . like some Greek play. You just have to feel it.'

'You're assuming you can't feel the play,' Adam countered. 'Euripedes didn't write the *Bacchae* so that undergraduates could pore over its grammar. He wrote it to make you howl with fear at how cruel the gods can be.'

He often said those sorts of things, and Jonah had learned to ignore them. 'I'll see if I can improvise something.'

Adam rocked forward, his hands clasped around the water glass. 'Pythagoreans thought that music was the underlying order of the universe. They thought through music you could reach a transcendent state, a sort of oneness with creation. Have you ever experienced that?'

'Yeah,' said Jonah, truthfully. He felt a spark of connection with Adam, a barrier removed. But when he looked at him, the face behind the long hair looked sad.

'On drugs?'

Jonah wasn't sure whether to be offended, or if it was just another part of the teasing he got for being a musician. Adam brushed the hair back from his face and met his gaze. 'I'm serious.'

'Sometimes.'

'I read a book.' Adam's tone was clipped, matter-of-fact. 'The Greeks had a goddess called Demeter. Goddess of grain and harvests – probably a manifestation of some kind of primitive, great-mother-earth fertility goddess. They worshipped her with mystery rituals that apparently produced a kind of frenzied divine ecstasy.'

'And you think they were dropping Es?'

'The ritual to Demeter involved drinking a mix of wine and barley. She was a goddess of grain. There's a fungus that grows on wheat called ergot, which apparently has psychotropic effects.'

'A fungus? Are we talking about magic mushrooms now?'

'It doesn't matter.' Adam stood, his face set. 'I thought you might understand better than the others.'

Jonah crumpled his beer can and tossed it in the bin. 'It's like the music. You can't just read about this stuff in books.'

A thin smile. It was the only smile Adam had: the bleak, resigned look of someone who'd looked at the world from every angle, and come away irretrievably disappointed. Someone who knew it was all absurd, but had resolved to make the best of it.

'That's why I'm having my symposium.'

He paused at the door, as if he'd just remembered something. 'How are things with you and Lily?'

'Fine.'

'It can't be easy, trying to make a go of it here.'

'We're fine.'

London

Julian had come from work. Pinstripe suit, lavender shirt, silk tie and shiny brogues. Standard-issue city uniform, complete with gold cufflinks and a belly sagging over his belt. Yet above the collar, nothing had really changed from ten years ago. He still looked like a plus-size schoolboy, a mop of black curls that he never combed, wide eyes and a face that reminded Jonah of a cream bun.

He shook hands.

'God, I'm sorry about Lily,' he said again. 'Let me buy you a drink.'

He hustled Jonah into the pub and almost pushed him into the seat. He came back from the bar with four pints crammed between his hands.

'Happy hour.' He set them down, slopping beer over the table. 'Ironic, under the circumstances. But might as well take advantage.'

Even among Lily's friends, Julian had always been at one

remove. When the others did doctorates and climbed the ivory tower, Julian took his degree from Oxford – *a gentleman's 2:2*, he called it – and made straight for his father's law firm in the City. Each time they met up, Julian would be there with a new car and a new girlfriend, buying all the drinks, slapping them on the back and dismissing any attempt to talk about his work. Then they wouldn't hear from him for months, until the next reunion. But he bought every CD that Jonah's band put out, and never forgot a birthday.

Jonah knocked back his beer. 'Did you find Adam's number?'

Julian gave him a compliments slip with a gilded letterhead and a phone number scrawled across it. 'God knows if it still works.'

'You haven't spoken to him recently?'

Julian shook his head through a mouthful of nuts. 'Not much since he went all Byronic. Why are you after him?'

'He sponsored the dig where Lily worked. She went to see him last week.'

Julian might play the public-school buffoon, but he wasn't obtuse. He looked up sharply from his drink.

'Adam's a bloody monk. And a mate. He'd never.'

'He was in love with Lily ten years ago.'

'Weren't we all? Broke all our hearts when you showed up. Now yours too. No bloody consolation. Have another drink, it's the best medicine.'

He went to the bar. Jonah got out his phone. He entered the number but didn't dial it.

Adam had funded the dig. Lily must have known all along, and never told him.

What else hadn't she told him?

He balled up the paper and stuffed it in his pocket. His thoughts were a mess; he didn't want to talk to Adam now.

However much courage the alcohol gave him, it wasn't enough for that conversation.

The screen lit up. Adam's number disappeared as a text message arrived. He didn't even have to open it: the phone previewed it automatically. Only the first two lines, but that was all there was.

Stop looking for me. I'm not coming back. {o} L

He was still staring at the phone when Julian sat down with two large glasses of whisky.

'News?'

Jonah slid the phone across the table.

'Christ.' Julian banged down the whiskies so hard they spilled. 'When did this come in?'

'Just now.'

Was it real? For the last three days, he'd been convinced someone else had been sending the messages. He'd even suspected Richard. But perhaps there was a simpler explanation.

Certainly, Julian didn't doubt it. 'None of us saw this coming. You and Lily, you seemed so perfect together. Do you know if there's another . . . ?'

Jonah gripped his glass as if it was the only thing mooring him to the world. 'You saw the message. That's all I know.'

But that wasn't true. They'd all tried to tell him.

Ruth, the policewoman: *Were there any issues in your relationship? Any problems?*

Sandi: *I thought she was one of the good guys.*

Charis: *She isn't missing, darling. She's left you.*

And he'd ignored them, shutting his ears because he was so certain they were wrong. He loved Lily; she loved him. He hadn't thought anything else mattered.

The screen flashed again – the phone was ringing.

Hope stopped his heart as he saw the number: *Lily's Mum*. He stumbled out of the pub. In the doorway, he jostled two men in suits coming in: they shouted something, but he didn't notice. He stood in the middle of the pavement in the current of commuters and answered the phone.

'Jonah? It's Julie.'

Hope crumbled, but he clung to the pieces. 'Is Lily there?'

'No.' She rushed on. 'I had a message from her just now. She said she's staying away for a while. She said she wants to be alone.'

She slid in the last word like the point of a needle, trying not to hurt him while she delivered the poison. It had to be done.

'I had a message too.'

A bus roared by. Jonah felt the weight of it in the wind that blew by. He imagined it colliding with him, the release of oblivion. He took a step back from the pavement. He didn't trust himself.

'I'm sorry,' Julie said.

But she was Lily's sister, and that limited her sympathy. If something had happened, there had to be sides; if there were sides, she wasn't on his.

'Keep in touch.'

He went back in the pub. At least he didn't have to explain anything to Julian. Time slipped by. Julian talked, Jonah drank, until at last Julian looked at his watch.

'Time to get you home, old friend. I'm afraid I'm booked at a party.'

'Anyone I know?'

Julian's face squirmed. 'Bit embarrassing, really. You've heard of Sugar Daddy parties?'

'No.'

'For chaps like me. Cash-rich, time-poor, not enough hours in the day to go a-wooing. Chance to meet girls who are willing to come to an arrangement.'

'Hookers?'

Julian looked appalled. 'God, no. Just girls who want a bit of security, to know they're not wasting their time. Nothing unsavoury.'

'But you pay them?'

'Christ you're rude when you're drunk, you know that? You don't pay them. You make them feel appreciated. We're all grown-ups.' He shot out his arm and waved his credit card at the barman. 'We weren't all as lucky as you and Lily.'

'Lucky?'

'You had ten good years. God knows what you did to upset her, but she adored you to the end. No one else could get a look in. Come on, I'll drop you off.'

All he remembered of the trip back was Julian ushering him into a taxi and giving the driver Jonah's address. A short ride and slamming the door. Staggering down the steps to his apartment, juggling the key. Collapsing on the sofa. He found the bottle of vodka still on the table where he'd left it. He splashed some more into the meltwater from the old ice cubes, then looked at his watch. Only half past nine. How did he get so drunk so soon?

He knew he had to keep it going as long as possible. He looked at his phone, wondering who he could call. Was Alex back yet? Shadow?

The phone was like a needle, defying him to use it. He knew he shouldn't. He knew it would hurt. He did it anyway. He opened up Lily's last message and read through it again. Just to keep the pain fresh.

He was still staring at it when, for the second time that evening, it started to ring. *Withheld number.* Suddenly, he was deathly sober again. It was Lily, calling to tell him it was all a mistake, to apologise. Even to explain would be a start. If he could just talk to her.

His clumsy fingers fumbled with the phone. 'Yes?'

'Is that Jonah Barnes?'

A woman – not Lily. He almost hung up right there. 'Who is this?'

'A friend you haven't met yet.'

'How did you get my number?'

'I want to help you. Can you come to Athens?'

Now he didn't know if he was sober, or drunker than he'd ever been. He held the glowing phone away from his face and studied it like a specimen from another planet.

'Why?' he said to the empty air.

'To meet me.'

'Why?'

'Because I know who took your wife.'

Nineteen

Anyone who lets himself to be taken prisoner may as well be abandoned to his enemies; he's their lawful property, and they can do what they like with him.

Plato, *Republic*

Imagine our situation something like this.

There's a cave. There are men inside it, collared and chained so that they can't move, can't even turn their heads. There's a fire behind them – which they can't see – and puppets dancing in front of the fire. All the prisoners see is the shadows thrown on the cave wall.

It's not that bad. I'm collared and chained, but at least I can turn my head. I'm in a long, high cave that curves to a point like a conch shell. The entrance is wide and open to the day, so a little sunlight creeps in. There are no fires and no puppets.

Puppets would be good, actually. I could use the entertainment.

There are forty-three of us chained up in the cave this morning. Last night, there were forty-seven. The morning before, only forty-one. I count them obsessively. Perhaps Archytas could extract some sort of meaning from the numbers: I just play games. I make little rules for myself and test the predictions. If there are forty-five when the guards bring supper, I'll get extra bread; if it's an even number when the sun touches the opposite wall, they'll free me. None of it comes true – but it gives the waiting some kind of purpose.

Shadows fall across the cave as two guards come in. Red cloaks, black helmets, a roaring lion on their belt buckles. My heart races as they approach, though I don't dare look up. Then relief and despair as their boots go past. Chains are unlocked, a man pulled out. When the boots return, there's a pair of shackled feet dragging between them. I try not to hear the sounds that go with them: gibbering, weeping, pleading. He's screaming about the light hurting his eyes.

Nobody knows where they go when they leave. We don't talk about it. All we know is they're free, one way or another. But do we want that kind of freedom?

Now it's forty-two.

When I was twelve years old, Athens decided to conquer Syracuse.

On the face of it, that was an odd decision. We'd been fighting a war against Sparta, on and off, since before I was born. Sparta's landlocked, a few days' march from Athens. Syracuse is on the east coast of Sicily, almost the edge of the world. Sparta threatened us every year; Syracuse just wanted to trade. But somehow, aristocratic hubris combined with democratic enthusiasm to launch us into an expedition to Syracuse.

It was a fiasco and a tragedy. Fifty thousand troops went out, barely two hundred came home. And the hero who dreamed it up? His name was Alcibiades. Before he left, on a drunken dare, he profaned the mysteries of Demeter and ran about Athens smashing all the good-luck herms in the city. When the government found out and recalled him, he jumped ship at Thurii and defected to Sparta. He told them exactly where the Athenian army was weakest. In short order, our fleet was sunk, our siege broken, our army routed and massacred. Seven thousand captives were brought back to Syracuse and shut up in the quarries for seventy days without food or water. The dead lay where they fell, until Dionysius got bored and sold the survivors into slavery. Alcibiades, meanwhile, offended his Spartan hosts and was next seen as special adviser to the Persian king, telling him how to defeat Athens.

Once upon a time, though I'm too young to remember it, Alcibiades was Socrates' star pupil.

Forty-two prisoners. If there's an odd number at sunset, I'll be freed. That's what I told myself. The sun's creeping back down the cave. Dust from the quarries outside swirls in the beam, though there's no actual quarrying going on. They've got all the stone out: now they're just enormous holes in the ground. Useful for dumping things you don't want.

I don't know what happened to Polus and his smugglers: we were split up early on. I don't think they're in this cave. The prisoner next to me is mumbling to himself nonstop. When I catch snatches, it sounds like Aeschylus. Perhaps he's an actor. Opposite is a man who swears he's a survivor from Alcibiades' expedition, though I don't believe him. No one could have survived here that long.

I'm covered in bruises. Getting me here involved a certain amount of casual violence: being beaten, kicked, punched, hauled and dropped. The advantage of being a big man is that people usually think better of trying to hit you. The disadvantage is that when they do, they feel they have to make it count. The shackles and collar have chafed my skin open; there's a welt around my neck where they tore off the gold chain; fleas have bitten me raw. At night, I can't sleep for trying to fend off the rats. Soon, I'll be too tired to bother.

Even Socrates can't reach me in the depths of this cave. I

try to speak to him, but he doesn't reply. I've got all the time in the world, but there isn't a thought in my head.

Next time, the guards don't throw shadows. The first I know is the slap of their boots. My heart lurches into panic, the familiar routine, but even as it speeds up it's already slowing down in anticipation that they'll go past.

They stop in front of me. I'm face to face with the roaring lion on an iron buckle. One of them grabs my neck so he can unlock the collar that ties me to the wall. Then they hoist my arms onto their shoulders and drag me away. After a week in the cave, my eyes shriek at the daylight, even at dusk. Dark spots blur my vision – or perhaps they're bloodstains on the rocks outside.

In the cave behind me, forty-one prisoners watch me go. Forty-one. It's an odd number.

The guards don't say anything and I don't ask. They bundle me into a cart with a canopy over the top and set off down the hill. It's a bouncy, stop-start journey. Early on, I can hear traffic and crowds around me; later, there's just a roar like blood in my ears, punctuated with shouted challenges and answers. The cart wheels ring loud on the stone road.

The cart stops. The guards pull me out. I'm in a high place surrounded by massive walls. To my right, I can see the sun setting blood-red over the sea, but there's no time to admire it. More guards are waiting for me; these ones have gilded armour and hard faces. The men who brought me from the prison salute and hurry away as quick as they can.

There are doors and there are rooms. The last one isn't the biggest, but it's clearly the most important. There are no windows, nowhere for secrets to leak out. Seven guards stand to attention around the room. None of them carries any obvious weapon, but their arms look big enough to do the job.

In the centre, on a golden chair, with armrests carved like

crouching lions and a radiant sun above his head, sits the tyrant. He's bigger than me, with golden-red hair and a face freckled like a barbarian. He's as notorious as they come – and yet, looking at him, he can't be any older than me. One hand is balled into a fist.

His name is Dionysius. At this point in time, he's the most controversial man in the Greek world. A military genius, a bulwark of civilisation, a usurper, a murderer, a tyrant – his name is debated in every agora from the Pillars of Hercules to the Black Sea. It's almost disappointing to find out he's simply a man.

He sat still, studying me. I stared into his blue eyes and tried to find the humanity in their depths. I didn't touch bottom.

He seemed to expect something from me, though I had no idea what. I waited.

'Do you know who I am?' he asked at last.

'I suppose you must be some kind of criminal.'

'*What?*'

He didn't expect that. I gestured to the soldiers spread around the chamber. 'You must be dangerous, if it takes so many men to guard you. I only need two.'

A short, barking laugh. 'Very good – and quite right. I am dangerous. They told me you're quick.'

He waited for me. After eight days in that cave, I was in no rush to say anything.

'If I was in your position, I'd be on my knees begging for mercy,' he suggested.

'If I was in yours, I'd already have freed me.'

The words seemed to come from somewhere outside me, like an unfortunate echo that had just happened to bounce out of my mouth. How else could I be mad enough to speak to the tyrant of Syracuse like that?

'I hear you knew Socrates.'

How did he know that? From the moment his men captured me on the mountain, I hadn't told them anything. Nobody asked.

'In fact, didn't you write an account of his trial? I'm sure I've read it.'

My courage fled. Suddenly, I wasn't an anonymous prisoner with nothing to lose. I was known.

'I wrote it,' I admitted.

'Then you know what happens to philosophers who speak out of turn when they're on trial for their lives.'

'Am I on trial? I thought we must have skipped that when I ended up in prison.'

'You can go back there if you like.' He jumped down from his chair and advanced until we were face to face. My guards, anticipating a hit, tightened their grip on my arms.

Dionysius opened his fist and thrust it out – but he didn't touch me. A thin gold cylinder on a gold chain lay cupped in the hollow of his fat hand. *Was that why he brought me here?*

'What is this?' he asked.

'I don't know.'

'Where did you get it?'

'A friend gave it to me.'

'Where did he find it?'

'I don't know.'

'What was his name?'

'Agathon.'

I assumed the name would mean nothing to him. If I'd had any inkling he knew Agathon, I'd have lied. But Dionysius' face lit up in recognition.

'You're a friend of Agathon? What a shame he didn't know you were coming. You've just missed him.'

Horror. 'Agathon was *here?*'

'I'm a famous patron of the arts. Every philosopher, poet, artist and playwright comes through here eventually.'

I didn't believe him. Agathon hated tyranny; he was more likely to pop up in a Kerameikos whorehouse than here – unless it was with a knife to slit Dionysius' throat. Or, if he had no choice in the matter.

I'd tried to follow Agathon to Rhegion. Perhaps I'd followed his footsteps all too well. 'Did you kidnap him like you kidnapped me?'

Behind the throne, the guards smirked.

'He came of his own free will.'

'Why?'

'The same reason everyone else does. For my money.'

Agathon didn't care about money. In all the time I knew him, I never saw him touch an obol. We often had to buy him bread to make sure he didn't starve, or new boots when winter came. But the gleam in Dionysius' face said he was telling the truth – to a point.

'He wanted the money to buy a book.' A guess, but I was right. That was why Agathon went to Rhegion – to find Dionysius and beg his patronage. Or maybe Timaeus lied, and Agathon came straight here. How badly must he have wanted that book?

'Did you give him the money?'

Dionysius studied his fingers. I remembered the temple at Locris, Timaeus' babbling in the heat.

– Who bought the book?

– A Lydian trickster, a sorcerer, with golden hair and perfumed locks, and the flush of wine on his face.

He'd told the truth, I realised bitterly, and I'd been too stupid to notice. He'd been quoting Euripides. The Lydian trickster was the disguised god – Dionysus.

'You found out why Agathon wanted the money and bought the book for yourself.' One more reason to hate the smiling tyrant in front of me. 'Where did Agathon go?'

Dionysius' face was innocence itself. 'He disappeared.'

He put the gold chain over his head and hung the locket around his neck. It seemed to signal an end to something – but he wasn't in any rush to send me back to the cave. He lifted two fingers, and the guards stepped away. I could hardly carry my own weight, let alone the manacles. I fell hard on my knees.

'You don't think much of me.' It wasn't a question. 'Are you one of those democrats who thinks everyone should decide everything?'

The conversation had become unreal. I looked for evidence that it wasn't a dream, and couldn't find any. But I understood the rules. Worse to retreat in front of a tyrant than to stand your ground.

'Democracy's a charmingly chaotic form of government. It treats all men equally, whether they deserve it or not.'

He was clever enough to catch the sarcasm. He liked it.

'Don't you value liberty?' The last word came out coated with a fur of distaste.

'Liberty's all very well. But the more people have of it, the more they want. In the end, they resent anything that remotely circumscribes their freedom: laws, customs, even social conventions. It's anarchy.'

'But you don't approve of rule by one man either?'

'In a democracy, everyone's appetites run amok. In a tyranny, it's just one man's. Neither makes for a well-ordered state.'

He liked that less. For a man who claimed absolute power, he was sensitive to criticism.

'Homer says, "We can't all be kings: one man must be supreme."'

'Homer says a lot about chariot-driving too – lean to the left, drive on your right-hand horse with shouts and the whip and so forth. Does reading Homer train you to be a charioteer?'

His lip curled. 'So you don't want the people and you don't want a tyrant. Who do you want? Some sort of committee of nobles and worthies?'

'That just breeds factions.'

'Who, then?'

I took a deep breath and forced myself to stand tall. My head spun with the effort; the chains threatened to break me. I gathered up my strength and tried to remember a sentence from the pamphlet I'd been working on before I left Athens.

'Until philosophers are kings, or kings and princes are philosophers, we'll never cure our states – or indeed the human race – of its evils.'

Dionysius burst out laughing.

Of course, I didn't think I'd change his mind at once. Even so, I was disappointed. Dionysius was no fool. I'd hoped he might at least engage with the argument.

'We're both the same,' he told me. 'Great men think great men should be in charge, philosophers think philosophers should run things, and anyone with no other qualifications believes in democracy.'

'I don't want to be a tyrant. I want the world to be a just place.'

'Don't you think I'm just?'

'Justice isn't a trait. It's a discipline. It needs constant exercise.'

I thought he'd laugh me off again. Instead, he changed the subject.

'Do you know what Euripedes says?'

'"Dionysus is in the building – get down on your knees!"'

'Very quick. And you know what Dionysus does to the man who doesn't recognise his power?'

I nodded. In the play, King Pentheus scorns Dionysus. The

god lures him to a mountaintop where he's torn to pieces by women and eaten. His own mother brings his head back to the palace like a football.

'I was thinking of a different tag,' said Dionysius. '"Tyrants are wise when they associate with the wise."'

It must have been a favourite phrase – it almost gleamed with polish. I thought of repeating what I'd said about taking advice from poets, but decided against.

'You're a wise man, so tell me this. Would keeping you here be a wise thing for me to do?'

A satisfied smile. He was cleverer than I thought, and he knew it – like the god in the play, who gives King Pentheus all the rope he needs to hang himself.

'Socrates was wiser than I am,' I said carefully. 'And he said he was only wise because he knew how little he knew.'

Dionysius frowned. 'Does that mean you're not wise?'

He was toying with me.

'If you were wise, you'd judge for yourself.'

'You want philosophers to be kings.'

'Or kings to be philosophers.'

'Do you think you can make me a philosopher?' The question yawned open, a wide and dangerous trap.

'Socrates said he never taught anyone anything. He merely helped them find the knowledge waiting to be brought out from inside them.'

'I don't care what Socrates said. I want to know what *you* say.' Dionysius crossed the room and took a scroll out of an alcove. He skimmed through it. There's a knack to reading quickly, getting the motion of the wrist so that the scroll flows from one spindle to the other without creasing or tearing. Dionysius did it with an educated turn, not the clumsy fumbling of an illiterate. They say he was a scribe before he turned his hand to politics.

'"Anyone who really cares about justice, and wants to stay

alive for any length of time, needs to keep out of public life,"'
he read aloud.

The scroll was my little pamphlet on Socrates' trial. I wrote
it to defend his memory. Now it was a weapon in the hands
of a tyrant.

'Are you still minded to sit out public life?'

'My thinking's developed since then,' I admitted.

'How convenient.'

I'd bent so far that the sap was squeezing out of me.
Dionysius knew it. If I broke, he'd throw me onto the fire
without another thought.

'Philosophy is about life,' I improvised. 'Politics, commerce,
war – they're all part of it. It would be strange to divorce
one from the other.'

I think I got it more or less right from what Archytas
said.

Dionysius scratched his chin. I waited to see if he believed
me or not.

'So if I gave you the chance to make your model ruler,
would you take it? Or is it all just so much *theory*?'

'You want me to teach you?' It would be like being locked
in a cage with a lion. Some of that sentiment must have told
in my tired voice. Dionysius snapped around.

'There's always the quarries if you prefer.'

'I'd be happy to teach you whatever I can.'

'Not me.' *I know what I know*, his face said. *The rest can
go to hell.* He didn't bring philosophers and poets here to
learn from them, but to own them.

'I was thinking of my son. Perhaps you can make something
of him.'

I nodded. What else could I do?

'They say Socrates often debated whether virtue and
wisdom could be taught. Now's your chance to find out. It's
fair to say your life depends on it.'

He clapped me on the shoulder and bared his teeth, delighted with himself. He could quote Homer and Euripides, or debate laws and constitutions with a subtle intelligence. But at that moment, I realised, I was in the hands of a psychopath.

And what had he done with Agathon?

Twenty

Jonah – London

The last ten seconds of his old life ticked away on the sofa – ten blank seconds while his mind warmed up out of sleep, before he remembered. He felt a brief, almost euphoric moment of weightlessness as every atom of his body twisted itself to the gravity of this new world he'd dropped into.

Then it hit. *She's not coming back.*

He looked around. His phone lay on the floor by the sofa. His wallet sat on the table, the credit cards spilling out. Had he been robbed? He rubbed his eyes and glanced at the door. Still locked and chained.

Was there someone else in the flat?

'Hello?' he called. No one answered. He looked into the other rooms; he even pulled open the bedroom cupboards just in case. No one there.

On the carpet, the phone beeped reproachfully. Jonah pawed the screen.

Three new voicemails, one new e-mail, it told him.

He listened to the messages first. Yesterday, he'd have had his heart in his mouth hoping for Lily. Today, the hope was gone.

Julian: *Hope you got back all right. Look after yourself.*

Charis: *So sorry about Lily, darling. Would you like to come and stay with me and Bill in the country for the weekend?*

Richard: *Glad to hear Lily's safe. I'll tell the police.*

Julian must have told them after he'd gone. Anger flared inside him; he felt embarrassed that Julian had been spreading rumours about him.

It's not a rumour if it's a fact, said the cruel voice in his head.

For thoroughness, he looked at the e-mail as well. *Flight Reservation Confirmation,* the subject said.

If he hadn't still been a little drunk, he'd have deleted it straight away as a scam. Instead, he tapped on it.

He read it through three times. First, because his tired eyes struggled to read the tiny screen; then because he must have read it wrong; then because it made no sense.

It said he had a flight to Athens booked that afternoon. He kept reading, waiting for the hook. A request for him to confirm his bank details, or wire ten thousand dollars to a travel agent in Nigeria. There was none of that.

Your card ending xxxx-0427 has been charged the full non-refundable amount.

He picked up one of the cards from the table and read the last four silver numbers.

0427.

Did I do this?

Panic. He dropped the phone and jumped up. The moment he stood, a hundred-ton weight in his brain knocked him back. He looked at the scattered beer cans and the vodka bottle, as if their pattern might hold some meaning. He needed to remember, but the heaviness in his skull crushed all thought. And he was dying of thirst.

The fridge was empty. He ran the tap as cold as it would go and poured a glass of water, drained it, poured another.

Dreams and memories dribbled back. The phone ringing. Running down a dark tunnel, pursued by a force that would devour him if he once looked back. Someone asking, *Can you come to Athens?* Swimming in blue water, stretching for Lily's hand but she was always out of reach.

I know who took your wife.

That must have been the dream. Lily hadn't really been taken. She'd run off and left him, the way marriages ended every day. Eventually she'd get in touch, they'd call lawyers, meet other people and move on.

But the Lily of his dreams, the Lily he'd married, would never leave him. He scraped the credit card over his stubble like a razor. He'd believed the dream enough to book a flight. Why stop now, just because he'd woken up?

He thought of a line that Adam once gave him, from an ancient philosopher called Heraclitus. *Awake, we see our dreams; but whenever we go to sleep, we see death.* He'd used it in a song.

For the second time in his life, he had nothing in the world but a broken heart and a ticket to Athens. He went to the bedroom and threw some clothes in a bag.

There were moments, writing songs, when it all came together. When all the false starts and wrong notes suddenly resolved into something vital and true. One moment he was stumbling through chaos; the next, it all made sense. He could glimpse the whole – not every detail, but the essence of the thing. Just a glimpse, and long hard hours ahead to capture it. But enough to know where he was going.

The phone call had been one of those moments. A single word that tied it all together. *Athens.*

Lily flew to Athens the week before she disappeared.

Adam was based in Athens and came back with her.

The Eikasia Foundation's headquarters was in Athens.

If you rationalised it, there was nothing there. Lily went

to meet the people who were funding the dig; Adam came back to deal with firing Sandi. No great mystery. Except that right afterwards, Lily vanished.

If they wanted Lily off their case, they'd give her a plane ticket and a payoff and an NDA.

He was looking in the wrong place. A meteorite had hit his world, and he was trying to understand it by staring at the rubble at his feet. He needed to look up. Whatever happened in Sibari, it had come from Athens.

In the heat of the night, in the grip of alcohol and emotion, it had been so real he could almost touch it. In the cool of the morning, exposed to daylight, he could see how shabby the argument was. But by then it was too late. The joy of the modern age was that however drunk, however dumb, however deluded you might be, with a credit card and a few taps on a screen, you could have whatever you wanted straight away. Even if it was crazy.

Jonah touched down in Athens at eight o'clock local time. A lone border guard waved the queue through, barely glancing at the passports. The crowds had gone: Jonah's flight seemed to be the only one. His footsteps echoed down the empty corridors. In the long baggage hall, carousels turned but no bags came.

He left the other passengers waiting for their luggage and went through customs. He called Adam from the arrivals hall, using the number Julian had given him.

'Yes?' It was a long time since he'd heard Adam's voice – he'd forgotten how much it unnerved him. Cool, hard and clear, not coloured by any sort of accent or emotion. Disembodied by the phone, it existed in a sort of pure, acousmatic sound-state.

'It's Jonah.'

A long pause. Talking to Adam was like dealing with one

of those chess-playing computers, calculating every possible sequence twenty moves ahead.

'I heard Lily turned up. That's good news.'

They all know, he realised.

'There was a text message. She hasn't actually come back.'

'No,' Adam agreed.

'I'm in Athens. I want to talk to you.'

A longer pause.

'OK.'

'A bed for the night would be good too.'

'Of course.'

'Can I come by?' With anyone else, he'd have added an apology. With Adam, there was no embarrassment. Only problems and solutions.

'OK.'

'Where's your house? I'll get a cab.'

'They're on strike. Trains are no good, either.' Problems and solutions. 'I'll come and get you.'

'You don't have to . . . '

But he'd already hung up.

Oxford

Jonah wasn't there for Adam's symposium: he had to work. One of the bar staff had called in sick; his manager told Jonah to cover the shift or lose his job. He didn't get out until almost midnight, onto freezing, empty streets and a light snow falling. He almost went straight home.

But he wanted to see Lily, and he'd promised Adam. He walked down St Giles', head bowed against the snow, to the row of high terraces where Adam lived with Richard and Julian.

He thought the party must have finished. The house was

dark, all the curtains drawn; no music, no conversation. He pressed the bell and heard it chime inside the house, but no one answered. Snow fell in the streetlights and gathered on his scarf.

He rang and knocked again. He tried calling the house phone – he could hear it ringing through the windows, on and on into the winter's night – but nobody picked up.

Just as he was about to hang up and go home, Julian answered. 'Who is this?'

'It's Jonah.'

'Jonah?' His voice sounded slurry and dazed, as if he'd just woken up.

'I'm standing on the mat getting snowed on – can you open the door?'

'I don't think you should come in.'

'What do you mean? Is Lily there?'

'She's . . . Christ.' The voice trailed off. 'I'll come down.'

Julian opened the door wearing nothing but a pair of chinos. His belt ends flopped limp and loose; his hair was a mess.

'It's a bad time.' He sounded high. Jonah sniffed the air for pot.

'What's going on? Where's Lily?'

'I don't think she's really—'

Jonah pushed past him, up the stairs to the first-floor living room. Soft light glowed inside, but when he tried the door, something blocked it. He had to squeeze round to get in.

The room stank of incense, sweat and vomit. Three single beds and a sofa had been crammed into a square around the edge of the room, draped with blankets. That was what had blocked the door. The whole room was lit by candles. A joss stick smoked on the bookshelf, and a sock dangled from the ceiling to stifle the smoke alarm. A bowl of olives lay over-turned on the floor, next to a Pyrex casserole dish half-full of wine, and a kitchen knife. Dark stains marked the cream carpet. Was that wine? Blood? It was too dark to tell, and he couldn't find the light switch. The lyre stood in the corner, untouched.

'Jonah, darling?'

Charis lay sprawled on one of the beds. She was wearing what looked like her gap-year sari, though it had unravelled in some disorder. He could see the dark smudge of a nipple where one breast had slipped out of the dress. She didn't seem to care. Her eyes were open but they didn't move; red lipstick was smeared around her mouth.

Richard sat on the bed opposite, head in his hands, dressed in a toga that had fallen off his shoulder. Even by candlelight, his hairless chest looked pasty-white.

'What the *fuck* happened here?'

'He spiked the wine,' Richard said.

'*What?*'

A spasm went through Richard's body, like a frog in a biology class. 'He didn't tell us.'

'Where's Lily?'

'He didn't tell us.' Richard groaned and put his head back in his hands.

'Upstairs,' Charis said from the couch behind him. 'She's with Adam.'

He took the stairs two at a time – three flights, to the very top. Adam's room looked empty without its bed. In the blue light of a lava lamp, Lily sat hunched up against the bare wall, cradling Adam's head in her lap. She was wearing what she called her Aphrodite dress: a wispy, sleeveless number she'd bought in Greece. Adam was naked.

Her tired, weeping eyes looked up and saw Jonah. She had a scratch on her cheek.

'Can you get him a glass of water? He needs to drink.'

Jonah didn't move. As his eyes got used to the dimness,

they made out long streaks that looked like blood caked up Adam's arms. He didn't really process it. All he could see was Lily.

'What—?'

'It's not what you think,' said Lily.

Jonah ran.

Afterwards, no one spoke about it – at least, not that Jonah ever heard. The secret to their type-A, fast-tracked Oxbridge lives, he realised, was selective memory, and they were ruthlessly good at it. When you aimed to climb so high up the ladder, there was no point looking back; if emotional baggage weighed you down, you discarded it. At the same time, you couldn't just cut off your friends. So you made-believe, and nothing bad ever happened for long.

But he always wondered about the others, and what they really remembered.

Athens

The silver Audi arrived outside the airport forty-five minutes later.

Jonah pulled up an imaginary photo of Adam as a student, and tried to match it to the man in front of him. The long black hair had been shaved back to the scalp: people who didn't know him well wondered if he'd had cancer. As far as Jonah knew, there was no medical reason. He'd just shed it one day, along with ten kilos, like a theorem being pruned back to its truest expression. Occam's razor, Richard called it. They'd had to explain that one to him.

But the dress sense hadn't changed. He got out of the car wearing a tight black V-neck T-shirt, loose black cargo trousers and black boots. The eyes were the same too – except, perhaps, more so. With no hair or fat to distract, you couldn't escape them. Watery grey, examining the world with withering intensity.

He saw Jonah and got out of the car. He moved gracefully, like a dancer. Jonah knew some people were convinced he was gay.

His handshake was firm like ice. 'Short notice.'

'Julian got me drunk. It seemed a good idea.'

Adam accepted it without judgement. 'She isn't here.'

The announcement came so unexpectedly it took Jonah a moment to process it. Then, because it seemed like the logical reply: 'Do you know where she is?'

'No. You're not the only one worried about her.'

He pointed to Jonah's bag. 'Is that all your luggage?'

Jonah knew, because Lily once told him, that the airport stood near the site of the Battle of Marathon, where nine thousand Athenians held back the full weight of the Persian empire. After the battle, the Greeks' fastest runner, Pheidippides, ran back to the city to deliver the news. The distance was twenty-six miles, three hundred and eighty-five yards, and he'd just fought a battle: he died as soon as he got there. No one recorded his time.

But the spirit of Pheidippides seemed to possess Adam as he piloted the car along the empty highway, the digital speedometer rock-steady on 180 km/h. Jonah wondered if the traffic police were on strike too. He watched the roadsigns fly by, the strange names in a strange alphabet. The same letters – the same language – as someone had pressed into a gold tablet 2,500 years ago.

Adam didn't do small-talk. Jonah piled right in.

'Lily came here last week to see you.'

Adam nodded, keeping his eyes fixed down the tunnel of streetlights.

'She wanted to talk to you about the gold Orphic tablet they dug up.'

'Did she tell you about that?'

'I found out about it.'

Adam didn't ask how – or mention the non-disclosure agreement. It had failed its purpose; it didn't exist any more.

'After she came here, you went back together and fired Sandi McConn, the conservator. Why?'

'That's not relevant.'

The speedometer slipped to 179, then jumped back to 180.

'I think it is. You wanted to do something with the tablet. Sandi McConn didn't approve, and I don't think Lily did either. That was Tuesday. By Friday, they'd both left the dig.'

'That's an explanatory hypothesis.' Adam swerved the car past an ancient BMW dawdling up the hard shoulder. 'You know the difficulty with hypotheses? You can never prove one. You can stack up all the evidence in the world to support it, but all it takes is one piece of negative evidence and the whole thing's refuted.'

'I'm right, aren't I?'

'The point being,' Adam continued, as if he hadn't spoken, 'if the foundation wanted to hide the tablet – and assuming Lily didn't, which is also untrue – why did she steal it?'

'She didn't.'

Did she? A tired voice in Jonah's brain told him he couldn't keep denying everything forever. But if he accepted what they were telling him, he was letting go of everything he'd ever believed about her. And everything he'd believed about himself.

Is it her you won't let go of? he asked himself. *Or are you just clinging on to a version of yourself that doesn't exist any more?*

They plunged off the highway, into a warren of narrow, double-parked streets. Jonah hung on to the seat and braced himself for impact, while Adam piloted the car through the asteroid field of motorcycles, pedestrians and other drivers.

'And they call it the birthplace of civilisation,' Jonah muttered.

'Plato complains about the crazy traffic in the *Republic*. Nothing's changed.'

They pulled into a parking garage and went up to the flat.

A lifestyle magazine – in the unlikely event one ever visited Adam – would have called his flat minimalist. A Spartan from ancient Greece might have found it a bit functional. The word that came to Jonah's mind was 'empty'. The furniture was white and low, designed to disappear; the table was glass and the chairs were thin, spidery steel. Even the walls were transparent, floor-to-ceiling windows that gave a panorama onto every side of the city. To the east, he could see a yellow moon rising behind the floodlit Acropolis.

'You must be hungry,' Adam said. He took noodles and vegetables from a white cupboard and began to stir-fry them. The smell crept through the apartment like the tendrils of some exotic vine. Jonah wandered around, though there wasn't much to see. The whole flat was one open room on the top of the building, except for a bathroom tucked into one corner. The bedroom was a futon on the floor with crisp white sheets; the living room was the sofa. A line of cupboards at knee height presumably stored a lifetime supply of black clothes.

He stopped in front of a large painting hung on the bathroom wall. In the stark space, it blazed like a planet. An engraving of a dahlia filled the middle of the canvas, though it was almost invisible under a violent red crayon scrawl, as though a two year old had tried to obliterate it. Below, slightly cutting it off, a crimson blood-blot stained a dirty strip of canvas where thin, washed-out letters spelled VENUS. It was the only colour – the only decoration – in the whole flat, so vivid it made him uncomfortable.

'Cy Twombly,' said Adam. He tipped out the stir-fry onto a white plate and put it on the table. He didn't take any himself. He sat down opposite and watched Jonah eat.

'Why haven't you asked the most obvious question?'

'What's that?' Jonah asked through a mouthful of noodles.

'If I was having an affair with Lily. If she left the Sibari dig and came here because she's left you for me.'

'Because it's not true.' He tried to remember what Adam had said earlier. 'It's not a "valid hypothesis".'

'No,' Adam agreed. 'But you can't falsify it. Doesn't that worry you?'

'I know I'm right.'

'I think the word you're looking for is "axiomatic".'

Jonah leaned low over his plate and sucked up a noodle. 'How's work going?' he asked.

'Fine.'

'Sandi said you're the program director. It sounds important.'

'It's just a title.'

Silence.

'How's the band?'

'We just finished a tour. It might be our last.'

'I'm sorry to hear that.'

Jonah shrugged. 'All good things come to an end.' He heard himself say it and winced. *Not all things*, he told himself. *Some things should be forever.*

He finished his meal; Adam took the plate to the kitchen area and washed it in a gleaming porcelain sink. 'You can have the bed. I'll sleep on the sofa. I've got some work to do before I go to sleep.'

The last thing Jonah saw before he shut his eyes was

Adam curled on the sofa with his laptop. His disembodied head floated in the screen's sea-blue glow like a drowning man.

When Jonah woke up, the sofa was empty and he was alone. In the stark flat, he felt like a mariner shipwrecked on a desert island. The only evidence otherwise, the footprint in the sand, was the hiss of steam coming from the bathroom, and the light rattle of a saucepan on the hob.

A white egg sat on the counter next to a pan of boiling water. Jonah dropped the egg in the water, set the timer, and watched the sun rise over Athens.

Two minutes later, Adam emerged from the shower. Naked, you could see how gaunt he'd become. Jonah wondered again about those rumours he'd been ill. Unselfconsciously, he pulled on a pair of black suit trousers, a black shirt and a pair of black loafers from a white cupboard.

'What are you doing today?' Adam asked. The egg timer beeped.

'Maybe I'll catch the sights.' He really had no idea. Twelve hours in, coming to Athens was already beginning to feel like an indulgent fantasy, the dying notes of a song that had already ended.

'Be careful. Athens isn't safe these days. Communists, anarchists, fascists, demonstrators – and the police are almost as bad. Stay away from the Parliament building in Syntagma Square. The tear gas is usually worst there.'

'You're better than TripAdvisor.'

In the Oxford vernacular the others used, Adam had 'taken a double first' in Physics and Philosophy. After graduation, he'd started a doctorate in the Computer Sciences department. The degree didn't work out, reasons unknown, but it had permanently affected the way he spoke. Every sentence seemed to emerge in ones and zeros, each word meaning neither more nor less than had been programmed into it. Or perhaps he'd always spoken that way.

He handed Jonah a round steel pebble. 'The *ostrakos*,' he said. Jonah didn't know what that meant. 'Wave it at the door if you need to get back in. I'll be back around nine. Will you be staying tonight?'

There was no subtext that Jonah could detect. No implication Adam wanted to get rid of him, nor equally any suggestion he'd like him to stay. Just a request for information.

'If that's OK.'

'Of course. Just be careful.'

Three minutes after he'd left the building, Jonah's mobile rang.

Twenty-one

We mustn't be panicked by the arrival of the tyrant and his henchmen; but go and poke around every corner of the city, observing carefully, before we rush to judgement.

Plato, *Republic*

When the guards struck off the shackles, I thought I'd died. I felt weightless without them, as if my soul had been separated from my body. Though if I'd actually started to float away, I'm sure the guards would have stopped me.

They took me out of the chamber, down corridors, and across a wide open courtyard. It was the first time I'd seen the stars since I was captured. On the far side, another door led into a barracks block, up a flight of stairs, and into a small, unpainted room with a bed and a window.

As soon as the guards had left me, I sat down on the wooden bed and put my head in my hands. Violent shivers ripped through me; the sea seemed to pour through the window and roar in my ears. I didn't hear the door open.

'I knew you'd come here.'

The triumph in his voice was out of place. So was the voice itself, though I didn't know why. It sounded off, the wrong string plucked on a lyre so that even the tone-deaf notice.

Euphemus stood in the doorway, wearing a gold-trimmed

robe and a smug smile that vanished as he saw the welts on my neck, the bruises, the ragged tunic and the dirt caking me.

'What on earth happened to you?'

'Your patron.' With Dionysius, my voice had seemed to belong to someone else – someone fearless and sure. Now it belonged to a corpse.

'How . . . ?'

'They caught me on the mountain outside Rhegion. They put me in the quarries.'

I watched the information work its way through him, the contortions of a man adjusting to a new reality. In the end, he fell back on self-righteousness.

'I told you not to go.' A pause. 'Did you find Agathon?'

'Dionysius said he was here.'

He looked surprised. 'I've been here a week and I haven't seen him. But I didn't know you were here either, until they told me just now.' He spoke quietly, as though something profound was happening inside him. Then he remembered himself. 'You look terrible.'

I had no strength. I followed Euphemus like a sheep as he found a bath and hot water, oil and fresh clothes. Nobody stopped us moving around the palace. Within the hour, I looked almost human again.

He helped me into bed. 'Are you hungry?'

I shook my head. Probably I was ravenous, but my stomach hadn't caught up yet.

'I'll get some bread and milk in case you want them in the night.'

'Stay with me,' I said. After so long in the prison, I wasn't ready to be alone yet.

Euphemus sat down on the window ledge and blew out the lamp.

★　★　★

When I woke next morning. Euphemus had gone. A basin of cold water sat on the windowsill where he'd been. I splashed my face and looked down at the sea foaming against the rocks. I wouldn't get out that way. But when I tried the door, it opened to the touch.

'Up already?'

A guard was standing there, square in front of the door, as if he'd been just about to knock. He gave me an ugly smile.

'It's time for your first lesson.'

On the parade ground outside, men in Dionysius' red tunics practised in the shadow of a huge stone lion. Among the clash of arms and sticks, I heard a melee of unknown languages. Even the Greek was barely recognisable.

'A cosmopolitan bunch,' I said.

'Dionysius buys the best,' the captain told me.

I shuddered. 'Slaves?'

'Not any more.'

I don't approve of slavery. But giving slaves freedom and weapons so they can tyrannise the society that owned them doesn't seem an improvement. Except, admittedly, for the slaves.

We climbed a staircase and emerged into a raised garden, with curved steps at one end like the tiers of an empty theatre. A fat boy sat there, dressed in a thick purple robe that was too heavy for the hot day, munching his way through a bowl of almonds.

'This is Dionysius' son, Dionysius,' said the guard.

Of course a tyrant names his son for himself: it's the thing he loves best. Though looking at the boy, I doubted his father loved him much beyond the name. At eight years old, he was a poor knockoff of his father, like the pottery copies of Phidias' sculptures you can buy at Olympia. The cheap material softens the features, blurring the character and the purpose of the original.

He peered at me as if seeing the world through a mist, and offered a formal greeting. In spite of who he was, I actually felt a small measure of sympathy with him. We were both prisoners of the same man – and only one of us had any hope of escape.

'His father says to give you whatever you need. Books, tablets, pens . . . ' The guard looked at me for guidance. As our eyes met, I realised neither of us had the least idea what you need to teach an eight year old.

What could I do?

Too late, I understood the cruel beauty of Dionysius' game. Like his namesake the god, he barely had to lift a finger. He'd given me all the rope I'd need.

'I'll want two tablets and a stylus,' I told the guard. 'And some books.' I turned to the boy. 'What have you been reading?'

A blank look.

'What did your last teacher give you?'

'The *Iliad*.'

That sounded hopeful. 'You've been reading Homer?'

'He told me the stories.'

'Can you read?'

He looked at the ground. 'Some.'

'I presume you have a grammatist to teach you reading? And other specialists for music, gymnastics and so on?'

A glum nod. I didn't envy the man who had to teach him gymnastics.

'Then I'll concentrate on your moral education.'

A clatter as the guard came back and dropped two tablets on the steps. He leaned against the wall, smirking.

I'd never improve the boy's character with that brute glowering over my shoulder.

'Can you leave us alone?'

He pretended to be horrified. 'You? Alone with the boss's son?'

'Really, the only danger is that I'll bore him to death.'

He considered the threat seriously. I shouldn't have tried irony.

'Make sure you don't,' he warned me, and sauntered away.

'Now,' I said to my new pupil. 'Where shall we begin?'

'I liked hearing Homer's stories,' he offered hopefully. 'They were exciting.'

'I'm sure they were.'

The Greeks are a scattered people – divided by dialects, gods, seas, mountains, food and politics. Against all that, the only thing that unites us is two poems written by one man in the ancient darkness between myth and history. I don't deny that they're powerful stories and masterful poetry but, as the basis for any kind of virtuous civilisation, their cast of vain heroes and petty gods leaves a lot to be desired.

But I didn't want to get off to a bad start with my new pupil. 'What stories had you learned?'

He stood, puffed out his chest and recited:

> *The crashing bones before the sword gave way;*
> *In dust and blood the groaning hero lay:*
> *Forced from their ghastly orbs, and spouting gore,*
> *The clotted eye-balls tumble on the shore.*
> *And fierce Atrides spurn'd him as he bled,*
> *Tore off his arms, and, loud-exulting, said—*

'Enough, enough,' I flapped. 'Who on earth taught you that?'

Sullen-faced, the boy pointed past me. Quick footsteps were coming across the courtyard. I turned and saw Euphemus, still wearing his absurdly overembroidered robe.

'You've changed your tune,' he huffed, before I could say anything.

'Sorry?'

'"I hate tyrants and I'm too good for politics." Now look at you. I thought you were a man of principle.'

'What?' He was acting as if the night before had never happened. Perhaps clean clothes and a wash was all it took to make him forget the wretch I'd been. In his world, after all, reality is what you see. Or choose to ignore.

'Anyway,' I said, 'you don't believe in principles.'

'Very clever.'

'What is it that you think I've done?'

'You've taken my job.'

'*Your* job?'

He pointed to the boy, who had sat down and was watching us from behind his bowl of almonds. '*I'm* supposed to be tutoring him.'

If he hadn't been so obviously upset, I'd have laughed.

'Dionysius dragged me out of the quarries – he didn't give me a choice.'

'Everything you said about standing up to tyranny. Was that just so much *shit*?'

I glanced nervously at the boy. He looked delighted.

'You were the one who told me to engage with the world. And you are famously persuasive.'

I'd meant it as flattery (mostly). Perhaps there was a hint of sarcasm around the edges. Euphemus didn't miss it.

'Snide as well as hypocritical. It doesn't suit you.'

'I didn't—'

'I thought you were better than that. He turned to go, then remembered something. 'And good luck making any progress with *him*.' He shot the boy a venomous look. 'You both deserve what you're getting.'

I picked up one of the tablets and made a show of writing something down while I tried to compose myself.

'The trouble with poetry,' I explained to the boy, once Euphemus had disappeared, 'is that poets thrive on watering desires that would be better left to wither. Their whole art is showing us men in extreme states of passion, and making us feel what they're feeling. In fact, of course, we shouldn't be indulging our feelings. We should restrain them.'

A blank stare. Restraining his feelings didn't seem to be a problem.

'Let's go to the library and find something more suitable.'

'Once up on a time, a Town Mouse went to visit his cousin in the country. This cousin was rustic and a bit simple, but he loved his urban relative and welcomed him in. He didn't have much food – just salt, olive oil and bread – but he offered them freely.'

I looked up to check the boy was listening. About the best to be said was that his eyes were open.

'Aesop's fables have a lot to commend them,' I encouraged him. 'Socrates spent the last days of his life thinking about them.' Capricious to the last, he put them into verse. I think it was the only thing he ever wrote down.

We stood in Dionysius' library, in front of wide open windows looking out to sea. The shelves around us were packed with scrolls, stacked like amphorae in the hold of a ship. Where Dionysius got them, and how, I dreaded to imagine, but somewhere on those shelves lay the book Agathon had wanted to buy from Timaeus – *The Krater*, he'd called it, a book of Pythagorean secrets worth a hundred drachmas. I was itching to rummage through the stacks until I found it, but a vigilant librarian and two guards by the door made me think better of it for now.

Instead, I was stuck with Aesop.

'The Town Mouse turned up his nose at the simple food he was offered.

'"How do you eat this terrible stuff?" he said.

'"It's all we have here in the country," his cousin apologised.

'"Then come with me, and I'll show you how to live. After a week in town, you'll wonder how you ever managed to tolerate life in the country."

'The two mice set off and arrived at the Town Mouse's residence late at night.

'"I'm starving," said the Town Mouse. He took his country cousin into a grand dining room filled with cakes and jellies and wine. The Country Mouse ate so much he felt sick, not being used to so much rich food.

'Suddenly they heard a terrifying growl.

'"What's that?" said the Country Mouse.

'"Only the cats," his cousin said through a mouthful of food.

'"*Only!*" squeaked the Country Mouse. The door flew open, and in came two huge tomcats. The mice had to run for their lives and just squeezed through a hole in the floor before the cats got to them. The Country Mouse scampered to the door.

'"Goodbye, Cousin," he said.

'"Going so soon?" said the other. "But what about the cakes?"

'The Country Mouse shook his head. "I'd rather eat salt and bread in peace, than cakes and wine in fear."'

I put down the scroll.

'What do you think the fable's trying to say?'

The boy shook his head.

'Which mouse was the more virtuous?'

He gave it some thought. 'The Town Mouse.'

'Why?'

'He was braver. The other one ran away.'

'Ah,' I said. 'I can see why you think that. But although the Country Mouse ran away, he was actually doing the right thing. Being virtuous isn't an unthinking reflex. It means acting appropriately, depending on whether something should be pursued or avoided.'

He didn't understand. 'Isn't courage a virtue?'

'Yes.'

'And cowardice isn't.'

'Yes, but—'

'So the Town Mouse is virtuous.'

'I think it would be better to take the fable allegorically,' I said hastily. 'This isn't about the mice. It's about the societies they live in. The Town is a society which has every luxury, but its citizens live in fear for their lives.'

I looked around the room, letting my gaze linger on the guards at the door, hoping he would make the connection.

'The Country, on the other hand, may appear simple and uncivilised. But it has the greatest luxury of all – freedom from fear.'

'But they have cakes and jellies in the Town.'

'Those are ephemeral,' I explained. 'They taste good for a moment, but they have no lasting value.' I could see he didn't believe me. Not surprising: he was round as a pudding. 'The wholesome fare in the Country is much more nutritious.'

'Bread and oil is boring.'

I tried to stay patient. 'We're not really talking about food. We're talking about virtue. You have to set up your life for maximum control over your own appetites if you're to win loyal friends and subjects – or how will they be able to trust you?'

He still looked confused. I tried to put it in terms he might understand.

'Wouldn't you rather be in a place where you could live your life without worrying you'd be eaten by cats?'

He scratched his ear. 'Not if I was the cat.'

A door opened. A warm breeze blew in. The boy's face lit up and, for the first time, I saw some trace of his father. He pushed past me, ran across the room and threw his arms around the new arrival.

'Dion!'

The newcomer was around twenty, tall and strong with tousled hair and a solemn face. Whatever his relation to Dionysius, he looked far more like the tyrant than the feeble son. The same confidence, the same certainty. But Dionysius had a black aura, menacing you with his power. In Dion, the power flowed golden.

'You must be the new tutor,' he greeted me. 'I'm his uncle Dion. His mother is my sister.'

The tyrant's brother-in-law. Even that didn't chill the warmth I felt from him. *Everything that moves makes music*, Archytas said. That must include people. We don't hear it with our ears, but I think we catch the resonance when we come close. The music that accompanied Dion was perfect harmony, a sparkling bright melody underpinned by deep seriousness.

'I hear you knew Socrates,' he said.

They'll put that on my tombstone. 'Perhaps some day I'll be known for something else.'

He flashed a smile that was bright as the sun, that made my reply sound peevish. 'Tutoring my nephew to be a great ruler, I hope.'

I nodded and tried to smile. If Dion noticed my lack of enthusiasm, he didn't say anything. He tousled his nephew's hair. 'Run along.'

The boy slipped out of the door, followed by a guard. Dion rolled up Aesop and put him back on the shelf.

'Let me show you around.'

If you ever go to Syracuse, here are some facts to orient you.

It's a huge city, sloping down from a limestone ridge to two harbours which are divided by a tongue of land. The peninsula is called Ortygia, a low hump like a tortoiseshell that used to be shipyards and warehouses. When Dionysius overthrew the democracy, this was where he came. He walled off the slips and turned the warehouses into cellars for the new citadel he threw up. He cut the peninsula three times over, and gated the bridges. Because he didn't dare go out among the citizens in the agora, he built a new monumental core on the highest point of the island: two vast temples standing side by side, dedicated to Athena and the Goddess.

And that was where Dion led me. The Temple of the Goddess was wrapped in scaffolding for repainting: we climbed to the top, and came out among the gods on a little balcony in front of the temple's pediment. On the neighbouring temple, Athena's gilded shield burned in the sunlight like a flaming eye. They could probably see it in Greece.

'What do you think?' Dion asked.

I could see the whole city. The causeway with its massive gates and drawbridges; the warships riding at anchor in one harbour, and the merchantmen in the larger harbour to the south. In the distance, lowering over the city, the ridge where the stone for all this building had been quarried out. Where forty-two prisoners (more or less) sat shackled to a wall, awaiting their fate.

'Very impressive,' I said.

Except for one thing. Dionysius had built his own model city on Ortygia, but he didn't trust anyone to live there. In Athens or Corinth or Thebes, this would have been the city's living heart: lawyers and legislators, sophists and prostitutes, merchants and hawkers all haggling, bargaining and brawling together. Here, if I looked straight down, everything was immensely empty. I could see a few clerks hurrying across the square with bundles of documents, and the ever-present red-cloaked guards posted outside the temples. Otherwise, no one. The palace wasn't even old enough for ghosts.

Dion leaned on the stone balustrade. 'How are you getting on with my nephew?'

I tried to think of a reply that wouldn't make things awkward. 'He's less intimidating than his father.'

He understood what I meant. 'You can't judge his father by Athenian standards. Sicily's been at war for generations. It needed someone with his courage to take charge.'

The yawning streets below contradicted him. Dionysius wasn't courageous. He'd walled himself off from the world he ruled because he didn't dare face it.

'How many years' peace have there been since Dionysius took over?' I asked.

'Not many. But you can't blame him for that. He took power when the Carthaginians had taken almost all of Sicily. However often he beat them back, they kept coming.'

'But Carthage made peace, eventually.'

'Yes.'

'So why is his army camped outside Rhegion now? Why does every colonist in southern Italy look over his shoulder when you say his name?'

No answer.

'A tyrant comes to power claiming he wants to rescue the state from some sort of crisis. And in the early days, he's full of smiles and promises. He forgives debtors and doles out land, wanting to be so kind and good to everyone. Except that when the crisis is over, he finds he needs another threat to justify his position. So he starts another war.'

Dion didn't contradict me.

'Of course,' I went on, 'some people complain. Criticism threatens him, so he gets rid of them. There's a war on, after all. But the more people he gets rid of, the more enemies he creates, the more he has to purge them until there's no one with any courage or ability left.'

We were in a high place. Perhaps I thought no one could hear us. Perhaps the dazzling false sun of Athena's shield blinded me to the dangers of discussing tyranny in a tyrant's palace with the tyrant's brother-in-law. The truth is, I wanted to trust him.

Dion looked down. Perhaps he'd never heard anyone speak so plainly before.

'Is this your first time in Syracuse?' he asked.

'It's the same everywhere.' Like one of Archytas' mathematical laws, the same numbers always add up.

'They said you didn't care about politics.'

'I don't.'

'You obviously think about it a lot.'

'Because I hate it.'

'That's different. Not caring *for* something isn't the same as not caring *about* it.'

'How old are you?' I asked.

'Nineteen.'

'All you've ever known is your brother-in-law's rule. I've seen both sides of the coin. When I was twenty-three, my uncle had the same idea as Dionysius.'

Strange to think, in that year Dionysius had already taken power in Syracuse. The tyrant and I are almost exactly the same age. When I compare the callow, unsure youth I was with the brutal confidence he must have had to overthrow the *polis* at twenty-one, I think we might as well be different species.

'My uncle didn't last long,' I said. 'But he left me with enough taste of tyranny to last a lifetime. Five years later, his enemies executed Socrates, and I knew the world was irredeemable.'

I looked out to sea, thinking of all the miles between me and Athens. 'Socrates thought if you avoided public life and cultivated virtue, that was what mattered. He opted out. The sophists who justify rapacious self-interest are just flattering the system. Democrats make it a free-for-all; tyrants keep it under their thumbs. But it's still broken.'

'So what's the solution?'

He'd turned to look at me. His face glowed gold with the reflected light from Athena's shield, but it was the hunger in his eyes that really shone. He wanted to know – and he thought I could tell him. Was this the way I once looked at Socrates? Surely Socrates never felt as awkward as I did then. He loved the attention.

'We have to go deeper. The selfishness that the sophists teach is just Heraclitus on a human scale. Have you read Heraclitus?'

He shook his head.

'He said there's nothing constant in the universe. Everything's in flux. And if you believe that, self-interest makes perfect sense. There's nothing but ourselves to pin our behaviour on.'

I could see from his face he understood intuitively.

'There has to be something else. Something fundamental to the universe that's outside ourselves.'

'Yes.'

'There's a man in Taras called Archytas. He thinks that fundamental thing is mathematics. Mathematics refutes Heraclitus: it proves there are things which are constant in the world. A triangle is always a triangle; two and two always make four. A string twice as long as another always makes the octave.'

'Hard to argue with.' Our eyes met. He'd heard the catch in my voice.

'Archytas is on the right track. But nobody's going to change their life to solve an equation. Music can change our mood, but it doesn't change our life. At best, it's a metaphor.'

I remembered Diotima. *Either our senses aren't made to appreciate perfection – or else the perfect world that mathematics describes isn't our world.*

'Pythagoras discovered that music is mathematics turned

into sound. There are laws behind it, truths. If the strings obey those laws, the result is harmony. If we could only find the same laws for ourselves, society would be harmonious and the result would be . . . '

' . . . Virtuous?' he suggested.

'Beautiful.'

'So what are these laws?'

The song in my ears stopped suddenly. A cloud covered the sun on Athena's shield, and the world became less bright.

'I haven't got there yet.' I rubbed my eyes. 'When I do, perhaps there'll be no more tyrants.'

'Is that what you're going to teach my nephew?' A smile with a warning behind it. 'That would be brave.'

'Socrates said that courage is what happens when you get rid of wrong thinking. For him, wisdom was a sort of cleansing process, stripping away error until you got to truth.'

It was a wistful sort of thought. It reminded me why I'd come to Italy in the first place.

'A friend of mine came here from Athens. Agathon. Did you see him?'

Dion scratched at a loose piece of stone in the balustrade. 'He wasn't here long. He wanted money; Dionysius wouldn't give it to him.'

'You'd have enjoyed speaking to him.' Agathon was nearer Dion's age: I could imagine the two of them in the gymnasium, sharing a couch, taking long earnest walks along the coast. Ridiculously, the thought made me hot with jealousy.

'And Dionysius just let him go?'

'Why not? He's not some monster who devours everyone who enters his castle. He's a man trying to get things done.'

The piece of stone came free. Dion turned it over in his hand, then tossed it over the edge. I didn't hear it hit the ground.

'Were you using Aesop's fables to teach my nephew?' he asked.

'It was the best I could come up with.'

'Do you know the story of the old lion and the fox?'

'It's a long time since I read Aesop all the way through.'

'You should read it.' It seemed important to him. 'The lion's teeth had fallen out and his claws were blunt. His legs were tired; if he chased prey, it easily got away. So he made sure the other animals all knew how weak he'd become, then retreated to his cave. One by one, the animals came in to offer their sympathy. And the lion, who wasn't as feeble as he'd let on, ate them all up.

'One day, a fox came to the cave. The lion saw the shadow by the door and asked, "Why don't you come in?"

'"It's terribly kind of you," said the fox, "but no. I can see lots of tracks going in, and none coming out."'

I laughed. 'Why are you telling me that? If you're warning me not to go into the lion's cave, it's too late.'

Dion didn't laugh with me. 'Aesop says the moral is: *take warning from the misfortunes of others.*'

I didn't understand why he'd told me that. But the sun had gone in, and Dion was looking over his shoulder like a man who has to be somewhere else.

'It's easy to talk about these things in bright high places. But be careful when you go down. There are a lot of corners in the palace, and you never know who's listening in the shadows.'

'Don't worry,' I said. 'I'm not as brave as Socrates.'

He smiled. 'But Socrates never left Athens.'

The guards had gone when I came down, though it didn't make any difference. I'd seen Ortygia's defences, the rings of walls and water: I knew I wouldn't escape. Perhaps that was what Dion had wanted me to see.

I sat down on a bench. A slave appeared, unasked, and offered me cool well-water. I drank it thirstily, spilling some over my tunic. Even behind a cloud, the sun baked the courtyard and the high walls trapped the heat. I felt light-headed. This time yesterday I'd been a prisoner in the cave. Now, I was tutor to the tyrant's son. At least in the quarries you know who your enemies are.

'Do you mind if I join you?'

A fat man had appeared: balding, sweating heavily in his thick formal robe. Even with his size, he moved precariously, like a bird with a damaged wing. Without waiting, he lowered himself onto the bench.

'"See how men blame the gods for what is after all nothing but their own folly,"' he said unexpectedly. He said every word carefully, looking me right in the eye.

'I'm sorry?'

'Leon,' he introduced himself, as if he hadn't spoken that strange line from Homer. 'Just back from a trip to the country. You must be our new Athenian.'

'Don't hold that against me.'

His laugh exploded like someone dropping a plate. He mopped his brow. 'Dear me, no. As it happens, I have plenty of friends in Athens.'

The laughter dried up as suddenly as it had erupted. He shot me a penetrating look.

'Did you bring any letters?'

'No.'

'Really?' He jerked his head to one side, as if trying to clear wax from his ear. 'You're tutoring the boy, I hear.'

I nodded.

'A bright pupil?'

'I'm sure one day he'll be the mirror of his father.'

Another eruption of laughter. 'Very well put. Very *apt*. Your reputation does you justice.' He sucked his finger. 'You're sure you didn't bring any letters?'

'None.' And then, though it wasn't relevant: 'I was ship-wrecked on the way here.'

'Ah.' He nodded vigorously, as if that solved a mystery he'd been puzzling at for hours. 'How is Athens?'

'The same as always.'

'And you're enjoying your stay in Syracuse?'

'I was brought here against my will, beaten, and held in the quarries for a week. Other than that, it's very pleasant.'

He looked shocked. 'That's terrible. Did they find the letters?'

'I didn't have any letters,' I repeated wearily.

'That was lucky.'

And with that, he left me.

I had nowhere to go, so I stayed on the bench. The sun had come out again; bees rummaged around the flowers and the world was a long way away. I'd almost fallen asleep when urgent footsteps brought it back with a jolt.

It was Dion again – but not the smiling, earnest boy who'd talked philosophy on top of the temple. When he stopped, water pooled around his feet. Had he been swimming?

'What is it?'

He wouldn't meet my eye. 'It's your friend.'

'Euphemus?'

'Agathon.'

Twenty-two

Jonah – Athens

He stared at the phone, shaking and glowing in his hand like some exotic fish trawled from the depths of the ocean. Around him, Athens sprawled away through the windows of the glass box.

The phone stopped moving when he answered it. The voice on the other end reminded him of something he'd almost forgotten, like sniffing rain at the end of a long dry summer.

'I'm glad you came. I wasn't sure you'd remember.'

'Who are you?'

'*Don't* you remember?'

'Did you call me in London? Two nights ago?'

A sigh, as if he'd disappointed her somehow. 'Did they drug you that thoroughly?'

Listening to her made him wonder if he was back in his dream. 'Nobody drugged me. I just had too much to drink.'

'Alcohol's a drug. They don't even have to inject it.'

He had no answer to that. 'Did you tell me to come to Athens?'

'You're here, aren't you?'

Talking with this woman whose name he didn't know, he wasn't sure of anything. He looked out the window to get his bearings, and came eye to eye with the Acropolis. Suddenly, it looked absurd – as if he was in a film, and the director had called for the most obvious establishing shot to show the audience that Jonah was in Athens. Except in a film, the Acropolis would be a backdrop stretched across the studio wall.

'Are you there?'

'Still here.' He'd been studying the Acropolis, looking for creases. The haze in the air made it wobble and shimmer. He wondered if it was the infamous Athenian smog – or tear gas.

'Are you going to tell me who you are?'

'Do you know Elefsina? It's an archaeological site, on the coast beyond Piraeus.'

'OK.'

'Meet me there at twelve. Make sure they don't follow you.'

'Who?' No answer. 'Why would I go there? I don't even know who you are?'

'Then come and find out.'

'How will I recognise you?'

'I'll know who you are.'

In another world, Jonah wouldn't have been sitting on a bus lumbering through suburban Athens on the strength of an anonymous phone call. He wouldn't even have been in Greece. But that world didn't exist any more. Its destruction had been seamless, but irreversible. He remembered the empty gates in the field at Sibari, the chill on his shoulders as he stepped through. Was that when it changed?

The bus rattled down a long, straight street full of tyre-change garages and hardware shops. Even at his stop, nothing said 'ancient site' except the driver shouting at him in Greek and pointing down a nondescript side street. At the end, a man in a kiosk sold him a ticket that was covered in dust, admitting him to a large, open square surrounded by broken pieces of tombs and buildings. Column stumps marked the remains of a monumental gateway that had been cut down. A scrubby hill rose behind it, topped by a clock tower that said twelve o'clock.

Beyond the ruined gate, a path wound around the side of the hill to yet more ruins. Lily would have known where to go. She would have cast an eye over the ruins and brought the whole thing alive, pulling the stones up out of the dust until he could see them in their original glory. He wished she was there.

'Are you looking for a guide?'

She seemed to have appeared from nowhere – he was positive there'd been no one there a second ago. Even now, right in front of him, there was something temporary about her, like a bird that might fly away at any moment. Large sunglasses and a baseball cap shaded her face. It was a warm day, touching thirty degrees, but she wore a long-sleeved cardigan buttoned all the way up, and lightweight trousers. About all he could say for sure was that she seemed slim, small-breasted, and delicate. She barely came up to his chin.

A dizzying sense of déjà vu hit Jonah, like the feeling he'd had the day he met Lily. Not recognition – he couldn't see anything to recognise – but familiarity. A sort of harmony resonating between them.

'Are you looking for a guide?' she said again. She spoke perfect English, a hint of an American accent. Was it the voice from the phone? Suddenly, he found he couldn't remember how it had sounded at all.

'Did you ask me to come here?'

The low cap hid her face completely. 'I'm a guide.'

Two possibilities. Either she was the person he was supposed to be meeting, or she wasn't. If she was, and wanted to play coy, so be it. If she wasn't, at least it would pass the time. Maybe he'd learn something.

Two hypotheses, as Adam would have said. All he could do was let the evidence stack up until one turned out to be false.

'OK.'

He followed her over the threshold.

'There are three parts to this mystery. The loss, the search, and the ascent.'

She'd led him up the path that curved round the hillside, past a cave, onto a wide terrace that overlooked the sea and the island of Salamis. It had once been one of the holiest sites in Greece. Now, tankers and freighters clogged the sound; gantry-cranes and chimneys jagged the horizon, tangled with pipes and smoke from an oil refinery. Across the water, the twin horns of the mountain on Salamis made a perfect crescent against the sky. They reminded Jonah of the mountain at Sibari.

'In ancient Greece, you had the public religion that people grew up with – gods like Zeus, Athena, Poseidon and so on. And then you had the mystery religions, secret rituals you had to be initiated into. The mysteries of Eleusis were the most famous of all. They ran for something like a thousand years, from dark-age Greece right through the Roman period, until Christianity finally killed them off.'

'What was the mystery?'

'Nobody ever said. Once a year, the worshippers walked the twenty kilometres here from Athens. They came into this shrine, where the priests performed the ritual. They saw sacred objects, and were taught sacred truths. It transformed their understanding of the world.'

'OK.'

They walked across the terrace. Half of it had been cut into the side of the hill, the other half built out on a massive stone platform towards the sea. His guide pointed to one of the column bases poking up through the earth and dead grass.

'The building was supposed to be like a forest, full of columns. They crammed the initiates in here a thousand at a time. They'd been fasting for days; they'd walked twenty kilometres in the heat; they were in the dark, disoriented, dazed. There was smoke, incense, torches. Some scholars think they might have taken psychotropic drugs, like magic mushrooms.'

For a moment, he was back in the house in Oxford, the beds and sofas, the blood and the snow. He imagined how different it would have been here at Eleusis: the dark cavern, flickering lights, sweaty bodies jammed together, waiting for the moment when the god would come down and touch their souls. And music. There must have been music. He wondered what it had sounded like.

Rows of banked benches ran along the back of the terrace, cut out of the cliff like steps. The guide sat down.

'No one's found out what the rituals involved, exactly. But the basis for them was the cult of Demeter. Do you want to hear the story?'

She was looking away, across the terrace and out to sea. The cap and glasses still hid her face; she'd said nothing that wasn't appropriate to a tour guide. But the longer he spent with her, the more sure he became that she was who he'd come to meet. There was a mystery about her, something hidden, waiting to be taken out of its box and revealed at the right time.

'Tell me the story.'

She curled her legs under her on the stone. 'There was a maiden who was the daughter of Zeus and Demeter, the goddess of the harvest. She was a wild girl who lived in the shady depths of the forest, a child of nature. Ivy wrapped itself in her hair; at night, the grasses lay down for her mattress and trees knitted together their branches to shelter her. All the gods wanted to marry her but her mother refused them.

The King of the Underworld, Hades, wanted her too, but he knew she'd never agree to come down to the underworld. She was life, and living things need the sun.

'So Hades went to his brother, Zeus, the king of the gods, and Zeus agreed to help him. He told his brother he could snatch the maiden while she was picking flowers in a glade.'

'Wait a minute,' Jonah interrupted. 'I thought you said Zeus was the girl's father.'

'And her mother's brother. It's all a bit incestuous.'

'No kidding.'

'So the maiden went to the meadow, braiding flowers into a crown. But when she reached to pull up one of the narcissus flowers, a great rift opened in the earth. Hades rode out in his golden chariot. The maiden screamed, but the god grabbed her and dragged her down to Hell.'

Jonah's chest tightened. As the story played out in his mind, it wasn't a forest glade in Greece, but a baked plain in Southern Italy under a forked mountain. And the hole in the ground had people in it, opening up the earth five centimeters at a time.

'Her mother heard the scream and came flying, but the crack in the earth had closed. She scoured the earth for her daughter, but no one would say anything because they all feared Death. At last, Helios, the sun who sees everything, took pity on her and told her. When she realised that Zeus had betrayed her, she tore off her crown, covered her head, and wandered the earth as a mortal. At last she came here, to Eleusis, and collapsed in the shade of an olive tree, next to a well. When the local king's daughters came to fetch water, they saw her and took pity on her: they brought her back to life. Later, she taught them her mysteries, and ordered them to build her a temple on this spot. But she was still wasting away inside.'

Across time, across the bridge between myth and reality, Jonah felt the goddess's emptiness inside him.

'Meanwhile, without Demeter, the rains didn't fall, the crops withered in the fields and turned to dust. The whole earth starved. And not just people. Because they had no food to make sacrifices, the gods became desperately weak too. One by one, Zeus sent the other gods to Eleusis to beg Demeter to return to Olympus and bring back the harvest. They offered her every imaginable gift, but the only thing she wanted was to see her daughter again.

'When Zeus saw he had no choice, he sent his messenger down to the underworld to make Hades set the maiden free.'

'I think I've heard this story before.' Jonah searched his memory. 'This is Orpheus and Eurydice, right?'

The guide shook her head. 'That's another legend. Orpheus is similar – but he was a mortal, and his story ends differently. When Zeus's messenger reached the underworld, Hades didn't argue. But before the maiden went, he gave her a few pomegranate berries to eat, so she wouldn't get hungry on the journey home. In her excitement, she forgot that if you eat the fruits of hell you can never be free of it. Which is why, forever afterwards, the maiden spends eight months of the year with her mother in the light, and four months in darkness with her husband. And for that season, Demeter keeps the earth hostage and no crops grow.'

'Does this woman have a name?'

'The ancient Greeks didn't dare say it aloud. They called her *Kore*, which means maiden. Plato refers to her as *Pherepapha*, the "goddess who understands". You probably know her as Persephone.'

He barely caught the name. She'd lowered her voice, so that all he heard was soft consonants rustling like grass. As if, even now, she was afraid of what the name would conjure.

'She has various other cult titles. The ancient philosopher Empedocles refers to her as *Nestis*. Perhaps you've heard of her?'

Jonah stared. She met his gaze, but all he saw was his own reflection mirrored in her sunglasses.

'Why are you telling me this?'

'Aren't you looking for the maiden too?'

She unbuttoned the cardigan and peeled it away. Underneath she wore a black top with thin straps, revealing golden-brown arms. A lotus-flower tattoo blossomed on her shoulder.

Déjà vu hit Jonah all over again. Except this time it was real, a true memory. A beautiful woman sitting on a patio, fairy lights twinkling like stars. Jonah rushing by to get to the boat across the water. The tattoo. *Nestis*.

'You were at the hotel in Sibari the night Lily disappeared.'

She nodded.

'You called me in London. You brought me here.'

She nodded again. Jonah felt that he'd been straining on a rope which had suddenly come undone so quickly he'd lost all balance.

'Who are you?'

'My name is Ren.'

That didn't begin to answer his question. '*Who are you?*'

'Do you mean *Why?* Why was I in Sibari? Why am I here? Why did I call you?'

'Why. Who. Everything.'

'Because I can help you.'

He remembered what she'd said on the phone. *I know who took your wife.* A wild thought struck him.

'Did you take Lily?'

'No.'

He was flailing. He got up from the steps, walked a brief circle on the terrace, and stood facing her. She watched him patiently.

'Why did you bring me here? Why the charade about being a guide?'

'I wanted you to understand what this is.'

'What *what* is?'

'Eleusis.'

He gazed at the terrace, the dry grass growing through the stones, the signs and barriers for visitors who didn't come any more. 'What is it?'

'A place for revelations.'

'Revelations,' he repeated. 'Do you mean like *truth*?'

'Truth's a problematic concept.'

She had a way of avoiding questions that made him want to grab her shoulders and shake the answers out of her. But an equally powerful force prevented him. An aura surrounded her, something inviolable. He knew, without having to be warned, that if he touched her in anger, bad things would happen.

'Why were you in Sibari? Did you know what was going to happen to Lily?'

'Of course not.'

'Why, then?'

She took off the baseball cap and shook out her hair. It fell past her shoulders: long, dark and glossy. She lifted her sunglasses to hold back her hair, revealing a pair of almond-shaped eyes. For the first time, Jonah wondered how old she was. She didn't look much more than twenty, but her eyes were as old as time.

'Have you ever heard of Socratis Maroussis?'

'Is he related to Ari Maroussis, who owns the *Nestis*?'

'His father – and the richest man in Greece. Not that that means so much these days, but don't be fooled. The crash didn't touch him. His fortune's in London, his ships are registered in Panama, and his clients are mostly in China.'

'OK.'

266

'He's the money behind the Eikasia Foundation. He funded the Sybaris dig. He employs your friend Adam Shaw.'

'How do you know about Adam?'

'The old man's probably a psychopath, if you want to be clinical. You don't get that rich worrying about people's feelings. He's destroyed more people in the last fifty years than you've played gigs.'

She knows about the band, Jonah noted.

'Other people's souls have wells of compassion, sympathy, altruism. In Maroussis, they've been poisoned by greed and ambition. But he's old fashioned: he still lives by some sort of code. Ari, on the other hand, inherited all his father's vices, but none of the restraint. Have you read Plato?'

The question caught him off guard. 'Should I?'

'He captures Ari well.' She said it matter-of-factly, as if a Sunday magazine had assigned Plato to write a profile. '"He lives in clouds of incense and perfumes and garlands and wines, and all the pleasures of his dissolute life only make him mad for more. And if he finds anything good in himself, any merit or kindness or vestigial sense of shame, he wipes it out until his madness is perfected."'

On the warm stones in the noon sun, Jonah shivered. Ren's words framed a cave, a jagged gash in a barren hillside. The stench of rotting flesh wafted out; discarded bones lay at its mouth. From inside, he could hear the screams of unspeakable things. The thought that Lily was in there made him want to throw himself into the sea.

'You said you know what happened to Lily.' His mouth was so dry he thought he'd choke.

Her eyes shimmered like oil: sometimes green, sometimes blue, sometimes so dark they lost all colour. 'Socrates said, "All the truths in the universe have always existed in our soul." We just need a guide to bring it to the surface.'

Frustration erupted in anger. 'For God's sake, can we cut

through the mystique and the games? Just tell me what happened.'

Ren didn't move, didn't even change her expression. She was a rock; against it, all his emotion was just froth and spray. For a moment, her permanence whipped his fury to a new, savage peak. Then he realised it was pointless.

And as his anger slipped away, he understood she was right. He had all the pieces he needed. In the straight beam of Ren's stare, they all came together.

'It started with the gold tablet,' he said slowly.

'A long time before that. But keep going.'

'The others wanted to keep it secret – I don't know why. They sacked the conservator, but Lily wouldn't play. So they got rid of her.'

'How?'

The ancient philosopher Empedocles refers to her as Nestis. 'The boat. They took her away.' And he'd stood there on the dock, watching the wake churn the sea, knowing what was happening but not understanding it.

Without thinking, Jonah leaned down and broke off a stalk of grass. He wound it around his finger, watching the tip flood red as it went tight, then drain when he let go. His thoughts ebbed and flowed.

'What's so special about the tablet?'

Ren shook her head. Her hair swayed as though a breeze tickled it. 'Do you know about the Orphic religion?'

'I've heard of it.' Written on a card at the British Museum. *Gold tablet with an Orphic inscription and the pendant case that contained it.*

'It was a mystery cult, a lot like Eleusis. It was concerned with a journey to the underworld, too.'

Charis: *The tablets are directions to the underworld.*

'Like a lot of billionaires, Socratis Maroussis suffers from *ennui*. There's nothing he can't have, but he still wants more.

268

He's also an old man, and he's not well. He's obsessed with ancient philosophy, and the Orphic cult in particular. Everything the Eikasia Foundation does is to try and understand its secrets.'

'Wouldn't he be better spending his money on a cure for cancer, or whatever?'

'Do you remember the last line of the tablet? *No longer mortal – a god.* You don't need the tablet to *find* the underworld – we're all headed there anyway. The tablet is to help you escape. That's what the Orpheus cult promises. Immortality.'

The sun warmed his back. The ancient stone dug into his hands. A beetle crawled slowly up his trouser leg. He didn't notice any of it.

'But the tablet's not unique,' he said at last. 'There are others. I saw one in the British Museum.'

Ren watched him and didn't speak. After a moment, Jonah understood that she was waiting for him again.

'There must be something different about this one. Something the other tablets don't have.'

She nodded.

'But Charis translated it. She said it was the same as the others.'

'Do you trust her?'

'She's my friend. Lily's friend.'

Sandi: *Don't you get it? They were all in this together. All college friends, all in each other's pockets.*

'What about the others. Richard, Adam? Are they part of this?'

She shrugged. The lotus flower on her shoulder shivered.

'Adam Shaw is very close to Maroussis. It would be surprising if the foundation did something without Adam knowing about it.'

'Or Ari could have acted alone.' *Acted alone.* He felt as if he was covering someone else's song. The words belonged in a story, in a cop show or a crime novel. Not in his universe.

'Maybe.'

'And Richard?'

'Richard Andrews has lived his entire life by the rules that other people set for him.'

It was all too much for him to comprehend. He stared at Ren, wondering if he was about to wake up from a dream.

'What about you?'

'What about me?'

The question was so deep and so broad, he almost had to laugh at the futility. 'You – everything. You've brought me here, you've told me this amazing story.'

'You told the story.'

'You've told me I can't trust any of my friends. Why should I trust you?'

She sat perfectly still, her head cocked to one side as if listening to the wind in the dust. The silence lasted so long that Jonah wondered whether she'd say anything again, or if he'd offended her in some obscure but irrevocable way.

'Do you think she's . . . ?' He couldn't bring himself to say it.

'Does it matter?'

Anger flared inside him. 'Does anything else?'

'Weren't you paying attention to the story I told you? Wherever Lily's gone, you'll find her. The real question is: can you bring her back?'

Twenty-three

When your opponent has you 'stuck down the well', as the saying goes, trapped by a question with no good answer, what will you do?

Plato, *Theaetetus*

The boy was about ten and naked. His damp hair clung to his scalp, though the sun had already dried his skin. He had a length of rope tied around one ankle, and a small amphora of wine lay on the ground beside him on a wet patch of stone. Soldiers milled around.

Agathon lay next to the amphora, sprawled out like a drunk in a stage comedy. Except this was tragedy. His bare skin was raw and bloated. Even trying not to look, I could see clouds of bruises spread over him like inkdrops in water. One leg stuck out at a right-angle: it must have broken somewhere on his journey to the bottom of the well. His head lolled the other way, mercifully hiding his eyes.

'The boy found it when he dived for the wine,' Dion told me. 'We leave it down there in the summer to keep it cool.'

I nodded, as if what he was saying mattered.

'He must have fallen. Perhaps he'd been drinking and lost his way in the dark.'

'Perhaps.' The well was in the kitchen garden, a long way from guest quarters. Its wall was knee high, with a wooden cover leaning against it. And Agathon never drank.

271

'I'm sorry. I know he was your friend.'

This is what happens when tyrants rule. Men disappear in the dead of night; corpses turn up in unexpected places; friends fall down wells. Tracks go in to the cave, but none come out.

The moral is: *take warning from the misfortunes of others.*

Now I understood what Dion had been trying to tell me. I turned to face him.

'You knew.'

He was too young – and not quite innocent enough. The look he gave me aimed for bewildered ignorance, but didn't quite get there.

'He fell down the well.'

'All that time we were talking about virtue, when you were so interested in what I had to say. Is this what you were thinking about?'

I looked down at the corpse again. It was a horrible thing: broken, flabby, empty. The soul had left it; so had the intelligence and the beauty. Everything that was Agathon.

Even so, I couldn't bear to leave him there with the men who'd killed him. He looked so lonely, so lost. Without thinking, I knelt down and lifted him up. He was heavy – heavier than he'd ever been in life – but I wasn't going to drop him in front of Dionysius' mercenaries.

I carried him through a gate and all the way back to my room. I laid him on the bed and pulled a sheet over him. Then I went to find the man responsible.

Nobody tipped Socrates down a well. He died as he lived, publicly, surrounded by a crowd hanging on his every last word. I wasn't there: I was ill. That's what I tell people.

It's not exactly true, not the way they think. I wasn't lying in bed, or breathing in vapours at a steam pool. I was standing on the beach below Cape Sounion, holding a basket of rocks. I'd tied a small end of rope to the handle, and looped it around my wrist so I wouldn't let go when I passed out.

My heart was broken. I was so empty, I needed the stones to weigh me down. If Socrates could be murdered by a mob, then there was nothing left in the world for me. I refused to inhabit it.

I remember that morning as if it were the only day I ever lived. The smell in the air, the ripples of light on the sea bed. I remember how calm the sea was, and how pleasant it was to have it cooling my feet. A fisherman sat hunched up on a rock on the point, but he didn't seem to notice me.

My friends said Socrates drained the cup calmly and easily. He scolded the others for crying like women: he wanted to die in peace.

The numbness started in his feet and rose. He walked around to stir the poison, then lay down when his legs got too heavy. The executioner provided a running commentary, prodding his ankles, his calves, his thighs; asking him what he could feel. When it got to his belly, he lifted the veil briefly and said his last words.

At Sounion, a gull swooped down from the headland and plunged into the water with a shock of spray. I felt a pain in my chest and knew the poison had reached his heart. Socrates had left the world. I gripped the basket tighter and prepared to follow him. The laughing waves tugged at my legs like children, encouraging me on. It was a calm day, but the wind and the sea seemed to roar in my ears like a storm.

I couldn't do it. I slipped the rope loop off my wrist and let the basket sink. I waded ashore and collapsed on the beach, unable to move. The fisherman who found me thought I was dead.

Was that courage or cowardice? Socrates said that to be properly courageous, you have to understand the true nature

273

of the dangers. Of course I didn't understand death. But I didn't think that life would be this hard either.

That night, I had my drowning dream for the first time.

The guards didn't try to stop me. They could spot a man bent on his own destruction – why bother to get in the way? Some even opened doors for me, with mocking bows and grins that said they didn't expect to see me come back.

I came to the great bronze doors with the snarling lions and pushed them open. The windowless room looked no different in daylight, but the throne was empty.

I turned around. A knot of guards had bunched in the open doorway to watch. Their faces said getting out would be harder than coming in. I kept turning, like a hanged man twisting on the rope. Like a man spinning in the air as he drops down a well-shaft.

Dion pushed his way through the guards. He must have run: his hair was askew, his face red. He looked like a boy again.

'What are you doing here?'

'I wanted to see Agathon's murderer. I wanted to call him a killer to his face.'

'What would that achieve?'

'It's telling the truth.'

'And if he executed you for saying it – would that make it better?'

I dropped my head. 'It's my fault.'

The moral is: *take warning from the misfortunes of others.* I'd come to the tyrant's palace, and never noticed Agathon's footprints leading me in. I'd insulted Dionysius, and thought there was nothing he could do to touch me.

'Dionysius was sending me a message.'

'Then listen to it,' Dion implored me. 'You're a wise man. Don't step into the trap he's set for you.'

274

'Socrates could have run away. He was completely innocent. But he took his punishment bravely.'

'And did that make anything better?'

The question lingered in the open room, until heavy footsteps chased it away. The guards at the door separated, slipping into their lines as Dionysius came in.

He walked towards the throne as if I didn't exist. But I was in his way. For a moment, it seemed he'd walk straight into me, like a trireme on a ramming course. I felt an invisible tide tugging on my body, the Voice of Reason yelling that I should move. But the Voice of Will kept me rooted in place.

Dionysius stopped, an inch from my face. The same height, the same build, the same age – it was like looking at myself in a tarnished mirror.

'I hear your friend fell in a well.'

Off his shoulder, Dion shot me a fierce stare. I didn't trust myself to speak.

'He should have been more careful.' A smirk turned the corners of Dionysius' mouth. 'There are plenty of dark holes on Ortygia where visitors fall and are never seen again. We wouldn't even have heard the screams. It's tragic. A waste.'

He wanted to provoke me. The Voice of Desire said *let him* – that the only way I could honour Agathon was to sacrifice myself on his tomb. Against it, the Voice of Reason was a small bleating, too easy to ignore.

Socrates said that no one can do a wrong thing once he's been told the right thing. I think Socrates underestimated the human capacity for self-destruction. But this time, his argument held. I didn't react.

It disappointed Dionysius. 'You can mourn your friend.' All magnanimity. 'Tomorrow, I want you back tutoring my son. If not, your position is terminated.'

I nodded.

'You can go.'

For a moment, we faced each other down like wrestlers. Then the Voice of Reason took charge, and I stepped around him. His men let me go.

Halfway down the next corridor, I heard someone hurrying after me and Dion's voice calling my name. I ignored him until he was right behind me, then spun around, forcing him back.

'You told me Agathon left.'

'I saw him go.'

'Obviously, he came back. Did you know *that*?'

His eyes dropped. 'Yes.'

'When? Where had he been?'

'He wouldn't say. He came back a week ago, but he was different.'

A week ago. While I was chained up in Dionysius' quarry. 'How was he different?'

'As if he'd been in battle. Not wounded – but like sometimes you see men who've taken a blow to the head, or who've panicked under a charge. As if something's been shaken loose inside them.'

'And you don't know where he'd been?'

'Not too far away. He'd only been gone a few days.'

'Did he say anything else?'

'He said he had to look up a book by Empedocles in the library. Then he was going to catch a ship to Thurii. He had to meet a friend.'

That was me. 'Then what happened?'

'I didn't see him the next day. I hoped he'd caught his ship.'

I tried to snatch out facts from the chaos in my head. 'If he came back a week ago, and was only here a day, where's he been since?'

'Where we found him.'

That couldn't be right. 'Last night I stood in Dionysius' hall and called him a tyrant to his face. Today, this happens. Is that a coincidence?'

'Agathon was dead before you got here,' he insisted. 'Before Dionysius knew you existed.'

He could see I didn't believe him. 'Have you ever seen a drowned man pulled out of the water?' he said.

'Not until today.'

'I have. Look at the state of the body. Agathon was in that well for days.'

I didn't believe him – but why argue? 'Does it matter?'

'If you're blaming yourself.'

'He's still dead.' I'd come so far looking for my friend, and now his corpse lay under a sheet on my bed. That was the end.

'We should bury him,' said Dion pragmatically.

'I won't bury him on Ortygia.'

'You don't have a choice.'

I turned away. This time, Dion didn't try to stop me.

Twenty-four

Jonah – Athens

Jonah took the bus back to Athens, staring out the window at the miles of concrete and dust. The bus was slow; the sun was setting by the time he got back. A six-pack of Mythos beer had appeared in the fridge. Adam didn't drink; Jonah supposed it was for him. He certainly needed it. As he opened a can, he remembered what Ren had said.

Alcohol's a drug. They don't even have to inject it.

He left the beer and stood at the window, letting the orange light blast through him. He closed his eyes and pressed his face against the glass. The sun filled the horizon: he thought if he opened the window, he could step right into it.

The first time he'd spoken to Ren, he'd been on the phone and drunk; this time, face to face and stone-cold sober. Yet both times, afterwards, the memory faded like water drying in the sun. He struggled even to remember her face. If he had to pick her out of a photograph, he wasn't sure he'd manage, though in person, even in a crowd, he'd know she was there without a doubt.

He hunted for a piece of paper and a pen but couldn't find them. In the end, he had to use the back of his bus ticket and a pencil he found at the bottom of his bag. He scribbled down everything he could remember, worried that he'd wake up and find he'd lost it all.

Maroussis.

Ari.
Nestis.
Orpheus
Underworld

There wasn't much room on the back of the ticket – it was about the size of one of the gold leaves, in fact. He wondered again about the hand that had incised those tiny letters into the flimsy metal, cramming the words in with such desperate urgency. Hard-won revelations they couldn't afford to forget.

You don't need the tablet to find the underworld. The tablet is to help you escape.

He thought about what Ren had told him, but his brain couldn't process it. It sat in his mind, a giant rock that had fallen from the sky. Too big to understand: he could only chisel away at it with the one question that mattered.

How do I find her?

Ren had stood up when he asked that. 'Stay with Adam. If they think you know too much, they might act unpredictably.'

Before Jonah could ask what 'unpredictably' meant, she slid the sunglasses over her eyes and pulled on the baseball cap. After that, the memory flickered and went dim, like an old film reaching the end of the reel. The next thing he knew, he was at the back of the bus, grinding through the traffic into Athens. And now in Adam's flat, eyeballing the setting sun.

Staring at the sun hurt his head. He drank a glass of water and lay down on the bed. When he woke, it was dark outside and Adam had come back. He moved around the kitchen quietly, chopping vegetables and dropping them in a pan of boiling water.

'What did you do today?'

Adam spoke softly, almost tenderly. *Adam Shaw is very close to Maroussis.*

'I went to Elefsina.'

'Eleusis,' Adam corrected automatically, using the ancient name. Jonah remembered the attitude from the dig: permanent disappointment with the present. For Adam, like the archaeologists who'd displaced whole villages to get at the ruins underneath, modern Greece simply got in the way of its own history.

The knife cut a staccato rhythm as he chopped a carrot and threw it in the pan. 'What took you there?'

'Lily talked about it once,' Jonah lied.

'I hope you weren't expecting much.'

Jonah shrugged. 'It's not the Acropolis, I suppose.'

'It's everything that's wrong with this country.' Just for a moment, there was a glimpse of emotion in Adam's voice. 'It's a sacred place – a place of revelation. But they've made it a wasteland. The oil terminals, the factories, the refineries.

A place of revelation. Hadn't Ren used that phrase?

'It's jobs, I suppose.'

'Jobs.' The word came out sticky and filthy, like a seabird plucked from an oil slick. 'Everything that's ugly in the modern world gets justified by *jobs*. Find something beautiful, a mountain or a meadow or a stretch of coastline – promise jobs, and you can bury it under as much concrete and plastic as you like.'

'I didn't know you were an environmentalist.'

Water boiled over the side of the pan. Flames hissed up where it met the burning gas.

'I don't care about rare species of beetle, or protecting a tree that some woodpecker nests in. It's the human environment. The life around us that provides the context for our soul.'

He turned down the gas and put the lid back on the pan.

'Do you know why politicians love to talk about jobs?'

'So they can collect the taxes?'

'Because work is the best tool of oppression they've ever

invented. Better than drugs or religion or television or secret police. It keeps us plodding along, believing we're achieving something, when all we're doing is clock-punching our life away. And we don't even notice, because the first thing it does is stop us from thinking.'

'Pays the rent, though.'

Adam missed the humour.

'The Greeks prized the civilised man. The curriculum they invented included maths, writing, music, sport, astronomy. We pay lip service to the same virtues, but it's a lie we tell our children. Look at everyone we knew at Oxford. The best and the brightest. From four years old, they'd worked every hour they had to get into the best school, the best university, the best job. They'd done music, sport, drama, clubs – everything to be a well-rounded individual. And then they finished, and they found out that none of that mattered. All society wanted was for them to become drones, automata serving the machine. It's not living.'

Jonah didn't disagree. Adam served up the food and carried it to the glass table by the window. Without asking, he poured Jonah a beer from the open can and put it by his plate.

'All the great leaps in human thought came from men who had the time to think.' With Adam, a conversation never lapsed. He could pause it like a CD and resume hours, sometimes days, later. 'In ancient Greece, three or four generations of philosophers sketched out a whole scheme of reality that we're still coming to terms with. Why? Because they had the leisure to think, to drill down deep into the wells of existence and tap the truth. It didn't make them rich or powerful. Some of them became famous, and some were executed because people couldn't handle the truths they told. And none of them had jobs.'

Jonah sipped the beer. It tasted pretty good. 'Didn't they have slaves?'

'A well-ordered society is like the human body: each part is necessary, but it's only the brain that's capable of thought. Everything else serves that function.'

Adam's face was pitiless. For some reason, it reminded Jonah of the statue of the goddess in Charis' house. The deep levels of existence they inhabited were cold places. Kindness couldn't survive.

'We're different, you and I,' Adam said. 'We saw through the gilded lie. You followed your muse; I followed my . . . calling.'

'Is working for the foundation a calling?'

Adam nodded. A smug smile touched the sides of his mouth, and it made Jonah angry.

It would be surprising if the foundation did something without Adam knowing about it.

'Tell me about it.'

'I'm the program director.'

'What does that mean?'

'I exercise oversight on the projects we fund.'

'*Exercise oversight?*' Jonah swigged his beer. 'Is that your calling? To "exercise oversight"?'

Adam chewed a mouthful of vegetables to pulp.

'You can't look down at all the poor sods who have to work for a living, and then tell me that your life's purpose is to "exercise oversight". Even if the money's good.' He waved at the apartment. 'I suppose you do all right out of it.'

Adam peered at him, like a man listening very hard to a quiet television. 'You're angry. I know you're frustrated about Lily. If you want to take it out on me, I understand. But it won't make it better.'

'I just want to know what makes you so special.'

'Socrates said, "If I have any wisdom, it's knowing that I know nothing."'

'Socrates didn't get a double-first from Oxford.'

'That's a specious comparison.'

'Lily was working for your foundation when she disappeared. I want to know what it's about.'

'*It?*'

'Your office in London said you fund all sorts of research. Physics, geology, history, philosophy. How do you "exercise oversight" on all those different things?'

'I have a pretty good degree in physics and philosophy,' said Adam drily. 'The rest of it, we have expert panels who review the technical merits of the applications.'

'Which makes you . . . what? Some sort of rubber-stamp bureaucrat?'

Adam sat upright in his chair, so stiff he didn't touch the back.

'I wouldn't say that.'

'What is it then?'

'You want to know what the common thread is?'

'That's what I'm asking.'

'*Eikasia* is the Greek word for "illusion". Plato uses it to describe the most unreliable levels of the world, the shadows and reflections that our senses perceive. We're trying to get past all that to understand true *reality*. That's why we investigate it from every angle we can.'

'Isn't that kind of vague?'

'Only if you think vaguely.'

'Doesn't every scientist on the planet investigate reality?'

'Not really. They're looking at shadows. They can't accept how tenuous our sense-reality is.'

Jonah patted his hand on the table, rattling the plates. 'It seems pretty solid to me.'

'Not as much as you'd think.'

Jonah had no comeback. Two weeks ago, Lily had existed in his reality; now she didn't. The change had been as abrupt as a door slamming.

She still exists. It frightened him how quickly he'd begun to doubt it. *I just have to find her.*

They ate. Jonah took a sip of his beer and realised he'd finished it. He didn't ask for another.

'Will you be staying much longer?' Adam asked. 'I'm not sure there's anything more for you in Athens.'

Jonah thought for a second, wondering if he had anything to lose. Nothing he could think of.

'Your boss, Ari Maroussis. He was there when Lily disappeared. I'd like to speak to him.'

Adam put down his knife and fork and stared across the table, concentrating furiously.

'Where did you hear that?'

'At Eleusis. It's a place for revelations, apparently.'

Adam nodded, assimilating the information. 'You know who Ari is.' Not a question, just establishing some parameters.

'And his dad.'

'Ari has nothing to do with the foundation.'

'Then what was he doing at Sibari? *Exercising oversight?*'

'He was a tourist.'

Jonah let the silence play like an open note, sustained so long the audience almost forgot about it. So that the chord-change came as a shock.

'I don't believe you.'

Adam speared a piece of broccoli onto his fork and crunched down on it.

'I want to meet him,' Jonah insisted.

'I'll see what I can do.'

'What about his father?'

'He's an old man in poor health. He's confined to a villa on Spetses. He hardly ever leaves, and he's been forbidden from receiving visitors.'

'Perhaps if I call the police and tell them his son kidnapped my wife, he'll agree to see me.'

'Don't do that.'

'Because it would embarrass you?'

'Because you'll end up either in prison or deported. Maroussis is the richest man in Greece, and the police haven't been paid in five months.' No emotion, just more facts. Adam gathered the plates and carried them over to the sink. He pulled on a pair of yellow washing-up gloves, tight rubber snapped over his fingers. They were the brightest thing in the apartment, like the first daffodils after a hard winter.

'I'll make you an appointment with Ari.'

Twenty-five

*How can you prove whether right now we're sleeping, and all
our thoughts are a dream; or if we're awake, and talking to
one another in real life?*

Plato, *Theaetetus*

I knew Diotima was there before I opened my eyes. I could
smell ripe figs blowing through the air in the room, drowning
the smell of the corpse.

She stood in front of me wearing a long white dress. It
clung to her body so tightly that she seemed to be naked,
except for a piece of ivy around her middle like a belt.

She reached down and pulled me to my feet. Even on that
warm night, her hand was cool to the touch. She looked at
the bed. Her marble face trembled.

'We have to move him. There isn't much time.'

'What about the guards?' I'd lain awake for hours on the
stone floor, listening to the march of their footsteps, regular
as a heartbeat, and the shouts as they changed watch every
hour. The last change only seemed five minutes ago.

'Help me,' she said.

I didn't ask how she'd got there. In the dream, it didn't
matter. I took Agathon's shoulders, Diotima his feet. He felt
much lighter than when I'd carried him back from the well.

'Where are we taking him?'

'To rest.'

A handcart was waiting in the courtyard outside. A tall, bare-chested slave helped us lay Agathon down in the back, then took the handles. He moved quickly, a graceful half-run that made me think of a centaur. Diotima and I followed.

'What about the guards? What about the gates?'

She moved like moonlight, flitting across the courtyards and through the porches unchallenged. Past the temples, past the lions and the arsenals where Dionysius' power slept. The cart's wheels had cloth tied over their rims and didn't make a sound.

We reached the first gate. The massive doors seemed to rise all the way to the stars, but Diotima whispered something to the guards and they pushed back the bolts without question. The bronze pegs spun, the doors swung open and a gaping chasm opened in front of us.

Three times that happened; then we were off the island and in the town. A lonely dog bounded across the road, perhaps chasing a rat. An owl hooted from the plane trees in the agora. Apart from that, the streets were empty.

We carried on through the vast and dark unknown. The axle squeaked, the wheels grumbled softly. Syracuse passed behind us. The starlit landscape opened around me: looming shadows suggested hills, fields, trees. A primitive world.

Then fire came into it. I saw it from some way off, like a candle through an open door. As we approached, it separated into a constellation of tiny lights. A group of people stood in a circle inside a poplar grove. They wore long white robes, and veils over their faces. Each of them cupped a lamp in his hands, holding it chest high like a glowing heart. They made me think of the *Odyssey*, of Homer's 'thin, airy shoals of visionary ghosts'. But they didn't frighten me. They seemed reverent, not bloodthirsty; at peace with the world, not jealous of it.

Agathon's cart stopped in the centre of the circle. The

slave had vanished. I stepped into a gap in the circle and realised I'd closed it. Hands put a cloak over my shoulders and a lamp in my palm, though they left my face uncovered.

Diotima raised her arms and chanted an incantation to the goddess. Someone had put a jewelled wreath on her head, golden leaves bearing fruits of garnets and pearls.

> *Maiden who anchors the eternal world in our own,*
> *Immortal, Blessed, crowned with every grace,*
> *Deep breasted Earth, sweet plains and fields, fragrant grasses*
> *in the nurturing rains,*
> *Around you fly the beauteous stars, eternal and divine,*
> *Come, Blessed Goddess, and hear the prayers of Your children.*

A piece of gold flickered in her hands. She reached down and laid it on Agathon's tongue. It caught light from the lamps, glowing in his mouth like the last ember of life. I thought of the broken tomb at Taras, and the gold tablet he'd stolen. Now the tomb had claimed him back.

Had he found what he was looking for at last?

> *Only those who've paid Persephone the price*
> *For the pain, for the grief, of long ago –*
> *Theirs are the souls that she sends,*
> *When the ninth year comes,*
> *Back to the sun-lit world above.*
> *And from those souls, proud-hearted kings will rise,*
> *And the swift and the strong, the wisest of the wise.*
> *And people, for the rest of time,*
> *Will hail them as heroes, to be held in awe.*

She put a myrtle crown on his head. Six men came through the circle, carrying a clay coffin. They put it down next to the cart and lifted the body into the coffin. I stepped forward to help, but Diotima gave me a glance that said *stay where you are*. A soft wind blew through the trees.

When Agathon was in the casket, a girl brought a wide *krater* that seemed to be filled with ashes. Diotima took a handful and scattered them over the coffin. As they fluttered down, I saw they were leaves, olive and poplar, mixed with barley grains that rattled on the coffin floor.

The six men closed the coffin and lifted it onto their shoulders. The circle broke open to let them through, then flowed in behind the coffin. The procession moved off, until I was left alone with Diotima.

'Should I follow?'

'Not yet.'

She held my hand. We stood side by side in the centre of where the circle had been and watched the lamps recede. They faded, then vanished suddenly, as if some deeper hole in the darkness had swallowed them.

All I remember of the journey back is rushing wind and the sound of doors slamming. Then I was in my room and Diotima was with me, standing close.

'Do you understand what you saw tonight? Where you went?'

I didn't understand a thing. 'The thing you put in his mouth. Was that the gold tablet?'

'He needs it for his journey.'

'But Dionysius took it. Did you—?'

'There are others.'

The full moon shone over the sea and through the open window, trapping us both in its beam. She examined me like a tailor measuring out cloth for cutting.

'You found Agathon,' she said.

'Yes.'

'Now what are you looking for?'

'I don't know.'

Perhaps that was the wrong thing to say. She stepped back into the shadows, almost invisible. Her hands flashed in the moonlight as they moved to her throat; I heard something flutter to the floor. Had she vanished?

She moved forward again into the shaft of moonlight. She was naked. I thought I'd seen everything at Dimos' house, but now I realised how much her transparent dress had managed to conceal. It had blurred the lines, softening reality like smoke. Now every inch of her body was stark and clear. If you could walk up to a statue of the goddess and rip off her Olympian robes, this is what you might see. Though you wouldn't live to tell of it.

She untied my belt. I lifted my tunic over my head and threw it away. She put her hands on my shoulders and pressed me down onto my knees. I kissed her stomach, her hips, the inside of her thighs. She twined her fingers in my hair, moving me where she wanted me, and I obeyed.

She slid down onto her knees so that she straddled me. With one hand, she fed her breast into my mouth. I bit down and she gasped. She pushed me back onto the floor. Staring up at her in the moonlight, her body was flawless, the most beautiful thing I've ever seen.

I slid into her. She moved against me, and the whole earth shifted. The world peeled away and I stood on a sea-less beach of endless sand, under a cloudless sky. I looked for shade but there was none, not even my own shadow. The sky was perfect blue, but I couldn't see the sun. Only light.

Diotima leaned back, her arms on the floor. She hooked her knees around me and pulled, squeezing herself into me and rocking back. Sweat ran down my chest. Lines of light raced through me. I gazed down at her: head tipped back, teeth bared, hair flowing down her back, eyes closed in a trance.

She laid me back onto the floor. She leaned forward, letting her nipples brush my chest, dappling my face with kisses. Dazzling colours swam through my head as if she'd painted them straight onto my eyes. My skin stretched so tight I became an instrument, resonating like a lyre. Every sound in the world rang through me, the mad mountain music that the bacchantes dance to. I writhed and twisted, pinned between her thighs; I kicked my feet against the stone floor. I raked my nails down her sides until I drew blood and still she wouldn't let me go. She smiled at me, and it was as if I suddenly understood everything I'd ever wanted to know.

My soul swelled inside me until my body couldn't contain it. I emptied myself into her, shuddering, and the convulsions split me open like a clay mould struck by a hammer. The halves of my body fell apart. Nestled inside, released, I saw a figure like a sleeping child, burning with the brilliant white light of pure gold. Beauty Itself.

Diotima rocked forward with a moan that seemed to come from the depths of the earth. She grabbed my hair and pulled me up and buried my face in her breasts. I wrapped my arms around her back and clung on. My body was an empty husk. She cradled my head against her and I was lost in darkness. Her breast pressed into my mouth and I tasted the sticky, milky flavour of figs on my tongue.

By my ear, I heard a sigh that sounded almost like laughter.

Twenty-six

Jonah – Athens

He was standing in a wasteland, a red desert filled with scrap metal and rubbish. Tottering towers of rusted cars rose impossibly high around him, further than he could see, scraping the clouds. A light, powdery ash rained down on him.

Engines screamed from above. A burning plane crashed out of the sky, smoke billowing behind it. Lily was on board – he had to stop it before it hit the ground.

He started to climb one of the car towers, but it swayed so much he couldn't go fast enough. And the plane kept falling: down, down, down, spinning like a sycamore seed in a high wind . . .

When he opened his eyes, the sun was up and Adam was gone. A white business card lay on the granite counter with a note scrawled on the back.

Come to the office at two. Ari will see you.

The address was on the front of the card, underneath the Eikasia Foundation logo and Adam's name. *Program Director.*

Under the title, Adam had written, 'I exercise oversight.' It was the first joke Jonah could remember him making.

Did you oversee Lily being kidnapped? It was a crazy thought. He said it out loud to see if it made any more sense. All he could think of was the hospital in Aegion, Lily's face white

292

as death, Adam sitting beside her bed. He saved her life. He loved her.

Ten years ago.

He tried to think about Ren, though it was like trying to describe music you'd never heard. He thought of the story she'd told him, how Zeus had betrayed his own daughter (who was also his niece) to his brother Hades.

It's all a bit incestuous.

The address on the card was on another long street that spilled out towards a big square, not far from the flat. Even before he got there, Jonah could tell something wasn't right. There was smoke in the air, black and chemical, a haze that made the sun glow red and his nose run. The Eikasia Foundation office windows were shuttered up to the third floor; so was every other building around it. The entire street, a major boulevard that cut a straight line through a good mile of Athens, was empty. Not empty as in 'quiet', empty as in 'deserted'. In the distance, he heard a roar like a wall of water gathering pace down a mountain.

What's that sound? In his head, he heard Buffalo Springfield warning him away, two haunting notes cycling ominously back and forth. He buzzed the entryphone, but no one answered. He rattled the door. In desperation, he picked up an empty Coke can from a pile of uncollected rubbish on the kerb and threw it against the shutters. It bounced off with a hollow clang, but no one answered.

He got out his phone – no missed calls, no messages – and rang Adam.

'Where are you?' said Adam.

'I'm at your office. Where's Ari Maroussis?'

'Are you joking? If he went down there today, the mob would string him up from the nearest lamppost.'

293

'*The mob?*'

'The demonstration.' A click of the tongue as something fell into place. 'Didn't you get my message? You need to get out of there now. It's going to be ugly.'

The wave that had been building out of sight suddenly came around the corner. A wall of people, with a red banner stretched in front of them like the scoop of a bulldozer. More banners waved overhead, hand-painted with angry slogans, hammers and sickles, clenched fists.

Jonah shoved the phone in his pocket. Individually, you could have picked anyone out of the crowd and seen nothing threatening at all. Many looked like pensioners out for a Sunday stroll: men with neat white moustaches and tweed suits; widows wearing black dresses and headscarves. They didn't look like a revolution.

But Jonah had seen crowd trouble once before, at a big festival in the Netherlands that had got out of hand. He knew what thousands of people moving in one direction did if someone got in their way. They filled the street like water in a pipe. No way for Jonah to squeeze past, not even a doorway in the shuttered shops to shelter in. All he could do was run.

A block away, the street opened into a wide square. It looked like a battlefield. Rubble lay scattered across the broken pavement like blast debris, and the plane trees that grew over it cast no shade because their leaves and branches had burned away. Further up, a crowd massed in front of the Parliament building: more shouts, more banners, while megaphones distorted and amplified the anger. A line of white-helmeted policemen stared them down from the steps, shields locked in a Perspex wall.

Jonah felt giddy, as if he were standing on the rim of a vast bowl. Warm petrol fumes blew over him. If anyone lit a match . . .

The marchers were coming up behind him. He turned left,

looking for a way out, and for a moment he thought he'd lost his bearings completely. There were the marchers again, a wall across the street pushing forward into the square. He rubbed his eyes and pain flared as if he'd been stung. He turned again. The marchers were still coming. Turned again. There they were. Through the tears, a part of him noticed that these protesters had a yellow banner. Wasn't the other one red?

He had no time to think. His eyes itched like mad, but he knew if he touched them it would be ten times worse. Smoke and tears cut off the world. If he stayed where he was, he'd be crushed.

On the side of a building, he noticed a street sign, printed in Greek and English for the benefit of tourists. Syntagma Square.

Stay away from the Parliament building in Syntagma Square, Adam had told him. But he'd sent him there anyway – and now he didn't have a choice.

Five lanes of road ringed the square, but the only evidence of cars was burning tyres. Jonah ran across, trying not to trip on the stone blocks littering the way, and found himself at the foot of a tree beside an empty fountain. Perhaps it had boiled dry. Behind him, the red banners and the yellow banners poured in to add their weight to the crowd in front of the Parliament. The roar doubled, tripled. More megaphones joined in, cranking up the volume in blaring competition.

But some sounds cut through everything – like the sound of breaking glass. Jonah heard it and followed the sound. A hundred feet away, a cloud of flame roared up from a broken bottle on the ground, as though a gas vent had opened in the earth.

Molotov cocktail, his brain said. But it couldn't pass the information to his legs. All he could do was watch as a gaggle of young men in jeans, balaclavas and gas masks ran across the square to join the crowd. *Who brings their own gas mask to a demonstration?* Some of the protestors tried to push them away, but the men in hoods forced themselves through to the front. Sparks flared; burning bottles flew through the air and smashed on the Parliament steps. More flames. From his right, Jonah heard a flat pop, like a cork coming out of a wine bottle.

Everything changed. The police line came to life and advanced down the steps towards the protestors. Batons swung; clouds of yellow smoke blossomed in mid-air as the tear gas fell. The shouts turned to screams, though one or two of the megaphones kept going, shouting resistance even as the crowd disintegrated. In an instant, the wall of people shattered into thousands of panicked fragments.

Perhaps this was how drowning felt – except that in the sea, the currents were vast and constant. Here, he was part of the chaos: one among thousands going wherever terror took them.

Another word swam from his memory: *kettling*. The currents ripping him weren't random. Somewhere, some intelligence was closing down possibilities, directing the crowd with sticks and rubber bullets. Herding them. Through the smoke ahead, he saw the dark mouth of a Metro entrance leading underground. Hundreds of protesters jammed the stairs, so thick they were no longer people, just bodies and limbs and heads. He wondered if they could even breathe. Some tried to get away but the police beat them back, funnelling them into the hole like rabbits in a sack. More police lined the railings around the steps, watching the chaos. Their gas masks gave them bulging eyes and strange rubbery snouts, as if demons from the underworld had come up to enjoy the sport.

Terror gripped him. He knew, with irrational but absolute certainty, that if he went down that hole he'd never come up. A white-helmeted policeman leaned over the rail, aimed his gun down and fired a gas grenade straight into the hole. Smoke fumed out; the crowd convulsed, but the pressure was too great. They couldn't go anywhere but down.

He tried to turn. He knew he was going the right way when every other face was against him. Bloodied, weeping, contorted faces: the legions of the dead pouring past. He lashed out, flailing his arms like a swimmer, but for every step forward the crowd pushed him back two.

The tear gas was so thick he could hardly breathe. His throat had closed up, his nose ran, his eyes burned. He forced them open to see where he was going: if he closed them, even for a second, he'd be sucked into the hole. His lungs felt as if they'd burst. He ripped off his T-shirt and held it over his face like he'd seen other people do.

A gap opened in the crowd where someone had fallen. A woman, long brown hair trailing down her back. She tried to push herself up, but the crowd knocked her down again. If he was quick, he might get over her and build up some momentum against the crowd.

The woman had hunched into a foetal ball on the ground. Through the smoke, he saw a strand of hair curled across her cheek, and for a moment he wasn't looking at a stranger, but at Lily, curled up in bed.

He remembered himself. He stepped over, planting his feet either side of the woman and shielding her with his body. The crowds beat against him; for a second, he thought he'd fall and die with her. But he held. The herd felt the obstruction and shifted its flow, just a fraction, following the course of least resistance. Jonah hauled the woman to her feet. She looked dazed. She started to drift away, towards the mouth of the cave, but Jonah grabbed her arm and pulled her after him. One hand holding her, one hand pressing his T-shirt over his nose and mouth, he shouldered his way through the crowd. The bodies thinned out, the way got easier. Even the air seemed clearer, though the chemicals still burned his face.

But escape wasn't that easy. After the crowd came the police, snapping at their heels with batons and shields, driving them on like demons. One saw Jonah coming and stepped back, inviting him through. Half blind, Jonah didn't have time to think. The hit came as a complete surprise. The demon swung his stick and connected with Jonah's hip: pain exploded inside him. He screamed and let go the woman's arm; he tried to breathe, but the scream had filled his mouth with gas and nothing would come in.

He fell to his knees. A steel-capped boot prodded his side. Straining his eyes open, he saw the demon raise his stick over his head. He tried to protect himself, but his body wouldn't respond.

A firebolt sailed through the air and hit the policeman in the face. Glass shattered; suddenly, his head burst into flames.

The scream of a man strapped into a burning rubber mask isn't something you ever forget. Jonah watched him reel away, clawing at the mask. The riot helmet kept it on. Four youths in black T-shirts and gas masks raced up to him, knocked him to the ground and started kicking him. Other police waded in to help their colleague, who vanished in a cloud of fists and batons and gas.

Jonah ran.

Twenty-seven

*No one would argue that the only thing lovers want from each
other is sex. Clearly, there's something else which the lover's
soul needs but can't put into words, dancing around it in obscure
riddles.*

Plato, *Symposium*

I lay in my bed. Every muscle ached as if I'd fought a wrestling match. I had bruises on my shoulders, and swelling at
the back of my head where I must have banged it on the
floor. I reached to check for blood.

The moment I touched myself, the dream rushed back at
me. Diotima. Her body wrapped around me and mine in
hers. I blushed. For the first time in ten years, I couldn't help
a smile spreading across my face.

Then I remembered the rest of the dream. I looked around,
though I should have realised much sooner. I was in the bed
where Agathon had lain – and I was alone. The body had
vanished.

I threw back the cover and jumped out of bed. I was naked.
I rubbed my finger and thumb together and smelled figs. In
the corner, my belt and balled-up tunic lay where I'd thrown
them.

It couldn't have been a dream. But it couldn't have been
real. I remembered Diotima appearing suddenly in my room,
the high gates flying open and the slave pulling the cart. In

reality, we'd never have got out of Ortygia, let alone back in.

So where did Agathon go? And why did my bruised skin glow all over, as if I'd gone ten rounds in the ring and won them all?

The creak of the door made me jump. Whatever had happened in the night had cleaned me out. My ears heard, my eyes saw, my skin touched with freshly minted senses. The world felt brighter, louder, more real. As if I'd just arrived.

Euphemus peered around the door. As new as I felt, he looked older: his skin had sagged, his eyes had receded, as if some spirit within had punctured and deflated. Even his silver mane of hair seemed flat. He started to say something, then broke off as he saw the empty bed.

'What happened to Agathon?'

I wish I knew. 'I buried him.'

Euphemus glanced at the open window, calculating whether you could force a body through. 'How are you feeling?'

I couldn't possibly explain. 'I'm fine.'

He didn't believe me. 'What they did to Agathon—'

'I'm fine,' I repeated, so loudly that Euphemus backed away.

'Dionysius sent me to tell you that it's past time for your lesson with his son. Otherwise . . . '

I didn't care about Dionysius or his feeble son. I didn't even care about Agathon. All I could think of was Diotima. My whole soul pulsed like a throbbing artery.

Euphemus misconstrued my reluctance. 'I know you're upset, but . . . '

Upset?

' . . . if you want to stay alive, you'd better teach that boy some Homer until the tyrant gets bored and lets you go.'

Of course I wanted to stay alive. How else could I dream of seeing Diotima again?

★ ★ ★

Euphemus escorted me through the palace. I resented him for it – I wanted to be left alone to nurse my feelings.

'It must be nice, being so at home in the tyrant's castle,' I told him, purely for the sake of being rude.

I'd expected he'd ignore me. Instead, he dropped level with me and leaned over close to my ear. 'I'm trying to help you,' he hissed. 'Mouthing off to tyrants, grandstanding for your own satisfaction: it may make you feel better than the rest of us. But it doesn't make anything better in the real world. If you really want to change something, to avenge Agathon . . .' He broke off as a knot of officials came around the corner. 'I'll talk to you later.'

My pupil was waiting in the library. He looked disappointed to see me – and, presumably, to be denied the entertainment of watching me led back to the quarry in chains. I grabbed the first thing I could find – I think it was Aeschylus' *Niobe* – and told him to read it, then asked the librarian to bring me a copy of Empedocles' *On Nature*. He looked doubtful – but tyrants' servants aren't used to disobeying. I stood at a lectern by the window, scrolling through, pretending I couldn't see Dionysius doodling a trireme in the margin of his text.

If you've never read Empedocles, he can be hard going. He lived on Sicily about fifty years ago, one generation after Parmenides and two after Pythagoras. Like Parmenides, he wrote his treatise in mock-Homeric poetry, which might make it more artful but does nothing for the clarity of his ideas. Not that they're all that clear to begin with.

Several passages had been marked in ink.

You will bring drought from a storm,
And then from drought, streams pouring out of the heavens,
And you will lead forth from Hades the spirit of a dead man.

And this:

Behold the sun, warm and bright on every side,
And whatever is immortal is bathed in its radiance.

And, near the end, one more:

Far from the Blest, this is the path I tread:
Exiled from heaven, a wanderer.

Next to it, someone had scrawled two words in the margin.
Stay away.

I stared. It looked like Agathon's writing, though I couldn't
be certain. Why did he come back here, risking his life? What
did he think he'd find?

Or did he come to deliver a warning?

'How's the pupil this morning?'

The voice made me jump. I turned around guiltily, taking
my hand off the scroll so that it rolled up with a snap. Dion
had come in and was peering over the boy's shoulder.

'Making progress.' From the corner of my eye I could see
he'd progressed to carving an obscenity into the bookshelf
with his penknife. 'He's working on Aeschylus.'

'Yes?'

'"The gods sow flaws in a great man, when they want to
destroy his house",' the boy recited, with an innocent smile for
his uncle and a spiteful look at me when Dion wasn't watching.

I grimaced, wishing I'd chosen something more innocuous.
I hadn't expected the boy to actually read it.

'And you?' Dion turned his head to read the ribbon on
the end of the scroll-staff. 'Empedocles.'

'I thought I should read something Sicilian.'

'You know Empedocles killed himself in the volcano?' Dion
said.

I'd heard the story – but I didn't interrupt. I sensed Dion had come to make peace, after yesterday. And I found I didn't want to be angry with him any more.

'He told his followers he'd become a god, then marched up Etna and threw himself into the crater.'

The crater. I thought of the krater that Diotima had held in my dream the night before, scattering black leaves and grain from its bowl. The krater we'd sipped at Dimos' symposium while a bunch of heartless men argued about love. Then the book that Agathon had tried to buy – *The Krater.* What was mixed in that *Krater?*'

Dion was waiting for me to say something.

'I've never seen a volcano close up. I was wondering how much its crater looks like the cup, in reality.'

He smiled. 'I'll take you up some time so you can see for yourself.'

'Is it safe?'

'As long as you don't plan on trying to immortalise yourself. You know, all they found of Empedocles was one bronze sandal. I've seen the place,' he added, proud to have some first-hand experience to salt the story. 'It's not as far up the mountain as you'd think.'

'I heard the mountain belched out the sandal because it couldn't digest it.'

His face fell. 'You knew the story.'

'Only parts,' I assured him. 'And I'd love to see where it actually happened, if your brother ever lets me out of his castle.'

'But that's what I came to tell you. He's given me permission to take you out this afternoon.'

'To Etna?'

'On a boat trip.'

We went down by a water gate and rowed across the south harbour, threading our way between the merchantmen and freighters at anchor. Painted eyes peered over the ropes that bound the hulls tight, like monstrous fish that had come up from the depths. Conversations drifted down to us from the decks, sailors joking and singing and telling stories while they waited for the wind. Some of the voices sounded Athenian. For the first time in my life, I missed home.

'I'm surprised Dionysius trusted me outside the palace,' I said, trailing my hand in the water.

Dion smiled. 'I had to guarantee you'll come back.'

I took my hand out of the water and wiped it on the hem of my tunic. 'That was kind.'

'It wasn't my idea.'

'His?' But that didn't make sense. 'Whose?'

'You'll see.'

We left the harbour and rowed into the mouth of the river that feeds it. Soon warehouses gave way to farms, then fields to forest. I leaned back in the boat, breathing in the trees and the filthy stink that came off the slow-moving water. I suppose I was glad to be out of the palace, but that day, I hardly noticed. Every silence, every pause, all I could think about was Diotima. Sunlight burned through the overhanging leaves and soaked my clothes with sweat. Wild figs on the riverbank teased me with the scent of memory.

The boat turned towards the shore. I thought we would crash, but at the last moment I saw a narrow channel almost covered by the undergrowth. I pressed myself flat in the bottom of the boat as willow branches brushed and scratched me. Then we were clear. I looked up.

The first thing I noticed was the colour. The muddy water had turned a deep, majestic blue: a small lake hemmed in on every side by greenery. It was a beautiful, restful place. Poplars, wild figs and vines tangled the banks. Above them spread a broad and lofty plane tree, and a high chaste tree cast in full blossom. Its purple blooms burst into the sky like splattered paint and filled the air with its fragrance. A mossy altar stood at its foot, knocked crooked by the roots. From the statues and votive offerings around it, I gathered this lake was sacred to some nymph or goddess. Even without the altar, I think I'd have known.

At the water's edge, clusters of plants I'd never seen before brushed the water with their spindly fronds. As we rowed closer, I saw they had strange, triangular stems, firm and waxy to the touch. I squeezed one between finger and thumb.

'Gently,' Dion said. 'Someday that might make you immortal.'

He let me ponder his riddle, then answered it for me. 'It's a papyrus.'

I squeezed it again, enchanted by the touch. I've spent half my life with papyrus, but only ever in the dry, processed sheets you get from the booksellers. It doesn't grow in Greece. It was so lushly alive I almost felt guilty for all the pages I'd covered with my scribblings.

The boat nosed up to the shore and ran gently aground. Dion stayed in his seat.

'This is where you get out.'

I stared at the wilderness. 'Are you abandoning me?'

'I'll wait for you on the river.'

'And if I don't come back?'

He smiled – though there was a strain behind his eyes.

'Make sure you do.'

I splashed through the shallows and clambered onto the muddy bank. Dion rowed away until the boat vanished through the hidden passage in the reeds. I was alone with the birds, and the insects darting across the blue pond. The water freshened the air; a summery hum answered the cicadas' chorus. I found a grassy bank, just right for resting my head, and lay down.

She moved so quietly that I didn't hear her come. Even

when I caught her scent, I thought it must be one of the wild figs dropping its fruit. It was only when she stepped on a reed behind me, snapping it, that I rolled over and saw her shaded against the plane tree.

Joy flooded into me through openings I thought had hardened shut. Visions of the night before overwhelmed me, and suddenly I was certain they were memories, not dreams. I leaped to my feet, pulled her against me and kissed her hard.

She pulled away. 'Not now.'

I felt like Icarus, stripped of his wings and dropping back to earth. I sat down hard on the grass. Diotima lay beside me and put her head in my lap. *This intimacy*, she seemed to be saying, *but no more*.

'Did you ask Dion to do this?'

'He's a sweet boy.' She turned her face into the sun and closed her eyes, while I seethed in silence. It was easy to imagine her with Dion – two beautiful bodies, his young curiosity insatiable for her mystery.

'Why did you bring me here?'

'I wanted to see you.'

I reached down and risked stroking her cheek. She turned her head, nuzzling my fingers.

'Did Dion tell you where we are?' she asked.

I shook my head, enjoying the touch of her lips against my hand.

'This is where Hades snatched Persephone.'

I stared at the deep blue water. It looked too beautiful for such a violent crime.

'A friend was with her, the nymph Cyane. When Cyane tried to grab hold of Persephone, to save her, Hades turned her into this spring.'

The lake was clear and beautifully pure, just the place for girls to play. I tried to imagine the King of the Underworld creeping through the thicket, his red eyes smouldering with desire. Snatching the maiden while she braided flowers into a crown. The screams of frightened girls, then nothing except water bubbling out of the ground.

'What happened last night?' I asked.

She opened her eyes. 'Was it that forgettable?'

I blushed. 'Before that.'

'We sent Agathon's soul on a journey.'

'Was it real?'

'His soul?'

'What I saw.'

She smiled her sphinx-smile. 'Did it seem real?'

I sat up. The clear lake made a perfect reflection of the sky, but everything around it was thorns, knots and dark places.

'How did you get to Sicily the same day we found Agathon?' I said.

'I've been here a few days. Just after you left Thurii, I had a dream. Agathon was in trouble: he told me to come to Syracuse. So I did.'

'Do you always act on your dreams like that?'

'I was right.'

I couldn't deny that. 'And the palace? How did you get in and out?'

'The guards know me.'

I didn't believe her. I understood that she was trying to help me, offering explanations I could accept. *This is not important,* her eyes said. But the Voice of Reason wouldn't let go.

'Are you a nymph?'

'I'm a woman. As you well know.'

I played with one of the papyrus fronds, wrapping it around my finger. 'Am I mad?'

'Does it matter? Sometimes madness is a blessing, a divine gift. Haven't you ever been in love?'

I took a leap. 'I am now.'

Her deep eyes watched me solemnly, but her mouth twitched at the corners. Was she trying to stifle a laugh?

'How does it feel?'

'Agony.'

She rolled off me and lay on her back on the grass. 'When we were created, our souls had wings and we soared with the gods in the aether. But when we came down to earth, the wings withered and fell away like leaves in autumn. The stumps scabbed over; hard scars formed, and the veins that had supplied them went cold. When we fall in love, the process reverses. Love warms our souls like spring sunshine. The flesh softens, the scabs melt and blood begins to flow. The feather-roots put out their shoots, and the wings start to grow again.'

'It sounds painful.'

'It is,' she agreed. 'The wings have to push through openings that have been closed for a long time, and it hurts. You feel like a child cutting her teeth, aching and itching and tingling all over. But when you're away from your lover, it hurts even more. The pores dry up again, and the sprouting feathers are trapped halfway. The pain drives you wild. When you see your lover again, your soul opens up and it's the sweetest release, even though the quills still hurt. And when you're apart, you can hardly bear it. It drives you mad.'

I thought about that, even as the spikes tore open the holes in my soul.

'Did you love Agathon?'

Was I so petty I could envy a dead man – my friend? Was the madness so irredeemable? Or was I really asking: *Do you love me?*

She nodded. No apology, no embarrassment. The knots I'd tied inside me tightened, and suddenly I didn't know what she meant. It was ridiculous to think that Diotima, as cool and mysterious as the spring, could feel the hot pains ripping me apart. I flushed, ashamed and confused.

'Did he love you?'

A look that made me freeze. 'Agathon understood that love is just a way to open up the soul. Love lets the wings grow, but Agathon wanted to fly.'

'Is that why he died?'

No answer. She stared into the water as if waiting for something to sink.

'Agathon was my best friend. If you know why he died . . .'

Instead of answering, she pointed to the pool, the blue water so lucid and calm. 'Why do you suppose Hades turned Cyane into a spring? She couldn't have stopped him taking Persephone – he was a god, after all, and she was just a nymph.'

'I don't know.' I didn't care.

'He was worried she might tell someone. He didn't want anyone to follow him down.'

Deep in the shade of the chaste tree, a nightingale began to sing. I listened for a moment, following the flow of the song up and down its register.

'Agathon found something out,' I tried. 'Something he was killed for.'

I took her silence for consent.

'What was it?' Still silence. I thought back through my own long journey across Italy, from the day the sea spat me out at Taras. 'Agathon was looking for something. The tablet was part of it. The book in Locris was too, and Empedocles, and the Pythagoreans. And so were you. Then Dionysius got involved.'

I'd followed his path like a dog sniffing through the forest – and, at the end of it, all I'd found was a corpse. Suddenly, I hated Agathon for dragging me here.

'What was Agathon trying to find?'

'The same as you.'

'I was looking for him.'

'Is that all?'

'Until I found you.'

Diotima frowned; she didn't like the compliment. 'What does love crave more than anything?'

I remembered her at Dimos' party, almost naked in the middle of those hungry men. The memory answered the question. 'Beauty.'

'And?'

'Immortality.'

'Love draws you to Beauty. Beauty leads you to Truth. And Truth is immortal,' she said. I wasn't really listening. Jealousy had planted a thought that set my mind on fire. I tried to resist, then blurted out, 'Are you pregnant?'

She gave me a look that would have made a gorgon think twice. 'No.'

I reached out and felt the hard, triangular stalk of the papyrus plant. I remembered Dion's riddle. *Some day this could make you immortal.* I rubbed it between my fingers and imagined the farmer coming to harvest it, the curved blade peeling away the fibres and laying them down, pressing and drying the woven page. Whose book would be written on the plant I was holding? Whose hands would hold it after mine?

'Was Agathon writing something?'

'No.'

'What, then?'

I wasn't sure she'd answer me. A slow knife turned inside me as I wondered if she'd lost patience with my fumbling answers. When she spoke, I still couldn't tell.

'What do you believe about the soul?'

Talking to her was like chasing butterflies. Each time I

thought I had her, she danced away. All I could do was run after her.

'According to Homer, the soul is the impression we leave when we die – smoke lingering in the air when the fire's burned out.' I tried to think of something more original, and failed. 'Even Socrates didn't know.'

His trial, the closing speech after he'd been condemned: Either death is oblivion, or it's a migration of the soul from this world to another.

I tried again. 'The soul's a metaphor, a way we talk about the "self" we feel inside us. The Voice of Reason – the rational, intelligent part of us. We know it exists because it's always talking to us. But really, we're just talking to ourselves.'

'You think the soul is *reasonable*?' Her eyebrows arched up, as if I'd proposed some outrageous act.

'Reason is what we are.'

'Isn't love what we are too?'

I stroked her hair. 'Yes.'

'But we just said love is a form of madness. And madness is the opposite of reason.'

'I suppose that's why we try to control our appetites.'

She grabbed my hand and pulled it away, mock offended. 'Are you saying you want to control love? That you want to love less than you possibly could?'

She'd trapped me like a sophist. I felt betrayed. 'Does it matter? Whatever we say about the soul, we can never prove it. We'll never even see it, until it's too late and we're all shades moaning in the underworld.'

If you can't win the argument, rubbish it.

Again, the gorgon look. I wanted to take back what I'd said, but she wouldn't let me. She leaned over and snapped a reed off its stalk. Holding it like a pen, she pricked a small hole in the damp earth, then drew a circle around it.

'What do you see?'

'A wheel? An eye?'

'Geometrically.'

'A circle with a point at its centre.'

'Or it could be a cone, seen from directly overhead.'

'If you're trying to tell me the world is deceptive and our senses are inadequate, Heraclitus got there first.'

She gave a small nod, as if something had been established to her satisfaction.

'There are walls around us that box us in to our world. We can't see beyond them – and so we assume there *is* nothing beyond them. In the end, we stare at the walls so long we don't even see them. We forget they're there.'

I tried to understand the connection. 'Is that what your picture represents? An individual surrounded by a wall?'

I don't think she heard me. 'The wall isn't as solid as it seems. There are hidden doors you can get through. Pythagoras found one, so did Empedocles and Parmenides.'

I didn't know if we were talking about a real place, or some sort of metaphor. For safety's sake, I decided to stick with the metaphor.

'Agathon wanted to find this gateway?'

Her face said: *almost.*

Hades was worried the nymph might tell someone.

'He found it.'

Twenty-eight

Jonah – Athens

Two blocks away, the battle was just distant noise, like a television in another room. The loudest sound was the ringing in his ears. Had he dreamed it? A part of him almost wanted to go back to the square and have a look. He wondered what had happened to the woman he'd rescued, if she'd made it. But the blood on his face was real, and so was the pain in his knee every time he put his foot down. He kept going.

It was only when he felt the phone vibrating in his pocket that he realised how little he could hear. He pulled it out and answered, shouting as loudly as he could. All he heard was a tiny voice, his own, coming from the end of a long, dark tunnel. He turned the phone volume all the way up, but couldn't make out any words.

Whoever it was hung up. Almost before he had time to despair, a text message appeared on screen.

Where are you?

He glanced up and saw the street signs on the side of the buildings. His hand was shaking so badly he could hardly tap out the message.

Corner of Perikleous and Voulis

Almost at once:

I'm coming

Five minutes after that, a motorbike pulled up.

Ren drove him down to the Piraeus and stopped outside a fish restaurant by the harbour. Jonah was bloodied, bruised and topless, but the owner, reading a newspaper at a table out at the front, didn't register an expression. Perhaps he was just glad of the business.

Jonah found the bathroom and stuck his head in the basin. He ran cold water over his eyes until he couldn't feel the pain. Ren brought a two-litre bottle of mineral water: Jonah gargled half of it and drank the rest. He looked at himself in the mirror. His hair was wild, and he had a wide cut across his forehead. Ren dabbed it with a towel and bought hydrogen peroxide from the pharmacy next door. It stung, but at least it felt clean. She'd also managed to get Jonah a new T-shirt from the Piraeus' last souvenir shop. I ❤ ATHENS.

Across the road from the restaurant, a few tables sat under a plastic awning overlooking the water. They sat down, the only customers.

'Adam told me to go to his office but it was shut. I got caught in the riot instead.'

She nodded. He could hear things now, but still from a great distance. Bad feedback screeched in his ears.

'I told him I knew about Ari Maroussis. I suppose he wanted to warn me off.' He remembered the yawning mouth of the Metro station, the dead souls flooding down. 'Or get rid of me.'

She nodded again. The waiter brought them menus and stale bread. Jonah chewed over the crust and didn't say anything. He was in a place beyond words. If he tried to

314

think about Adam, he felt so much fury he wanted to break something. Thinking about Lily was worse.

'Do you want to go home?' Ren asked.

He knew what home was. An empty flat, a silent phone and a river whispering Lily's name every minute of the day.

'I want to find Lily.' He remembered what she'd said. 'I want to bring her back.'

The waiter returned. Ren ordered for both of them, a list of Greek dishes Jonah didn't catch.

'Do you have a plan for where we go next?' he asked.

'Spetses.'

'Maroussis' villa.' As the adrenaline faded, a killer headache had begun to rack his skull. 'You said he's one of the richest men in Greece.'

'*The* richest.'

'He must have guards. Fences.' He held a bottle of water against his forehead and added unnecessarily, 'I'm a musician.'

'I can get us in.'

The waiter brought their food. Bubblegum pink taramasalata, fat peppers bursting with rice, and a plate of tiny fish you ate with the heads on. Jonah glanced over the railing into the harbour, wondering how local the fish were. A scum of Styrofoam and effluent bobbed around the concrete pilings.

'Do you need anything from Adam's apartment?' Ren asked.

A part of him would have loved to go back to the flat, to get his bag and dangle Adam off his Acropolis-view balcony until he told him everything. Another part – some vestigial organ left over from a world view that had become extinct – thought about calling the police. He tasted the gas on his tongue, remembered the demon with his head on fire, and shook his head.

He had nothing but the clothes he was wearing, his phone,

his wallet and the passport in his pocket. Seven summers touring Europe had taught him you never knew when you'd need it.

'I'm ready to go.'

Through different eyes, eyes that weren't still red from tear gas, Spetses was probably a beautiful island. White houses with red roofs clustered around the port; to its right, a Greek-Edwardian hotel that looked like the Brighton Pavilion strutted its dilapidated grandeur on the seafront. Behind the town, forested slopes rose towards a central ridge that gave the island its spine. The low sun shone down behind it, soaking the island with gold and making the mountains in the distance a purple watercolour of peaks and slopes, endlessly repeating into the haze.

Standing on the pier where the hydrofoil had dropped them, Jonah scanned the houses on the hillside. 'Which is Maroussis's?'

'The other side of the island.'

'When do we go?'

'When you've recovered.'

'I'm ready.' His hip still ached each time he moved his leg; he could feel the bruises coming up all over his body. But he could handle it. To get to Lily.

Ren hoisted her beach bag onto her shoulder. Wrapped in her scarf and sunglasses, he had no way of knowing if she believed him.

'We can't go until it's dark.'

They got a room at the big hotel on the waterfront and sprawled out on the bed. Outside the window, the mountains slipped into the haze; an old bell chimed; a loudspeaker on the church broadcast a liturgy, mysterious lines rising and falling in some ancient, eastern mode. Jonah watched the ceiling fan spin away reality.

'What kind of a name is Ren?'

'Japanese.'

He examined her face. Her hair was straight and dark, her skin a light brown, but that was about as close as it got. 'You don't look Japanese.'

'No,' she agreed. Perhaps she'd had this conversation a thousand times before. But she'd led him to Greece, to Eleusis and now to the island, and he still didn't know the most basic things about her.

'Where do you come from?'

'It's complicated.'

'Why are you doing this?'

'What?'

'Everything.'

'I told you: I want to help.'

He stared into her dark, almond eyes, trying to force more out of her. She was immune.

'What were you doing in Sibari?'

'Following Maroussis.'

'Why?'

'I was afraid he would find the tablet.'

'How did you know it was there?'

But it was all he was going to get. She rolled over and studied her fingernails, as if looking for chips in the polish.

'Do you believe in reincarnation?' she asked suddenly.

'You mean like, if we're bad in this life, we'll come back as a cockroach next time?'

'There doesn't have to be a moral logic to it.'

Jonah thought about that. 'Would it make any difference? I mean, if I've *already* been reincarnated, I don't remember it. And if I haven't, then there's nothing to remember anyway. So either way, we end up in the same place.'

'The same place can look very different depending on how you get there. If you thought you might come back as a cockroach, you'd make sure you behaved.'

317

Jonah watched the fan spin. 'If I did come back as a cockroach, all I'd know was that I was a cockroach. I wouldn't know I'd been in a band in a previous life, or that I could have been a dolphin if I'd been nicer. I'd just be a cockroach and want to not get squashed.'

'That's quite a limited horizon, don't you think?'

'Comes with being a cockroach.'

'If that's what you are.'

She swung her legs off the bed and stood. Without warning, she lifted off her T-shirt, unzipped her skirt and stepped out of it. She folded them both neatly and put them in the wardrobe. When she opened the door, the mirror on the inside reflected everything back at Jonah. She wasn't wearing a bra.

Jonah stared. Her eyes caught his in the mirror and trapped his gaze. And he realised again that he didn't know a thing about her.

'I'm not really . . . '

But was that true? He'd been underwater for weeks and his lungs were bursting. He was desperate to break the surface, to emerge into the sun and feel her soft dry skin against his. He wanted to put his head between her breasts, feel her stroking his hair, calling his name. To feel whole again.

She turned – or perhaps the cupboard door swung a fraction. A bow of light flashed off the mirror, so that for a moment she disappeared.

She's not real. Neither was his desire. It was an image in a mirror, an inversion. In that flash of clarity, he understood it was a test, that if he followed her into the looking glass he'd be lost forever.

'No.' One short word. It shouldn't have been that hard.

As if nothing had happened, she reached into her bag and pulled out a pair of black jeans and a black long-sleeved

T-shirt. She put them on as carelessly as she'd undressed, then pulled another black shirt from the bag and tossed it to Jonah.

'Let's go.'

They went down to the old harbour and found a water taxi. The captain argued furiously when Ren told him where they wanted to go, but a hundred-euro note settled the matter. The engine made conversation impossible: they sat in the back, staring at the black water and the spidery white wake behind them.

They came around the tip of the island and saw the full moon rising in front of them. Jonah thought it was the biggest moon he'd ever seen, a perfect circle, buttery yellow as it hung over the horizon just a few hundred yards away. There were fewer lights on this side of the island: a handful of fishing villages, a couple of big hotels booming music across the water. The captain throttled back and steered closer to the shore, scanning the water ahead.

They passed a point and came into a broad cove. A few metres off shore, the captain idled the engine. Barefoot, Jonah and Ren scrambled over the side and splashed through the shallows onto the beach. Tiny waves raced up around them. When Jonah glanced back, the boat had already reversed and was chugging away into the night.

'Isn't he going to take us back?'

Ren didn't hear him. With the lap of the waves, the scratching of the cicadas and the wind brushing through the pines, you had to listen carefully. Further round the cove, where the dark land tapered to a point, a light glowed among the trees like a wrecker's lamp.

A steep slope rose towards the trees at that end of the beach. A coil of barbed wire blocked the way, but when Jonah touched it he felt rust flake off in his fingers. Following it, they found a gap where they could squeeze through into the woods.

'I thought you said this place would be impregnable.'

'You said that.'

Ren went ahead, still barefoot, silent on the sandy soil. Moonbeams flooded through the branches, feathering the ground with shadows.

There's no such thing as moonlight.

Adam had said that, on a moonlit night on the banks of the Cherwell. *The moon's just a mirror in space. It's sunlight we're seeing – not the real thing, but a dimmer and colder reflection.* Did that mean the world was different too? A dimmer, colder reflection of reality? A mirror-world in a looking-glass light? It was the only explanation he could think of.

Did you ever wonder why the world doesn't look backwards at night, if we're seeing it all by reflected light? It was the sort of question Adam often asked back in Oxford.

He remembered Ren in the hotel mirror, and shivered. In a backwards world you couldn't trust anything.

The light he'd seen from the beach glowed through the trees ahead. Jonah tugged Ren's T-shirt, but she shook her head and kept going. Jonah hung back. He thought he saw the outlines of a figure behind the light, a tall man standing stock still. Was he holding a gun?

The trees ended and he saw clearly. The light was a sunken floodlight shining out of the ground; the figure a statue in front of a ten-foot wall. Even on his pedestal, he was barely taller than Jonah: a grotesque dwarf with a pug nose, bulbous cheeks, a cheeky grin and an erect penis that almost touched his chin. Two goat horns curled back out of his forehead, and he held a set of reed panpipes.

In daylight, the statue might have been comic – endearing, even. The contrast between the erection, bursting with hope, and the sad ugly body was almost pathetic. But in the flare of the floodlight, the face became cocky and cruel. The phallus wasn't desire, but a threat. And the dark wall behind him looked impassable.

'Where now?'

A warm breeze tickled the back of his neck. From somewhere nearby, Jonah thought he heard soft music rising and falling. The wall seemed to ripple. When he put out a hand, he felt branches and leaves yield to his touch. Not a wall, but a hedge.

A few yards along, a more perfect blackness showed a gap.

'Is this the way in?'

The black mouth smiled at him. Beyond, he could feel the tangled darkness waiting to swallow him – the same way it had swallowed Lily, a black hole from which nothing ever came out. Was it possible to feel *nothing*? To be terrified of *nothing*?

An owl hooted from the trees. He swayed and took a step back; something touched him; he almost screamed aloud. It was only Ren's hand feeling for his in the darkness. Her slim fingers closed around his.

'Whatever you see, don't run off. Don't let go.'

She pulled him in.

The moon didn't penetrate the high hedges. They walked in darkness, their world defined by shifting limits they touched but never saw. Deprived of sight, Jonah's other senses went into overdrive. He heard branches rustling; scratches, whispers and sighs; the thud of his footsteps on the earth like a heartbeat; snatches of the same mournful music he'd heard before. The sticky, private smell of the hedge filled his nose; his fingertips grew so sensitive he could feel every vein in the leaves he brushed. Soon he began to dread the touch. He imagined the foliage coming to life, wrapping itself around him, forcing itself down his throat until it choked him. He'd never suffered claustrophobia, but now he couldn't escape the thought of the walls slowly pressing in, squeezing him between them.

Suddenly, light flared around them. Another buried flood-light, exploding like a mine when they stepped over it. Rubbing his eyes, he looked around to see if they'd been caught.

The only creature watching was a black stone animal, sitting on its plinth like a cat in the sun.

'Guard dog?'

'It's a sphinx.' In the floodlight's glare, they could see they'd come to a fork in the path. One way led left, the other right. In front of them, the sphinx stared dead ahead and offered no clues.

'Which way do we go?'

'That's the riddle.'

'Do you know the answer?'

She tugged him down the right-hand path. The light faded behind them, leaving him blinder than before.

They stumbled on through the maze. Each time they came to a fork, light flared to reveal a choice and a statue. A goddess draped in diaphanous robes, bending her bow towards them; a terrifying Medusa with snakes writhing out of her hair; a solemn-faced boy with broken stone where his genitals should have been. Each time, Ren chose right.

'How do you know?'

'"The Mansions of Night, the right-hand spring",' she quoted at him. 'You always go right. Maroussis knows that.'

It sounded too easy. And at the next fork, his fears came true. When the light came on, there was a black sphinx staring at them.

'We've gone round in a circle.' Despair flooded through him, washed on by a wave of terror that he'd be trapped in the maze forever. 'You led us the wrong way.' He pulled away, but Ren gripped his hand until her nails almost drew blood. Her strength surprised him.

'It's not the same statue,' she said fiercely.

'Are you sure?' Jonah examined it, but saw nothing that identified it.

'If you start to doubt yourself, you'll never get out.'

'What about the floodlights?' Each time, the light hit him like a gunshot. 'If we keep setting them off, someone's going to see. They'll know we're in the maze.'

She shrugged. 'They know anyway.'

'Then why don't they stop us?'

'That's not their job.'

They carried on. Now he could hear a scratching sound, all around, as if they'd wandered into a colony of crickets. The path twisted and turned, ever tighter, until he could hardly tell which way was forward. The noise got louder.

And then they were out. He'd passed the exit before he knew it; the hedges vanished and spacious night opened around them. A wide lawn ran up to a low, square-built house silhouetted in its own light. Sprinklers spun glistening arcs of water across the grass, making the sound he'd thought was crickets.

There was nowhere to hide. A wide stone basin, like a birdbath, cast the only shadow on the lawn.

'How do we get to the house without being seen?'

'It doesn't matter.' Still holding his hand, Ren led him across the open lawn. The wet grass yielded to their feet without a murmur. The sprinklers turned, soaking them with a fine spray. By the time they got to the other side, Jonah's legs were wet through. He barely noticed.

As they reached the edge of the house, the sprinklers suddenly shut off and sank back into the lawn. The night came alive with the patter and rustle of living things. Below the house, where the promontory fell away to a hidden beach, Jonah could hear waves brushing the shore.

They crouched behind a row of bougainvillea that guarded the top of the slope. Above, Jonah glimpsed the arches of a whitewashed colonnade, and a set of French windows opening onto a balcony. Dim lights glowed inside. His chest tightened. Was Lily there?

A shadow broke the line of the windows. Jonah froze. A man stood on the balcony puffing on a long cigar. At first, Jonah took him for another statue. Lit by the moon, in a grey three-piece suit, with a handkerchief tucked in the pocket and a grey silk tie, he could have been cut out from an Edwardian photograph.

A red ember flared on the end of the cigar. The photograph turned to colour. A cloud of smoke blew out into the night. The man looked down, staring straight at where Jonah and Ren were hiding.

The smell of tobacco mingled with the flowers and damp earth. Raising his voice just enough to carry, the man in the suit called down from the balcony.

'I suppose you have come to see me?'

Twenty-nine

*'And what's more, I have to say, so far you've only understood
a small fraction of the difficulty which this involves . . .'*

Plato, *Parmenides*

*Love draws you to Beauty. Beauty leads you to Truth. And Truth
is immortal.*

For a moment, I felt as if I'd broken through the clouds
and was standing on a mountaintop bathed in sunlight. The
love in my heart fused with the longing in my soul and I
thought I understood everything Diotima had told me. I was
flying.

'What did Agathon find when he went through the door?'

Diotima lay back in my lap and gave me a strange, dissat-
isfied look. 'I've told you as much as I can.'

The sun went in. I landed with a bump. 'But you haven't
told me anything. Just riddles and metaphors.'

'Words are part of the wall we have to get through.' She
pointed to the circle she'd drawn in the earth. The damp
ground had already begun to ooze shut, muddying the shape.
'We call this a "circle". But if we called it a "straight line",
it would still be the same thing. Language is a weak tool: it
describes things, but it doesn't get to the *being* of the thing.'

'There you go again,' I complained. '*Walls, tools* – more
metaphors.'

'Metaphors are the closest we can come. To put it into

words brings it down to the level of language – and all that languages *are* is metaphors.' She bit her lip, frustrated with me. 'Didn't you ever have an experience that seemed to go beyond words?'

'Last night.' Even thinking about it sent small tremors through me.

'So describe it to me.'

I blushed – but she wouldn't let me off the hook. 'Well, um, you undressed, and then I took off my tunic, and then I put my . . . ' I mumbled away into nothingness. 'This is ridiculous.'

'You see? Some things are too real to be put into language.'

'But I need to understand.'

She turned away and began walking into the trees, brushing past the papyrus fronds. I called after her, 'Did Agathon find it in the book? *The Krater*?'

A rustling in the reeds across the lake made me look back. Dion had returned with the boat. He gave Diotima a shy stare that stayed on her while I clambered in. He started to row away. Diotima stood on the shore and watched us go.

'Wait,' I called. I could feel something being pulled out of my heart as the space opened between us. 'Aren't you coming?'

'I can't come to Ortygia. There's a lion in that cave who'd gobble me up if he got his hands on me.'

She said it frivolously, like a little girl playing pretend. But the grimace on Dion's face was real enough, and all too grown-up. I wondered again about his place in things. Where were his loyalties?

My thoughts were a mess as we rowed across the lake: a tangle of frustrated questions and ignorance. Diotima's mysteries had set me on fire; I had to know them, however much she wrapped them up in riddles and allusions.

What was Agathon looking for?
The same as you.

But was it the secret Agathon discovered that killed him? Or was it the nymph he fell in love with?

As we approached the landing, I saw a guard hurrying up the steps to the palace, presumably to report to the tyrant that I had come back as promised. Or perhaps to tell the boy to get back to the library. When I got there, I found him still staring at the same scene of Aeschylus I'd set him that morning.

I gave him some Aesop – the fable of the Fox and the Grapes, nothing controversial – and told him to compose two columns on the moral. He scowled, which was something. I stared out of the window, at the crimson sky and the sea, and tried to put my thoughts in some sort of order.

Was it the mystery I wanted, or Diotima? Did I think that by possessing one I could understand the other? The Voice of Desire screamed so loud I couldn't tell what it was saying.

Too many metaphors, the Voice of Reason complained. Wings, walls, nymphs, souls: every question I asked, Diotima obscured it in clouds of words.

Socrates, baiting a sophist: 'I don't want this "if you like" or "that's your opinion" sort of argument; I want to prove the real *you and me.'*

Metaphors insinuate and suggest; they mislead the mind like a painter's trick of perspective. You think they add meaning, but all they are is images. They create similarities where none exist. They're illusions. Lies.

From now on, I resolved, I'll steer clear of metaphors and other figures of speech. They're too dangerous for the situation I'm in.

When the lesson was over, I found Dion on one of the terraces overlooking the harbour. His hair was oiled and combed, and he wore a vividly dyed robe. Lesser men would have looked pretentious in it – I'd have felt ridiculous – but Dion carried it off easily. I guessed Dionysius was hosting a dinner that night, though I hadn't been invited. If the tyrant had really wanted to torture me, he'd have made me go.

We greeted each other, and talked warily around a few general subjects – the weather, the theatre, common acquaintances. The impact of our first meeting had cooled to second thoughts: now, neither of us trusted ourselves. Or each other.

Two bushy cypresses grew at either end of the terrace, filled with starlings. The screech of their chatter made it impossible to eavesdrop on us. And I had to believe that the golden youth I'd glimpsed, thirsty for virtue, was still there inside the shell.

'Your brother bought a book from a man in Locris called Timaeus,' I said.

'He buys a lot of books.'

'This is one he paid a hundred drachmas for. It's called *The Krater.*'

He shrugged.

'Do you know where it is?'

'Most of his books are in the library.'

I turned and looked Dion in the eye. For all their confidence, there are still ways of asserting authority over eager young men. Socrates taught me that much.

'Do you know the book I mean?'

Suddenly, like athletes at the starter's call, the starlings rose off the tree in a cloud. They flew out over the water, spiralling and twisting in the air like smoke.

The soul is the impression we leave when we die – smoke lingering in the air when the fire's burned out.

No metaphors, I reminded myself sternly.

Dion picked up a leaf and began pulling it apart.

'The book was gibberish. The ravings of a madman.

Dionysius was so furious he'd spent a hundred drachmas on it, he ordered it to be burned.'

I gripped the balustrade and stared at the foamy water swirling below, hoping there was more. 'And?'

'I don't like to see knowledge destroyed. I persuaded him to send it to the temple treasury instead.'

'I need to see it.'

'There's no point. My brother was right: it's nonsense.'

Words are part of the wall we have to get through.

'I'll judge that for myself.'

Dion straightened a fold in his robe. 'Then you'll have to ask Dionysius. No one except the chief priest enters the temple sanctuary without his permission.'

Dion went in to dinner; I headed back to my room. In the colonnade by Dionysius' ball court, I met Euphemus and another man coming the other way. The companion was short, fat and balding, sweating from trying to keep pace with Euphemus. He smiled as if I should remember him.

'We were coming to find you,' Euphemus said.

'Our new Athenian,' his companion added. 'The scourge of tyrants.'

The moment he spoke, I remembered who he was. The strange man who'd found me in the garden the day before, who'd thought I should have brought him letters. So much had happened since then I'd almost forgotten.

'Did you get your letter from Athens?' I asked.

'That was a misunderstanding.' He chuckled, then abruptly broke off. 'Or perhaps not.'

'Leon thought you were me,' Euphemus explained.

'An Athenian, a philosopher, the boy's tutor – you can see why I was confused.'

Another smile, eager to please. I didn't care. Euphemus was the least of my worries now.

Leon glanced over his shoulder and licked his lips. 'I'm glad we found you. There's a passage of Herodotus we'd like your opinion on.'

He unrolled a book and fussed until he found the line he wanted. He pointed a fat finger to it, inviting me to read.

'To yourself, if you don't mind.'

I leaned over. *When night fell, Gyges took his knife and hid behind the door. Then, when the king had fallen asleep, Gyges entered his room and struck him dead.*

I looked up, surprised and confused. 'What do you want to know?'

'We'd just like your opinion.'

I tried to think of something intelligent. 'There's a variant of this story I've heard,' I said. 'Gyges finds a magic ring which makes him invisible, which lets him sneak into the king's palace.'

'How quaint.'

'It poses the ethical question: do we behave well because it's the right thing to do, or just because we're worried we'll get caught?'

I glanced at Euphemus, expecting him to launch into one of his monologues. But he stayed quiet. Instead, Leon exclaimed, 'But that's precisely what we wanted to talk to you about. Ethical questions.'

'I'll try.'

'Now this passage here . . . ' He rolled the scroll on and pointed. I read, silently, *It was a heavy blow to Croesus to learn that his son was dead, because the stranger whom he had sent as the child's guardian had turned out to be the murderer.*

I was missing something. I checked with Euphemus again, but he wouldn't meet my eye.

'You keep on talking about a question.' I looked from one to the other. 'Well? What is it?'

Leon fiddled with his thumbs. 'Really, you've hit the nail on the head already. Is a good man willing to do the right thing? Even if he might get caught.'

'I think you misunderstood. If he's doing the right thing, he doesn't have to worry about being caught.'

'Well, that's just it, isn't it? Good and bad, right and wrong. Tricky.' He nodded twice more. 'That's why we came to you.'

'Socrates would have said that a man who knows what's good could never do something bad.'

'Take Thrasybulus,' Euphemus said suddenly. 'Would you say that what he did was right or wrong?'

I stared, trying to make sense of the question. Athenian history was so far from my mind that it took me a moment to put the pieces together. Thrasybulus is the general who came out of exile to overthrow the Thirty Tyrants, fifteen years ago. He led the Democrats in the battle where my inglorious uncle Critias died.

At first I thought Euphemus was simply mocking me again, trying to get a rise with an old argument. Then the penny dropped.

I looked up and down the corridor. I lowered my voice. 'Are you asking . . . ?'

'Will a good man do a bad thing in a good cause?' Euphemus nodded grimly. Leon jabbed a finger at me, in case I had any doubt which good man they had in mind.

'You've changed your tune,' I said to Euphemus. It was easier than answering the question. 'I thought you admired . . . *him*.' I didn't dare say the name aloud.

'Let's say I changed my mind.'

'And you?' I turned to Leon. 'What's your part in this?'

Euphemus answered for him. 'Dionysius has had a long reign. Do you think Agathon was the only one to suffer?'

I looked at Leon more closely. Suddenly, his constant motion, the awkward laughs and sudden twitches, seemed

331

less like a clown and more like a man trying desperately hard to shift a weight he couldn't bear.

I pitied him, whatever he'd endured. But it wasn't my business.

'If you want to do this thing, go ahead and good luck. But without me.'

'We need you.'

'Why?'

Leon pointed back to the scroll, still open in my hands. I read it again.

. . . the stranger whom he had sent as the child's guardian had turned out to be the murderer.

A line of sweat trickled down my spine. A pain started spreading through my chest.

'It has to be done,' Leon said. 'No point killing the lion and leaving the cub.'

'We need someone with access to the boy,' Euphemus added.

I looked from one to the other. I looked at Herodotus and thought about Gyges' ring. What *would* I do with it? Would I creep, invisible, into the tyrant's bedroom and stab him in his sleep, safe in the knowledge no one would ever know?

Diotima: In their hearts, all men think that behaving badly will get them further than doing the right thing. Good men are just too frightened of getting caught.

The day before he died, I went to visit Socrates. He sat on a stone bench in the prison, his feet shackled to the floor, his head slumped over in sleep. Summer heat made the place stink like a toilet. Outside, the Scythian guards were unusually quiet. I'd been there so often that month I'd got to know them well.

He looked so peaceful that, even with the urgency of the moment, I couldn't bear to wake him. I sat by his feet, toying

332

with the key the warden had thoughtfully left on a hook outside. I wondered what he was dreaming.

'I can't believe you can sleep at a time like this,' I murmured.

'At my age, there's no point resenting the fact that I have to die.'

I'd spoken so softly I'd barely heard myself. But Socrates was sitting up, wide awake. His face – his bulbous, florid, beautiful face – looked down on me like a child in a crib. Even there, at the end, no malice or hurt clouded his eyes.

'Have you been here long?'

I shook my head. 'Everything's prepared. The warden's gone out to the agora and won't be back for half an hour. The guards have been called to a fire in the Kerameikos. Simmias and Crito are waiting outside with a fast horse, and we've paid off the informers so that even if someone sees you go, they won't remember it.' I knelt to unlock his shackles – but Socrates stopped my hand.

'Do you think I should change the principles I've taught just because the circumstances have changed? Or was that all just *for the sake of argument*?'

'But you can't die like this,' I raged. 'It's . . . It's . . . *absurd.*'

For once, he didn't say a word: just twitched a bushy eyebrow. *Do you think absurdity ever stopped anything?*

I begged him to come with me. I told him he was betraying his children, though I really meant he was betraying me. I told him he was participating in an injustice. The charges were false, the trial was a sham, the sentence was barbaric.

'Didn't we agree that you should never intentionally do something you know is wrong? Isn't wrong always wrong? Or have recent events changed your definition, so it's acceptable to do wrong sometimes, or in some ways, but not others?'

He went on for a bit, developing his theme. He made a lot of the fact that he'd lived all his life by the laws of Athens, so it would be hypocritical to break them now just because

333

they'd been turned against him. He said that virtue was everything to him: more than reputation, more than family, more than the shifting opinions of men. 'Whatever happens to us, whether things get worse or better, a wrong is never justified. And wrongdoing always discredits the wrongdoer.'

I didn't listen. I couldn't. When he'd finished his lecture, he asked if I had anything to say that might make him change his mind.

'I have nothing to say, Socrates.' My last words to him, the end of our conversation. And even though he only had hours to live, I could see he was disappointed.

Euphemus and Leon waited for my answer. I stared down the corridor, at the dark shadows lengthening between the arches. I imagined Socrates' ghost waiting behind one of the columns, listening.

'I have nothing to say.'

Leon tutted and shook his head; Euphemus looked furious.

'What about the things you said to Dionysius? What you said to *me*? Was that just *rhetoric*?'

'You should know. At the time, you were selling me the glories of Dionysius' enlightened rule and explaining how there's no such thing as good and bad.'

'What about Agathon?'

He was trying to provoke me – and he nearly succeeded. I remembered Agathon's dead weight in my arms and the wounds on his body. I thought of Dionysius watching him in the dungeon, egging his torturers on. Using him to bait me.

But then I thought of Dionysius the son, my pupil. He might be dull and lazy, but should he die for that? I tried to imagine myself wielding the knife, his piggy eyes staring at me in terrified surprise. The picture went red and I shuddered.

'Two wrongs don't make a right.' Words might be empty, but they're a good place to hide.

'Is anything ever right for you? You think you're above all this, too good for the real world. Did Socrates teach you that cowardice is a virtue?'

I stepped back, as if physically distancing myself from them would get me out of their plot. 'Say it happened. Who would replace *him*?'

They shared a glance. 'Someone you admire, I think,' said Leon.

The answer was so obvious I was surprised I hadn't seen it at once. 'Is he in on this, too?'

'Absolutely not.'

'Dion's like you. Too good to get his hands dirty,' Euphemus said. 'At least he's loyal to his brother-in-law. What are you loyal to?'

'Truth.'

I thought he'd spit in my face. 'I can't believe we're here talking about . . . *this* . . . and you want to turn it into a philosophy exercise.'

'Philosophy is about life.'

'You accuse me of twisting arguments, making black white and good bad. But you're worse. I don't dress up what I'm saying as some sort of absolute truth. I'm honest.'

I've never been good in debate. Rather than argue, I turned and fled down the long corridor. I kept waiting for them to call me back. But you can't shout about trying to overthrow a tyrant in his own house – not if you want to live.

Is cowardice a virtue? Socrates could have spent a whole day discussing the question, teasing out my position, trapping my inconsistencies, hammering my opinions into something firm and true-to-purpose. But in the end, they were just words.

Language is a weak tool: it describes things, but it doesn't get to the being *of the thing.*

Was Socrates really better than the sophists? Or just more consistent in his arguments? I tried to remember a single conversation that had reached a decisive conclusion, and found I couldn't. Endless debate, endless questions – and never any answers.

Euphemus' taunts rang after me out of the past.

While you're sitting on your mountaintop drawing triangles, we're down in the law courts and the Assembly wrestling with the problems of real life.

No metaphors, I reminded myself.

Thirty

Jonah – Spetses

Socratis Maroussis pointed to a staircase. Jonah didn't move.

'Do you want to find out what happened to your wife?'

Jonah climbed the steps and came out on a wide balcony. A wicker table and three chairs had been arranged on the checkerboard marble tiles, with three glasses and a jug of wine on the tablecloth. As if he'd been expecting them. Jonah peered at the French windows, wondering what was behind the drawn curtains. One of the curtains swayed, as if in a gust of wind. Except the night was still, and the windows were shut, and Jonah could see a pair of black shoes sticking out below the hem.

Maroussis pulled out a chair and offered it to Ren. He took a second chair for himself and pointed to the third for Jonah. 'Please.'

Jonah sat. The gravity had gone out of his world; up and down had no meaning any more. He couldn't even summon the anger he ought to feel.

Maroussis poured three glasses of wine – simple tumblers, like you might find in any taverna. He slid them across the table. '*Na zisiste.* Your health.'

Jonah didn't touch his drink. Nor did Ren. Maroussis shrugged, drank, and set his glass back on the table. If he noticed Jonah studying him, he was too well mannered to show it. He seemed to make a fetish of old-fashioned *politesse*:

his perfect posture, the graceful way he moved the glasses across the table like chess pieces, even the angle he left his cigar dangling in the ashtray. *How old was he?* Seventy? Eighty? Age had tightened the face, not lined it: he reminded Jonah of an African sculpture carved from hardwood.

'You must be Miss Lamelle,' he said to Ren. 'My condolences for your sister.'

Ren stiffened.

'And you, of course, are Jonah Barnes. I was sorry to hear about your wife.'

He couldn't sit there and take that from the man who'd stolen her. Suddenly, he'd found his rage and his chair had tipped over and he was standing over Maroussis, holding the glass jug by the neck and shouting, 'Why don't you tell me what happened to her?'

Maroussis didn't move. 'If you are violent, my guards will come.'

Jonah looked around and saw no one. Even the shoes behind the curtains had gone. That didn't mean they weren't there.

'They didn't stop us getting in.'

'That is not their responsibility.'

'What are they for, then?'

'Their job is to keep me safely locked away.'

'You?' Jonah tightened his grip on the carafe, feeling the certainty drain away. Maroussis sat still, ankles crossed, calm as a man waiting for a train.

'I am as much a prisoner as you.'

'This doesn't look like a prison.'

'Only because you lack imagination. Please sit down.'

Jonah leaned back against the balcony rail. Suddenly, he was desperate for his glass of wine.

'I have – forgive me if you know this already – a son. A wayward son, you would say in English.'

'Ari?'

338

'I had hopes for him, but . . .' A wave of his hand consigned the hopes to history. 'I have taught him to desire the things I desire – but not to disregard the things I abhor. He is confused. He can recognise goodness, but he does not know why. He wants everything, indiscriminately, and he expects it because nothing has ever been denied him. Like a child, he cannot tell right from wrong or dreams from reality.'

Jonah decided to risk a drink. It didn't seem like he had a lot to lose.

'I don't care about your son. I want to know what happened to Lily?'

The wine was sharp and resinous. He still finished the glass. Maroussis poured him another.

'You know my excavators found a golden Orphic tablet. Your wife stole it.' He saw Jonah about to object and held up his hand. 'I am sure you will tell me her motives were honourable. But Ari did not see it that way. He wanted her to tell him where she had hidden the tablet.'

'He kidnapped her.'

Maroussis shrugged. 'I told him he had behaved recklessly. He called me a senile old man. He fought me.' He lifted his arm so that the sleeve rode back to reveal a heavily bandaged wrist. 'He no longer accepted my authority.'

'Wait a minute.' Jonah stepped forward, towering over the old man. 'You saw him? He came here?'

'He's still a child. When he has done something wrong, he comes to his father. Even if he cannot stand the punishment.'

'Did he bring Lily here?'

The old man pointed his bandaged hand down the slope towards the sea. 'He came on his boat. She was tied up just down there.'

Jonah's heart almost shut down. 'Is she alive? Where is she now?'

'She is in a place you cannot reach her.'

Ever since the maze, an oily scum had clouded his thoughts. Now, anger boiled it away and he saw clearly. He could taste blood in his mouth and he wanted more. He picked up the wine jug again, and this time he smashed it on the rim of the table. Wine and shattered glass splashed over the terrace, leaving a jagged edge in his hand. Now he had a weapon.

Maroussis stared up at him from his chair, eyes hard and calm.

'Do you know Euripides' masterpiece *The Bacchae*?'

Jonah didn't answer.

'The god, Dionysus, presents himself to King Pentheus as a man and pretends to submit to him. He gives the king every opportunity to treat him honourably; he even lets the king make him his prisoner. But it is an illusion. When the king begins to think he is greater than the god, he is destroyed. Dionysus' followers, the Bacchantes, tear him limb from limb and use his severed head as a football.'

Jonah wasn't listening. He had a weapon in his hand and he was going to use it. Music pumped in his ears, a frenzied drumbeat whipped on by stinging cymbals.

'She is alive, Mr Barnes. You still have something to lose. Or something to live for, if you prefer.'

The music stopped. Jonah stepped back.

'Where is she?'

Maroussis eyed the broken glass in his hand. 'I cannot talk to you while you are threatening me.'

The fury drained out of him; he sat down. Across the table, Ren watched him carefully.

'Where is she?'

Maroussis folded his hands together. 'You are asking the wrong question. Ari is not interested in your wife. He would like the tablet.'

'OK.' He didn't want to talk about the tablet – but he knew he had to calm down. 'Why is the tablet so important?'

Maroussis lifted his good hand and made a circular motion with his wrist. From around the corner of the balcony, a butler in a white jacket and black bow tie appeared carrying three more glasses and another jug of wine. He set them out and cleared away the empties, careful not to step on the broken glass at his feet. Jonah wanted to pinch the man to see if he was real, but didn't dare.

Maroussis fussed with his cigar. 'Have you ever read Plato, Mr Barnes?'

'No.'

'Are you familiar with this quotation: "All Western philosophy after Plato is simply a footnote"?'

'No.'

'An Englishman said that. Alfred North Whitehead.' The name rolled out of his mouth, exotic and mysterious in the Greek pronunciation. 'What he means, I think, is that any question you can think of, Plato thought of first. Perhaps he did not find the definitive answers, as we would like, but he framed the questions, and that is more important.'

Jonah was getting used to the old man's way of speaking. He sipped his wine and waited for the point.

'At the age of forty, Plato made a journey to Southern Italy. This we know, because he says so in a letter that survives. He does not say what he learned, but we can make an extrapolation. When he returned to Greece, his writings took a new direction. He is not writing little parables of Socrates any more, mocking the Athenians for their ignorance. His dialogues are complex and profound. He is like a man who has been paddling on a beach and suddenly has learned to dive to the depths of the ocean.'

Down below the house, the sea hissed against the shingle beach.

'Did he go to Sybaris?'

'He does not say. Anyway, this was a hundred years after

the destruction of Sybaris – he would have gone to the successor colony, Thurii. And I believe he did go there. He went to Greece to learn about Pythagoras, and Sybaris-Thurii was deeply associated with this man.'

He breathed out a cloud of smoke. 'There is no doubt Plato learned many things from the Pythagoreans. The mathematical basis of the universe. Concepts of the soul and metempsychosis. But I believe he found something from a time even more ancient. A source of wisdom that lifted his mind to another plane of reality.'

'The tablet?'

'The tablet is a signpost. It points the way.'

'To what?'

Maroussis changed tack again. 'Have you ever pondered the nature of reality, Mr Barnes?'

'It's Adam you need to speak to about that.'

'Your friend, Adam Shaw. I have spoken to him many times. You know, Plato divided the person into three parts – of Reason, Will and Appetite. I have made myself what I am through will; my son has more than his share of appetite. Adam Shaw operates in the realm of pure reason.'

'That's one way of putting it.'

'You think he is cold?'

'I'd rip his heart out, if I thought he had one.'

'We are all prisoners in a world of illusions. We are kept chained in a cave, staring at puppet shadows we mistake for reality. Plato was the man who escaped from the cave and saw reality as it really is. Adam Shaw and I would like to do the same.'

Jonah thought of Adam's flat, the glass walls and white surfaces. The emptiness, and the view of the Acropolis so clear it looked fake. He couldn't think of many places less real – except perhaps where he was right now.

342

Suddenly, like an animal taking fright, he banged the table, rattling the glasses. 'Isn't this reality?'

Maroussis picked up one of the glasses and held it next to his ear, listening to the resonance.

'We trust our senses – but we are pathetically ill-equipped to apprehend reality. Our ears hear only a fraction of the sounds the world makes. Our eyes have the resolution of a one-megapixel camera. From these feeble stimuli, we deduce the existence of an entire complex universe around us. But what is this information we call reality? Nothing except electrical impulses and chemicals flickering dimly in our minds.

He put the glass down. 'Do you know the concept of the shadow worlds?'

'No.'

'Perhaps you have heard its more popular name – multiple universes.'

'I'm not really into science fiction.'

'This is science, not fiction. Experiments have shown that there are an infinite number of particles in this universe which we can never perceive, which exert no perceptible influence on the world we know except in the smallest fringes of experiments. All our telescopes, microscopes, spectrometers, colliders and other tools can only ever find one billionth of the matter in this galaxy.'

'Does this have anything to do with Lily?'

'Similarly with mathematics. Physicists tell us that the world is governed by numbers. They think this is a novel insight, but in fact it is as old as Pythagoras. And as wrong. The mathematician Gödel has shown that no mathematical model, however complex, can comprehend all possibilities of numbers, because they are part of a living universe.

'My point is that we live in a reductive, materialist world.

We think everything is explained by things we can touch and count – yet even those we cannot properly *know*. Since the ancient times, we have always been lowering our sights. From Gods to men, from men to animals, to cells, nucleitides, atoms, particles. We sink into the mud of our own making, and wonder why we cannot get out. The universe plays us a symphony, and all we listen to is the squeak of the piano pedal. And we think that is everything there is to understand. Have you seen what is happening in Athens?'

Jonah rubbed the cut on his forehead. 'First hand.'

'It is terrible – but also inevitable. My country led the world into the age of civilisation. Now we are leading it out again. What is happening in Greece is only the logical culmination of centuries of Western thought, that the only purpose to life is material gain. If we decide that humans are merely animals, then eventually we will end up living like animals.'

Jonah said nothing. He wished he hadn't drunk the wine quite so quickly.

'Plato defined man as a soul in a body, but because we cannot measure the soul we dismiss it. All we are left with is the body, and bodies are fragile, unstable things. They make a fragile, unstable world. To make something stronger, we must build it on the eternal. The soul.'

'But . . . ' Jonah shook his head, trying to focus on what mattered. 'What does all this have to do with the tablet? With Lily?'

'When Plato went to Italy, he found something that blew open his thinking like a hydrogen bomb. Instead of just the piano pedal, suddenly he could hear the whole orchestra. He understood how to see not just the flickering phenomena of the visible world, but the permanent architecture of the universe. I believe this thing is still there, waiting to be discovered. And I believe that the Sybaris tablet shows the way.'

'But there are other tablets. I saw one in the British Museum, for God's sake.'

Maroussis reached in his jacket pocket and pulled out a slim, silver cigarette case. He laid it on the table and snapped it open.

'Here is another.'

Jonah leaned forward. Inside the case, a thin piece of gold foil gleamed in the terrace lights. The tiny letters spelled out their ancient message. Promising – what?

'Is this the Sybaris tablet?'

'No.' Maroussis snapped the case shut. The golden light disappeared. 'Only your wife knows where it is. Unless she has told my son.'

Whether it was the wine, or lack of sleep, or the sheer impossibility of the situation, Jonah had listened to Maroussis' visions as if drifting under a spell. The mention of Ari snapped him out of it. He remembered why he'd come.

'What did he do with Lily?'

'When he left here, he returned to Italy.'

'Where is she?'

A shake of the head. 'I understand you are a musician, Mr Barnes. Do you like Bach?'

He'd had enough of the old man's evasions. 'Where is she?' he said again.

'I suppose you would not. Most young men find him too mathematical. Not enough of the passion.' A chuckle. 'So, he is not Elvis Presley. It takes an old man to understand his art.'

Jonah stood. He looked for the jagged piece of broken glass, but it had vanished. The waiter must have cleared it away without him noticing.

'Bach is a master of the canon form. You know this? Like your English song, "Row Row Row Your Boat".' He hummed a couple of bars. 'The tune is a simple figure. It is only through repetition that you learn its full complexities – and it needs a genius like Bach to reveal them. Like a magician. He takes the theme and ties it in so many knots you do not know where you are. And then, with the lightest tug of the string, the knot comes apart and you are back where you began. Except now, for the first time, you understand where you are.'

'Where is she?' He'd become the theme, endlessly repeating while Maroussis spun his inversions around him.

'*Life is but a dream*, Mr Barnes. Is that not what your song says? It is time to wake up.'

Thirty-one

My first law will be about the robbing of temples, just in case anyone should dare to commit such a heinous crime. I can't conceive that any well-brought-up citizen would ever do such a thing; but slaves, and foreigners, and foreigners' slaves, might be tempted.

Plato, *Laws*

The moon had begun to shrink again. Only a fraction, shaved off the side: at a casual glance, you might think it was still full. But the circle had changed; it was no longer perfect. Every night, it would deform a bit more until it vanished completely.

Perhaps the world is like that moon. So close to perfect, you'd hardly notice if you didn't concentrate.

Either our senses aren't made to appreciate perfection – or else the perfect world that mathematics describes isn't our world.

But even reduced, the moon shone brightly enough. If I'd been walking home from a dinner party I'd have been glad of the help. Given that I was sneaking around a tyrant's castle trying to burgle his treasury, I wished it would go away. It sat obstinately in the cloudless sky like a – anyway, as it was – pouring down its light on lovers and thieves, exposing our crimes in black and white.

The philosopher Anaxagoras claims that the moon has no light of its own, but derives its brightness from the hidden

347

sun. If so, what does that make the moonlit world? Is it a poor cousin, a second-hand place lit by second-hand light? Is that why the moon makes men mad: the unreality of it all?

I must be mad. It's past midnight and I'm out of my room, stealing across the citadel from pillar to pillar, like Odysseus sneaking into Troy to get the palladion. I'm not a spy, and my military service was twenty years ago. It seems quite likely I'll get caught. Dionysius killed and tortured Agathon for less.

I can't even plead ignorance. I know the odds, the probable outcome, and I'm doing it anyway. That's the madness. An irresistible voice is driving me on: I have to know what the book says. Diotima said that madness can be a blessing and a gift. I'm not so sure. It was madness that made the Bacchante tear her own son apart, and Heracles kill his children.

Is it the book I want – or Diotima? Is there some sort of equivalence in my mind – if I get one I'll have the other? I don't know. The music in my soul is playing out of control, fast and dangerous; scattered notes, snatches of tunes, wild beats that erupt from nowhere and then disappear. As if someone's taken the sound out of the air, torn it up and thrown it into my ears anyhow.

All I know for sure is that I'd better not get caught.

The night sounds of the palace echoed the crazy music in my head. Boots, watchwords, hinges and bolts; fragments of conversations far too close. When an owl hooted, I almost surrendered. I crept around the exercise yard, across a broad garden, through the shadows at the foot of a watchtower and towards the main square. No gates or guards stood in my way. The weakness of an impregnable citadel, if you can call it that, is that it's too easy to believe your enemies are on the outside.

I reached the two temples and stood in front of them, like

a prisoner before his judges. The moonlight reversed reality: the fluted pillars shone airily, while the shadows between them looked solid as iron. On the pediment, Athena's golden shield had transmuted into silver.

With the moon up, I couldn't approach the temple without being seen. I cowered in my corner, clinging to the shadows.

This is madness, said the Voice of Reason.

You've come too far to go back, said the Voice of Will.

What's in the book? said the Voice of Desire.

The voices almost paralysed me. Then I heard real voices, and the jangle of armed men on the move. I ran across the square, into the shadows between the columns. I pressed myself against the stone and prayed they hadn't seen me.

The guards crossed the square. Perhaps, if I'd listened, I'd have noticed more than just two guards doing the rounds, or heard some tell-tale piece of conversation. But all I cared about then was: *where are they?* I tracked their progress by sound, holding my breath each time I thought they might be coming nearer, letting it sigh out each time they drifted away.

And then they were gone. I listened to be sure, counted to twenty, then approached the great doors and pushed. I'd hoped they were just for show, that on Ortygia Dionysius had no need for locks. Who would be mad enough to steal from the tyrant in his lair? Even if you did get something, no moneychanger or goldsmith in Sicily would risk handling it.

The doors didn't move. Even here, Dionysius wasn't so naïve. I don't know why I'd ever expected he would be. I kicked them in frustration and hurt my toe.

I remembered the way the island's doors had flown open the night before at Diotima's command. Then, I'd been flying. Now, I was tiptoeing around, terrified of every shadow. It was like a day at the theatre: first the drama, then the satyr play. I could almost hear the audience laughing.

I took a slow lap around the temple, feeling the sanctuary walls for any kind of door or window. The columns soared around me like a cage. By the time I came around to the front again, the Voice of Will lay cowering in a corner, while the Voice of Reason delivered a thorough kicking. If I could get back to my room undetected, I'd have got off lightly.

What about the other one? said the Voice of Desire.

I looked at the temple of the Goddess next door, shoulder to shoulder with Athena's and shrouded in scaffolding. Almost close enough that you could step from one to the other.

It's further than it looks, warned the Voice of Reason. But suddenly I was thirty feet in the air and climbing. The ladders creaked, the scaffolding swayed. When I glanced down, the moonlight left no doubt how far I could fall.

I reached to steady myself and felt the warm, smooth glaze of a roof tile. I'd reached the top. Breathing hard, I looked across at the Temple of Athena.

From the ground, it looked as though the two temples almost touched. Up here, the gap between them yawned like a chasm. Even a flying leap wouldn't make it.

The temple next door was slightly higher than this one. I could see under the lip of the roof and, tucked under the eaves, a narrow walkway, invisible from below.

Try a ladder, said the Voice of Desire.

I found the last ladder I'd come up by and hoisted it through the hole in the floor. It knocked and clattered against the scaffolding, startling a pigeon nesting in the roof. I hoped it hadn't disturbed anyone else. I swung it out into the void and pushed it towards the walkway on Athena's temple.

It reached.

You see, whispered the Voice of Desire, *the gods are with us.*

The gods lead us on to destroy us, answered the Voice of Reason. But I wasn't listening: I was on my knees, crawling across the narrow ladder. It sagged under my weight, lower and lower as I edged out; every time I moved, I could feel it tilt as if it was trying to shake me off.

And then I put out my hand and felt stone. Almost kicking over the ladder in my hurry, I hauled myself over the little parapet and dropped onto the solid base of the walkway under the eaves.

I was on Athena's temple. I offered a heartfelt prayer and hoped she'd watch out for a lost Athenian.

But I was still outside the main sanctuary. I looked along the narrow gantry I'd landed on and saw a yellow light, halfway down, glowing on the rafters. I hurried along to it.

The light came from a high window set into the sanctuary wall. Oil smoke warmed my face as I peered in. Far below, a sacred flame burned unattended in the floor. Behind it, Athena stood on her plinth in her armour, her face bowed away from me. Painted gods and heroes struck poses on the walls.

And even in the depths of night, I saw it all as clear as day. Not from the single flame, but by the reflection of the light off the thousands of plates and cups, bowls and caskets, statues, weapons, ingots, bangles and furniture piled around the room – every piece solid gold.

But all I wanted was the book – and even that was worth nothing if I couldn't reach it. Whether the window was just for ventilation, so the smoke didn't poison the priest, or whether Dionysius was so paranoid he even spied on the goddess, I don't know. But it wasn't meant as a way in. And I was a long way up.

I leaned through the window and peered down. The wall dropped away below me: sheer, but not smooth. Wide stone bars stuck out from the wall, almost like the rungs of a ladder. It took me a moment to realise they were marble frames around the paintings. I tried to work out how many there were, how far apart and how far down. Would they take my weight?

The Voice of Reason said it would never work. The Voice of Desire said I had to try. I turned around and manoeuvred my legs through the window, then slid through until I was dangling by my arms. My feet felt for the ledge and only touched air. I slid down a little more. Still nothing.

I lowered myself another couple of inches, as far as I possibly could. Now I was hanging by my fingertips, ten small pads of skin supporting the weight of a grown man. The weight of a life. And still there was nothing beneath me. The goddess watched from her plinth but did nothing to help. Her face said, *You've made your choice.* I hung there in perfect silence. Even the Voice of Desire had gone quiet.

Parmenides says that nothing can come from nothing. But sometimes, by stretching out your toe as far as it can reach, you might just find something after all. Resistance – the pushback of an object insisting, *I exist.*

I let go and slid down. The ledge rose against my foot, took my weight and held it. Pressing myself against the wall, flat as a fish, I tried to catch my breath so I could whisper a prayer of thanks to the goddess. Her cold face, almost level with mine, didn't acknowledge me – except perhaps the slightest raised eyebrow to say, *Don't thank me yet.*

There were two tiers of paintings, each framed in marble. Getting down without losing my grip or my balance was an ordeal, and the lower level was still above head height. I dropped the last few feet – there was no alternative – and landed on a set of golden plates with a crash like cymbals that echoed around the closed room.

I looked back up at the way I'd come. From the floor, the window was almost impossible to pick out, high above the topmost ledge. I'd never haul myself back up that way.

As I dropped my gaze back down the wall, I couldn't

help noticing the extraordinary quality of the paintings. If I hadn't touched the paint myself as I scrambled down, I'd have sworn some were sculptures. Three baby centaurs suckling their mother seemed to stick their bottoms out of the frame; Atlas' face, as he held up the whole weight of the world, was so miserable I wanted to offer to share his burden. I remembered Dion telling me they were by the great Zeuxis himself.

There's a story they tell about Zeuxis, I don't know if it's true. That he and his arch rival arranged a contest to see who was the better painter. Zeuxis painted a bunch of grapes so real that birds flew down from the trees to peck at them. Confident he'd won, he told his rival to unveil his own entry. The rival invited Zeuxis to do it himself. Zeuxis stood in front of the picture, reached for the curtain that covered it – and came away with paint on his hand. The curtain was the picture.

Never mind that, said the Voice of Desire. *Find the book.*

I turned and started digging through the treasure, trying to be as quiet as possible. It wasn't easy: a million drachmas in gold makes quite a noise. Even old King Croesus would have felt poor in that room.

Think, I told myself. You wouldn't keep manuscripts with the dinner service. I worked my way towards the back. In the shadows behind the statue, a dozen or more heavy chests lined the walls. I opened one – not locked – and felt around inside. Thick fabrics, lumpy with the jewels sewn onto them. I tried another one and found more of the same. Unwanted gifts, I suppose. For all Dionysius' faults, and his fabulous wealth, his personal tastes were commendably austere.

I opened the third chest and knew I was close. The sweet, grassy smell of manuscripts blew out of the open box. I reached in and heard a soft rustling as I moved the rolls, like the wind blowing through the papyrus at Cyane's lake.

The statue blocked the light. I dragged the chest back to the sacred flame, making a horrible noise. I began pulling out scrolls, unwinding a few inches to check the contents, hoping the recent additions were near the top.

The fifth scroll I tried was it. No different to any of the others, nothing obvious to say why it should be worth a hundred drachmas and a man's life. Not illustrated, or wound on a golden spindle. I held it up to the light, hardly able to breathe.

This is the testimony of Timaeus of Locris. He entered the crater which has neither bottom nor base; he went down to the furthest place, the inmost depths of the earth; he passed by the guardians and the sacred spring; and after years below, he returned to the land of the living.

My hand trembled. I was holding a book which men had died to read. I went on.

In the beginning, the universe was chaos. And the Creator wanted to bring order out of disorder, because he was good, so he took the elements of the universe, poured them into his krater *and mixed them together. He formed the soul from the elements and the physical universe in the soul, and brought the two together. The soul is eternal, and partakes of reason and harmony, and is the best of things created.*

A world with soul and intelligence. A world of harmony and reason to banish Heraclitus' chaos for good. The skin on my arms began to tingle.

God divided the mixture into as many souls as the stars, and implanted them in bodies so that they could feel sensation; and also love, in which pleasure and pain mingle; and fear and anger, and all the other emotions. And if they

354

conquer these feelings, men live righteously, and eventually take their place among the stars. But if they are conquered by them, and live unrighteously, then they walk lame to the end of their lives, and are sent back to the world below.

I felt a rush of clarity. For a moment, it seemed that all the things that Diotima had toyed in front of me were finally being handed to me in plain words.

But the more I read, the less clear things got.

Two things cannot be put together without a third, which is proportion. For in any three numbers, whether cube or square, there is a mean, which is to the last term what the first term is to it; and again, when the mean is to the first term as the last term is to the mean – then the mean becoming first and last, and the first and last both becoming means, they will all of them of necessity come to be the same, and having become the same with one another will be all one.

What did I think of that? Honestly – I don't know. I wanted to believe I was reading something profound: that the truth of the universe lay coiled up in that scroll. But the more I read, the less I was convinced. It was long on assertion and short on evidence. Stripped down, all you really had were more metaphors.

Some things are too real to be put into language.

Perhaps it was the circumstances. I couldn't concentrate while my eyes kept glancing to the door; or while the back half of my mind wondered how I would ever get out. But the hope of an answer, some explanation for what Agathon had found in this manuscript, wouldn't let me let go. I hurried on through it, skimming large sections. There was more about circles and harmony, some number theory that I didn't understand, and a great deal about triangles.

And then it ended. At the bottom of the last column, someone had added a diagram in different ink: two triangles with an arc swooping between them. No explanation. I wanted to throw the book into the sacred flame at the sheer waste of it all.

But the book didn't take up quite the whole length of the scroll: there were a few turns of blank papyrus left on the spindle. I unrolled it, just in case.

The gold leaf was so thin, I didn't even feel it. I pulled away the last few inches of papyrus, and there it was, curved flush against the spindle. Agathon's golden tablet. It fell into my palm with a whisper. The tiny letters winked at me in the reflected firelight. I ran back to the chest where I'd got the book and rummaged around. Among the soft scrolls, the metal chain and locket found my hand almost at once. I rolled up the tablet and tucked it into the locket, then hung it around my neck under my tunic.

Time to go, said the Voice of Reason. I tucked Timaeus' scroll in my waistband and started replacing the other manuscripts. Even with the sacred flame still hissing away at my back, the room seemed darker. The gold around me gleamed less; I felt cold. It was like waking up from a particularly depraved dream, with nothing but memories and shame. All I wanted was to go home.

But – too late. I heard shouts, muted footsteps coming up the stairs outside. I thought of hiding behind the statue, but that would have been undignified and futile, with treasures scattered across the floor and a box of manuscripts lying open.

The great door opened. A figure stood on the threshold, framed between the moon and the fire inside.

'I did warn you.'

Thirty-two

Jonah – Spetses

All he remembered of leaving the house was a gravel drive and an iron gate slamming shut. Two lions on the gateposts watched them go. Then they were climbing a dusty track, towards the ridge that divided the island. The moon had set; they walked by starlight, guided by constellations he didn't know. Ren slipped her hand in his and he took it gratefully. He needed the proof he wasn't alone.

He tried desperately to remember what Maroussis had said. The tyres turned in his mind, trying to gain traction, but the more they spun the more they destroyed the ground beneath them.

I spoke to him – the man whose son took Lily – and now I can't remember a thing he said. A hole opened inside him and he crumbled into it.

The track became a road, tarmac warm under his feet, climbing back and forth across the face of the hill. Back and forth, back and forth, like a vibrating string. He was glad of the slope. It gave him purpose.

They reached the ridge. The other half of the island unfolded below them, sketched in shadows; he realised there was light in the sky. He glanced back to see Maroussis' villa, but the trees made it invisible.

The world felt too heavy. He stepped onto a rock at the roadside, teetering off-balance. He felt giddy; he felt free; he felt if he slipped off the rock he could fly all the way to the sun.

'Where do we go now?'

Ren looked down towards the distant cluster of lights around the harbour. 'He told you.'

With the lightest tug of the string, the knot comes apart and you are back where you began. Except now, for the first time, you understand where you are.

'Italy?'

Over in the east, where Homer's sea lapped the horizon, the sun began to show its face.

Near Aegion, Greece

A bus. A road, winding between the mountains and the sea. That was all this country was, Jonah thought: mountains and sea. He leaned against the window, watching the Gulf of Corinth slide by. Not far from here was the site where he'd met Lily, the hospital where he'd held her hand, the hotel bed where they'd first made love. It disturbed him to be back here now. As if the story had finished.

The knot comes apart and you are back where you began.

Except the trench didn't exist any more. He'd watched the diggers pour in the backfill at the end of the season, piling up the earth like a grave. Two months' work undone in two days, and nothing to show for it but photographs and a few artefacts.

An arrow pointed down a sliproad labelled *Helike*. Curled up on the seat beside him, Ren stirred.

'You know Helike?'

How had she seen the sign? The last time he'd checked, her eyes had been closed, her cheek resting on his shoulder.

'No.'

'In ancient times, it was a great trading city. Then, in twenty-four hours, it was destroyed completely. An earthquake knocked down the buildings, the ground subsided, the sea poured in and the whole city drowned. Some people think it was the model for Plato's legend of Atlantis.'

'OK.'

The bus swerved across the divide into a contraflow. It seemed that half the road was still under construction, miles at a time, but all you saw were cones and signs. The workmen had vanished like a lost civilisation.

'Helike was the mother city to Sybaris. It was colonists from here who founded Sybaris, back in the seventh century BC. You know what happened to Sybaris?'

'Wiped out.'

'Flooded and lost. The same destiny for the mother and the daughter cities, two hundred years apart and for very different reasons. The pattern repeats.'

You are back where you began.

It hasn't finished, Jonah insisted. *I won't let it.* Out of the window, the flat water of the gulf gave no hint of the lives it had swallowed.

'Why did Maroussis say he was sorry about your sister?'

Ren twisted in her seat and put her head against the headrest, turning her back to him. 'He was being cruel.'

'Why?'

'It's not relevant.'

'If what happened to her was like what happened to Lily, it might be.'

'It wasn't.' A dark voice, sharp with a warning.

'Tell me anyway.'

She still wouldn't look at him. She might almost have been talking to herself. 'Valerie was a dreamer, always looking over the horizon. She saw this black-and-white world and wanted colour. When she was a teenager, it was crystals and incense; before she dropped out of college, it was drugs and Eastern philosophies. And sex,' she added drily. 'After that, she tried meditation, reiki, kabbala . . . the whole menu. Anything that offered a path out of this world.'

'What happened to her?'

Ren looked him straight in the eye. 'She fell in with the Maroussis family. She didn't survive. Whether that took her to another world, a better place . . . ' She shrugged.

Jonah didn't know what to say. 'Lily was nothing like that.'

'I told you it wasn't relevant.'

'Did Ari Maroussis—?'

'Yes.' She turned back, fixing him with an uncomfortable stare. 'There was a ship moored in the Piraeus, a decommissioned cruise liner waiting for the breakers. One night, a fire broke out. When the fire crews went aboard, they found her body in an abandoned cabin. Naked, no marks of violence, nothing to identify her at all. Just a gold tablet placed inside her mouth. A replica. They wouldn't waste the real thing on her.'

The bus went dark as it plunged into a tunnel. Jonah tried to kill the image in his head: the rusting cabin, the damp-stained mattress and the perfect corpse laid out, hair splayed around the face. In his imagination, it was Lily's face.

'Didn't the police—?'

'The ship belonged to Maroussis, so they went straight to him. The press never heard. There was no investigation.'

'So how do you know?'

'Persistence.'

The bus rumbled on. Jonah waited for the tunnel to end.

'I don't understand,' he said.

'What?'

'I want to find Lily and bring her back. What are you in this for?'

A mask of light struck her face as the bus came out of the tunnel.

'I want to hurt them.'

Italy

They caught the overnight ferry from Patras across the Ionian sea, and landed in Bari at dawn. From there, they took a train. Jonah dozed, slipping between dreams and memories. He had no idea how Ren passed the time. When he woke up, they were there.

In the ten days Jonah had been away, the season had started to turn. Persephone had begun the long retreat back to her subterranean husband: fields had been cut to stubble, smoke flavoured the air, and daylight already felt precious. There was no sign of a taxi at the station, so they walked. By the time they reached the lab, the evening had come on enough for them to see the lights inside.

They stepped through the open gate. Two cars sat parked in the lot: Richard's pickup, and the white Ford van with SOUTH PECKHAM CHURCH OF THE REDEEMER written down the side. Jonah had never been so happy to see it. He patted its flank as he went past, leaving a smudge in its dirt coat.

He tried the door and found it unlocked. He climbed the dark stairwell, trying to avoid the echo. At the top, light and the sound of piano music spilled through the lab doorway. It sounded like Bach.

Do you like Bach?

He stood in the shadow beside the door, straining to hear beyond the music. The antique heating system popped and clattered as it flexed pipes that had lain cold all summer. A loose shutter squeaked on its hinge. Anything else was hard to distinguish from the murmur of his imagination.

On the other side of the doorway, Ren nodded her head. *Go on.* Belatedly, Jonah wondered if he should have brought some sort of weapon.

The music stopped. A woman's voice came on the radio, murmuring something in Italian. Jonah went in.

The season had finished. The samples and instruments that had cluttered it two weeks ago now sat packaged in crates and boxes, ready to go into hibernation. The walls and pinboards had shed their paperwork. The skull still grinned on the table beside the sink, waiting to be put away; and a laptop trailed wires across a trestle table. Otherwise, the job was almost finished.

Richard stood at the table, squinting at the laptop. He didn't look up straight away – perhaps he was expecting someone, or lost in his work. When he did, he grabbed the table so hard he almost knocked it over.

'What—?'

Jonah didn't give him a chance. He crossed the room with two strides, pulled the table aside and swung a fist that connected hard with Richard's face. He collapsed; Jonah picked him up and hit him again, then dropped him on the floor.

'Where is she?'

'I don't—'

'I've spoken to Adam. I've spoken to Maroussis. I know they took her.'

Richard rubbed his mouth. Blood came away on the sleeve of his shirt. 'You saw Adam?' He glanced at the door. Ren stood there, arms folded, cutting off his escape.

'In Athens.'

Richard mumbled something pained and indecipherable. Jonah lifted him up by the collar of his shirt and put his face close. 'What?'

'Why didn't he stop you?'

'Stop me?'

'Adam.'

'He tried. He sent me into a war zone. Now I'm here.'

Richard pulled himself up and slumped on a stool beside the table.

'Can I have some water?'

Ren ran the tap and filled an empty coffee cup. Richard watched her warily, like a dog he didn't trust.

'Who's she?'

'A friend.'

Richard couldn't keep back the smirk from his bloodied lips. 'That didn't take long.'

Jonah thought about hitting him again, but decided not to waste the effort. 'Tell me everything. From the beginning.'

'From the *beginning*?' The word seemed to puzzle him.

'Why did you bring Lily here in the first place?'

'It was Adam. He came to me last November and told me his foundation was funding this dig. He said I should apply. Funding's rare as unicorns these days, so I jumped. Then I talked Lily into it.'

'Did you tell her what she was getting into?'

'*Getting into?* I didn't know myself. I mean, we weren't *getting into* anything. If we hadn't found that tablet, nothing would have happened. Just another season.'

'Did she know about Adam?'

'He told me not to tell her. He said it would be awkward if she knew he was funding her.'

'Go on.'

'Then we dug up the tablet. Word came down that they wanted it over in Athens. Obviously, that's completely illegal. Easy enough to do, with a piece that size – you could pop it in the post, for heaven's sake – but you'd be putting yourself out of bounds. No report, no publication. The conservator went ballistic and threatened to spill the beans; Lily wanted to quit.'

'And you?'

'I didn't like it either.'

'But you let her take the heat while you hid behind her.'

'I thought it would all fizzle out. Lily flew to Athens to see Adam. They came back together with Maroussis *fils*. Next thing, the conservator was off the dig. Then the tablet vanished.'

'When was that?'

'The night before you came. We didn't notice until the next morning.' A wounded note crept into his voice. 'Everything I told you in London is true. The tablet was in the safe, and only three people knew the combination. Me, Sandi and Lily. She must have stolen it. Christ, I probably helped her do it. I came to the lab that night to get some things and found her here by herself. I gave her a lift back to the hotel, for heaven's sake.'

'And the next morning?'

'It was one of those days. One of the volunteers fell ill. The osteologist turned up complaining that some of the finds had been mislabelled, and we spent half the morning sorting it out. Then the pump broke and flooded the trench. We started making jokes about King Tut's curse.'

'What about Lily?'

'She was on edge – but we all were. She'd been trying to get to the lab all morning, and she wanted to be ready for when you arrived. I assumed that was why she reacted so badly when Ari turned up.'

'He came to the trench?'

'To the lab. Lily was still at the trench. When she heard, she looked as if she could spit blood. She set off straight away, didn't wait for him to come down to the dig. Obviously she never made it.'

Another wave of anger rolled through him. Jonah rode it out and counted to ten. 'When did you find out? Were you in on it from the beginning?'

'Of course not.' The indignation of a guilty man clinging to fragments of pride. 'If I'd had any inkling, I'd have warned her.'

'And Adam?'

'I don't know. I still don't know what happened, exactly. Ari discovered the tablet was missing and hit the roof. Have you met him?' Jonah shook his head; Richard's eyes dropped. 'He's pretty wild. He must have guessed Lily stole it. He headed over for the dig just as she was coming here. When he saw her on the road, he grabbed her.'

'*Grabbed her*,' Jonah repeated. The phrase stuck in his mouth, alien and ugly. 'Just like that?'

'Ari's used to getting what he wants. I suppose he can afford to.'

All the pleasures of his dissolute life only make him mad for more.

'So when I got there – did you know?'

Richard looked genuinely miserable. 'I thought she'd gone to the lab. Honestly. No one told me anything until after you'd come.'

'And the text messages? Her mother's fall?'

A long, agonised silence. Richard stared at the table and fiddled with his hands. 'I sent them.'

More silence – more than Richard could bear. 'They gave me her phone and told me to do it. They thought I could make it convincing.' His cheeks flushed as if he'd been hit again. 'I promise you, I had no idea what it was about. Adam told me to get you away.' He glanced up, terrified of Jonah's reaction. 'For God's sake, I didn't want to.'

Richard Andrews has lived his entire life by the rules that other people set for him.

He knew he should be angry. Come to that, he *was* angry – but not with the all-consuming fury Richard deserved. Perhaps it would come later; perhaps the sheer enormity of Richard's betrayal had jammed his emotions.

Perhaps he didn't have the luxury of brooding on the past. 'What did they do with Lily?'

'Ari put her on his boat.' Richard fingered his collar, smearing more blood. It looked as though he'd cut his throat. 'I'm sure they'll let her go as soon as this is over. They're not bad people. They just want the tablet.'

From across the sea, Jonah caught Socratis Maroussis' eyes watching him from his island. As deep as the world, and as cruel.

'You really think they'll let her go? After all they've done to her?'

'I suppose they can pay her enough to keep quiet. You too.'

'What about the tablet?' Ren said from the door. It was the first time she'd spoken. Richard looked as surprised as if the skull on the counter had suddenly come to life.

Richard writhed under her stare. 'I don't know. I don't.'

'You were the only other person who had the combination.'

'Do you think Adam and Ari don't know that? Do you think they didn't work me over pretty hard.'

'He's right,' said Jonah. 'He'd never have stood up to them. You wouldn't even have dared take it in the first place.'

He sniffed. 'Some would say that's honesty.'

'So where is it?'

Jonah turned, trying to imagine Lily in the room. Late, dark – just like now – rushing to get the tablet out, scribbling down the words as urgently as the original scribe to preserve the memory. *I found her here by herself.* Richard's feet on the stairs, the squeak of the door as he came in. No time to put it back in the safe.

'She took the tablet, but she wasn't going to keep it,' he guessed. 'She wanted to copy the text, so that she'd have it if Maroussis made it disappear. You surprised her, so she didn't get a chance to put it back in the safe. That's why she was so desperate to get to the lab next morning. To put it back before anyone found out.

'But they searched her when they picked her up. She didn't have the tablet. It wasn't in her room, either. Adam said so.'

They searched her. Grim images came into his head, rough hands pawing at Lily, fumbling and groping and pinching. Were they violent? Were they *thorough?*

Ari's used to getting what he wants.

'Did Adam say if they've found the tablet since?'

'I don't know. I don't think so. I'm sure they'd have let Lily go if they had. That's all they want her to tell them.'

You really think they'll let her go? If Lily knew where the tablet was, he prayed to God she hadn't told them. If she had . . .

He forced himself to concentrate. He put himself back in Lily's shoes that night, copying out the tablet. He remembered the piece of paper, the awkward Greek letters and – in the top left-hand corner – a reference.

'Was R27 the number of the tablet?'

Richard shook his head. 'The trench. Every artefact is bagged up with a piece of paper that records the location we found it.'

Ren watched Jonah carefully, head tilted against the door-frame. 'What are you thinking?'

'The tablet isn't in the lab. It wasn't in the hotel room. She didn't have it with her.'

'Go on.'

'The only other place she went that day was the dig.'

'Why would she have left it there?'

'She meant to put it back in the lab, but Ari arrived before she could get there. So she hid it.'

'Where?'

'R27. The trench where she originally found it.' He turned to Richard. 'Have you got torches?'

Richard didn't move. A strange, unhappy look filled his face.

'What?'

'It's not that easy. The season's over, we've already started backfilling. And we turned the pumps off yesterday.'

The pickup's high beams shone over the hole, cutting a slice out of the night. Mist rose off the freshly turned earth. In the truck's cab, parked on the edge, Jonah could see how far the work of filling in the trench had advanced. It looked less than a third of the size he remembered. Heaped earth-mounds ringed the remaining hole like a crater; a digger's scoop dangled into the beam like the claw of some mud-dwelling monster.

Richard put the truck in low gear and nudged it forward until it was pointing down the slope, aiming the lights at the bottom of the hole. Jonah leaned forward in his seat.

The city had drowned again. A black lake covered the bottom of the pit, lapping its sides. The only remains were a few stone walls, barely breaking the surface. Jonah tried to remember how high they'd been before. A foot? Two feet?

Leaving the engine running, they grabbed two spades from the back of the truck and made their way down the slope. Damp mud balled under their shoes. They halted at the edge of the pool.

'Where was R27?'

Richard looked around uncertainly. Their shadows rippled on the black water. 'We took up all the markers.'

'Don't be cute,' Ren said. 'You know exactly where it is.'

'How?' said Jonah.

'Tell him.'

'When we survey the trench, we map every position with GPS,' Richard admitted.

'Where's that written down?'

'In the Field Journal,' said Ren. She took the battered notebook out of her bag.

'I thought we might need this. I grabbed it from the lab.'

Jonah shot her an admiring look. 'Did you bring a GPS reader too?'

'Everything you need is within you.' She slapped his hip pocket. 'Your phone will do just fine.'

She flipped through the notebook to find the right page. Jonah turned on his phone. He hadn't had it on since Athens, but there were no missed calls or messages. Only a text from the mobile carrier welcoming him to Italy.

Has everyone forgotten about me?

Ren read off the coordinates and he entered them into the phone. A red arrow glowed on the screen, pointing him into the water. Without bothering to take off his shoes or trousers, he stepped in.

It was warmer than he'd expected, and deeper. After two strides, it reached his knee. With every step, he felt the mud open under his feet, yielding and inviting. He had to use the spade to steady himself, digging in the blade then pushing off like a bargepole, gripping the phone in his free hand. The arrow wobbled as the digits crawled towards the coordinates Ren had given him.

The arrow became a green circle. He dug the spade into the mud so hard he couldn't pull it out.

'Throw me the other spade,' he called. It sailed out of the darkness and splashed into the water next to him. He put the phone in his pocket, grabbed the spade, and started to dig.

Almost at once, he realised it wouldn't work. The water was too deep and the spade was too large. He might turn over the tablet and miss it completely – or dislodge it, only to have it drift away. He stuck the second spade in the ground beside the first and dropped to his knees. The water surged up to his chest: he grabbed for the spade, missed it and almost lost his balance completely.

'Are you OK?' Ren called from the water's edge. 'What's happening?'

'Fine.'

Jonah forced himself to relax. He hummed a few bars of a song that had come into his head: *It comes down, down, down . . . like a divebomb.* He got his balance back, took a deep breath, and reached into the depths.

Down, down, down . . . His face broke the surface of the water before his arms felt the bottom. The moment he went in, buoyancy pushed his legs up, pitching him forward. His fingers touched mud. Lunging forward, he dug his hands in as deep as he could, clawing through the slime. It slithered through his fingers and kept its secrets.

He came up for breath, and to get his bearings. He'd already slid a few feet beyond the spade. He waded back.

Lily wouldn't have buried it far down. Just enough to cover it until Ari had left.

He dived again, keeping one hand on the spade so he wouldn't drift. He wormed his hand wrist-deep into the mud, then trawled it in a radius around the centre-point. A few pebbles, nothing to get his hopes up.

Soon he'd spent so long in the water he didn't feel it any more – only when he came up for air, when the night sucked the heat straight through his wet clothes. He actually preferred it underwater, blind but warm, the taste of earth burring his tongue. A worm wriggling through the mud. He lost count of the dives he made, snatched breaths and then back down. If Ren or Richard spoke to him in between, he didn't hear them.

The moment he felt it, he knew it was different. The hard edge stood out like a knife. He worked his fingers underneath

370

it, got a grip and rocked it free of the mud. He breached the surface gasping with triumph and squatted in the water to examine his treasure.

The headlights shone off old-fashioned letters printed in the metal. *Farrah's Original Harrogate Toffee.* It was the tin Lily used for her watch and wedding ring when she was digging.

A fit of shivering almost shook it out of his hand. He grabbed the spade handle and hauled himself to his feet. He opened the tin. No watch or ring, but a plastic bag folded so thick it became opaque. He lifted it out and held it up to the headlights at the top of the slope.

Golden words gleamed through the cloudy plastic.

Thirty-three

Though Dionysius was clever enough to know he couldn't trust anyone, he still hardly survived, for he had no reliable friends or followers.

Plato, *Letter VII*

I was caught red-handed. He stood in the doorway, a drawn sword in his hand. Another man lurked in the shadows outside by the pillars.

'Do you know what the penalties are for breaking into the temple?'

I didn't say anything. Even Euphemus would have struggled to talk himself out of this one.

Dion crossed the threshold. His companion – an old man with wild hair and a large key – followed and closed the door behind him.

'Do you have any idea how much danger you're in?'

'Pretty much.'

'Beyond the obvious.' He took the handle of the chest and dragged it back behind the statue. I followed with an armful of manuscripts. 'You don't know what's happened.'

'Are you going to report me to your brother?'

He looked up and I shrank back. There are few sights more chastening than a nineteen year old whose illusions you've shattered. 'Have you stolen anything?'

I took Timaeus' manuscript from my belt and threw it in

the box. I didn't mention the tablet. I folded my arms across my chest to hide the bulge of the locket under my tunic.

'No.'

'Then maybe you've done nothing wrong.'

I nodded to his companion, who I assumed must be the temple priest.

'What about him?'

'He's my uncle – he won't say anything. If you've upset the goddess, she can probably take care of you herself.' He glanced at the statue behind me and made a small, apologetic bow. She didn't look offended.

'How did you know I was here?'

'You weren't in your room. One of the guards reported he'd heard strange sounds coming out of the sanctuary, and I remembered our conversation.' He shook his head. 'I hope it was worth it.'

The box closed with a bang. I remembered the lid falling shut on Agathon's coffin. Did he think it was worth it, as Dionysius' torturers went to work on him? Had he found something I'd missed?

The book was gibberish – the ravings of a madman.

'Come on,' said Dion. 'We have to get you back.'

The great doors closed behind us. We hurried down the steps and back towards my room. A thought struck me.

'Why were you looking for me in the first place?'

'To warn you.' He ducked under a dark archway that led through to the exercise ground. 'Dionysius—'

The guard must have been waiting in a niche in the wall, invisible in the darkness. All I heard was a sudden clatter of armour and a sharp command.

'Come with me.'

Dionysius sat on his throne, leaning forward, every muscle tensed ready to pounce. Blood oozed from a scratch on his arm that hadn't been there yesterday evening. I half expected to see blood on his lips, too: he had the look of a wolf who's had a taste and wants more. His myrmidons around the room balled their fists and waited for the signal to tear me apart.

I glanced at Dion. Was he a friend – or one of the wolves?

Dionysius' gaze bored into me, searching for something. Guilt? Fear? There was plenty of both.

'My men went to your room half an hour ago. Where were you?'

My room must have been busier than the agora: everyone had been there except me.

'I'd gone to the temple of Athena. I wanted to pray.'

He curled his fingers, testing his claws. He examined my scraped knuckles, the streak of blood on the back of my hand. He was enjoying this. 'In the middle of the night?'

'I couldn't sleep.'

'It's true,' said Dion. 'I was with him.'

Dionysius shot him a dangerous look. 'Really?'

'He asked me to go with him. He couldn't wander around Ortygia alone.'

If I'd looked at Dion, my gratitude would have betrayed us both. I wondered why he was doing it. I wondered whether the lie would hold both our weights.

'And where was your friend while you were at the temple?'

Dionysius leaned back a fraction, inviting me forward. A smile opened on his face like the jaws of a trap. But I didn't understand.

'Dion was with me. He told you—'

'Your friend the sophist.'

'Euphemus?' I struggled. So much had happened in those last few hours. 'I haven't seen him since dinner time.'

And a second later, I remembered. The corridor, the laboured references to Herodotus and Gyges.

Then, when the king had fallen asleep, Gyges entered his room and struck him dead.

I gave the cut on Dionysius' arm a closer look. It was deep – worse than you'd get cutting yourself on a razor. If you'd happened to be shaving in the middle of the night, and accidentally mistaken your arm for your cheek.

'The sophist was out of his room tonight, too,' Dionysius said. 'He wanted to give me a lesson in Athenian democracy. He made some incisive arguments.' He twisted his arm so that the blood gleamed in the light.

'What have you done with him?'

'We agreed to disagree. Syracuse isn't Athens. It would never have taken here.'

Our eyes locked. I tried to read them: the animal cunning, the ponderous intelligence, the cruelty and the hunger for power. But in the end, after all, they were just eyes.

'It wasn't easy to persuade him. He found it hard to swallow his pride.'

'Where is he?'

'Lying down. He said he was having trouble breathing.' Some of the soldiers laughed. 'At least, I think that's what he said.'

I'd be lying if I said I wasn't frightened. Exhausted, confused and numb with shock, I still understood I could suffer a lot of pain before Dionysius finished with me. And I didn't hate my life so much I was willing to throw it away.

'I was at the temple,' I insisted.

'An Athenian makes an unannounced visit to my room in the middle of the night. At the same time, the only other Athenian here – his best friend – takes it into his head to leave his room so he can say some prayers. And you expect me to believe that's a *coincidence*?'

He'd half risen out of his chair, his fists clenched around

the lion's heads on the arms. Any further and he'd have thrown himself on me.

The locket seemed to burn the guilt into my chest. I summoned every scrap of strength I could find in my soul to resist. It still wasn't enough.

'Ask your brother-in-law,' was all I could say.

Still halfway out of his chair, Dionysius looked at Dion. Even without my life hanging in the balance, there would have been something elemental in the contrast. Dionysius, his meaty hands and blacksmith's arms, his burnt-red face etched with twenty years of sleeping with a dagger under his pillow. Dion, slim and dark and desirable, with the happy confidence of youth and the implicit promise you might see something wonderful if you followed him.

'It's true,' Dion said, so casual he almost sounded bored.

Did Dionysius envy his brother-in-law? Did it ever cross his mind to wish he had him for a son, instead of the dull, idle boy he'd fathered? Or are tyrants incapable of doubt?

Dionysius sat back down in his chair. Even he couldn't completely resist Dion's aura. I hoped for Dion's sake it lasted. I've known a few men who had that kind of addictive charm – Socrates, Alcibiades, Agathon. None of them died of old age.

'Take him to bed,' Dionysius told his guards. But he winked as he said it. I glanced at Dion as the guards led me away, and saw that he didn't know what it meant either.

The guards took me to my room, bolted the door from the outside and left me there, sobbing into my mattress. They didn't even touch me.

But they didn't take me the most direct way. Instead of going past the ball-courts, we diverted down a passage which came out on a small balcony right at the tip of the island. Waves crashed on the rocks below; the setting moon illuminated the ghastly scene with its unforgiving light.

Euphemus lay spreadeagled on a wooden cross on the ground. Leather ligatures bound his wrists and ankles to the wood; another one had been fastened around his neck, wound around a little spindle so it could be tightened slowly. It had cut so deep it had almost disappeared into the flesh: the head seemed to have swollen out of all proportion. Dead eyes stared up at the almost-full moon and looked for something that wasn't there.

The guards waited long enough to be sure I understood. Then they took me to my room.

It was the night that would never end. The next thing I knew, someone or something was scuttling around my room. I stiffened with terror. Had Dionysius changed his mind already?

'It's all right,' said a familiar voice. 'When they come for you, they won't bother to be quiet.'

It was Leon. I don't know how he got in past the guards. He put his lamp down and sat on the bed, rocking slightly forward. His eyes were bagged and bloodshot.

'What happened?' I asked.

'Someone overheard something. Dionysius was about to move against us, so Euphemus went to see him. He knew he wouldn't succeed, but he thought it might make Dionysius believe he was acting alone. He sacrificed himself to save us.'

'*Us?*'

'Me. Others in the court. You.'

'But I haven't done anything.'

'Do you think that matters here?'

I tried to reconcile that with everything else I knew. All I could think was: 'It seems so out of character for Euphemus.'

'Out of character?' The idea puzzled him. 'How well did you know him?'

His best friend, Dionysius had called me. We'd kept company almost all the way from the Piraeus to Syracuse. And now it seemed the only time I'd come close was when I'd teased him.

You say the world is a cauldron, all boiling against all. You say we use convention to mask the grasping, selfish truth. But I think you're hiding the opposite. Strip away convention and social expectation, like the ring of Gyges, and you might find you actually have some good in you.

'Euphemus was part of it from the beginning,' Leon said. 'Why do you think he came here?'

'Euphemus came to work for Dionysius. He admired him.'

'Is that what you thought?'

'He always spoke highly of Dionysius.' But was that true? Now that it was too late, I found I couldn't think of a single thing he'd said to praise the tyrant. He'd pumped Dimos and Archytas for gossip; he'd teased out the contradictions in my self-righteousness. But he'd never said what he really thought.

'So because he didn't fly into Ortygia telling the world what a super democrat he was, you thought he didn't care? You thought you were the principled one?' He took the corner of the sheet and wiped his face on it. 'For a philosopher, if I may say so, you're remarkably willing to take things at face value.'

I looked for a way to dispute it – and couldn't find one.

'Not that your theatrics did any harm,' Leon went on. 'Dionysius knew there was a plot brewing. When you arrived, he assumed you must be part of it. Well, you seemed to believe your rhetoric, so why shouldn't he?'

'Why did he put me in charge of his son?'

'You think he cares about the boy?' He considered his own question. 'Well, maybe. Were you ever alone with him?'

I thought back. The guards in the library, eying the books like so much kindling. The librarian himself. And, always popping in or dropping by . . .

'Dion.' That was somewhere I didn't want to go. 'I thought he was your great hope. The man to put on the throne.'

378

'Dion's handicapped by his sense of duty. Even Dionysius doesn't know if Dion's loyal, but he knows he adores his nephew.'

I wanted to die. I wanted my body to dissolve, and the gods to tear my soul to shreds like smoke in a high wind. While I'd been reading Agathon's book of nonsense, Euphemus had risked his life to overthrow the tyrant. And lost it.

You think you're above all this, too good for the real world. I couldn't deny it now. I'd rejected the world because I couldn't understand it, because my mind insisted there must be something better. Euphemus took the world as it was and gobbled it up, unashamed of his appetites. He didn't believe there was any such thing as goodness or virtue, yet he'd been willing to die for it.

Socrates said: *If I have any wisdom at all, it's that I know I know nothing.* I'd forgotten even that much.

Leon shifted his weight on the bed to remind me he was still there.

'So what happens now?'

'Dionysius is still alive. No one's safe.'

'Won't he be on his guard?'

Leon squinted at me. 'When we asked you to help a few hours ago, you refused.'

'I'm not refusing now.'

'Dionysius is off tomorrow on a hunting trip. The boy's going, so you will too.'

'Will he really take me, after all . . . ' I flapped a hand. 'This.'

'Dionysius knows Euphemus must have had accomplices in the court. As long as he suspects you, he'll keep you close in case you lead him to the others.'

'How do you know I won't betray you?'

He pressed his fingers together. 'Because the moment Dionysius thinks you're no use, he'll kill you.'

Thirty-four

Jonah – Sibari

It was 1 a.m. in Athens. Adam answered after three rings.

'I've got the tablet,' Jonah said into the phone.

The phone said nothing back. If it hadn't been for the music playing in the background, he'd have thought the connection had dropped.

'Where was it?' Adam asked at last, as if they were simply discussing a key he'd misplaced.

'Do you want it?'

'Very much.'

'Then give me Lily.'

Another silence. A breeze blew through his wet clothes, carrying the cold deep inside him.

'Where are you now?'

'Italy.'

'I'll need to make some arrangements. Have you got transportation?'

'Yes.'

'Head south. Leave your phone on. I'll call in a bit.'

Jonah handed the phone to Ren. His own pocket was soaked through, along with the rest of his clothes. He could feel the ice creeping closer to his heart.

'Where now?' she asked.

'Back to the lab. We'll get the van and head out.' He wanted to be gone as fast as possible.

'The truck might be more reliable.'

'I want the van.' Battered, rusted and conspicuous it might be – but it was a friend, and he needed friends now.

Richard glanced at his watch. 'What shall I tell them if they come here?'

'Tell them?' Jonah shook his head. 'You're coming with us.'

A plywood wall boxed off the back of the van, where they kept the instruments and kit. Jonah considered locking Richard in with them, but in the end he didn't bother. He didn't think Richard wanted to make himself a martyr by attacking him while they were driving. They all squeezed into the front and headed down SS106, the flat artery that connects the Italian heel to its toe. That late, they had the road to themselves. Their headlights opened a tunnel through the darkness, forever receding as they rushed into it.

'Why does Maroussis want the tablet?' Jonah asked.

Wedged in between Jonah and Ren, Richard squirmed. 'It's a priceless artefact.'

'Everything has a price,' Ren said. 'It's not even unique.'

'It must be,' said Jonah.

'Ask Adam. Do you think he tells me anything? He thinks I'm just a glorified shovel monkey.'

'He always overestimated you.'

Richard lapsed into a sullen silence, then said, as if it was something he'd rehearsed: 'Adam's a nihilist perfectionist. He's hard to please.'

A fragment of an old conversation dropped through time. We saw through the gilded lie. 'He's not a nihilist,' Jonah said. 'He's an idealist who can't find anything that measures up.'

The phone rang. Jonah put it on speaker.

'Do you have a map?' Adam said.

'Yes.'

'Just after Locri, there's a turnoff signposted to a village called Plati. Follow that road for twenty-eight kilometres. When you see a rockslide next to a chapel, turn right onto a track. That'll take you to a village.'

'And that's where you've got Lily?'

'That's where she'll be.'

'Who else?'

'I'm hoping to be there myself. To take delivery of the tablet.'

'No.' Jonah's foot pressed harder on the accelerator. 'You'll give me Lily. Then I'll tell you where I've left the tablet.'

'That's not acceptable.'

'Do you think I'm going to drive up to the middle of nowhere with the tablet in my hand and trust you to keep your word?' No answer. 'How badly do you want this tablet?'

'How badly do you want Lily?'

'There was a time when you'd have done anything for her.'

A pause. 'Just bring the tablet.'

The odomoter ticked round. Jonah half hoped the signal would die, letting him off the hook. *How badly do you want Lily?*

'OK.'

'One more thing.'

Jonah steeled himself. 'What?'

'The road's not in good condition. Drive carefully.'

He drove forever. At some stage, Richard climbed in the back and went to sleep; Ren dozed intermittently against her window. Jonah didn't feel tired. Hope, and the terror that hope brings, kept his blood racing through empty towns and silent roads. The darkness in his mirror softened to purple, then deep blue. Ren stirred.

'Do you mind?' Jonah asked.

She stretched. 'Sorry?'

'Giving back the tablet. You said you wanted to hurt Maroussis. Now he's getting what he wants.'

She stared out of the window. A pharmacy's neon green cross flickered on the glass. 'Your wife's more important.'

'Yes.'

'Tell me about her.' She put her bare feet up on the dashboard. 'Tell me why you didn't give up, when the obvious conclusion was that she'd run off with Adam. Didn't you doubt her?'

'No.'

'Why not?'

'Because . . . I knew.'

'How?'

He struggled to find the words. 'It's like when I'm playing with the band. When it's tight, when we're all in a groove, it just feels different. Sometimes I don't even know what's going to come out, but I know it's going to be right. It's like that with Lily. There's something inside her I hear, or feel, or sense, or whatever you want to call it. Something that's true.'

'You mean like her soul?'

He shrugged, embarrassed. 'You're the one who believes in reincarnation.' He tried to turn it back on her. 'Haven't you ever felt that way about someone?'

'No.' She wiggled her toes. 'Well, maybe once. But he was a long time ago.'

'What happened to him?'

She changed the subject. 'Do you know where we're going? The Aspromonte?'

'No.'

'It's like a piece of history that survived, a lost world from when this whole area was a Greek colony.'

'I thought that was ancient history.'

'It survived here. Deep in the Aspromonte, there are still villages which speak a dialect of ancient Greek. It's one of the most remote places in Italy.' She frowned. 'It's also the home of the N'drangheta. You've heard of them?'

383

'Mafia, right?'

'The name's a corruption of *Andron Geta,* which is Greek for "men of honour".'

Jonah steered the van past a dead dog on the roadside. 'Are we likely to meet them?'

'Maroussis' business is shipping. On the other side of the Aspromonte is Gioia Tauro, the biggest container port in Italy and also Europe's biggest port for cocaine. You think Maroussis doesn't have friends in this part of the world?'

Ahead, a signpost pointed them to Plati. As they turned, Jonah realised he could read it without the headlights.

Oxford

The morning after Adam's symposium, Jonah woke early. The snow from the night before had settled, a thin crust on the world that made everything different. On any other day, he could have sat by the window for hours taking it in. Not today.

The bed they shared was a student bed, a narrow iron frame with sagging springs. Lily wasn't in it. She wasn't in the kitchen either. Ice smeared the open window: he touched it, and realised it was on the inside of the pane. The air was so cold it hurt to breathe.

She hadn't come back.

He found orange juice in the fridge and drank half the carton. There were bananas in a bowl: he ate three. He wondered about boiling the kettle, but the thought of the taste of coffee made him sick.

There was a void where his mind should have been. He pulled on some clothes and boots, his army-surplus coat and scarf, and let himself out. Down the road, past the pub and the new housing estate, along Aristotle Lane and across the railway tracks. Beyond, the open space of Port Meadow glittered in the winter sun, with the dark river winding through the trees in the distance. A few dog walkers had braved it, but otherwise the snow was pristine.

Walking saved him having to think about the night before. The meadow had flooded and frozen before the snow: every step crunched through to the ice beneath, threatening his balance. He had to concentrate so hard, he reached the river almost without realising it.

He stuck his hands in his pockets and stared into the black water. A half-sunk log twisted in the current.

What happened last night?

The memories were too much for his fried, fragile head. He kicked away some snow and stamped his heel on the ice until it shattered, pulling away the shards and tossing them in the river one by one. They floated away like pieces of memory.

Her footsteps were so light they made no sound in the snow. He didn't hear her until she spoke.

'You weren't at home. I thought you'd come here.'

He threw the last piece of ice in the river, skipping it across the surface like a stone. 'Shouldn't you be with Adam?'

'Charis took him to the Radcliffe Infirmary.'

It wasn't what he meant, or the answer he expected. But anger and cold made his brain too sluggish to change course.

'What happened last night? You and Adam.'

He thought he was prepared. He'd let the cold flow in deep, icing him up before the bruises started to form. He was ready for the hit.

But not for what she actually said.

'He tried to kill himself.'

He turned around. The sun on the snow hit his tired eyes and he flinched back. All he saw of Lily was her negative, a ghost image behind his eyelids.

'Why?'

'A bad trip.' She shivered. Jonah couldn't see it, but he heard it in her voice. 'The stuff he put in the wine made him crazy. He was convinced he was trapped in a dream, that the only way to wake up was by dying.'

'Did you drink it too?'

'It made me sick. I think most of it came back up.'

'What about the others?'

'They're OK.' Another tremor. 'They were just watching, laughing at him. Julian opened the window and told him to fly away.'

Shielding his eyes, he risked another look back. Lily was crying.

'It's not your fault.'

'He did it for me.'

'That's the most fucked-up thing—'

'He wanted to get to the truth.'

'What truth?'

'He got the idea that we're prisoners of our selves, that the drug would smash down our conscious walls and reveal our true feelings.'

'Why?'

'He thinks I love him.'

They'd come to the place he'd first thought, after all, but from a different direction and he wasn't prepared for it. All he could do was stay frozen still and try not to fall into the white void around him.

'And?'

'I love you,' she said simply.

In the dead trees on the island, a crow cawed. The ice inside him started to drip, but that was worse than frozen. He wasn't numb any more. He was cold and wet and he'd been standing still too long.

'I'm going home,' he said. 'Back north. This was the wrong thing.'

'Because of last night?

'Because of . . . everything.'

'Are you saying *we're* the wrong thing?'

She was nothing but a voice, a goddess speaking out of the ice. He couldn't bring himself to look at her. He told himself it was the glare.

'I don't belong here.'

'You do when I'm here.'

'It was easy on holiday. Oxford . . . ' How to explain it? The dislocation and hours of solitude. The feeling of things happening just out of sight, that you were peering in the window of a mansion hearing words and laughter drift out, no hope of a key.

'This isn't a good time for this conversation.'

He turned and started walking. The snow crunched under his feet.

'If you leave, you won't come back,' she called after him.

He knew it was true. He knew he was pushing her to breaking. He kept walking.

'If you don't turn around now, you'll never see me again.'

Jonah kept going, slouched against the cold. He knew he was wrong. He knew he'd regret it. He could already feel the hurt beginning to form, ice creeping across the edges of his soul. But there was a darkness inside him, lumpen and proud, which refused to turn. Even if it was the biggest mistake of his life.

Something cold and hard hit him smack on the back of the head. He spun around, just in time to catch the next snowball clean in the face. Snow ran through his hair and fell down his collar.

'Why'd you do that?'

Her face was flushed, her bare hands wet with snow. The scratch on her cheek from the night before was livid.

'Because I wanted you to turn around.'

'That's cheating.'

'You can keep going if you want.'

But he didn't. Without really thinking, he was walking towards her. They met on the riverbank and embraced, a hot kiss that melted the snow on his face and made it trickle down his nose. Whatever had been inside him dissolved away. In the distance, among the spires, a bell chimed.

He licked meltwater off his lips and tasted salt. Lily was crying. He kissed her on the forehead, then softly on her lips again.

'Promise me one thing.'

He leaned back and looked into her eyes, shining blue as the winter sky. 'Anything.'

'If I ever walk away from you – because I'm proud, or hurt, or stupid, or anything – promise me you'll follow? You won't give up on me too soon?'

He buried himself in the folds of her scarf and whispered his promise.

Italy

At first, the road wound along a stony river valley. Then it began to climb. They went through a village and the road got steeper, switching back every fifty yards or so. Rocks littered the surface, big enough to damage the van. Off the road, huge concrete drainage channels made steps down the mountain, and strange fists of rock erupted from the trees as if the titans below the earth had begun to break out from their captivity.

Jonah swung the van hard around a corner and slammed the brakes. Three concrete barriers blocked the way, staggered like tank traps. Beyond, the road broke off abruptly in a tangle of mangled asphalt and steel rods where a flash flood or subsidence had taken a giant bite out of it. The only way through was a narrow strip of sand, barely wider than the van. Or maybe not quite as wide.

He edged the van forward, stalling three times. He winced as one of the barriers took a swipe at the paintwork. He put it close enough to the mountainside that the wing mirror scraped the rock. He still wasn't sure he had enough room to cross the gap.

He opened the door and jumped down. After five hours in the van, his legs had cramped badly. He took two steps, swaying dangerously near the ravine. The mountain's silence left him breathless.

The makeshift repair filling the road was about four feet wide. The van was wider. Only a matter of inches – but they were non-negotiable.

'How far are we from the turn?' said Ren.

Jonah stuck his head in the cab and checked the mileometer. 'We've come about eighteen miles from the main road.' It seemed so little for the effort involved – it had taken the best part of an hour.

'That's almost twenty-eight kilometres,' Richard said.

'We have to be close.' Jonah took the tablet, his phone and a bottle of water out of the van, then backed it up so it wasn't blocking the way in the unlikely event anyone else wanted to come through. The only other car he'd seen was a wreck gathering rust on the edge of a precipice.

They crossed the infill and carried on up the road. As soon as they got around the next corner, Jonah saw they needn't have bothered worrying about leaving the van. A landslip had broken through the concrete retaining wall, completely blocking the road. Just before it, beside a small chapel, a dirt track led off into the trees.

'Adam seems very familiar with this neighbourhood,' Richard said.

'Or someone he knows.' *You think Maroussis doesn't have friends in this part of the world?* He put his hand against his trouser pocket, feeling the toffee tin against his leg. *A golden ticket*, he thought. *My ticket to Lily.*

'Do you really think he'll go through with it?'

'What's he got to lose?'

Without waiting, Jonah set off up the dirt track. Ren fell in behind him. A few moments later, so did Richard.

The three of them walked in silence, along the edge of a defile that led around the shoulder of the mountain. Below, the slope fell away towards the distant sea. A dawn breeze blew cool air around them. Jonah didn't notice. His eyes had disengaged: all he could see was Lily, a blur rushing to meet him. Nothing else.

Ren glanced at the dry earth underfoot. 'No footprints or tyre marks.'

'They'll come.'

The sea vanished. The path turned a corner and suddenly the world closed off. They were in a high valley folded between two massive arms of the mountain. Ren pointed to the cliffs opposite.

'The village.'

He had to squint to see it. Even then, he wasn't sure. The red-brown houses hovered against the red-brown cliffs like an illusion, almost vertical.

'Who the hell would live there?'

The path wound up to the village, climbing higher and higher. The sun had come out and there was no wind in the valley: Jonah began to sweat. His hair plastered against his forehead and fell over his eyes, so that, even as they came closer, the village never grew clearer.

At last they arrived at a stone arch at the top of the slope. Jonah wiped the hair back out of his eyes and stared. The village was a ruin: empty windows, hinges without doors, skeletal beams stretched across gaping roofs. Bright red flowers blossomed from the cracks in the stone.

'It's a ghost town.' The silent houses echoed Richard's voice back at them.

'What time did Adam say?' Ren asked.

'He didn't.'

Would he come? He wandered on through the village, leaving the others behind. At the very top, looking down on the cascade of broken houses, stood the church. It was the only intact building he'd seen. It even had its bell, still hanging in the tower, and a pair of stout wooden doors padlocked shut.

He hammered on the doors until his knuckles bled. The knocking rang around the valley, but no one answered.

'Have a look at this.'

Ren had come up behind him. She took his hand, and led him down the hill to a house he hadn't noticed before, sunk below the road on the downhill slope. It was the only building that showed any signs of repair. The windows and doorway had been filled in with cinderblocks, and corrugated iron sheets thrown over the bare rafters at one end. Looking down into it, he could see straw covering the floor, and an iron ring bolted to the wall. Perhaps a local goatherd had used it as a makeshift stable.

The mortar was new, and no rust grew on the iron ring. Jonah knelt, braced himself between two roof-beams and jumped down.

Smells of dung and urine came up from the straw at his feet. He paced around the tiny enclosure, ending up at the ring. The old stone around it was scratched, fresh white scars that made his heart race. Then stop.

Near the mess of lines where the ring had chafed the stone, a mark stood out. A simple piece of graffiti, a heart surrounding two initials. JB LW.

Jonah Barnes, Lily Wilson.

Ren's face appeared above him, dark against the sky. 'Did you find something?'

'This was where they kept her.' Shock was already distilling into anger, a raw fury that they'd treated her like this. Penned up like an animal. He felt the claustrophobia, the stink of the filthy straw rising in his mouth. An evil place.

What did they do to her?

He needed to get out. The wall wasn't high: he could reach the top. Lily probably could have too, if she hadn't been chained up. With Ren pulling, he hauled himself back out onto the road above.

'Lily was here,' he said. Ren wasn't listening. 'What?'

'They're coming.'

She pointed down the slope. Across the valley behind the trees, a column of dust spiralled into the clean morning sky from the track they'd come up. If he listened hard, he could hear the drone of an engine.

'Where's Richard?'

'He was tired. He waited by the gate.'

Jonah glanced down into the empty house and took another hit of anger. Dark music played in his head.

Turn it down, he told himself. *You won't save her that way.*

'Last chance,' Ren said. Over the valley, sunlight flashed off the cars coming up the track. Jonah clung to the music.

They walked back down through the deserted village. The trees hid the cars, for the moment, but the engine noise grew steadily louder, like a giant insect circling its prey.

'I suppose we'll never know why Maroussis wanted the tablet,' Ren said.

'He's crazy.'

'Perhaps.' Ren halted. 'Can I borrow your phone? And the tablet?'

Jonah gave them to her. She spread the gold leaf on a flat

stone in the shade of a house, and held the phone a few inches away to take a photograph. 'A souvenir.'

An image of the tablet appeared on the phone's screen. Ren spread her fingers to enlarge it. The pressed letters swelled into shape.

'The world's first text message,' Jonah said, trying to break his own tension. Ren stared at the screen, her eyes flitting back to the gold tablet, until Jonah couldn't stand it.

'You can read it when I've got Lily.'

She looked up, though she hadn't heard him. 'This is different.'

'What do you mean?'

'The tablet. It has a different text to the others.'

'Are you sure?'

She fiddled with the phone. 'This is one from the museum. You can see the letters of the opening line – ΜΝΗΜΟΣΥΝΑΣ. Now look at yours.'

Jonah held the tablet in the palm of his hand and stared at it. He didn't speak a word of ancient Greek, but he could see the letters were different.

'Every other tablet that's been discovered begins the same way. ΜΝΗΜΟΣΥΝΑΣ. *Mnemosyne, Memory.*'

'But Charis said . . . ' A dreadful thought began to shake him. The cars were louder, too – they must be almost at the gate. He snatched his phone from Ren, found the number he needed and dialled. No one picked up; he dialled again. This time she answered.

'Six five eight oh.'

Who else answered their phone like that any more? 'It's Jonah.'

'Darling, it's six o'clock in the morning. Even the children don't wake me up this early.'

'The tablet I gave you. The transcript. Why did you tell me it was the same as all the others?'

A sigh. 'Can't this wait?'

393

'The tablet has a different beginning. Why didn't you say so?'

'I don't know.' A pause. 'I don't keep it on my bedside table.'

'Did you tell Adam? Did he tell you not to tell me?'

'I didn't . . . ' She trailed off into a long silence that ended with a sniff. 'Adam's always been better at Greek.'

Crouched beside him, Ren was mouthing something.

'What do the extra words say?'

'Darling, I have to go. Xander's waking up.'

'*What do they say?*'

'Where hundred-headed Typhos shakes open the earth, I went down into the bosom of the goddess.' She spat it it so quickly, she must have been chewing on it for days. A sob swallowed the final words, and he imagined the tears running down her face. He felt no pity.

A car door slammed, not far away. He gripped the phone tighter, trying to keep hold of her. 'Did you give Adam the whole translation?'

Another stifled sob. 'He knows everything. He always does.'

Realisation dawned, blood-red and ominous. 'But if you told them what the tablet says, they don't need it.'

'What? Who doesn't need it? What are you talking about?'

He wasn't speaking to Charis any more. He hung up and stared down the mountain. The jeeps' plumes of dust had begun to settle; the engines had stopped.

'Adam already knows what the tablet says,' he told Ren. 'He isn't going to bring Lily.'

'What will you do?'

Could he be sure? *If you turn around now, you'll never see me again.* The empty houses gaped at him, dead souls envious of the living. Even their pain.

'Let's see what they say.'

She gave him a look that was half despair and half admiration. 'Whatever they've done with Lily, they'll do it to you too.'

'I have to find her.' He kicked at a stone and watched it roll over the cliff. 'It's too late for anything else.'

Two small 4x4s had pulled up outside the village gate. Five men stood around them. Four wore dark suits and sunglasses, wide bodies and hard faces. The fifth was Adam. Standing a little in front of the others, in his black jeans and black turtleneck, he looked like their prisoner.

Jonah descended the slope towards them. Ren hung back.

'Where's Lily?'

'We'll take you to her.'

'You said you'd bring her here.'

'Did you bring the tablet?'

Jonah considered bluffing. But he could see the white sleeve of Richard's shirt hovering just behind the gateway, and Richard would have told them everything. There was no reason to lie.

'You know what it says already.'

Adam nodded.

'Why do you need the tablet?'

'We don't.'

'Then why did you bring me here?' A vast space had opened around him and he felt as if he'd fall forever. His words vanished into the mountain sky.

'I didn't think you'd believe me if I told you the truth,' Adam said. A noise in the sky chopped up his voice, the drumming of rotors coming closer.

'What's that?'

'I'm going to take you to Lily.'

Thirty-five

Visitor: There are two main kinds of hunting on land
Theaetetus: What are they?
Visitor: You can hunt tame animals, or wild ones.
Theaetetus: Does anyone really hunt tame animals?
Visitor: Yes – if you count human beings as tame.

Plato, *Sophist*

I'm in a low grey room filled with people. Diotima is there, and I have to talk to her, but the people around me keep getting in the way.

All the other people are me: prior versions of myself, hanging over my shoulder. A great crowd of us. They look slightly shame-faced – they know I don't want them there – but they won't leave. Every time I move towards Diotima, they fall in behind like a flock of sheep.

I woke up.

'Were you dreaming?'

Dion's hand reached out and touched my bare arm. On the far side of the tent, young Dionysius snored and snuffled like a pig.

'Diotima says that Etna is a good place for dreams. She says souls creep out of Hades through the vents, and whisper truths in our ears.'

'It wasn't a good dream.'

'Then let's hope it isn't true.'

I rolled over, trying to shake off the image of my other selves. 'How well do you know Diotima?'

He thought about that. 'I don't think anyone knows her well. She comes and goes without reason. She pops up where you least expect her, and then she's never there when you want her.'

'Want' has various meanings. 'She's afraid of your brother-in-law,' I said.

'I think he's more afraid of her.'

'Why?'

'She's got power. Dionysius can sense it – he's good at that – but he doesn't understand it. So he feels threatened.'

I didn't disagree – I'd felt it too. But I wanted to hear Dion's opinion.

'What sort of power?'

'She can read dreams.' The mattress rustled as Dion turned onto his back. 'She's a Sicel, did you know that? One of the prehistoric tribes of Sicily. The village she comes from is a sacred place. They say the temple there is to Demeter, but really it's to Hybla, an old Sicel goddess. She gives dream oracles. If you go there, the priests interpret them for you.'

'Are they accurate?'

'I've never been. It's not far from here, actually.'

'Here' was Etna, our camp in the forest on its middle slopes. We'd reached it yesterday at sunset after a hard day's riding. From mid-morning, ever since we came down from the hills north of Syracuse, it had dominated our horizon: its snow-capped summit puffing smoke into the blue sky. I'd barely spoken a word. Dion rode at the front with Dionysius and his son; I picked up the rear with the spear-carriers and grooms. I'd spotted Leon in the party ahead of me, but we pretended not to know each other.

It had been a good day to be alone. The night before had ended, at last, but I hadn't slept. I felt like sand in the ring:

bruised from the impact of heavy men falling, unable to move. Everywhere I looked I saw Euphemus' corpse, except that each time his lolling head grew more inflated, until the bulging eyes were bigger than his hands. I couldn't escape the accusation in those eyes.

I don't dress up what I'm saying as some sort of absolute truth. I'm honest.

Outside the tent, an owl hooted; another replied. I imagined the bird like the ones they mint on our silver drachmas – short and stout and round-eyed, sitting on a branch and listening for mice or toads. How close was it to our tent? Was it sitting on the silver birch opposite the door – the one with the hollow in its trunk? If it looked carefully with its big round eyes, could it see the gleam of steel deep in the tree where I'd hidden the knife?

I rolled over again and tried to sleep.

Tyrants love trumpets. Dionysius' woke us at dawn – so loud, they must have scared off every animal on the mountain. Perhaps he wanted to give them a sporting chance.

In a glade nearby, we sacrificed at an altar to Artemis. The stone looked ancient, worn smooth in the middle where so much blood and wine had poured down its sinkhole. The ends of the altar curved upwards, like horns or the tips of a bow.

Dionysius disembowelled a hare his men had trapped and laid the innards on the altar. 'Mistress maiden, ruler of the stormy mountains, let us cross the threshold of your realm and return with success.'

I looked at the tiny organs oozing onto the altar, the blood like red gloves on his hands, and thought of the knife in the tree. Could I really do that?

I can't believe we're here talking about . . . this . . . and you want to turn it into a philosophy exercise.

We milled around when the ritual was done, while slaves sharpened the spears and folded the nets. Hounds smelled the blood in the air and strained their leashes. Across the glade, I saw Leon drinking from a wineskin. He caught my eye and gave a small nod. Wine dribbled out of the side of the bag and splashed his tunic red.

I turned to look for Dion. Instead, as if he'd been stalking me, I found Dionysius right behind me.

Every man has his natural habitat, the context where he makes sense. Take Achilles out of battle, or Socrates out of the agora, and they look ridiculous. Here, in the wild, was where Dionysius belonged. His shaggy mane of red hair, his dangerous energy and wary eyes fitted the mountain forest perfectly. It didn't make him any more pleasant.

He clapped me on the shoulder. 'You look nervous. Are you ready for the kill?'

Animals watch us with dumb eyes, but we never know what they see. Did Dionysius know what was going to happen? Was I as doomed as Euphemus?

'Make sure you keep an eye on my boy. I don't want him getting hurt.' He hung on, twisting my shoulder like a promise of things to come. Then he let go.

'It should be a good day's hunting.'

Socrates had a routine he sometimes used, comparing hunting pigeons to the hunt for knowledge. I've no idea how he came up with it: he must have got chatting with some trapper in the market one day. The idea of Socrates crawling through the forest with lures and snares beggars belief.

The metaphor never really worked for me. I love knowledge, but I hate hunting. That day, I hated it more than ever. The sun beat down through the forest; branches tore at me; my head ached from the hounds baying. The knife I'd strapped to my thigh chafed my legs and made me sweat horribly. In the end, I untied it and tucked it into my boot, hoping no one would notice.

Quickly, our line stretched out across the mountain. Around mid-morning, we heard shouts from the distance.

'They've picked up the boar's scent,' said Dion. 'Let's see if we can corner it.'

In fact, there was little danger of that. Young Dionysius would have struggled to overtake a tortoise. His face burned, his nose ran, his lungs wheezed and coughed. As long as we stayed with him – me, Dion and two guards – we'd be lucky to see the boar before it was on the spit.

But we had to show willing, and so we went on. The trees thinned; the air grew cooler. The sweat we'd built up in the climb now chilled us. Dionysius looked miserable, though I don't suppose I looked any happier. I knew what was coming.

We paused in a glade ringed by pale green trees. Back below, we'd sought out the shade; now, we chased the sunlight. It shone brightly, but somehow weaker than before. I stood in the middle of the clearing and tipped my face upwards, turning this way and that as I tried to catch the warmth.

As I did, I found myself looking straight up the mountain through a gap between the trees. It framed the ridge above, where two hills erupted out of the slope like boils pushed up by the heat of the fires below. Perfectly symmetrical and perfectly conical. Silhouetted against the sky, they made a pair of triangles, with the dip between them like an inscribed circle.

Cold sweat iced my skin as I remembered the picture I'd found on the manuscript in the temple.

'What are those hills?' I asked Dion.

He laughed. 'The locals call them Hybla's breasts. It's actually the place I told you about, where they found Empedocles' bronze sandal.'

I took out the gold tablet and unrolled it.

'What's that?' Dion asked.

The tiny words swam before my sweaty eyes.

Travel further down the sacred road
In glory, with the other initiated souls.
Folded in the breasts of the Queen of Hell.

I looked back at the hills, shading my eyes. 'Is there a temple there?'

'An old Sicel shrine: it's mostly ruined. Only—'

A trumpet interrupted him, blaring through the forest from further around the mountain. Not a fanfare or a rallying cry, but short, panicked blasts.

'Something's happened!' Dion grabbed his spear and started running towards the sound. The guards followed. On the edge of the clearing, Dion glanced back and shouted to me, 'Stay with the boy. Make sure nothing happens.'

Their footsteps died into the forest. Behind me, young Dionysius sat on a boulder in the shade and picked apart a twig. Even the sudden rush of danger didn't seem to have excited him. I could hardly bring myself to look at him.

I pulled the knife out of my boot. Sunlight bounced off the blade onto the boy's face, and he looked up. We both stared at the knife, equally surprised, as if an unreal object had suddenly appeared between us. Even with my fingers curled around the handle, the weight in my hand, I didn't really understand that it was real. That it would cut real flesh, and a real life would end.

I took three steps towards the boy and faltered. He stared at me, eyes wide.

Can a good man do a bad thing in a good cause?

Hunting knowledge isn't the same as hunting pigeons or boars. Or men. I looked at the knife again, still trying to comprehend it. Two brown eyes stared back at me out of the polished blade – my own. We examined each other, I and myself, wondering what I was capable of.

Something long and sharp whistled through the air and plucked at my arm. I dropped the knife and spun off-balance, clutching my arm in pain.

One of Dionysius' guards stood on the edge of the clearing. *How did he get here so fast?* He was dressed for battle, not hunting, with a helmet on his head and a sword at his side. His spear quivered in the earth just beyond me.

I started stammering some kind of excuse, but neither of us believed it. He drew his sword and walked towards me. I searched his face for anger, hatred – any emotion that would add some meaning to the end of my life. He just looked like someone concentrating hard.

A stone the size of a fist sailed out of the trees and struck the soldier's head. His helmet rang like a gong. His knees buckled; he staggered forward, but recovered his balance and turned to see who had attacked him.

It was all I needed. The stone had rolled past him almost to my feet. I picked it up and crossed the clearing. His head was still ringing from the first blow: he didn't hear me coming. With my good arm, I brought the stone down on his head again, and again, and once more to be sure. He collapsed in a heap.

Can a good man do a bad thing in a good cause? Apparently so, if his life depends on it and there's a good-sized rock handy.

A rustle in the trees. I lunged for the dropped sword, but my hand was shaking so badly I could hardly pick it up. Blood flowed down my arm where the spear had cut it. I was defenceless.

The trees parted. Diotima emerged from the forest, moving softly as a fawn. She hurried over to me, tore a strip off the fallen soldier's tunic, and bandaged my arm.

I looked at the rock. 'Did you . . . ?' Her slim arms, bare to the shoulder, looked too delicate to have thrown it so hard. 'How—?'

'Dionysius knows. He sets spies on his spies, and guards to guard his guards.' Blood had already soaked through the bandage. She tore off another strip and wound it over the first, then picked a few stems from a plant growing under one of the beech trees. 'Chew on this. It'll help the bleeding.'

The leaves were bitter and made me dizzy. I sat there, stupefied, while Diotima cocked her head and listened. All I heard was birds.

'The assassination failed. Dionysius will be here soon.'

I struggled to my feet. 'I have to get away.'

A cool look that seemed to mock something inside me. 'It isn't you Dionysius wants.'

'Who?' I searched her face. '*You?*'

'You were the bait.'

'And you came anyway.'

She kept my gratitude at arm's length. 'I didn't want you to end up like Agathon.'

She turned her head again, and this time I heard it too: the crash and snap of heavy animals breaking their way through the forest.

'You have to get down off the mountain. Head for Katane. It's Carthaginian, so Dionysius can't go there. You'll find a ship going to Athens, or at least to Thurii.'

'What about you?'

'I'll find you.'

I hated to leave her – but there was no time to argue. I could hear the hunt coming closer. I turned to go, and saw young Dionysius still cowering behind a tree, too frightened to move.

'What about him?'

Diotima shrugged. 'Are you going to kill him?'

The knife lay on the ground where I'd dropped it, the

curved blade like a coiled snake in the middle of the glade. I shuddered.

'No.'

'Then let's go.'

We left him. Diotima glided into the forest, while I staggered and stumbled in the opposite direction. My arm burned, my head swam, my mouth ached for water and I had a stitch like a spear through my side. The golden chain bounced and swung around my neck. It snagged on a branch and nearly throttled me.

I stopped, panting hard. My sweating, panicked hands struggled to disentangle the chain. As it came free, I almost hurled it away.

But something stopped me. The golden locket seemed to throb in my hand. I knew I had to keep running, but I couldn't move. All I could think of were the twin hills I'd seen from the clearing, the valley between them and the picture on Timaeus' book. I heard its song in my ears: dark, ecstatic music calling me in.

You have to get down off the mountain, Diotima insisted. I saw the harbour at Katane, and the ship waiting for me, its high-beaked prow turned towards Athens. I saw Glaucon standing on the cape at Sounion like old King Aegeus, shielding his eyes against the glare on the water as he looked for my return.

What are you looking for, in the dark shadows of Hades? the tablet whispered. Have you come this far to give up? Don't you want to know?

Stay away, Agathon warned me. But it was too late.

I turned up the mountain.

The hunt was in full cry: baying, barking, closing its net like in one of my nightmares. I climbed and climbed, never resting, but each time I heard the pursuit it was closer. At least Diotima might have got away. The slope steepened. The stitch spread through my body like a crack. The ground became loose, crumbling underfoot, so that with every step I'd already slipped halfway back before I could take the next.

I staggered over a rise and stopped. The two steep hills loomed over me, left and right. A silver birch grew in the saddle between them, and underneath it stood the temple.

It was a simple building: a small white house, flat-roofed, blank-faced. Two columns supported a porch over a black doorway, with a marble garland winding across it and a black stone altar in front. Ants crawled over the altar, making a hairline procession into the bronze cup someone had left there.

I touched the gold locket. It seemed to tremble, like a metal bowl placed next to a vibrating string. The birds had stopped singing.

The Mansion of Night, the tablet said.

'What's inside?'

Come and see.

As I reached the steps, a white hound bounded out of the trees. I thought it would tear me apart but, just in front of the altar, it suddenly skidded to a halt, legs splayed, ears back, barking and growling. I didn't look twice, but dived into the temple.

The moment I crossed the threshold, something changed. I could smell it in the air. Dark as incense and sweet as poison. As the darkness covered my eyes, I saw a dull glow at the back of the empty room, a square hole lit by flickering flames from within.

A black and nameless terror welled out of the hole. At the same time, shouts drifted through from outside, voices from another world. I remembered something Socrates said.

If you're out of your depth, it doesn't really matter whether you've fallen into a little bath or the middle of the ocean. You still have to learn to swim.

I went down.

Thirty-six

Jonah – Etna

He was flying. A long way down, the blue sea raced by. Ahead, almost at eye level, the cone of Mount Etna swelled into the sky, a giant mouth exhaling a long plume of smoke.

He looked over at Adam. 'Are you going to drop me in the volcano?'

They hadn't given him a headset: Adam couldn't have heard him over the clatter of the rotors. But he got the sense. He gave a tight, inscrutable smile and shook his head.

Up front, the pilot glanced back and muttered something into his microphone. Adam peered forward between the seats at the smoke coming off the volcano, thick and black like an oil fire. A thin film of ash clouded the helicopter's canopy.

Jonah remembered how an Icelandic volcano had closed down European airspace a couple of years ago. Lily had been at a conference in Florence, trapped with the millions of others who'd suddenly woken up into a world where easy air travel no longer happened. If a volcano a thousand miles off could be so dangerous to jets, what about flying a small helicopter a few hundred yards away?

He looked around the cabin – the three guards, dark shades over scarred faces; Ren; Adam, like the Angel of Death in his black clothes and bulging black flight helmet. *And you're worried about some ash?*

The helicopter buzzed over the side of the mountain. Jonah had never been so close to a volcano before. Black lava fields, miles wide, spilled down the slopes. Further around, a vast crater had been blown out of the mountainside, leaving a bare plateau of knotted lava. Strands of smoke and cloud blew past the helicopter, while a row of serrated peaks guarded the mountain's flank. It felt like a lost world.

As they came around to Etna's southern face, Jonah saw the mountain spreading down to the Catania plain beyond. Well past the point where the slope levelled off, a series of rounded hills bulged out of the landscape.

The helicopter banked and headed towards a pair of the hills which rose out of the middle slopes of the mountain. There was a strange, geometrical symmetry to them: each like the other, and both almost perfectly conical. Their tree-covered hilltops stood out like a pair of fertile islands in a frozen sea of rock.

The pilot put them down on the tarmac road that wound up the mountain, below the hills. A black Mercedes 4x4, as long as a house, had parked across it to block off the traffic. Jonah gazed at it as if it were a creature that had sprung from his nightmares, remembering the rush of air as it blew past him on the road outside Sibari. He didn't have long to look. The shades bundled him into the car, Adam jumped into the front seat and the helicopter flew away. Soon, the Mercedes was grinding its way up a track that led towards the twin hills. They were taller than they'd looked from the air.

'Is this where you're keeping Lily?' Jonah shouted. His ears were still ringing from the helicopter.

'This is the place in the tablets. *Where hundred-headed Typhos shakes open the earth, I went down into the bosom of the goddess.* Typhos was a titan who was chained underneath Etna.'

Jonah looked out through the window. On the ashy track, a plume of fine black dust streamed out behind them. A smoky red haze covered the sky, like a solar eclipse or the end of the world. Sharp black rocks and spiky brown plants were the only things that grew here.

He thought of Lily swimming; the moistness of her mouth; her skin softened by years of gentle English rain. This place was as far away from her as you could get.

Ren leaned forward. 'Is the volcano erupting?'

'On the other side,' said Adam. 'We're too far away for it to matter here. Even if it does come, we'll have plenty of warning. Etna's lava moves at about four miles an hour. You can walk away from it.'

The car stopped in the valley between the two hills, at the edge of a trench excavated from the flow. In the bottom, white ashlar blocks lay where they'd been cut free from their lava prison. They made a simple rectangular foundation, with two round column bases together at the front like cats' paws. At the back of the chamber, a second hole sank into a deeper darkness.

'Did you do all this in the last week?'

But even as Jonah said it, he could see that wasn't right. The trench's edges were weathered smooth; the rubble heaped up by the edge wasn't nearly enough to have come out of the hole.

'The original temple was buried in an eruption around 400 BC. The Italians excavated that in the seventies. We got here three days ago.'

'Do they know you're here?' said Ren.

Adam shrugged. 'This is Italy.'

He skirted around the edge of the pit to a green tent that had been pitched beside it.

'I've brought them,' he said through the canvas.

The flap lifted and a man ducked out. He was bigger than

Jonah and built like a boxer: a short thick neck, a flat face, olive-black skin and bloodshot eyes. A mop of dark hair hung in lank ringlets almost to his shoulders. Jonah had never seen him before, but he knew him from his nightmares.

'Ari Maroussis,' said Adam.

He didn't even look at Jonah. 'The tablet – you got it?'

Adam gave it to him. The fragile leaf vanished in a fist the size of a brick.

'I knew your sister,' he said to Ren. He turned to Jonah. 'And your wife.'

Be still, Jonah told himself. He tried to imagine holding a chord, sustaining it as a single line against every dictate of rhythm, against the movement of the crowd and the fluctuating world. Perfect stillness.

'Where is she?'

Ari licked his lips, letting his tongue linger where a berry-red scab split the flesh.

'You will find out.'

The chord broke. Jonah launched himself at Ari. But he was tired, sore – and Ari was ready. He put out an arm and grabbed Jonah by the throat, holding him back. Jonah struggled, but Ari was strong as a horse.

Hands grabbed his arms and held him from behind. Ari tightened his grip, squeezing Jonah's neck so hard he thought he'd crush it. His sight misted over; he couldn't breathe. An arm's length away, the red-veined eyes stared at him with childish delight. Ari was smiling. Nicotine stained his teeth yellow.

'*Stamata!*' said a voice from close by. 'Stop it!'

With a final squeeze that nearly snapped Jonah's windpipe, Ari pulled back. The hands holding Jonah's arms let go. He collapsed in a heap on the ground.

When he was able to look up again, a new figure had appeared. Socratis Maroussis, still dressed like an Edwardian gentleman who'd been snatched out of time. Two of the shades flanked him.

Jonah spat out a gob of bile. 'I thought you were a prisoner on your island.' Every word was like drawing a fat steel cable through his throat.

'We have reconciled. Always, the son comes back to the father in the end.'

Standing beside him, Ari glowered. His dark skin flushed, a child who'd been caught out.

'Where's Lily?'

Ari began to say something, but Maroussis stopped him with a wave of his hand. 'You have nearly found her.' He glanced at Adam, who had come out of the tent with a pile of ropes and harnesses. 'You are ready?'

'Five minutes.' Something like thunder rumbled through the ground, though the only clouds in the sky were smoke. Adam looked up at the mountain.

'Can you check the instruments? See if we've got any readings?'

Maroussis and Ari went back into the tent. Ren and Jonah stayed outside, watched by the shades. Adam coiled the rope, each loop the exact circumference of the last.

'Do you remember the oracle at Delphi?' he said suddenly.

Jonah remembered it. What surprised him was that Adam did. Sitting squeezed into Lily's car, singing along to ELO with the windows wide open. Surely it was a different Adam who'd been there.

'A long time ago.'

'You remember it sits on a fault line?'

'Gas seeped out. The woman got high and told fortunes.' He rubbed his neck. 'Does it matter?'

'The point is, I don't think Delphi was the only place it happened.'

'OK.' He couldn't believe he was having this conversation.

410

Perhaps his brain had lost too much oxygen. Perhaps it was easier than thinking about Lily.

'Do you think it's a coincidence that the world's most profound philosophy sprang out of southern Italy? Pythagoras, Parmenides, Empedocles – even Plato, it wasn't until he visited Italy in his forties that his ideas really took flight. Somewhere underneath this mountain, there's a place the ancients knew. A portal to a higher plane of existence, where we can see the mysteries of the universe firsthand.'

When Plato went to Italy, he found something that blew open his thinking like a hydrogen bomb.

'Are you familiar with the work of Timothy Leary? The LSD philosopher?'

'Tune in, turn on, drop out.'

'He developed a theory of drug use, that there are two variables that determine the experience. The *set* and the *setting*. The *set* is the physical compound – the drug you choose and its biochemical effects. The *setting* is the environment in which you take it, not just your surroundings but also your state of mind. Your mood, your emotions, your expectations. The Greeks would have understood it as a ritual. Drugs don't just write themselves onto your subconscious: they open a conversation.'

'OK.'

'Take Ecstasy. For years, psychologists prescribed it thera-peutically. Patients popped it on the couch and it helped them relax. Work through their issues. Then someone discov-ered that if you take it while you're dancing with a thousand other people, listening to overpowering music, it becomes the gateway to something transcendental.'

'So I hear.'

'Our minds are made for so much more than we use them for. We rely so much on our senses, by the time we're grown up they completely own us. But they're pathetic. We're like supercomputers connected to a dial-up modem. There's a world out there, and we get thumbnail images drip-fed into our consciousness. We need to find a way to rip open the connections, to increase the bandwidth so we can understand the full spectrum of reality.'

'You tried that once before. It didn't work out so well.'

Adam ignored him. 'The problem with drugs is that they're unreasonable. You can't control the experience. They throw you into the ocean of the unconscious, but there's nothing to steer by.'

'Some people would say that's the point.'

'You know Pythagoras discovered the mathematical under-pinnings of the universe. Parmenides is known as the father of logic. Plato maintains that the only way to understand his forms is through dialectical reasoning.'

'They must have been off their faces.'

Adam missed the sarcasm, probably didn't even hear what he'd said. 'Whatever's down there, it doesn't bypass our critical faculties like drugs. It liberates them.'

'Does that matter?' said Ren.

'What's the point of experiencing the full spectrum of the world if you can't make sense of it?'

Jonah stared at the small, square hole that had been excavated from the bottom of the pit. *Where's Lily?* He wanted to scream it with all his voice, shake Adam until he told him or the whole mountain broke down. But, at the same time, he was afraid of the answer.

'Isn't there something you're forgetting.'

Just for a moment, a line of uncertainty cracked Adam's mask. 'I don't think so.'

'In all these myths, nobody says they went to some blissed-out heaven where they lay on a beach and contemplated the universe. They say they went to Hell.'

Adam stared at him with his deep, soulless eyes.

'That's why we sent someone down to see if it's safe. A canary in the tunnel.'

'You're going to send me down to breathe the air and see if I lose my mind.'

But he'd misheard.

'*Sent* – past tense.'

He still didn't get it. Adam steepled his fingers, a doctor putting on his white coat to deliver the bad news.

'She's already down there.'

Thirty-seven

In the hollows beneath the earth flow subterranean streams,
both hot and cold; and great fiery rivers; and streams of liquid
mud, thick and thin, just like the rivers of mud in Sicily, and
the lava-streams which follow them.

Plato, Phaedo

Down I went.

A passage stretched ahead of me, deep into the mountain. High enough that it barely touched my head, just wide enough to fit my shoulders. Lamps lit my way, hundreds of them, set in the walls in paired niches every few feet. It was an eerie effect; I wondered who had lit them. Their light showed many pairs of footprints in the black dust that smothered the floor. Were some of them Agathon's?

The air in the passage got hotter. After fifty paces, my clothes were heavy with sweat. After one hundred, I stripped off completely, wriggling like a snake shedding its skin. I left the clothes behind.

The heat got worse. The sweat tapped every drop of moisture in my body and drained it out. It reminded me of being in the exercise yard at noon, high summer, sticky with oil and sand, throwing each other while the instructor screamed instructions and abuse. One in particular, a veteran of the Spartan wars, used to make me lie face down in the sand with a long leather bag on my back. He filled the bag with

rocks, heavy as a man, and told me to do a hundred press-
ups.

A memory. The bag crushing me into the hot sand, scalding
my naked skin. Just lifting myself off the ground saps all my
strength. By the third press-up, I think my arms will snap.
The other athletes in the gymnasium stop what they are
doing and gather round to watch.

When I reach thirty, he fetches a basin of water. He puts
it on the sand in front of me, so close I can almost touch it
with my tongue. He stands over it, daring me to give up. *All
you have to do is roll over. The water's fresh from the well, lovely
and cold. Let the bag go. No one's going to judge you.* I keep
going. Sixty. Seventy.

I reached one hundred. I barely had the strength to tip
off the bag, let alone to stand, but somehow I did. I looked
down at the water in the bowl, and then I kicked it over. I
still remember the hiss the water made as it boiled off the
sand.

Jonah

He wanted to take one of Adam's bright blue ropes and wrap
it around his throat until his neck snapped.

'You sent Lily down there?'

A canary in the mine.

Adam tossed him a head-torch. 'No one's entered that cave
for almost two and a half thousand years. The gasses in there
could have built up to lethal concentrations. Or there could
be loose rocks.' Another tremor shook the earth. 'This isn't
a geologically stable region.'

'Really?'

'Do you think Socratis Maroussis is just going to crawl in
there like Indiana Jones?'

Jonah stared into the darkness in the ground. Despair washed through him and made everything he could do or say futile.

'Is she OK?'

'She's wearing a transmitter that's supposed to report back her vital signs.'

'And?'

'It stopped transmitting last night.'

Jonah tried to hold on, but it was like trying to squeeze broken pieces of glass together. 'It could be the rock, right? The signal can't get through?'

'Or a malfunction, or she broke it.' Adam flicked on his head-torch. 'That's why we're going down.'

Jonah took a last look at the sun. From the edge of the trench, Ren looked down from between the guards and gave him a small, vanishing smile.

'I'll come back,' Jonah said. He hated to leave her up there with Ari Maroussis and his father. He remembered the look Ari had given her, like a shark sniffing bait. But he had to.

'Find Lily,' she said.

The hole seemed to swallow the light around it, crushing the world down to two dimensions. He thought of Lily going down there. Captive, alone, one solitary light against the darkness of a billion tons of rock. A sacrifice.

'I thought you loved her, once.'

Ahead, Adam shrugged. 'Love is Truth. That's what we're going to find.'

Plato

My mouth burned. My throat ached. The passage continued down, and I wondered how close I was to the heart of the volcano.

416

A little way ahead, I saw a gap in the side of the tunnel on my right. I hurried on as fast as I could and stared.

A rough-hewn goddess, big-limbed and full-breasted, sat in an alcove, emerging from the rock like a face pressed against a sheet. Her lips, breasts, hands and eyes had been polished smooth, like black mirrors. Below her feet, a round pool of black water gleamed in the lamplight, with a bronze scoop lying invitingly on a ledge above.

I don't know where the water sprang from, or how it stayed full without spilling out. But I wanted that drink. More than I've ever wanted anything, I wanted to taste the water on my lips. I wanted to plunge my head in until I drowned.

I knelt and grabbed the scoop. As I leaned forward, the amulet around my neck swung out and knocked against the rim of the scoop. Gold chimed on bronze with a sound like a bell.

Euphemus' ghost's hand touched my shoulder. *Do you think it's safe?*

I looked again. The gold locket hung against my bare chest, covered in sweat. I took out the tablet and tried to read the words. The leaf was so hot I worried it might melt in my hands.

> *The Mansions of Night, the right-hand spring,*
> *Black water and a shining white cypress*
> *Where descending souls cool their fall.*
> *Stay away.*

The water winked at me and shimmered. The goddess watched me through polished eyes, mirrors of the pool below.

I put the scoop down and left the water behind. I didn't look back.

The long tunnel sloped down into the mountain. The walls bowed out then tapered together above his head, like a sea shell. The air was hot and dry. A row of shallow holes, about chest high, made serrated lines in the walls. When Adam trained his torch on them, Jonah saw dark patches staining the rock walls below.

'Oil,' said Adam. 'Originally, they'd have held lamps.'

There were dozens of them, maybe hundreds, as far as the torch-beam reached. Jonah tried to imagine them all glowing with flames. He tried to imagine who could have come down here to light them.

'Did you know this was here?'

'A flagstone covered the entrance and kept the lava out when the temple was destroyed. The original excavators got as far as the temple floor and stopped. They didn't realise, and no one ever came back to investigate. With modern imaging technology, we opened it up straight away.'

For something that hadn't been touched in thousands of years, the tunnel was remarkably clear. A heavy layer of soot carpeted the floor: otherwise, there wasn't so much as a crack in the walls. In the torchlight, they were a strange, pinkish colour, with undulating lines, as if a giant worm had bored through it.

'Is this natural?'

'Lava cools with exposure to air. The top hardens first, like a crust, but underneath it keeps flowing. Sometimes, when the eruption finishes, it flows right out and leaves an empty tube behind. A cave.'

'But this must have been here before the temple got destroyed.'

'It's a different eruption – thousands or tens of thousands

of years earlier. The later eruption came down over it. That's how Etna was made. It's a giant layer-cake of lava on lava.'

Adam paused. Ahead, on his right, the torch-beam shone off a black mirrored surface set in the floor of a little alcove. It was so smooth, Jonah didn't realise it was water until Adam touched it with the toe of his boot. Angry circles rippled out, so close to the rim Jonah thought they'd spill over.

'*The right-hand spring*,' Adam breathed. A golden glow bathed his face as he looked down at the tablet. Reflected light wrote tiny white letters on his skin. 'It's really true.'

'Is it safe to drink?' The heat in the cave had sucked Jonah dry. He was dying for a drink.

'*Stay away.*' Adam shone his light up. A nude goddess, black as night with gleaming black breasts, stared out of the rock. 'It's a trap.'

He knelt down and sniffed the water. A small mound of green bronze flakes lay next to the well, perhaps the decomposed remains of some long-lost vessel. Adam took a plastic test-tube from his pocket and filled it with water, careful not to touch it.

'How is it a trap?' Jonah asked.

Adam stood and screwed the tube shut. 'The key to Orphic philosophy is memory. They believed in the immortality of the soul, that it comes into this world again and again in its quest for perfection. How you lived your past life determines how you come back.'

'Isn't that Buddhism? Karma, or something?'

'Similar. In Orphism, the twist is that it isn't fate that determines how you come back. You get to choose – but you have to make the right choice. You pursue virtue in life so that when you get to the underworld, you've got the knowledge to make the best decision. And to do that, you have to remember what you've learned.'

Jonah rubbed his nose. Dust danced in the beam of his head-torch, just above his eyeline. 'Is that so hard?'

'The water makes you forget. That's why the tablet tells you not to drink it. You'll forget who you are and find yourself at the mercy of Hades.'

He looked down the passage. A little further along, the slope levelled out.

'Everything we are is memory. Without it, we'd live and die like goldfish. Do you know what the Greek word for "truth" is? *Aletheia. A* is the negative prefix and *Lethe* is forgetting. Truth is simply *not forgetting.*'

Plato

The passage levelled out, then began to rise. The lamps in the walls led me on. They didn't hiss or spit; none of them had gone out. Again, I wondered who kept the lamps filled and lit. Did they burn here in the dark, hour after hour, waiting for a traveller to pass? It was as if I'd arrived at a friend's for dinner, to find the tables ready but the house empty.

Though I didn't always feel exactly alone. Sometimes I thought I saw a pale circle of light dancing across the floor ahead of me. Sometimes, when I glanced at the walls, there seemed to be an extra shadow overlapping mine, a blurred edge that didn't belong to me. Every so often, the sound of my footsteps seemed to skip a beat, or add one, like a drummer playing out of time.

The passage ended suddenly in a round chamber. Cunning shadows hid it so well I nearly walked into the wall – or rather, into the statue facing out of it. A three-figured woman. One was the firm body of a young girl; the second, a woman in the ripeness of motherhood; the third, a withered crone.

Hecate, the witch-queen. She guards crossroads, keeping off

evil spirits and helping travellers choose the right path. Even here. The mother's head stared back down the passage I'd come by, while the daughter and the crone looked left and right down the two new paths that split away into the darkness.

I followed their gazes down the two passages. This was where the lamps ran out: everything beyond Hecate was darkness. Even the footprints couldn't guide me here. In front of the statue, and down the tunnels, the floor had been swept clean.

I took a tentative step along the right-hand passage. If anything, the air smelt even fouler than the chamber, as if some vast rotting carcass lay waiting at the end. I tried the left-hand passage instead. Here, the air was warmer but also dryer. My soul tugged me towards it, like a leaf turning towards the sun.

There are two ways, says Parmenides, *and one is impossible. Nothing comes back that way.*

I went back to the statue and stared into her faces for clues. The young woman looking left had smooth skin and wide eyes. The old grandmother looking right had a pointed chin, sunken eyes and deep lines scored across her face. Her shrivelled breasts hung low towards her belly, where thin ribs pushed against the papery skin. I shuddered, and marvelled at the sculptor's skill, chipping this hag out of the rock so deep below the earth.

Her eyes defied me with a lifetime's experience, hard won from the girl on the left. *This is wisdom*, they seemed to say.

I made my choice, and set off up the right-hand tunnel.

Jonah

They picked their way forward. Sometimes the roof soared out of reach like a cathedral; sometimes it came so low it brushed his shoulders. The walls bulged and shrank away, but the floor remained perfectly flat. He wondered how many feet must have walked the same path to wear it so smooth.

'The path should fork soon,' said Adam.

Jonah kept his eyes on the ground. His head-torch made a wan circle of light on the floor, chasing Lily's footprints into the darkness. Adam's boot-marks looked huge and square beside them, as though a toeless animal had pursued her into the cave.

'Stop,' he said. Before Adam could argue, Jonah pushed past him. 'I'll lead.'

Now there were only Lily's footsteps in front of him. He tried to imagine how she must have felt wandering down here alone. Was she lonely? Terrified? Hurt?

He paused and listened. The soft crunch of Adam's boots in the rock dust stopped behind him. Water dripped, and the mountain sighed as if it was breathing. Nothing else.

'What is it?' said Adam.

'I thought I heard footsteps. I thought it might be Lily.'

But that wasn't true. The footprints told him Lily was ahead. Whatever he'd heard, it hadn't come from up there: it had sounded almost beside him. Had it even been a sound? More like a feeling, a shadow flickering at the edge of his conscious. A ghost.

'It's a cave of illusions,' Adam warned. 'You have to keep a grip or you'll lose yourself.'

Twenty metres later, the path split. A three-bodied woman, chiselled from the stone, stared out and bared her breasts at them. Stone eyes riddled them like a sphinx.

'Hecate,' said Adam. 'The witch who guards crossroads.'

Jonah barely looked at her. He was halfway towards the left-hand path, following the footprints, when Adam grabbed his arm.

'That's the wrong way.'

Jonah pointed to the footprints. 'That's where Lily went.'

Adam's scalp glistened with sweat. Dust smeared his face. The confidence he wore so naturally in Athens had melted away. For the first time, Jonah could see the child he must once have been, wide-eyed, frightened of a world he understood so much better than everyone else, and yet not at all.

'She was supposed to go right.' His dry voice was almost a whisper. 'That's what I told her. That's the way the tablets say.'

'So why didn't she?'

'Maybe she lost her bearings.'

'Or she didn't trust you. Or maybe it was just a *fuck you*.'

They stared at each other, and the goddess stared at them and between them, utterly indifferent to the choices they made. In the silence that separated them, Jonah heard heavy footsteps echoing down the tunnel, a blind beast battering its way through.

'Ari's coming,' said Adam. Jonah ignored him.

'What's down the left-hand path?'

'I don't know.'

'You've got a guess.'

'Plato describes the path to the underworld in *The Republic*. The righteous take the path to the right, the condemned go left down to hell.'

'What does that mean?'

Adam shook his head. 'Bad, I suppose.'

'Then let's find out.' Jonah grabbed the arm that was holding him, locking it in place, and started dragging Adam towards the left-hand path. Adam struggled and jerked; he kicked and flailed; he tried to get the arm to his mouth to bite it. The goddess looked on, neither approving nor disapproving.

The footsteps came closer.

'Ari will kill you,' Adam warned. 'He'd have done it already if I hadn't persuaded him not to.'

'Like you saved Lily?'

'I did what I could. It's not my fault she went the wrong way.'

Jonah let go. Adam stumbled back and banged into the goddess. Down the tunnel, light approached from Ari's torch.

'Come with us,' Adam said. 'You can't save Lily, but you might save yourself.'

Jonah looked left, then right, and made his choice. Though, really, it was no choice at all.

Plato

In the dark, the stench was like a physical presence, dense and heavy – almost as real as the footsteps echoing behind me. I stumbled forward as fast as I could, never fast enough to outrun the footsteps. I flailed my arms against the emptiness. I waited to feel a hand around my neck – or a rock wall cracking open my skull. My heart beat so hard I thought it would burst out of me.

And suddenly there was nothing. Nothing in front of me, nothing around me and – crucially – nothing under me. I was falling.

I seemed to hang there for a long, long time. Out of context, out of time, out of every direction except *down*.

Was this how Agathon felt in the last seconds as he tumbled down the well?

No. Dion said he was dead before he—

I hit the water feet first and plunged in over my head. Water went up my nose and into my mouth and eyes. I gagged.

I left one nightmare and entered another.

Jonah

The path led down. The air got hotter still. When he put out a hand to steady himself on the wall, it came away caked with a strange, spongy residue. He shone the torch on it. An orange fungus covered the walls, almost to the roof, ballooning out in strange knotted shapes. Some of them looked like twisted faces, or eyes, or hands reaching out to pull him into the rock.

The condemned go left down to hell. Had it started already?

He kept his head down, torch on Lily's footprints, one arm up to protect his face. Hot air blew against him, and he wondered what moved it in the still caverns. Could it be the volcano? He remembered a film he'd seen, late at night in some hotel. Cardboard actors running through cardboard caves, computer-generated lava like melted cheese chasing them. He didn't think it happened that way in reality.

If he hadn't been looking down he'd have walked straight into the hole. As it was, he nearly missed it. A dark threshold in the floor of the passage: he had one foot over it before he realised it wasn't solid. It wasn't anything – just a yawning *nothing*. He jerked away from it, tripped and fell backwards. He hit the floor hard and the torch went out.

He lay still. When he could hear his breaths again, he counted off ten. Then ten more, half as fast as before. That brought the terror down to a workable level.

Think of Lily.

He patted around his head until he found the head-torch. Working by touch, he opened the battery compartment and pressed the batteries back into place. He tried the switch again.

The light came on – woozy yellow, no match for the profound darkness in the cave, but enough to see something. He wiped his arm on his T-shirt to get off the slime.

Lily's footsteps went straight to the edge of the hole and vanished. Dizzy from the fall, he crawled to the edge on his hands and knees and shone the torch down.

The hole was a shaft ten feet across and about thirty feet deep – hard to tell exactly, because of the steam boiling out. Through the clouds, Jonah could just make out something wet and glossy, bubbling and heaving at the bottom. Mud, oozing and simmering, releasing steam as its bubbles popped.

Didn't she have a torch? Her tracks had been straight and clear, not the erratic path of someone blundering in the dark. Did she see it in time?

He shone his light up to the top of the shaft. Among the shadows, he could see a dark hollow opening in the rock face opposite. A continuation of the tunnel.

But how do you get there?

He should have thought to take a rope. He examined the shaft more carefully. The rock was uneven, full of crevices and ledges. With a bit of skill, you might be able to climb around to the other side.

Jonah didn't have any skill. Shadow had taken him climbing a couple of times in the Peak District, but his wrists had been so sore afterwards he could hardly pick up a guitar. All he remembered were the basics: *hold on, don't fall off.* So much easier when you had a harness to catch you.

He looked back. He looked forward, at the footsteps going over the cliff. He tried to imagine any scenario where Lily had somehow turned around. There were no footprints going back.

You can't save Lily, but you might save yourself.

He got down on his stomach and dangled over the drop, stretching his leg out into the shaft until he felt a foothold. He moved his right arm over. Now he was splayed across the rock face like a spider.

Think of Lily.

He shifted his weight and pushed his toe out until he found another foothold. Then another handhold. Inch by inch, he worked his way around the shaft. It was wider than it looked. Steam made the rock slippery. Every time he thought he had a grip, his hand started sliding away. And always there was the mud, spitting and groaning below.

He risked a look ahead. He'd come more than halfway. But this was the hardest bit – a wide, shallow curve where the rock was almost perfectly smooth. He reached for a small bulge, almost as far as he could stretch. His fingers scrabbled, slipped, tried again and just got a purchase. Not even a grip, just pressure holding him in place.

He moved his leg towards the next foothold. Further, further – but he came up inches short. He brought the leg back. His fingers had locked up; the tendons in his wrist felt as if someone had them in a vice. He tried again, swinging his leg to make the extra inches.

His toe touched the rock – but slipped off. He tried to swing back again, but he'd gone too far. Unbalanced already, he couldn't support his weight. His left foot lost its purchase.

He hung by his fingertips, just long enough to feel despair obliterate his soul.

Then he slid off and fell, screaming, into the mud.

Plato

I've drowned so often in my dreams you'd think I'd be used to it. But nothing prepared me for the shock of falling into water from darkness. I went under and water rushed into me. I kicked out of instinct, but I didn't know up from down. At least in my dream I could see the sun.

My head broke the surface. I gasped, sank back, and kicked

so hard I almost flew out of the water like a dolphin. I gulped air into my lungs and choked again.

Breathe, I told myself. I forced myself to slow down my movements. Small circles with my arms, gentle motions of the legs. Like treading grapes.

When my breathing had calmed, I let myself sink experimentally with my arm extended straight up, until only my hand poked out of the water. Still no bottom. I swam back up.

This time I went sideways, trying to keep a straight line. A corner of my mind imagined swimming in circles, never knowing, until my strength gave out and I slipped under. I swam harder.

My hand brushed a wall: now my world had three dimensions I kicked my way along it, feeling for any gaps. The water was warm and stank of sulphur, leaving a powdery fur on my tongue.

I felt space and groped around. In front of me, there seemed to be some kind of lip or ledge, just above the water's surface. I hauled myself out. All I wanted was to lie down, but the ledge wasn't wide enough. I patted around and felt another ledge, higher and further back. Beyond that, another one.

Steps. Climbing out of darkness, into darkness.

I crawled up the stairs on my hands and knees. I counted ten steps. Where the eleventh should have been, my hand touched a flat rock floor. I stood up, wobbly as a child learning to walk, and explored the room with my hands. It was a big space: I felt column after smooth column, stretching away in every direction. Like being lost in a forest.

At least I didn't feel cold. The air in the cave was as warm as my skin, the dripping water as regular as my heartbeat. My body dissolved into it. All that remained was *me*, the person who exists when everything else is gone.

428

There are walls around us that box us in to our world. The body is one of those barriers, a wall around our soul. Hard to see past.

But not any more.

Jonah

He was still screaming when he hit the bottom. Hot mud filled his mouth as he went under. The pain was like nothing he'd felt before: choking, burning, suffocating him. His body shrivelled up like plastic tossed in a fire.

He'd stopped sinking, but he hadn't started to rise. In mud, he had no buoyancy – or perhaps there was no air left in him. He kicked frantically, though he no longer knew up from down. He lashed his arms and flailed his legs, but the mud wrapped him like a wet blanket. He still couldn't breathe.

I'm sorry, he said to Lily.

Air on his face. He'd broken the surface. He spat out a mouthful of mud and gulped down the air. Foul, steaming, sulphurous air – but it brought him to life.

Bicycling his legs to stay afloat, he opened his eyes. He could still see. That meant there must be light. He put his hand to his head and felt the head-torch, still strapped on. He wiped mud off the housing. The light got brighter.

He tipped back his head and looked up the shaft, trying to find the tunnel opening. One look said it would take a miracle to climb out. He tried anyway, stretching as high as he could. His slick hands slid off the stone; the mud sucked him back.

He wasn't going to get out.

Follow Lily, a small voice said in the back of his mind. She hadn't gone back, and he didn't think she'd managed to climb

429

across. He wouldn't let himself think her body might be somewhere underneath him, buried in the mud.

So where did she go?

He looked at the shaft, through the steam and bubbling mud. He palmed his way around the edge of the pit.

A shallow opening. Not much, just a few inches of clear space above the mud. Probably nothing more than a recess, but he stuck in his hand and felt back as far as he could reach.

Nothing.

He ducked down and tried to shine the light inside. Rock and darkness. He sniffed it, but all he smelled was mud. He listened, but his ears were clogged.

He didn't want to go in there. He went right round the chamber, squirming through the mud, feeling every crook and hollow for a way out. No luck. Five minutes later, he was back at the same place.

The knot comes apart and you are back where you began.

There wasn't any other option. And he wasn't going to last forever. Heat and fumes made him dizzy; his skin was flayed raw. Sooner rather than later, he'd pass out and go under.

He took a deep breath and turned onto his back. He slid under the opening like a patient going into a scanner, his mouth just sticking out of the mud. The air was a super-charged fog of fumes and steam compressed into the narrow gap beneath the rock ceiling.

Light meant nothing in that tunnel. Mud bubbles popped against his back. Mud fingers reached into every fold of his body. Muddy air coated his tongue, his throat, his lungs. He was an earthworm, contracting and expanding, wriggling blind. He ate mud; he excreted mud; he became mud. All that was left of him was a single imperative: *Go on. Go on or die.*

And then he touched something. Something that didn't ooze away when he touched it, but resisted him. Something hard and real. Something blocking his way.

A rock wall. Was it a dead end? Panic began to bubble through him but, before it could take hold, his scrabbling arm felt something else. *Nothing* else: not mud, not rock, just . . . space. Air, as far as he could reach.

He lurched up from the mud and sprawled, gasping, on a rocky ledge.

Plato

Imagine our situation something like this . . .

I'm lying in a cave. The hard floor bruises my bones; a knot in the rock digs into the back of my head. But even the pain fades eventually. The stone swallows me, the warmth of my body melting me into it.

Poets rhapsodise about the silence of the grave, but they're beautifully misinformed. It isn't silent. Water drips into the chamber. The stone hisses with the melody of the earth turning on its axis.

In the dry air, I catch the impossible smell of ripe figs. The goddess must be near. There's a sweetness all around me, like honey on my tongue. My nostrils open, my mouth relaxes, every pore in my body seems to dilate.

The darkness gives me strange sight. I can't see my hand in front of my face, but I can peer over the rim of the world and see all space combined. I can dip in my hand and scoop up bubbles of time, twisting them this way and that to see how they catch the light. In a glistening bowl, I see the gilded city, its temples proud on the high rock of the acropolis. There are ships in the harbour beyond the walls, but I can't see the flags. Is it Athens?

I think about how I got here.

I can hear the silence and see through darkness. I'm awake and dreaming. I'm dead, and more alive than I've ever been.

A door opens and spills light into the room. It's dim, from down the end of a long deep tunnel. A shadow appears against it. Far away, I see a man coming towards me. He's short and stooped, moving awkwardly. It takes him a long time to reach me, though the only instrument I have to measure it by is the beat of my heart. The closer he comes, the brighter the light gets, like a star coming down to earth, until by the time he reaches me I can barely stand to look at it.

And as he gets here, I realise he's been with me all the time.

Jonah

He reached up to turn on the head-torch. All he felt was mud-matted hair. The torch must have slipped off somewhere in the tunnel.

But a worm can still read the dark by the twitching of its hairs. He found steps. He slithered up them. He felt space, sweet air spreading around him like a clearing in a forest. After the tunnel and the mud, it made him feel as if he was floating. He could smell fruit in the air, the first green thing he'd encountered since he left the mainland.

A sudden and irresistible tiredness hit him. He felt himself sinking. The rock had opened below him, soft as a mattress, and he was falling into it. He tried to stay awake, certain there was something he had to remember just out of reach.

Everything we are is memory. Who said that?

A door opened in the ceiling. Dull orange light spilled through, and the sound of rushing water. He was still sinking, but the light was getting brighter. It hardened the mud that caked his skin, baking him into it. Through the holes around his eyes, he saw a figure walking towards him out of the light. Was it Lily? The light behind her was too bright. He tried to reach out to her, but the clay coffin wouldn't let him move.

She smiled. The coffin cracked open and flew into a thousand pieces of light.

Thirty-eight

Many men have risked the descent to the underworld in hopes of being reunited with their loved ones. So should a true philosopher, convinced the wisdom he loves is in the underworld, still fear death? He should know that only by dying can he find wisdom in her purest form, and so begin his journey gladly.

Plato, *Phaedo*

White light, filling my horizon. Featureless brightness, nothing else. So perfect, there's nothing for the eye to catch on. No perspective, no distance, no edge or shape to limit it. It could be right in front of my nose or a million miles away, but it wouldn't matter because it doesn't change. It simply *is*.

What is it? says the Voice of Reason.

Where are we? says the Voice of Will.

How do I get it? says the Voice of Desire.

My questions vanish into the light. The voices burn away like mist. All that's left is me and the light, like conjugating verbs. *I am. It is.*

The world realigns. I'm lying on my back staring up at the sun. By rights I should be blind, but in fact I can see more clearly than ever, as if I've spent all night in a smoky room and just stumbled out into a spring morning.

I sit up. I'm in a grassy meadow among asphodels and daffodils. There are no trees. A river flows by, winding gently towards a lake in the distance. High mountains ring the horizon.

And there, standing over me, is Socrates. He's exactly as I remember him – only more so. The memory fixed in my mind was a statue: this is the living man. His cheeks and forehead bulge even more than before. His nose is wider, his beard wilder, his stance more bandy-legged than ever. And his eyes are bright as dawn.

I'm still wondering whether I dare touch him when he reaches down, pulls me to my feet and claps me in an embrace that seems to last forever. Like two halves of a circle coming together without a join.

'You came,' he says. 'I'm so happy.' He stands back, holding me by my shoulders. He can hardly reach – I'd forgotten how short he is. 'You look well.'

I'm surprised. The last time I checked, my body was a mess of bruises, grazes and cuts. Now they've all gone and my skin is clean. The wound on my arm has healed with only a thread of a scar.

Socrates is in a hurry. He leads me down to the river, where a flat boat waits tied up on the bank. We get in. I sit in the middle, while Socrates stands in the back and poles us along.

The water is a deep, nourishing brown, rich with sediment. 'What river is this?' I ask.

'It's called Acheron.'

I lie back and stare at the sky. It's different to what I'm used to. I can see the curve of the heavens like a glass dome bending down to the mountains that surround the plain. The sun looms much larger than it does in our world; lower, as if pressed against a ceiling.

'I'm sorry you had such a difficult journey,' says Socrates.

There's an awkward question between us, but I feel I have to broach it. 'Am I dead?'

The pole catches in mud, and Socrates nearly goes overboard. When he's righted himself, I can see he's smiling. I've asked the right question.

'What is it that's inside the body that makes it alive?'

'The soul.'

'And wherever the soul resides, it brings that thing to life.'

'Yes.'

'And the opposite of Life is . . . ?'

'Death.'

'Good. Now, do you think that any concept can admit its opposite?'

'What do you mean?'

'Well, in numbers we have a concept of Odd and a concept of Even.'

'Yes.'

'Is there anything odd about Evenness – or vice versa? Or are they totally incompatible?'

'I suppose they're mutually exclusive.'

'Indeed. Three is never and in no way Even, and two is never Odd. Now, we said that Death is the opposite of Life. Can there be any aspect of Life that admits Death?'

'They're mutually exclusive.'

'So the soul, being Life, can't contain any portion of Death?'

'That follows.'

'Which makes the soul . . . ?'

I've never considered it before, but now the word comes out as naturally as breathing. 'Immortal.'

'Not like Homer's shades, which are just ghosts or reflections of the man who died. I'm talking about the real soul who lived on earth. The person we are.'

I try to comprehend the vastness of what he's said. But there are also practical implications. If the soul is immortal . . .

'I can't be dead.'

436

He nods.

'That's reassuring to know.'

A shadow crosses his face, though there isn't a cloud in the sky. He leans hard on the pole. 'Not as much as you'd think.'

He sat up. The world turned and came to rest under the feet of the woman in front of him. The red sun soared up above her and he could see her clearly at last.

Lily.

She wore a sleeveless summer dress brightly printed with orange and silver flowers, her hair tied back behind her neck. Her feet were bare, her smile brighter than the sun.

He felt as though he'd been waiting for this moment all his life. He tried to get up, but then Lily was kneeling beside him in the grass, arms around him, planting kisses over every inch of his face. She found his lips and opened them, fusing her mouth with his. Cool as spring water.

He didn't know how long they kissed. Afterwards, when she released him, he looked into her face. It was different. Subtle lines, marks that had crept in over the years, had vanished. She was more innocent, more hopeful, than the Lily who shared his life now.

She was Lily the way she'd been when he first met her, he realised.

After another kiss, she pulled him up and led him to the top of a ridge that looked down into a river valley. A square, flat-roofed house sat at the bottom next to the river, in the shade of a white cypress tree growing beside it. Two pillars framed the front door. A little way off, a line of black poplars grew straight to the sky. Something about them made him uneasy.

'What's over there?'

Anxiety made her face even paler. 'You have to stay away from there.'

437

'Why?'

'It doesn't matter.'

They went down to the house. Lily opened the door. Jonah crossed the threshold between the pillars – and came home.

He was standing in the front room of their flat in Wandsworth. Everything was exactly as he'd left it, down to the stack of papers he'd left on the floor looking for his passport, and the empty cereal bowl from his last breakfast.

But not quite everything. There was an empty space on the wall where his CD rack had been, and the guitar in the corner had been replaced with a potted rubber plant. Music played from the kitchen, mariachi horns and Johnny Cash lamenting how he'd fallen into a ring of fire. Had he left the radio on?

'Is this real?'

Lily went to the kitchen and got two cans of beer from the fridge. They sat together on the sofa. Jonah took her hand in his and stroked it. The beer can had left it ice cold.

'I looked for you everywhere,' he said.

He stared into her eyes. Her pupils were wider than he ever remembered, deep wells he could forget himself in forever.

'How long can we stay here?'

'As long as you like.'

In the kitchen, Johnny Cash gave way to the Righteous Brothers and '*Unchained Melody*'. Lily stood up and extended her hand.

'Shall we dance?'

He was too tired, but he didn't want to hurt her feelings. He held her and shuffled in awkward circles around the room. *Step, step, step, step*. She sagged into him, but however close he hugged her something seemed to muffle the feeling.

The Righteous Brothers played out. A DJ mumbled something that led on to Elvis Presley, '*Heartbreak Hotel*'.

Jonah went to the kitchen and turned off the radio.

'I like that song,' Lily protested, without force.

He put his hands on her cheeks and held her head still, trying to find the bottom of her poppy-black eyes. All he could see was his own reflection.

'Who are you?' he asked.

'What do you mean? We're together again.'

She stepped away. She bent her arms behind her back and unzipped her dress. It fell to the floor and she was naked underneath: the same firm, young body he'd seen the first time he ever undressed her. Except for her skin, which was pale white, as if the Mediterranean sun had never touched it.

Jonah felt himself go hard. Over her bare shoulder, he saw the kitchen door swinging shut, caught by a breeze. It didn't matter. In a moment, he'd never have to open it again.

Lily had teased apart the fly of his jeans and slipped her hand in. He closed his eyes, but he couldn't concentrate on her.

'When did you forget how to dance?'

Her hand stopped moving. 'What do you mean?'

'You used to be such a good dancer.'

'I forgot.'

'How about swimming? You still remember that, don't you?'

'Of course I do.'

But she sounded frightened. He pushed her away and stared into her eyes.

'Prove it.'

The back door was nearly shut. He ran to it and jammed his foot in the gap, just before it closed.

'The neighbours,' Lily said. 'I'm naked.'

'They won't see.'

He forced open the door and stepped outside. Lily didn't

439

follow. She stood in the doorway, covering herself with her arms.

'I can't go out there.' She sounded terrified. 'Come back inside.'

A boat had been tied up at the bottom of the steps: a punt, one of the flat-bottomed boats that students liked to drink and show off in at Oxford. Jonah scrambled in, shipping water over the side.

'Stay,' Lily pleaded from the back door, and the anguish on her face took him back to that icy Oxford morning. *If you don't turn around now, you'll never see me again.*

'I'm sorry.'

He untied the rope and cast off into the current. He didn't look back.

While we've been talking, the river's been carrying us forward. Now, we come around a bend and it opens out into the lake I saw earlier. From the boat, it looks like a small sea, sunk into an enormous crater. A breeze picks up, moving the surface of the lake. Not in waves, but round in an enormous circle, like water draining down a plughole.

Socrates poles hard to get out of the current and lands us on a red sand beach. Other boats are drawn up here, though I can't see any passengers. We scramble up an embankment, and suddenly we're high up on the cliffs and I can look down into the bowl of the crater to see the whole lake. The muddy Acheron empties into it on my right; another river, blue-grey, comes in from the left. And we're no longer alone. Hundreds of people, maybe thousands, have got here before us. Men and women, children, walking together like a festival crowd. They're all heading for a pair of giant stone pillars a little way off. Some of the people are dusty and weary, as if they've been on long journeys; others look radiantly pure. Everyone walks with his head bowed, as if contemplating some heavy decision.

'Who are these people?' I ask Socrates.

'Souls.'

'Where are they going?'

'Come and see.'

We fall in with them. A few people recognise Socrates and murmur quiet greetings, though they don't seem to notice me. Everyone's looking ahead to the massive pillars. Now that we're closer, I can see spidery lines covering the surface: at first I think they're cracks, then I realise they're tiny letters wrapped round and round the columns, covering every inch. It's written in an alphabet I've never seen before, but somehow I find I can read pieces of it.

The words of Memory, carved in stone

For the hour of your death . . .

Now we're near the front of the crowd. Between the columns, I can see two figures sitting on thrones. They're larger than life, clothed in white with wreaths on their heads and golden sceptres in their hands. As each person steps out in front of them, the sceptres twitch, left or right. The souls pass between the pillars, which are like the frame of an enormous door, and go where they've been directed.

'Who are they?'

'The Guardians,' says Socrates. 'But don't worry. For you, it's only a formality.'

And with that, it's my turn. The sun seems to be right behind the Guardians so I can't see them clearly, but I'm aware of their attention concentrated on me like a mirror. The golden sceptre hovers like the tip of a pen waiting to write my fate.

Why are you here?

I don't hear the voice so much as feel it, like the beat of a bass drum deep inside me. I look down and see the golden tablet has appeared in my hands.

'I am a son of Earth and starlit Sky
Drained dry with thirst, dying.
Let me drink quickly from the cold water
That flows from the pool of Mnemosyne.'

The sceptre inclines to my right. I'm moving again, through
the shadow of the pillars and onto the other side. A circle of
people are kneeling around a wide, grassy spring and drinking.
But when I look over my shoulder, to my left, I see others
being led away back down to the shore. I can't see their faces,
but they're staggering as if someone's just dropped a great
weight on their shoulders.

Socrates holds me back from the spring. 'It's not for you.
We have to keep going.'

Leaving the lake behind, we walk across open fields. The
next time I look back, the pillars and the Guardians and the
crowds have vanished.

He wasn't in Wandsworth any more. The river sped him along
through a wasteland of leafless trees and bare earth. Everything
he could see was a dead, grey-blue colour, as if the world
had asphyxiated.

He thought of Lily, standing at the door. The terrified look
on her face, as if without him she'd cease to exist. He wished
he could go back, but the river was strong and the punt had
neither oar nor pole.

Up a creek without a paddle.

The river widened out until it became the sea. High waves
tossed the boat. On the horizon, a water-spout twisted into
the air and spilled into the clouds. It seemed to suck in the
whole ocean, spinning around on its axis.

The current took him. For a frightening moment, he
thought it would drive him to the waterspout, like a needle
turning towards the end of the record. But then, quite

442

suddenly, it released him. The punt drifted towards the shore and washed up on a shingle beach. He got out, grateful for solid ground under his feet. Red bluffs rose in front of him.

He scrambled up the rocks and found himself at the edge of a sloping lawn. At the top, a square, whitewashed house looked down the garden towards the sea.

He'd been here before. He walked up the garden and climbed the staircase at the side of the house. He knew what he'd find before he got there. Wicker chairs and a table, and an old man puffing on a cigar. All that had changed were the two trees, poplars planted in huge terracotta pots that framed the table.

Night had fallen. Maroussis waved to a chair. The poplars rustled as Jonah brushed past.

'Why are you here?' Maroussis said.

'I've come for Lily.'

The cigar glowed orange. 'Of course.'

Maroussis snapped his fingers. A light came on suddenly under the balcony, throwing a cone of light. Lily stood in the middle of the lawn, dressed in a short, white summer dress with a daisy-chain crown in her hair. She looked around uncertainly, blinking. Shielding her eyes, she glanced up at the balcony and smiled.

Forgetting caution, Jonah vaulted over the balcony rail, dropped and landed hard. He ran to Lily across the dewy grass. She turned, smiling. He threw his arms around her. . .

. . . and felt nothing. Lily flickered and vanished, as if the projector had come to the end of the reel. His arms fumbled in air. He stumbled forward and fell face first on the damp lawn. He tasted earth on his lips.

Maroussis leaned on the balcony rail, flanked by the two poplars which rose into the darkness.

'Bring her back,' Jonah screamed. He jerked around, scanning the shadows and undergrowth in case she was hiding there. All he saw were flowers and statues.

'You cannot reach her,' Maroussis said.

The fight left him. He got to his feet and climbed slowly back up the steps. When Maroussis pointed to the chair again, he flopped into it without resistance.

Maroussis poured brandy into a deep-bowled glass and swirled it around. Orange light glowed from within.

'Let me tell you something about desire, Mr Barnes. When you have desire for something – sex, for example – you think it is the most pure, most absolute emotion it is possible to feel. You believe in the eternal – you cannot imagine ever feeling differently. You will do anything to have it. In normal life you are a respectable, balanced man, but now this is the only thing you can think about. Your first thought when you wake and your last before bed; your dreams, your being: everything is sex.

'Finally – she gives you sex. You have ten seconds of ecstasy. Then all you want is a cigarette.'

He drew a long draught from his cigar. 'You want a desire that is truly eternal? Take up smoking.'

'I quit.'

Maroussis rolled his cigar round the ashtray. 'Human beings are not made to get what they want. You are born for dissatisfaction. You are apes, looking at the fruit on the tree. You climb, you stretch, you reach it – and then you leave it half-eaten on the ground because you are too full. Your Tennyson says it is better to have loved and lost than never to have loved anyone. I say, better to love and never achieve it, because then you cannot lose it.'

'You're obviously not speaking from experience.'

'If you truly love your wife, let her stay here. Go back to your home – I will show you the way. You will miss her, of course. But missing her will become the best, most perfect expression of your desire. A pure longing, inside you forever.'

Jonah shook his head.

'You know, the Roman poet Martial joked that if Hades truly wanted to punish Orpheus, he would have given his wife back. Do you remember the first time you kissed Lily? In the hotel at Aegion? Have you ever loved her more than in the second before your lips touched hers, when what had been unattainable was suddenly yours?'

'Every day.'

'Then perhaps you think this choice will be too painful? That you cannot choose a life of endless sorrow? I can release you.' He slid the glass of brandy across the table. 'If you cannot have Lily, forget her. There will be others. Forget your pain, your past: become a new man, whoever you want to be. Every shameful thing you have done, every memory that makes you cringe, every guilty secret – gone.'

'I don't want to forget her.'

'Why did you come to look for your wife?'

'Because I love her.'

'Because you could not stand to be without her. Wondering every moment of your life – every knock at the door, every face in the crowd. You would go mad.'

Jonah didn't deny it. He remembered sitting alone in the flat, the silence, waiting for the phone to ring. Willing his life away, because every second spent was one less second to wait.

He picked up the glass. The brandy caught the light and flashed amber at him.

'Will it hurt?'

'It is as easy as swallowing.'

'And if I don't?'

A long plume of smoke exhaled into the night. 'There is

445

no alternative. Those are your choices. Remember her or forget. Live or die.'

Jonah sniffed the brandy. He turned the glass, making a vortex in the liquid that spiralled down into . . . *what?*

And where the liquid funnelled down into a single bead of light, he found the answer. He raised the glass to his lips. Over the rim, he saw Maroussis nodding encouragement.

'No.'

He let go. The glass slipped through his hands and shattered on the terrace. Without the light, the golden brandy became nothing more than a dark stain spreading across the stone.

Maroussis was half out of his chair. 'What have you done?'

'It's a false choice. Either way, Lily dies.'

'She is already dead.'

'Then I'll go with her.'

'It will be worse than you can possibly imagine,' Maroussis warned.

'I've got as long as it takes.'

'And if you do find her – what? You will have defined yourself by this one thing, this quest to find your wife. Your whole being will be contingent on her absence. If she exists, then you can not.'

'I'll take that bargain. Even if it takes forever.'

'*Forever*,' Maroussis scoffed. 'It's longer than you think.'

'I love her.'

Maroussis sighed and stubbed out his cigar. A wisp of smoke rose off the ash.

'It's your choice.'

Sharp, scaly hands grabbed him from behind and dragged him to the edge of the balcony. The rail, the garden and the sea had all gone: instead, he was teetering high above another river. Foul, black water, clogged with debris and sewage, rushing towards a dark hole yawning in the cliff.

446

He hung for a moment on the edge of the precipice, between the light above and the darkness below. Then he went over.

We've started into the mountains. They're barren, apart from a few thorn bushes that scatter the ground like sea urchins. A few of them flourish bright red flowers, much more vivid than the red stone around them. The going's hard, shards of loose shale that cut my feet and pull me back with every step. Without shade, I'm soon wet through with sweat. I remember the spring; I wish Socrates had let me drink.

'Why did you come here?' Socrates asks, in the tone that suggests he already knows.

'I was looking for Agathon.'

Socrates nods. 'I saw him – I'd forgotten what a beautiful boy he was. If I'd been thirty years younger . . . ' He laughed. 'Never as tenacious as you, dear Agathon, but very quick.'

'Is he here now?'

He shakes his head. 'There are various . . . procedures . . . to go through.'

'But he'll come back.'

'Oh, everyone comes back. The real question is *how* you come back.'

'How *do* you come back?'

He blows air through his lips. 'It all depends. It could be as a bird or an animal, or a beggar or a tyrant, or even a bean tree.'

I can't tell if he's teasing me. 'Is that true?'

'I wouldn't insist on it. But if I were you, I'd go along with believing that I've got it more or less right.'

A happy thought occurs to me. 'And how will *you* come back?'

'If you don't mind, I'd rather discuss the soul a bit more.'

He says it gently but firmly, a correction to steer us off a

447

dangerous course. I don't answer – but Socrates has always taken silence for consent.

'Earlier, we agreed that the soul is life. Life cannot be death, and therefore the soul must be immortal.'

'I remember.'

'And this gets you out of a spot of bother you've had with the sophists – the sort of riddle they love to flummox people with. They say it's impossible to learn about anything, because if you know what it is you're trying to learn about, then you already know it, but . . . '

' . . . if you don't know what you're trying to learn about, you don't even know what to look for,' I finished. 'I'm familiar with the argument.'

A sad silence as I think about Euphemus. Socrates lets the moment pass, before he continues.

'It's a false dilemma. Because the soul's immortal, it's already learned and understood everything there is in the world. So the things we think we're learning in our lifetime, really, we're just recalling them. What is knowledge, after all, but the memory of something we once understood to be true?'

'I hadn't thought of it that way.'

'The soul is immortal and comes into the world already knowing everything it needs. So what sort of knowledge must that be?'

'I don't understand your question.'

'Is the soul going to know about the weather? Or what's for supper?'

'You're being ridiculous.'

'Because those are fleeting things that affect the body. What are the things that concern the soul?'

'Virtue. Truth.' I think of Diotima. 'Beauty.'

'So these are the things that the soul must have knowledge of.'

'Yes.'

'And since the soul is immortal, what quality must these things have – beauty and truth and so on?'

'I suppose they'd have to be immortal, too.'

'And if they were immortal, would they ever change?'

'No.'

'And could they ever diminish?'

'No.'

'So, logically . . . '

I have the feeling he's handed me the key to a door I've been trying to force for a very long time.

'These things our souls understand – Beauty, Goodness, Truth – must exist in some form which is infinite and unchanging.' I can almost see them in my mind: pure existence, shining above the chaos and paradox of our world. Absolute standards which our souls can achieve, even if our bodies are riddled with compromise.

Socrates is smiling at me. 'I hope I've given you something to think about.'

'But we forget it all when we die.'

'But we can remember. What we call reason is simply a tool for navigating these deep memories – a way to remember things we've forgotten we ever forgot. All we need is one memory to start from and reason can do the rest, chipping away at the darkness. That's why the sophists' question is false. You can learn about anything because you already know about everything. Providing you're active and inquisitive, and don't lose faith in the search.'

'Everything you need is within you.'

Socrates beams. 'Exactly.'

We've reached the top of the slope. We're in a high place, looking out over a dry, red plateau surrounded by more mountains. A river flows through it towards a gaping hole in the centre, and from out of the hole a column of white light erupts into the air. It reaches all the way to the dome of the sky, which bends it back across the earth like a vast rainbow whose colours have fused into a single, perfect brilliance. It binds heaven and earth like the cables girding a trireme. It's the most extraordinary thing I've ever seen.

Socrates lies down and scoops up a mound of earth for a pillow. 'We'll make our camp here tonight.'

I stare out at the pillar of light. 'Am I dreaming, Socrates?'

He turns onto his side and closes his eyes.

'Do you know what makes dreams so convincing? It's the fact that they look just like reality.'

The river whipped him down, corkscrewing round. 'Things' in the water bumped and scraped him: some were soft and clammy, others hard and sharp; some clung on to his skin and tried to drag him down, so that he had to fight to wrestle free; others knocked him into midstream, where the current was worst.

In the brief moments where he could look up, he glimpsed an endless tunnel lit by a sulphur-orange glow. Yellow-brick vaults curved overhead; sometimes, where they met, iron ladders like portcullises hung down to just above the water.

Would he be spat out? Or was he trapped in an infinite labyrinth, no centre and no exit?

He kicked until he was facing forwards. At least now he could see what was coming. One of the ladders rushed towards him: he grabbed for it, missed, tried the next one and touched it, but the current pulled his slimy hand away before he could get a grip.

What if that was it? What if that was the one way to Lily, and he'd missed it? Panic made him lose momentum. He sank, gasped, and took a mouthful of sewage. He spat it out, heaving and gagging to get the taste out.

Another ladder was coming up. He spread his arms to slow

himself, waited, then lunged. His fingers closed around the rung. The water sucked on his legs, trying to drag him off, but he held on.

His left hand joined his right and he hauled himself up. It got easier as he climbed further out of the water. At the top of the ladder he could see an iron manhole cover. He put his shoulder to it and – miracle – it lifted free. A circle of light opened over him.

He crawled through the manhole to see where he'd arrived.

Next morning, we scramble down a long, broken slope onto the desolate plain. The earth is dry and cracked, even near the river. The heat is terrible. Red sand scalds my feet, but Socrates doesn't seem to notice. He hurries ahead, gliding over the desert, while I trudge along behind him as always.

'Can I ask you something?'

'Of course.'

'Was Euphemus right? Am I a coward?'

'Not at all.' The answer comes straight back, like a song you've been hoping to hear. 'You wouldn't have come here if you were a coward. You'd never have left Athens.'

'*You* never left Athens.'

He ignores my teasing.

'But Euphemus' broader point was correct. Philosophy is about life. You shouldn't have tried to abandon one to pursue the other.'

'You said that anyone who really cares about justice, and wants to stay alive for any length of time, needs to keep out of public life.'

'I think *you* said that, actually. In your pamphlet about the trial. I'm sure I wasn't nearly so eloquent at the time. And be that as it may, you're forgetting something else I said. *To fear death is to think oneself wise when one is not.*'

'I wasn't frightened of dying. I just didn't see a way through.'

'Earlier we agreed that the soul is life. Philosophy is the study of things which are good for the soul, so we should also study things that are good for life. Even public life.'

'Now you're playing with words.'

'It's true. Cities, states and nations can be good and well ordered, just as much as individuals. One proceeds from the other. If we can establish what makes good people, then good societies will follow.'

Red dust kicks up around my feet. 'Are you saying I should have killed the boy Dionysius?'

'Do you think you should?'

'No.'

'You probably did more good reading him Aesop's fables. So much wisdom in those little stories.'

I don't care about fables. 'How am I supposed to win? You're saying I shouldn't remove myself from the arguments of daily life – but when I do try to get involved, you say I shouldn't do the bad things that they require.' This is Socrates at his sanctimonious worst: offering you choices and then demolishing each one in turn. I'd forgotten how infuriating he can be.

'You're assuming that if you enter the stage, you have to play the script they've written. Why not give them something better?'

'What?'

'What was the basis of the method I taught you?'

'Eliminating hypotheses to reach the first principle.' I scowl at him: it's not helpful just now. 'I feel as if I've destroyed all my assumptions, but not found anything to replace them. I'm stumbling around blind.'

'You're nearly there,' he encourages me. 'There are two ways of being blinded. Either coming out of light into darkness, or coming out of darkness into light.'

'Which way am I going?'

'The right way.'

'I hope I get there soon.'

He sweeps out an arm at our surroundings. 'We spend our lives in the hollows of the earth, clustered around its puddles like frogs around a swamp. It's a dark, misty place: no one can see clearly. And because it's all we know, we assume it's all there is.'

'Is there a point to this?'

'There's another world above – a true heaven and a true earth, beyond our drab perceptions. The philosopher's job is to get to the upper limit of our cave – and then pop his head through to the world above.'

An objection's lurking at the back of my mind, but with Socrates in full spate I can't put my finger on it. He makes everything sound so straightforward.

'Now this true world up on the surface is a wonderful place. Out in the sunlight, everything is dazzlingly bright. The plants, the trees, the fruits, even the rocks are infinitely clearer than what we see normally.'

I see the image, but I don't understand the metaphor.

'The philosopher can't stay out in the paradise he's found. He has to go back down.'

'Why?'

'Because having seen what's above, once your eyes adjust to the cave again, you'll see ten thousand times better than the people who live there. You'll be able to help your fellow men distinguish between good and bad, right and wrong.'

'Do they want the help? Athens didn't appreciate yours.'

'If you leave public affairs to men who are only in it for themselves, who think that politics can somehow redeem their moral failings, it'll be a disaster. They'll spend all their time fighting for office, and the ensuing conflicts will bring down the government and the state to boot.'

'That sounds familiar.'

I've noticed the change of person – from *he* to *you*. With anyone else, it would just be a different turn of phrase. But Socrates has always been obsessively precise about saying what he means.

'You have to go.' He says it gently, and suddenly I realise that the metaphor is about me.

A pang of heartache, an echo of the beach at Sounion. 'I've already lost you once. Can't I stay?'

He shakes his head. There's a certain amount of regret, but I think it's on my behalf rather than his. 'You have to go back.'

'I don't want to.' Kicking like a child. 'Go back to Athens, set myself up as an authority on . . . *what?* What am I supposed to tell them, when I don't even know myself? Where do I begin?'

'Everything you need is within you.' He chuckles. 'The trick – and, if I may say so, the pleasure – is finding it.'

We've reached the column of light. It emerges from a vast chasm in the ground, a mile wide at least. The river we've been following pours in over the edge and disappears from sight; on the opposite side, I can see the blue-grey river cascade over in a waterfall that goes on for ever. Lower down, other rivers spout out from holes in the cliff-face. The light makes rainbows in the spray.

A wind blows the spray onto my face. I lick my lips: it's warm. Looking down into the chasm, I can see the cliffs are riddled with holes. They make windows into the caves behind, layer upon layer, like the galleries of a mine. I can see Sisyphus pushing his boulder up a slope to the rim of the chasm, only to have it roll back past him: if only he could get it over the edge, into the void, he'd be free of it forever. Through another window there's Tantalus, up to his chin in water but unable to bend his neck to drink because it's strapped tight to a post. I see murderers and tyrants being whipped with thorns

454

by savage, fiery-looking men; a woman trampled face down in mud; another trying to fill a leaky bucket with water from a sieve. And in the background, on every level, there's tousle-headed Orpheus, searching frantically for his wife but finding only images and ghosts.

I look up. Oscillating bands appear in the column of light, brighter and darker, so that the whole pillar looks like a rising staircase. Seen from the bottom, it makes a perfect triangle tapering towards a point in the impossibly distant heavens.

Socrates embraces me. Even here, his head only comes up to my chin. I cradle him like a child, though it seems the wrong way round.

'Remember what you've learned.'

I step into the light.

Thirty-nine

He was back in Syntagma Square, but not as he'd left it. The battle that Ren had rescued him from, days or lifetimes ago, had continued in his absence. The wounded and dying lay everywhere, naked and blood-soaked. Every stone in the square had been torn up and thrown somewhere else; the surrounding buildings had been ripped open like envelopes. A canvas sky stretched blood red across the heavens, bulging in the middle where the smoke pressed against it.

He looked down, wondering if there was a way back. But the manhole cover had vanished.

Probably, you will not even find her.

There was no way back; there never had been. Searching for Lily was all he was.

So look for her.

A scream tore into him. He spun around and saw a woman staggering forward, being chased by a policeman. It was the demon from before, masked and suited, only now it wasn't just his head on fire but his whole body. The flames didn't seem to hurt him. He lashed the woman with a whip made of burning barbed wire. A crowd watched, gaunt faces weary with horrors, but no one moved to help. Before Jonah could try, the woman and the demon disappeared into the smoke.

Lily's somewhere down here.

He set out, drifting wherever he saw knots of people, scanning the faces that emerged from the smoke. In the beginning, his heart skipped each time he saw one. Later – he didn't know how long – he started to hate the people around him, their sad faces and feeble bodies, the way their bones pressed through their skin. He wanted them to go away, to leave him alone, because each figure in the distance meant he had to keep hoping.

Don't stop, he warned himself. *Don't forget.*

In patches, the paving stones had been lifted to reveal sand underneath, as if the square stood on a desert that had started to break through. In one of these places, he came across a row of heads planted in the sand like carrots. Some of them managed to bend their necks forward enough to touch the ground with their tongues, trying to lick any drop of moisture off it. Blood streaked the sand where it had rubbed their tongues raw. Jonah wanted to rescue them, but they had no arms, and when he tried to pull one out by his ears the screams drove him away.

Was it better to find her? Or to be allowed to keep hoping she might not be there?

Missing her will become the best, most perfect expression of your desire. He told himself it wasn't true.

I step into the light, but I don't fall. The light catches me and spins me up, weightless, right to the very pinnacle of the sky. From here, I can look straight down into a spindle that hangs in the column of light. Eight vast whorls are cupped around its axis like nested bowls, all different colours and widths, some turning one way and some the other. Their rims are flush, so that seen from above they look like eight concentric wheels spinning against each other.

All things that move make music: we just need the ears to hear it. Each of the rings makes a single note, so that turning against each other they play the most perfect song I've ever heard.

And as I listen to the music, bathed in that burning white

light, the pores open in my soul and knowledge floods through.

These are the things that I understand.

I understand Time. That there is no 'was' or 'will be', only 'is'. I understand Beauty. I understand that it doesn't blossom or fade, not like a woman who's beautiful in youth but not in old age, or like a boy who has beautiful eyes and a crooked nose. Beauty is the same from every angle, up close or far away, whatever you measure it against, as lasting as time. Everything on earth draws its beauty from the common pool of Beauty, but they can't increase or diminish it because it's infinite. You pour more in and it never overflows; you draw some out but the level never goes down.

The whorl spins faster, bending the circles and sounds and colours together. I understand that there is Good, like Beauty, and everything that is good in the world has a share of it. Heraclitus and the sophists were wrong. Pythagoras came closest, but he didn't go far enough. His numbers don't add up; perfect intervals create an imperfect scale. The numbers are just another level of metaphor which *describe* the world but don't *explain* it. The skeleton of the universe but not its soul.

Our souls are life and life is not death and never can be. Everything we need to know is within us – we were born with it – but creation is chaos and as we pass through we forget it. If we live in the world of the senses, we become creatures of the senses. Fallible, partial and ephemeral. It's only if we set our minds on Beauty and Truth and Goodness, not with the senses but through pure thought, that we rediscover the certain eternal knowledge of our souls.

And that is the path to wisdom.

He couldn't tell how long he walked. There was no sun; the sky never changed. He'd lost sight of the buildings. But,

458

gradually, he noticed a different orientation. All the people he passed were facing the same way, like trees leaning away from a wind. As if there were something at the centre of the world they had to avoid.

A clang at his feet. He looked down. A broken guitar lay on the ground: the neck had snapped off, and loose strings tangled in a bird's nest around the bridge. He sat down cross-legged and picked it up. He stared at it, as if he'd forgotten what it was; he tried to jam the splintered halves together, like a child with a broken toy, but they fell apart in his hands.

He unwound one of the strings and pulled it free. He wrapped it around the broken neck, looped it through the sound hole and fed it out through a crack in the back. He tied it off. Now the string held the instrument together, precariously, like a bandage.

He tightened the remaining strings. He thumbed them softly, bending each pitch to where he thought it ought to be. When he had them all in tune, he strummed a chord. Dark, hopeless with loss and longing.

Ren's voice whispered in his ear. *Remember who you are.*

'Who am I?' he said aloud.

He played another chord, and the answer came from Maroussis. *You will have defined yourself by this one thing, this quest to find your wife. Your whole being will be contingent on her absence.*

Something hard and sharp tugged at his cheek. He put up his hand and it came away soaked in blood. A burning man stood over him, cracking the barbed-wire flail which had torn open his skin.

Jonah screamed and dropped the guitar. The knot unravelled; the string came loose and the instrument fell in two with a boxy thud. He fled, feeling the flail pricking at his back.

But an idea had begun to grow, spreading through him

459

like music in an empty room. He ran, heading against the crowd flowing away from the centre of the square. The guards didn't try to stop him.

If she exists, then you can not.

He went on through the smoke and the petrol-fires burning on the ground. Past horrors he could never imagine and afterwards never forget, against the faceless tide.

The crowd thinned, then disappeared. The fog thickened. He was running alone, now – but he knew where to go.

Quite suddenly, he arrived at the place he remembered. A blue Metro sign hung from a bent pole, flanked by two burnt and limbless trees. Between them, under the sign, a flat square hole gaped open.

He stepped towards the hole. The world shuddered, like a rusty wheel that had just begun to move.

'*Jonah!*'

He turned back and saw Lily running towards him out of the smoke. She staggered as the world moved again, almost falling as loose paving stones rattled across the ground. The Metro entrance became a circle, widening out like oil welling from the ground. In the distance, the buildings started to turn.

Lily stopped two feet from him. He reached out tentatively, like trying to catch a feather in a breeze. She hesitated, as if she'd tried this before and couldn't believe he was real.

Their eyes met. Their hands touched. Their fingers meshed into each other. It was too late.

He leaned back over the void, her hand his only connection with the world. He stared into her eyes, willing himself to remember the moment for the rest of his life, even if that was only a few seconds more.

'I love you,' he said.

He let go her hand. Felt a moment of weightlessness as his body reached the perfect equilibrium between *something* and *nothing*, between *is* and *is not*. Then fell.

The trees collapsed. The buildings crumbled. The roof of the sky pinched together and rose up, like a dust-sheet being drawn off the world. He could hear music, deep organ pipes groaning as if they hadn't played in centuries. The sky twisted around in a pillar of light. The world sank into the spiralling void. The organ bellowed rage.

If she exists, then you can not.

He was falling, spinning, and the rushing in his ears was the man in black laughing at him.

I went down . . .

The spindle's turning so quickly now that the colours have fused into a white light that bleeds into the brightness around it. The music plays so fast that the notes become one and all I hear is a single pitch, the fundamental frequency of the universe. The plain below is a blur. Trying to fix on something solid, I look across to the mountains.

The mountains melt. A dark line smears off from a peak and billows across the sky. It catches on the hook of the spindle and starts gathering on it. The rest of the world is drawn in behind. The mountains unravel; the plain pulls apart. Threads of reality fly in and wind around the staff: sea-blue, golden, white as snow, every colour more vivid and more beautiful than anything I've ever seen.

I start to fall. The whorl spins around me, inches away: if it catches me, I'll be thrown off and spun out of existence, but it can't catch me because I'm the axis it spins around. I'm the point at the centre of the circle, and everything in the universe is within arm's reach.

With a flash of pure, perfect light and a thunderclap to shake the heavens, the light vanishes and I'm in darkness.

Forty

Now imagine the man is reluctantly dragged up a steep and rugged slope, and forced into daylight: won't it be painful and disorienting? As he approaches the light, his eyes will be dazzled, and he won't be able to see anything at all of his new reality.

Plato, *Republic*

He landed so hard the impact forced his eyes open. He was lying on a hard floor in the dark. But not blind. A dim red light glowed a little way off, just enough to hint he was still alive.

He tried to move his arm and found he could. Then his leg. Dried mud cracked and flaked off his skin as he bent his joints. When he stood up, he put his hand over his head and felt the rock ceiling a few inches above his head. Warm to the touch.

He moved towards the light, palming off the columns like a swimmer. He'd almost reached the light when his foot tripped against something. Not rock: something soft and yielding, something that grunted when he touched it. Something human.

He stepped over it, as best he could, and bent down to pick up the light. A head-torch. He found the switch and moved it. The red glow became a white beam cutting the darkness.

Adam lay stretched out at his feet, flat on his back, arms

462

folded across his chest like a corpse laid out for viewing. He seemed to be asleep, but his eyes were wide open, his pupils dilated to the very edge of the iris. As if they needed to capture every glimmer of light in that dark place.

Jonah looked around. Through the columns, he could sketch in the outlines of a square stone room. Two stone staircases led down from opposite sides. Mud had pooled near one of them, perhaps where he'd been lying. Steam rose off it.

How long was I asleep?

Socratis Maroussis and his son lay on the floor beside Adam, in the same wide-eyed trance. Ari's face was drawn into some kind of angry snarl; his father's stiff with fear. Adam, perhaps for the first time in his life, looked perfectly happy.

The floor trembled. A bass rumble, like a low-flying jet, rolled through the chamber and made the columns shiver.

Despair hit him. Was this all just another level of the dream? He waited for the world to fly apart, to dissolve into a new reality and pitch him back into Syntagma Square. Or somewhere worse.

The tremor stopped, though the noise lingered. Like the sounds you sometimes heard in a cinema, explosions from the next-door film.

I'm underneath a volcano. He needed to get out, and he wasn't going back the way he'd come.

Two staircases, and one was impassable. He shone the light around again. In one wall, he saw a stone frame that might once have been a door, but it was blocked by a tongue of basalt that must have flowed in during some long-ago eruption.

The only other exits were the stairs. He turned back to the second set, opposite where he'd come up. A sulphurous, rotting smell blew out of it, but after so long in the cave he barely noticed.

He went down. There were only ten steps: at the bottom, a pool of cloudy water, milky white, lapped the steps and reflected the torch back at him. A stone shaft rose above it, a mirror image of the shaft he'd fallen down into the mud. With one crucial difference.

Ropes. Two blue climbing ropes snaking down the far wall into the water. He followed them up with the torch-beam, to a rocky ledge above that looked like the mouth of a tunnel.

Another tremor, louder than the first. The water rippled; bubbles popped the surface. He dipped his toe in the water and wondered if it was safe to swim in.

He looked at the ropes again. Adam, Ari and Maroussis must have come out the tunnel at the top, down the ropes and across the pool to the steps. Easy enough to retrace their route.

Aren't you forgetting someone?

The guilt would have crippled him – if he'd had time. He ran back up the steps to the cave, flashing the torch wildly as he hunted for her. Past Adam and Maroussis and Ari, still sleeping. Past the blocked doorway, through the forest of columns.

The last place he looked was where he'd begun, where a mud outline on the floor imprinted the spot where he'd lain. Another dark shadow lay beside it, so close he thought he must be seeing double. Except that when he shone the torch on it, the shadow didn't move.

Lily lay in the light, curled on her side, just the way he'd seen her a thousand mornings before. She was covered in mud, every inch of her body. Except her eyes, which stared across the floor, blindly open. All the time he'd been dreaming, she'd been right beside him.

Jonah knelt beside her. *Don't disappear,* he prayed. *Whatever reality this is, please stay long enough for me to touch you.*

He licked his finger and tried to clean some mud off her

face. He felt her: not the cold, pale skin from his dream but warm, tanned by the sun, with smile lines creeping out from her eyes and mouth. He leaned over and kissed her.

The floor trembled. He shook her shoulder gently, then – when that did nothing – harder.

Her eyes didn't move.

He lay down and wrapped himself around her. He started to speak, but her ear was clogged with mud.

Another rumble. Dust showered down off the ceiling, and he covered her naked eyes with his hand to protect them.

He sang to her. His parched throat could barely make a note; his dry mouth struggled to form the words. But he dragged the sound out. He sang the songs he'd written for her, and songs he wished he'd written for her. He listened to the roar of the mountain cracking apart, and hugged her closer.

'I love you,' he whispered.

She blinked, stirred and rolled over.

'Jonah?'

The light went out when I opened my eyes. I was in darkness, lying on a warm hard floor. Every muscle in my body ached, but my skin tingled with the aftermath of the golden dream.

I closed my eyes again, trying to hold on to the dream. I wondered, if I fell asleep again, would I be back there with Socrates in the whorl of light, drinking in the mysteries of the universe? I could already feel the memories receding like the tide. It made me despair.

A rumble shook the cave. 'Wake up,' a voice whispered in my ear.

You can't stay here. You have to go back.

I opened my eyes again. Diotima was leaning over me. I couldn't see her, but I could feel her breath on my lips.

'How did you get here?'

'We have to get out.'

Her hand gripped mine and pulled me off the floor. How long had I been dreaming?

The ground shook again. Rock dust came loose from the ceiling and rained over me. A roar echoed through the cave, like wind on a mountaintop. Diotima led me by the hand, weaving through the forest of columns with unerring blind-sight.

'Duck,' she warned me.

I put up a hand and felt flat, hand-worked stone just over my head. The walls squeezed in and I was in a tunnel, a narrow passage rising through the mountain. Far in the distance, I saw a spot of light. Just a pinhole, but growing slowly larger. I wondered if reality was collapsing again, if Socrates would come walking out of the light to lead me back into my dream. But there was no one ahead of me except Diotima.

The tunnel climbed steeply. The light came closer: a strange, bluish glow, as if it was shining through water.

'Close your eyes,' Diotima said.

I felt a shuffling and a bumping as she squeezed behind me. She put her hands on my back and steered me forwards. Round a sharp corner, and suddenly I felt warmth on my face: not the sapping, second-hand air of the cave, but the direct heat of the naked sun.

I opened my eyes and went blind again.

He wanted to hold her forever. Another roar from the moun-tain said that might not be very long.

'Can you walk?' he asked.

Lily stood, wobbling like a newborn calf. 'Where am I?'

'Nowhere we want to be.'

He put his arm around her waist and helped her across

the cave. It wasn't how he'd imagined it would be: no joy, not even time for triumph. Survival was all that mattered now.

Lily looked down as the torchlight swept over the sleeping figures. 'Is that Adam?'

Jonah hurried her on. Down the stairs to the milk-white pool. The hanging ropes swung in a nonexistent breeze: if you held them straight in your gaze, it looked as if the whole mountain was swaying.

'Can you swim?'

Something like a smile cracked the mud around her mouth. 'Swim, yes. Climb . . . '

They lowered themselves into the water, gasping at the heat, and splashed across. Treading water, Jonah tied a loop in one of the ropes and put it around Lily's waist. Then he grabbed the other and started to climb. Steam made the nylon slippery; the heat sapped his strength more than he'd thought possible. A couple of times, he lost his grip and slid back, burning the skin on his hands. The lost inches hurt more than the pain.

At last, he hauled himself over the top. There was no time to rest. The sound in the background had changed: deeper, angrier. He put the rope around his waist to give himself more leverage, leaned back and hauled. Wet clothes made Lily heavy; the rope bit into his raw palms. He sucked in the pain and forced himself to hold on. Hand over agonised hand, he hoisted her up.

He brought her over the edge. His numb fingers plucked at the wet rope but couldn't untie the loop: he just pulled her out of it. Leaning on each other, they stumbled up the passage and came to the three-faced statue guarding the fork in the tunnel. A wizened old woman stared out at them.

'This was the right-hand path,' Jonah realised. 'They both end up in the same place.'

They followed the circle of torchlight on down the passage. Down to the black pool watched over by the goddess, then up. The noise was so constant now that Jonah barely heard it.

The torch began to fade. Jonah tapped it, then realised it was light from ahead that made it seem dim. They were almost at the entrance. He smelled smoke.

He didn't need the torch now. He pulled it off his head and dropped it. He stood under the entrance, a square window into the world, and looked up. A red sky churned above him, just like the sky above Syntagma Square.

What world is this? What would he find if he went up there? He clung on to Lily, terrified he'd lose her.

'Whatever's up there,' he told her, 'I'll never let you go.'

She managed a tired smile. 'Neither will I.'

He cupped his hands and made a stirrup for her. She stepped on and he lifted her, teetering, towards the light. Even then, she was too weak to pull herself through the hole. He had to push her through, sending her sprawling out onto the ground. He pulled himself up after her.

It looked like the old world he remembered, after all. The bleached-white stones of the excavated temple, the basalt trench walls. Lily had already started climbing the metal ladder out of the trench. He followed her up, so fast he almost knocked her over when he reached the top.

She'd stopped, staring back up the mountain and shielding her eyes against the light.

A wall of burning rock swept towards them.

I sat down on the mountain with my head in my hands. I felt as though a lightning bolt had split open my head, burning out my skull. Tears fell from my sightless eyes.

'I can't see a thing.'

'You will,' Diotima said.

'Can't I go back into the cave?' Suddenly I longed for the comfort of the darkness, to slip back into the dream and hear that eternal music again. Through the ringing in my ears, I thought I could still catch a faint echo of that fundamental note that incorporates all harmonies.

You can't stay here.

The earth shook under me. I realised the rock I was sitting on had become hot, and the noise in the distance wasn't the music of the universe, but an angry bellow like a wounded giant.

'What's that?'

'The volcano,' Diotima said calmly. 'It's erupting.'

'Are we going to die?'

'If we stay.'

Even then, I might have stayed – if dying meant I could go back to my dream. Then, through the noise and the music and the ringing in my ears, I heard a voice. Not Socrates or Diotima, but – of all people – Euphemus.

While you philosophers sit on your mountaintops drawing triangles, we're down in the law courts and the Assembly wrestling with the problems of real life.

I found Diotima's hand and let her lead me down.

Lava flowed down the mountain. In daylight, it didn't look like much: the consistency of mud and the colour of rock, with just an orange rim at the edge giving away the heat inside. In fact, a scientist could have told you, it was emitting plenty of light, but mostly ultraviolet, invisible to the human eye. The pyrotechnics would come with nightfall.

It moved slowly, a rocky surf rolling over itself, filling in every cave and crevice in its way. It reached the two conical hills and funnelled between them, always taking the path of least resistance. A tree toppled over and burst into flame. A tent turned to ash; a temple collapsed. A petrol tank exploded

469

and blew a fountain of molten lava out of the stream. Through the smoke, through time, you could see shadowy men and women running ahead of the flow: a tousle-haired Orpheus and his wife hobbling on his shoulder; a broad-shouldered wrestler tripping like an old man; a fleet-footed goddess leading them down.

We live our lives between the mountains and the sea, between adamant truth and the endless changing of the tides. We play in the foothills, but we rarely risk the climb. The mountains are too massive, too permanent to contemplate.

But even mountains change sometimes. Stone melts, and the mountains run like water, fired by the heat of a new world coming into being.

Forty-one

That was what happened on my first visit to Sicily, and the events I was part of. Afterwards, I came home.

Plato, *Letter VII*

Imagine our situation something like this.

There's a cave. There are men inside it, collared and chained so that they can't move, can't even turn their heads. There's a fire behind them – which they can't see – and puppets dancing in front of the fire. All the prisoners see is the shadows thrown on the cave wall.

They've been in that position their whole lives. They think the shadows are reality. How could they know any different?

But suppose one of them breaks his collar and escapes. Suppose he stands up and turns around and walks towards the fire. He'll be dazzled. He'll see the puppets and he won't know what they are; he'll assume they're an illusion, because the shadow-world of his reality can't possibly explain them. He'll shut his eyes and run back to his seat, lock the collar back around his neck and never look back again.

But if there are guards there to take him by the arms, to drag him up the steep mouth of the cave and cast him out into the sunlight – what then? He'll be blinded. He'll hurt so much he'll think the guards have pressed his eyeballs into hot coals.

But, slowly and painfully, his eyes will start to adjust. He'll begin by peeking at the shadows on the ground, which at least look familiar, though they're a thousand times sharper and more vivid than anything he's seen in the cave. He'll move on to watery reflections, then the objects themselves – rocks, trees, animals. They'll appear so beautiful and so real that he won't believe he's spent his entire life not knowing about them.

Finally, he'll dare to look up. First at the stars, then at the moon, and finally – last of all – at the sun itself, just as it is.

And he'll know the truth.

Thurii

The world looked different at the end of the summer. The wheat had been harvested. Some of the fields were white with ash where they'd burned the stubble; in others, gangs of labourers turned the soil, ready for the new seed. Persephone had begun her journey underground: I was on my way back, too.

I sat by the roadside, on the slope of the causeway, looking out over the swamp. The still water reflected the sky; beneath the surface, the drowned city settled deeper into its grave. On the breeze, I heard someone picking out a tune on a lyre.

I turned my head away, trying to deflect the wind and make the sound go away. I could hardly bear to listen to music any more. After the song I'd heard in the cave, everything else sounded like squawling babies.

'What are you thinking?' asked Diotima, sitting on the bank beside me.

'The same as always.'

We'd come down from the mountain a month ago. The moment I was sure we were clear of the volcano and Dionysius' men, I collapsed. All I had from the journey after that were dim, watery images: a cart, a city, a quick ship and then the large house in Thurii. I stayed indoors with the caged bird, too weak to go out and too frightened of seeing my step-brother. All I could think about was the cave. Awake, I played it over and over like an actor learning his lines; asleep, I dreamed it so often I no longer knew if I was awake or not. I felt the same way I did when Socrates died. The guests had gone, the lamps were out, and I was left alone in the empty room. I *was* the empty room.

The pink sky softened Diotima's skin; her dress had slipped down, leaving one shoulder bare. I wanted to kiss it, but I didn't dare. Since Etna, she'd only touched me to nurse me. She found ways of avoiding me: one night, when I couldn't stand it any more and went to her room, she wasn't there. The intimacy of Syracuse had vanished.

That was something I dreamed about, too.

'I was thinking about something Socrates told me. He said a philosopher's job is to go to the limit of this sensory world and then break through to the world beyond.'

Diotima nodded.

'But when I stayed with Archytas, he set me a riddle. A man goes to the edge of the universe and tries to put his arm through. If he does it, then there's space beyond and so he's not really at the edge; and if he can't, then there's something beyond blocking his way, so he can't have reached the very limit either.'

'It's a paradox.'

'Doesn't it negate what Socrates said? Is it possible ever to get beyond this world?'

She shrugged. 'Do you know why paradoxes work? Because reason can only take you so far before it ties itself in knots.'

Out in the marsh, a crane called, a lament that echoed over the water. I looked up, and caught the setting sun dead ahead. I winced. Even now, my eyes wept if I stayed out too long. By mid-afternoon each day, a familiar throbbing started up in my skull and lasted until I went to bed.

473

I burrowed my fingers into the wet ground, feeling the secrets that only worms know.

'Will I ever be able to go back to the cave?'

'Not that way. Not in this lifetime.'

'I don't know if I can bear that.'

'It's better like this,' she told me. 'The cave's a dangerous place, even to the initiated. You remember Timaeus?'

I did – the filthy, gibbering madman on the porch of the temple at Locris. Even with everything else I'd seen, it would be a long time before I forgot his hollow, scorched-out eyes.

'He found the cave, too; he spent two years down there. When he finally came out, the world was so bright he couldn't bear it. He burned out his eyes so he wouldn't have to see.'

A sigh – or perhaps it was just the wind on the water. 'There's only so much reality we can stand.'

'What about Agathon?' I said. 'Did he go into the cave?'

'I tried to warn him, but he wouldn't listen.'

'So why wouldn't you tell me?'

'To protect you. If Dionysius thought you knew . . . '

I fingered the bulge under my tunic, where the necklace hung. 'The things I saw – were they real?'

'They were images.'

'They felt more real than anything in this world.'

The longing told in my voice. Diotima gave me a stern look. 'The cave is a window. You can see in, but you can't get through. You have to find another way.'

'Where?'

'*How*,' she corrected me.

'How?'

All I got in reply was an impatient look that said I knew the answer already.

Socrates: What was the basis of the method I taught you?

Me: Eliminating hypotheses to reach the first principle.

But what then? In the cave, I'd gone right down to the very foundation of the universe. Where else was there to go?

There are two ways, says Parmenides . . .

The sophists use relentless questioning to break people down and confuse them. In a way, Socrates was guilty of the same thing, only on a more fundamental level. In Heraclitus' ever-shifting world, nothing stands up to scrutiny. Every time you think you've reached the bottom, it turns into a trap door that drops you further down.

But now I know there's a bottom. And a top. I saw the column of light rising towards the heavens, the spirals inside making the rungs of a giant ladder. It would be hard, painstaking work, but you could climb that ladder. One step at a time, all the way to the summit. And when you got there, the view would be all the more breathtaking for the effort.

But I couldn't do it alone. A conversation needs a partner. I reached for Diotima's hand.

'Come back to Athens with me.'

'I can't.'

'Of course you can.'

'For what? To become your wife, locked in the women's quarters tending my weaving and my children? Is that how you see me?'

'We could live together as equals. Like Pericles and Aspasia.'

'The gossip would kill us.'

'Then I'll stay here.' It had only just come into my mind, but I meant it with my whole being. 'I love you.'

A long, soft silence. She let it stretch over me, settling on my hopes until it smothered them.

'You have to go back.'

'I love you,' I repeated, as if it was an argument.

She smiled her sphinx smile. 'You've forgotten what I told you. Human love is only the first step on the way to understanding. You're beyond that now.'

475

'I don't want to be.'

'What's the true object of love?'

'Immortality,' I repeated wearily.

'For most people, love's the only way they can taste the immortality of the soul. But you've seen further. You won't be satisfied – and you shouldn't be.'

'I want to be with you.'

'It's impossible.'

Maybe she was right – but I hated her for it. I stood up suddenly and pulled off the locket. I wanted to be rid of it forever, and the golden scroll wrapped inside.

Diotima held out her hand, but I wouldn't give it to her. I held the chain and whirled it in a circle. It hummed in the air.

'If you lose that, someone will find it,' she warned me, though she didn't move to stop me. As if she'd already seen everything that would happen. As if she knew that late one night, mad with memories, I'd taken a needle and added my own text on the blank flap at the top of the golden canvas. So not everything I'd endured would be forgotten.

Where hundred-headed Typhos shakes open the earth, I went down into the bosom of the goddess. Next to it, I'd drawn the diagram from Timaeus' book, the two triangles linked by an arc.

I let go the chain. The locket sailed through the evening air and fell far out in the swamp. It barely made a ripple in the sky's reflection.

London

The SOUTH PECKHAM CHURCH OF THE REDEEMER van reached the end of its journey at three o'clock on a warm September afternoon. Another fifteen hundred miles had gone on its clock, though as no one knew how many times it had ticked back round to zero, that didn't count for much.

Jonah got out and went down the stairs to the basement flat. He'd called ahead; Alice had left the spare key under a flower pot. He unlocked the door, opened it – and paused.

He could hear music inside.

He stood on the doormat and stared between the posts of the open doorway. Wondering what he'd find.

'I'm dying for a drink.' Lily had come down after him. She pushed through into the living room.

Everything was as he'd left it. The beer cans on the floor, the vodka bottle and cereal bowl on the table, his guitar in the corner and his CDs on the wall. The radio was playing in the kitchen, Tom Petty and the Heartbreakers saying they wouldn't back down. He must have left it on the whole time.

Lily poured a glass of water and turned off the radio. Jonah shuffled around the flat, picking up the post that had come, tidying away some of the mess. They still weren't completely at ease. They'd come into a new world, and they had to get to know each other all over again. Like picking up a book you hadn't read in a long time, and didn't remember as well as you thought.

The phone rang. He remembered the despair of those empty hours sitting here, begging it to ring. Now he resented it. He ignored it.

'Better get it,' said Lily. 'I need to freshen up.'

She went into the bathroom. Unwillingly, Jonah picked up the phone.

'You're back.'

Ren's voice conjured mixed emotions. For a brief period, she'd been his only friend in the world: he owed her everything. Now, he couldn't think of anything to say to her.

'Where are you?' he asked.

'The Eikasia Foundation have issued a statement saying Socratis Maroussis and Ari died when their yacht sank off Sicily. I thought you'd like to know.'

'Not really. But thanks.'

They'd found Ren in the tent, ankles and wrists zip-tied together. The shades had run away; Richard had vanished. The camp was deserted. Jonah had ripped off the cords, frantic as the lava rolled nearer.

Lily had been almost unconscious. Her eyes were closed, her breathing shallow. But she was mumbling something. Jonah put his ear close to hear above the roar of the volcano.

'*Adam.*'

Jonah had turned back. But the lava had already spilled over the edge of the trench, and was dribbling into the mouth of the tunnel.

'It's too late.'

They'd hobbled down the hill, Jonah almost carrying Lily. As soon as they reached the road, they'd flagged down a car and called the police. But Etna was still erupting, and nobody would send a rescue crew to dig into a fresh lava field.

'He was asleep. He wouldn't have felt a thing,' Jonah had told Lily.

The lava must have flowed right down the open tunnel – at least as far as the fork. But he thought it wouldn't have got past the mud and the water into the cave. There'd be enough air in there for Adam to survive for hours, maybe days. Longer, if there were fissures in the rock it could seep through.

He thought of Adam, sleeping like a child. He thought of the deep peace on his face. Would he even wake up? Or would he just fade slowly into eternity? In a selfish corner of his soul, Jonah sometimes envied him – he'd gone on a trip and would never come down, never have to confront the shattered pieces of the real world. But then he'd look at Lily, and know he was in the right place.

'Are you going to be OK?' he asked down the phone.

'Yes. And so will you.'

He liked the certainty in her voice. He'd found Lily, but bringing her back would take time. He hadn't forgotten that in the old stories, women who'd been to the underworld never returned quite the same. There was an ache in Lily's eyes that hadn't faded as he'd hoped. She'd drift off in the middle of sentences, or wander away while he was speaking to her. Sometimes, in the night, he woke up with her screaming, clinging to him as if a giant tide was pulling her away. He cradled her, sometimes for hours, and sang her back to sleep.

'Will I see you again?' he asked Ren.

He was certain she'd say no. She'd come into his life from nowhere, and he sort of understood she'd disappear the same way. But she surprised him.

'Some day.'

She hung up. Lily came out of the bathroom, wrapped in a white towel that just reached her thighs. Her skin was scrubbed fresh, her wet hair pushed back off her face. Some of the light seemed to have come back into her eyes.

She kissed him. 'I need fresh air.'

They went to the back door. Jonah hung back, but Lily didn't skip a beat as she stepped over the threshold into the yard. *Idiot*, he told himself, but some dreams were hard to shake. He needed time, too.

They sat together on the riverbank and watched the water flow by. He put his arm around her and she leaned her head on his shoulder, two halves of the same whole. Neither of them said anything because they didn't have to. They were sharing a moment of eternity, and words couldn't touch it.

Athens

The grove is named for Academus, the ancient hero who helped rescue Helen when Theseus kidnapped her for his bride (much good it did her: as soon as she went home, the Trojans nabbed her instead). Inside the low wall, yews and poplars surround the gnarled olive trees that are sacred to Athena. A gymnasium stands between them, a weathered colonnade overlooking the running track and sandpits.

It's summer again. My journey back from Italy wasn't without its complications, but I'm home now. I've come down with Glaucon to see the festival; later, there'll be a torch race in honour of Prometheus, who brought fire down from the gods to men.

Crowds mill about, waiting for nightfall so the race can start. Young men, naked bodies oiled and gleaming, stretch their legs and check out the competition when their backs are turned. Over at the sandpit, athletes queue up to take turns at the long jump. It's a curious thing. Each one looks as if he's trying his hardest every time, yet each leap takes him a few inches further than the previous mark. How do they manage it?

'Odysseus returns!' It's Philebus, poling himself along on his walking stick, delighted to have caught me. 'Not captivated by sirens or seduced by Italian sorceresses?'

I force a polite smile and wipe away the spittle he's just sprayed over my face. There was a sorceress, and a siren song, but I'm not going to tell him about that.

'I did have a shipwreck.'

The jowls flap. 'Really. *Really?* You must tell me all about it. And so thin.' He pinches my stomach like a clucking mother. 'You must be the only man to come back from Italy having lost weight.'

'It didn't agree with me.'

'And the sophist? What became of him?'

'He died.' I've planted a gravestone for him on the road out of Athens, next to the one I bought for Agathon. I don't know what Dionysius did with Euphemus' body. I suppose Diotima would say it doesn't matter.

Philebus' eyes bulge. 'How *tragic*. Was it the food? Some other kind of . . . *excess?*'

'He tried to murder the tyrant Dionysius, and was strangled to death.'

He doesn't know what to say to that. Being at a loss for words is a painful state for him to be in, a sort of constipation of the lungs, so he makes his excuses and leaves.

Glaucon comes up to me, his mouth sticky with a honey-cake. I think he was hanging back to avoid Philebus. 'Are you regretting coming back, yet?'

'It's as if I never left.' But that's not true. Athens may be the same, but I'm not.

'This is where I'm going to come,' I tell Glaucon. 'This grove.'

He looks puzzled. 'You're already here.'

'Pythagoras had his school in Croton. Socrates had the agora. I need somewhere to instruct my pupils.'

It's a good place to start again. A measured mile from Athens – out of its intrigues, but near enough to be visible. The gymnasium brings plenty of young men here, who might want to exercise their minds once they've exhausted their bodies. And when the sun gets too hot, you can always retreat into the shade of the trees to rest.

'Are you going to take up teaching?' It's the first he's heard of it.

'We can't abandon the world to people like Philebus. We have to offer another way.'

'Socrates tried that. Look where it got him.'

'Socrates tried to fight error. I'm going to look for Truth.'

'You'll have your work cut out.'

'And we won't make Socrates' and Pythagoras' mistake: we'll write it down.' I point out a boy, about fourteen, standing by the colonnade watching the jumpers. He's in the bud of adolescence, aware of his beauty but not yet sure enough of it to be vain. He pretends not to notice the men prowling in the shadows, watching him and planning their attacks. One's already wobbling over to start a conversation. Philebus. The boy gives a shy smile, flattered to be noticed.

'That boy wasn't even born when Socrates died. People are already forgetting the things he said: soon he'll be no more real to them than Theseus or Orpheus. As for Pythagoras, all people know now is the triangles. If we're going after Truth, we need to make sure it gets remembered.'

What is knowledge, after all, but the memory of something we once understood to be true?

A year has tempered my optimism. I can still see the shining ladder leading into the heavens, but it seems higher than ever. I'm not sure if I'll ever reach the top. But I can point the way for others, and hope they'll get further. Even if Archytas is right, and the top of the ladder is only an infinitely receding paradox, it'll be worth it. You go further when you know where you're going, whether you get there or not.

'We'll talk about it later.' A wrestling match is about to start and Glaucon wants to see it. Left alone, I sit on the steps of the colonnade between two pillars. I want to think, but there's something uncomfortable sticking into my buttocks.

I reach down and pull it out. It's a wax tablet, covered in tiny writing, and a stylus.

The letters swim in front of my eyes. For a moment, my mind insists it's the text from the gold leaf; I scan the crowd feverishly for Diotima, in case she put it there, but don't see her.

I look at the writing again. It isn't the golden text, it's numbers. The gymnasiarch must have been doing his accounts.

The sun hasn't set yet: there's still enough light in the sky to see by. I smooth the wax with my palm, and start to write.

I went down to the Piraeus, yesterday, with Glaucon . . .

As for all the writers, past or future, who may claim they understand the deep mysteries I devoted my life to – whether from what they've heard or read, or from their own research – this is what I have to say for them:

They don't know a thing.

Plato, *Letter VII*

Acknowledgements

Beyond philosophy, Plato's dialogues stand as a monument to the pleasures of conversation and the search for enlightenment. For enlightening me with their wisdom, knowledge and conversation, I'd like to thank: Angelo Strano, who guided me up and into Mount Etna; Dr Andrew McGonigle of Sheffield University, and Professor Alessandro Aiuppa of the University of Palermo, who explained what's under the volcano; Professor Dora Katsonopoulou and the Helike Project for an unforgettable fortnight's digging; my archaeology buddies George, Savannah, Rund, Sandra, Courtney, and especially Sara Wilson, who answered all my questions afterwards; at the Foreign Office: Iona Thomas, Amy Cumming, and especially Clive Correa, who told me about missing persons; Seth Kim-Cohen, for good beer, stories about life in the band and permission to quote his song; Julia Kim-Cohen, for arranging an amazing six weeks in New Haven; Lucasfilm Ltd for their very kind permission to quote *Raiders of the Lost Ark*; the Saul Bass Library at Yale, the British Library in Boston Spa and London, and the JB Morrell Library at York University; Michael Ridpath, for encouraging me not to fear philosophy; Virginia Stewart-Avalon, for permission to use her elegant translations of the Orphic Hymns; Penguin Books, for permission to quote from Adam Beresford's translation of Plato's *Meno*; Oliver Johnson, for his Socratic wisdom and Syracusan banquets; the wonderful team at Hodder for all their efforts, especially Anne Perry,

Kerry Hood and Ellen Wood; Jane Conway-Gordon, the Voice of Reason; my sons Owen and Matthew, who followed me down into caves and up over volcanoes; and my wife Emma, who is Beauty Itself.

There have been (and still are) various excavations at Sybaris/Thurii, and several Orphic gold tablets have indeed been found there. The dig in the book is not based on any real-life excavation. Plato and his brothers, Socrates, Archytas, Eurytus, Dion and the two Dionysiuses really existed; all the other characters and their organisations, past and present, are simply shades of my imagination.